The Reborn
RUDE AWAKENING

KR. WHITE

Smooth
Operations

Disclaimer

A great percentage of this work is based around entertainment themes. Famous actors, singers, and other known artists are mentioned in passing as well as some song titles and a few movies. It is not the intention of the author to accept credit for, or otherwise profit from these persons and works of art. In the entertainment field these things are "household" terms and the author names them in appreciation only as this manuscript will show.

https://www.facebook.com/smoothoperationsarehere

ISBN 978-1-7325325-0-2 (print)
ISBN 978-1-7325325-1-9 (digital)

Table of Contents

Acknowledgements   *v*

I Didn't Feel a Thing   1
The Rude Awakening   5
In Her Shoes   19
Learning to Cry   23
A Red Wave   37
One Soul… Two Minds…   47
The House of the Second Sons   53
Miss Janet (If You're Nasty)   69
The Society of the Princesses   83
The Cost of Doing Business   91
My Soccer Name is Score   97
All Hail the New Kid in Town   101
A Class Within a Class   111
It's Beginning to Look a Lot Like… Fire   117
I'm Going to Disney Land   133
School's Out Forever   149
"Bust a Deal… And Face the Wheel…"   159
Playing Twister   171
Hollywood and Vine   179
Smoke on the Water   189
There's No Place Like Home   211
Give Me Shelter   229
You Got Your Mind Right?   249
The Devil Made Me Do It   263
Play it Again Sam   275
I'm Just on Vacation   287
Flash Back Who's That   331
And Those Hollywood Nights   347

About the Author   *375*

Acknowledgements

My first acknowledgment is to my mother. Our downtown Chicago day trips to the parks for concerts, water fountains, and festivals were my freedom to enjoy sights and sounds unknown in our neighborhood. At the museums we saw art, history, science, and stars being born. I promised myself that I would one day go to the Pacific Islands, Egypt, England and many of the other places studied on those days. Now I have. I love you Mom.

I only have a few true friends and Derrien Relyea is one of them. Not only is she an outstanding writer in her own right, but she turned out to be a very good editor and was instrumental in helping to make this work more readable. Look for the "Darque Legends" fantasy series to find her for yourself.

Thank you to Ariel Frailich for the brilliant cover work, manuscript formatting and his wisdom. Truly a bright light in a dark place.

The cover and promotion video are a collaboration between the lovely and multi-talented Francine White, Chuck Taylor of Izon Media Works, KR. White of Smooth Operations and Derrien Relyea. (A winning team) See video links for contacts and other information.

A special thankyou to Sparky Bell for helping to make these connections possible.

Dedication

This book is dedicated to my two sons, Paul Jr and Paul II who bear the name of my fathers' favorite uncle. Where there is life, there is time.

I Didn't Feel a Thing

I said I would never do this. I would not be one of those guys who would write his lies in a book for a last chance grasp at glory and fame before he's dead. In my world that kind of thing is forbidden. It could not only cost your job but your life as well. Your friends (if you had any), family, and the ability to perform your duty, were all at risk. That's why most guys like me never write until they are too old or too sick to worry about it anymore. Most who do write, soon mysteriously disappear and are forgotten. But it seems that I am at a point of no return (again), and since these days my new middle name is "Change", I feel obliged to note a tale that is at the very least fantastic, even for my standards.

For years I had been jotting down mental notes on my new challenges and my thoughts and opinions concerning them. So, it was only fitting that when I began to transfer this tale into a form of script, that I reopened the original files and immortalized those same emotions as I felt them at the time. So, forgive me if I seem to slowly evolve from what was once my version of conventional thinking, to something that is now admittedly unique.

I should start by saying that my name is Robert Blake. It's not but I've always liked the actor and it's as good a name as any. I was born 12 April 1940, and I was 69 years old when I died. I was assassinated three years ago by the very men who are hunting me today, but that is getting a little ahead of myself.

I will attempt to tell this story in a way that will be easy to understand but you may have questions. Some of these events, and the situations surrounding them will sound similar to events you think you know. If anything, this is a testimony to all the things that we thought we knew but really didn't.

I would dare you to look up what you can about the historical events I mention. It may lead you to find a greater insight about the world you live in. Some of these things can be easily found but the real details might be missing. Many once traceable reference sources are outdated and may have ceased to exist by now. Other questions have so many answers that there's no telling what is, and what is not, true anymore. Then again, the active search for knowledge is a conscious decision and that, in itself, is an action. These actions are what got me killed. Furthermore, it must be noted that this manuscript is not the entire story, and that these are only some of the events and a few of the ways, I was affected by them.

After starting this exercise in futility, I noticed that my style of writing slowly began to change. Initially, I wrote in the fashion I had always used to make my reports and investigations. As I was forced to broaden my strategies in order to survive, my long-standing perspective on life was also broadened and I was forced to adapt. It altered the way I saw myself and the style in which I would express it, on paper and in my mind. I changed from bullet statements and fact-filled notes on paper, to what evolved to something like a conversation with an old friend. I'm sure I didn't change everything I should have, so bear with this telling.

Three years ago, while on an inspection tour in Iraq, a roadside bomb (IED) destroyed my vehicle, killing myself and two other Inspectors. Others died in that planned hit, to include an important British dignitary who had the misfortune to be with us at the time. His escorts had vehicle trouble on that day. He, his Lebanese wife, and young daughter, were to fly back to England for an urgent matter of some kind. Since our route took us near Baghdad International Airport, it seemed to make perfect sense to allow him to fall in line with us for the added security.

I remember the vehicle rising into the air and flipping several times before the roof collided with the ground. The sound of the explosion and the landing came later. I was still alive at that time and I heard the sound of other explosions and weapons fire nearby. All my previous training told me to get away from that vehicle. The voice inside my head was yelling, "If you want to live, you have to MOVE, MOVE, MOVE!" That voice was never wrong.

But at the same time, the rational part of me knew that I had not been a soldier for a long time. Besides, the vehicle was armored. "Why should I expose myself to possible gunfire when I can let Security do the job they are paid to do?" Besides, the noise was deafening. I was so shaken up that I had no way of knowing what was going on in my own head, much less what was happening outside. So, for the first time in a lifetime of memories I hesitated but like the "Good Book" says, "He who hesitates, is lost."

In hindsight, it's possible that I could have given some support to the Security units with my weapon. I was always a great shot with a handgun in close quarters. I was carrying the tried and true 9mm Beretta. It wasn't my all-time favorite weapon but the 9mm ammo was so versatile that it was the wisest choice.

I was always sentimental to the Colt 45. It had been an extension of myself from my time in Vietnam but nowadays, nearly everything that didn't come out of a rifle used 9mm ammo. It was safe to assume that if you were in a long firefight and running low on ammo, the first or second dead body you came across would have some 9mm rounds on his belt.

In truth, even if I would have crawled over Mark Denton and James Case, my broken necked assistants, kicked open a window and started shooting through the dust like I was John Wayne in the movie Stage Coach, I wouldn't be shooting at Hollywood fake Indians. Besides, my mind was so rattled that I may have taken shots at our own guys. Still, I maybe would have been able to at least get out of the truck.

A second nearby explosion lifted the British vehicle into the sky and threw it down on top of ours to crush them and all the people inside both vehicles into one. I didn't feel a thing.

A number of people have tried to kill me, and this was not the first time I'd been blown the fuck up. My two ex-wives wanted me dead. Hell, even my kids hated me. I can't really blame them. I was never around much. It was the work that was my real life, and I had to focus on that. When world leaders wanted to know answers, I was the one who gave them the straight facts. What they did with those facts was not my concern. Take it or leave it, giving the truth, cold, hard, and raw, was all I cared about. It was what I was known for. It earned me both respect and contempt.

I've always had my own thoughts and opinions and when asked, I would express them. But if I couldn't justify them in facts, I would never put them in my reports. I was never hired to advise people on what they should do with their politics, I was hired to investigate and tell the truth about what I found, even when sometimes they would rather hear something else.

A gift or a curse, it has always been my desire to know the real truth about the things that mattered in the world. The wars, politics, religions, the beginning of the universe and whatever facts we think we may know, are mostly lies as a whole. Everyone knows that. What they don't know, is which of the things they thought they knew were true and which of the others were important enough to even care about. Me, I was gifted with the ability to uncover the truth, and that's what made me an important asset to my employers.

At first, I suspected everyone. I could give names and titles of certain individuals in CIA, FBI, Homeland Security, and a host of other offices, at home and around the world, that most people would never, and probably should never, hear mentioned. So, I won't. As I am still investigating this matter, I will keep most of the true names to myself. Besides, this is about me now, and what has happened in this time.

The Rude Awakening

I later recall waking to the strange sound of quiet, or I should say the absence of sound. There was no pain of any kind. There was also no feeling in my body. I thought to myself, "If I'm dead, why am I still alive?" I may have said this out loud in my sleep. I do remember the sensation of floating. When I awoke again, it was to the smell of antiseptics and flowers.

An unfamiliar male voice quietly said, "No honey, you're not dead." My entire body tingled so much that I could almost hear it. It was the first of what would be many new sensations. My vision was blurred more then it normally was. I was still as dazed and disoriented as I was the first time the lights went out. But that didn't upset me. Hell, I was surprised just to be alive. I was just wondering how fucked up I was, and why this 'Gay Mother Fucker' was calling me "Honey"! (Don't ask-don't tell). I let it go. I had other concerns, and this guy may have some answers.

I squeaked when I asked him, "Who are you, sir? Where am I? What is my condition? And why does my voice sound so crazy?"

"Well," he replied, "those are all very complicated questions that require very long and equally complicated answers. What I can tell you is that you were in a bad accident, but you will recover. In fact, you are already well on your way."

"But this weird tingling over my body is driving me nuts!" I continued, now challenging him, "Be straight with me man! Am I really going to be OK, or am I as fucked up as I feel?" At that point, he called for the nurse who quickly turned a valve on the IV and I was out.

I learned that I had to adjust my thinking if I wanted to survive this thing. I was used to being the Boss. I've been a one man show most of my life, but I was always, "The Man." When I told someone to jump, I would expect to see them in orbit later that night. Authority is a good thing. Most people would consider it to be the same thing as power but it's not. Power can come with authority, and authority can give you a lot of power. For me, I am of the mind that power corrupts most of the time, but power in itself is overrated. A man can make himself powerful just by offering a job or something to eat. Having authority on the other hand, can impound that man's car or put him in jail for life.

When I woke again, I felt the touch of hands between my legs. Through a dim light and a drug induced haze, I saw the face of a beautiful black woman in her 40s. She was in white and on her head was a cone of light that reflected from the white of the bedsheets back into her face. She smiled when she saw that I was awake and said, "Oh, I didn't want to wake you." She continued to work. "Your foley came loose and wet up everything. You're a real good sleeper, you know that? We changed you and the bed while you were just dreaming away. You're all good now. Just go back to sleep." She whispered, "And if you need to pee... just go ahead. Mama Meg's got you hooked up."

I squeaked, "I thought you were an Angel."

She laughed, "Child please! I been called many things, but never that. I like you. Now go on back to sleep before I get in big trouble just for talking to you."

"You can't talk to me?"

She laughed again, "Not unless you want to see me shot," and quickly disappeared from the room and into the darkness.

I was about to nod off again, but I was more than a little curious about what Meg was doing. She said something about a foley. That was a catheter. I knew about UCDs. A Urine Collection Device is a kind of cone that your penis will fit in. Pilots use them in fighter jets and patients would use them when confined to the bed. I had used them before and everyone I knew, to include myself, thought them to be uncomfortable to say the least. You could get used to it sure, but it was never something you looked forward to. I had them leak on me before, but those kinds of things came with the job. When I was wounded in 'Nam they called it a catheter. This one felt way different than any of those other times. I could have chalked it up to the tingles I was feeling, but they were a little less intense now. This felt like something was stuffed inside of me.

All of a sudden, I got it in my head that my dick was missing! "It was lost in the explosion," I thought to myself. How really fucked was I? I had pretty good control of my hands and arms now. They were weak, but I could move them. One was taped and had the IV attached, but my right arm was free. I found the catheter and to my horror, I was right! This thing was jammed inside of my body and I could not feel any part of a penis anyplace. (And believe me, I checked). It, along with my balls, were now completely gone. I started thinking that I was no longer a man. A man had a dick! Now what was I without one? I did have both my arms and legs, so I could not have lost much more. Still, for a man to lose his only member, is a curse!

I said to myself, "Maybe it was just a bad dream. I saw an Angel then my dick was missing." But, that's a nightmare I've never had before. Maybe I was still asleep in this nightmare. "It's got to be all the drugs I must be on", I said to myself, and tried to fall back to sleep. But, how could I?

It took about a week to find out what was going on. I used the old trick of pretending to be asleep when someone was talking, and then using that information along with some gentle coaxing with Meg the Angel, to find that my name was Faatina Britten, and that I would be turning 18 later this year.

I had never met Arthur Britten, but I knew he was a powerful man in England, as well as in many other places. Much later I learned that his line of the Britten clan was an old and wealthy one. They were instrumental in the creation of their country and can trace their lineage back to ancient times. It is a little known fact that their fame has been purposely downplayed in recent generations for security reasons. But those in the know have always respected their power and the influence they wheel around the world. These people were Lords, Knights and Kings from way back. You see them at world changing events and shake hands without knowing who and what they really are. They change outcomes and shape developments with readymade contingencies, to form the world according to a plan they set in motion centuries in advance. Some have said that they can trace a line even to Alexander the Great himself, and that being in his bloodline gives them a godlike autonomy over all things. But again, that's getting too far ahead of myself.

When the great religions began to take power, these people had to ally themselves, or be destroyed. They were hunted in World War I and decimated in World War II. That's when they went underground. Legends and rumors of secret societies begin and end at their doorstep. Secrecy, misdirection, and subterfuge, are their only true friends.

Those earlier demigods that played in the world of man, ruled for thousands of years. To keep the Great Lines as pure as possible, they interbred with each other. This practice, above anything else, nearly destroyed them. So, they decided to spread themselves out around the known world to conquer and rule but would still occasionally marry back into each other. This can be seen in some of the distinct facial features we note in portraits of the old noble families around the world. The same features that you can see in the wealthiest of people today.

Unfortunately for them, the strong noble blood separation has the same old side effect that it has always had in the past. They seem to have a hard time giving birth to healthy males, thus further thinning the line as well as its power. Lamees, the Lord's beloved wife, was a product of a Saudi and Lebanese breeding plan that involved 8 families and was 80 years in the making. She was a daughter from two princely Arab families known for birthing many boys. The few girls born to them were fantastically beautiful but not very intelligent. Their offspring would nearly always carry the features of the baby's father. With that kind of history, breeding, and the advancements in medical science, there would be more than an 85% chance that their first child would be a boy. Of course, this time it was not. Lamees was nearly godlike in her beauty and it looked as if her daughter Faatina would be the same. She could be married off into another side of one of the clans and the quest for a healthy boy could continue. But now, that too, can never be.

Faatina's body was badly damaged in the incident that killed her parents. Bone and muscle were crushed beyond repair. Really, only her head was intact. They saved her brain by removing it and placing it in stasis, while a body was rebuilt from suitable parts acquired from a few other girls around her age. The process was incredibly complicated but nothing that the scientists at this facility had not seen before. Drugs that will never be spoken of were used to stimulate the brain to remake pathways that did much more than were needed to retake the body. Even nanotechnology was employed in making the required connections from stem to spine. The body itself was animated long before the brain was reinserted. Her repaired original skin was wrapped around this rebuilt form that was already placed into an improved and much stronger framework, but Faatina will never bear a child.

Faatina is a walking collage. An artistic composition of elements shaped into a finely crafted cohesive whole. Parts of her are African, European, and Arab. If she ever were to get pregnant, there would be no telling what the baby would look like. She was purposely made sterile for that reason. She can still be married off or traded to another house for favors or something else. She could be gifted to another Lord as an expensive trophy or sex toy. And I'm sure she would have been well trained to perform in any of those capacities. But, other than that, she had little use to either family at this point.

In my mind, I was given a choice between 'the red and the blue pill'. I could tell them all that I was not going to fall for this hoax and that they should just kill me now. Or I could play along until I could somehow find a way to escape this situation. The first choice was death, but it was a quick one when compared to playing out a charade that could take months or years to find out if this was a good trick or a bad mistake. I took what I thought was the 'blue pill'. I was wrong.

I didn't really know how this kid was supposed to act. I saw the Britten's a week before the incident at a banquet in the US Embassy. The mother fussed over the daughter so much that it seemed like the child could do nothing on her own. Each time I glanced in their direction, I saw the kid looking at the walls. It seemed a little odd, then again most of the real pretty girls I've known in my life were airheads, too. So, during my rehabilitation I played the dumb role. I spoke very slowly and used a British accent. From time to time I would throw in some Arabic words, just for effect.

Doctor Stacy, a psychiatrist, was assigned to me, and with me for most of my waking hours. A pretty white girl who told me she was 32 and from California, she was one of those real touchy-feely kinds of people. I can say that she was very careful not to give up anything about where we were, or how long I had been there. She did talk to me about losing my family and being blown the fuck up. She called it a 'violent episode'. She kept trying to get me to cry. She said I was still in shock and that I needed to release. We also talked about my being reborn, and how special I was to be given this rare opportunity. (I kept thinking of that old black and white version of Frankenstein, but I was sure she had never seen it). I mostly listened to what she had to say. What a great hugger she was. It would have been annoying in my old life, but as they say, "when in Rome." She looked, smelled, and felt so good that it turned me on in a new and different kind of way. I wanted to cry just to please her, but I didn't know how.

Shifting from an old and respected man whose single word was golden, to a young lady who rarely said any words at all, was very difficult. Before, I spoke as I damn well pleased. Now, I had to plan and choose each and every little word I would say. God forbid I'd be found to be too smart, or too well informed. I was forced to learn new ways of communicating with others by incorporating facial expressions and body language. I was eventually able to craft a personality around it.

I was ultra-polite and said really dumb things in order to gather my information, and everyone thought I was innocent and oh-so-sweet. When I finally saw myself in a mirror for the first time, I wanted to scream out loud. With my now perfect vision, I could see that I truly was a little girl. Then I noticed how stunningly pretty I was. As young girls go, I would have to say that this one was strikingly beautiful. I had a childlike face, but for a kid of 17, I was outstanding. Age could only make me more tantalizing (if that were even possible), I thought. The doctors and scientists needed to be congratulated. Faatina was built to be a sex goddess in every way. I could see some of the Arabic in my face. The ample breasts and tiny waist were European products no doubt, but the big butt had to be African-made. She was somewhere between a pear shape and the greatly desired hourglass figure. Her eyes were bright green, and my skin was a kind of olive color. A little too voluptuous for my taste. A body like this should have come with a manual. This was the kind of girl that you could never let outside of the house for fear of starting a riot. With her thick legs, pretty face and wide hips, she reeked and leaked of sexiness. I couldn't believe that I was looking at a reflection. But, when I opened my mouth, so did she. When I moved my hand, she did also. It was crazy and at the same time more than fascinating. Maybe this is a trick, I thought. What did they want from me? I knew about mind games all too well. Hell, I was trained in them. But, just in case this was a legitimate mistake, I decided it was in my best interest to play along for now. To tell the truth, at that moment, I actually did need a hug.

She was so many things I hated. The Arabs will always be at war with us. They hate me, and I had never met one that I didn't think I might have to kill at some point. Europeans are snobbish, at best. I have little time for them. And who wants to be an African? Not even Africans themselves. But the worst had to be the fact that I was now a female. What the fuck was I supposed to do with that? I could hardly bear the thought of living like this. At least I wasn't part Asian. I would have killed myself with a sheet tied to the drapery rod and a nearby chair. My hatred for them goes all the way back to Vietnam. Still, if this body really was going to be mine, then I would have to find a way to adapt to it.

But, if these people can make me a girl, then maybe they can make me a man again. It had to be an elaborate trick of some kind. I decided that they (whoever they were), wanted me to give up some kind of info. But, what info could that be? If they want a little girl, then they'll get one, I said to myself. I would be the best 17-year-old, rich dumb girl they ever saw. I would find a way to work this in my favor.

The first thing I did was what I figured my enemies didn't want me to do. I dove into the fact that I was a weakened and pitiful little girl. I pouted and complained about little insignificant things. But, I was always polite and sweet about it. The people around me would bend over to appease me. (Amazing the power a pretty face can have). On the times that they didn't or couldn't satisfy me, I would refuse to speak to them for a while. That scheme really seemed to upset the women much more than I thought it should. They would actually feel bad about themselves, until I let them off the hook. It took a lot of patience to pull this off, but the reward was surprisingly joyful. I tried not to go overboard with it. I know how annoying that is, even from the prettiest of women. Still, it was my chance to test the limits of this new character I was now forced to portray, and I learned a lot from it.

I was initially bald, but I was starting to grow what looked like light brown hair on my head. Eyelashes and eyebrows grew in first but on this date, I still had no other body hair. Meg tied a long yellow and pink scarf around my head that I retied in a more Arabic style. During this time, I was also learning to use my hands. I was taught to touch every part of myself in order to know where my body truly was, and to understand what it felt like. I would be blindfolded. The challenge was to start at the top of my head and move all the way down to my toes. The trick was trying to use my fingers, knuckles, wrists, palms, the front and even the backs of my hands. This helped to sensitize myself to the reality of what was now me. It made a big difference! Before, I felt like Pinocchio. After a few of those exercises, I felt like a real person again. This person, whoever she is, is definitely a girl.

The doctors had an issue with my hormones. It seems that my brain was not putting out enough of the ones my new body was calling for. So again, they sent some nanomites to the rescue. Overcome by the tingles again, my senses instantly went haywire. I started feeling sensations no man had ever felt before, and I was hit with the mind-blowing reality of what this body was truly designed to do. For instance, I could smell all kinds of things I had never noticed before, in my past life. With eyes closed I could point to where items were around me because of the smell they gave off. Perfumes, soaps, and a person's individual body odor, could be memorized. I could see pictures or a symbol of what the scent was supposed to be and call the face of the person who was wearing it, even when the same fragrance was worn by two different people. That gave me the ability to identify who was coming to see me, long before they came close enough to hear. Foul odors made me feel sick and sometimes I would throw up if I couldn't get away from them. But, everything felt so much more intense. The fabric of the sheets, the gown I was wearing, and things I would put in my hands. Much to my amazement, these things all gave me an emotional reaction. I found myself drawn to the things that I thought felt, smelled, looked, and sounded nice. Yes, I found that even words gave me a reaction.

My body, as a whole, became more sensitive. Cold things became unbearable while things that were hot became hotter but also more enjoyable. These sensitivities were most notable in the erogenous zones, namely my lips, tongue, neck, breasts, (especially the nipples), anyplace near the vagina, and my rectum. Yes, even my butthole was a hypersensitive machine. The slightest touch near any of these areas by anything that came in contact with them, made me sweat, and I was sexually aroused. Obviously, this was part of a fool proof plan to make Faatina addicted to sex in all its forms. From that day on, I could have a small orgasm every time I went to the toilet. And I went a lot.

There I was, overcome with intense sensory input as well as a physical and emotional overload that I could not shake. This was a great acting challenge in that stage of my role playing. How should Faatina react to these changes? I knew I could later take these new gifts and turn some of them into useful weapons. But, the others could serve no real purpose and were just too intense to manage. I could see them to be nothing more than a hindrance at best. In fact, some feelings were so loud, that I was finding it hard to think over their bombardment. Maybe I could get the Doc to turn this sex part off, or just down some, I thought. When I could bring myself to ask one of the doctors about it, he advised me to speak with the Chief Managing Physician.

It took me many weeks to see him, and no one would give me a hint of any kind about this man. I wanted to have "something in the bag" that I could use, like, if he had a daughter, or someone in his family had died in the war but it was no use. At this time, I was still on liquids and connected to the IV. They had me standing but I was working with a walker. My balance was completely out of whack and I had a tendency to get dizzy and throw up. I guess it had something to do with an almost one foot difference in height. Everyone said that I was learning very fast, but it wasn't fast enough for me. So, when I saw Mr Salim Mujawar, AKA Doctor Frankenstein, I travelled to his office in a wheelchair, dangling bottles and all.

Doc Stacy was with me as always. She wheeled me through the many halls and security check points. She used 3 colored IDs, and a "Special Memo" along the way. She seemed worried and she talked the whole trip. I tried to listen, but she had nothing of use to say. I think she was more nervous than I was, and I didn't know why. I knew that this was a risky move. If something went wrong and my pretense was discovered, I was screwed with no means yet to escape. Doc Stacy knew my concerns, and I had hoped she would be the one to speak for me, but that was not to be.

Mujawar's office was less than generic. There was nothing to suggest that this middle aged Indian man, ever worked in this room. There were no wall hangings, no diplomas, no family portraits, and no files or books around of any kind. There was not even a skeleton in the corner. It looked as though this room was setup just for me and this interview. Now, I was nervous.

Mujawar said that he was not really the Chief Physician. He said that he could not tell me who any of the members of the team were, and that this was to be a one time meeting. He would not say where we were, or how long I had been there. He did confirm the things I had learned through my earlier investigations. Then he asked me what I wanted to talk about.

In my practiced quiet shy voice, I told him that Doctor Stacy could do a better job of explaining my feelings, but he wasn't having any of that. He wanted my concerns to come from my own lips. I purposely made myself sound as clumsy as I could. That was easy to do on account of I had no idea how to explain any of these female issues. The sensations, the emotions, the senses I was now overloaded with, and the countless other feelings I was having, were just too much. At a lesser intensity, a normal woman would be born to most of these things and be none the wiser. But, to literally wake up to this modified overload after 70 years of what now seemed peace, was overwhelming.

So, I told him that I thought my feelings were more intense then I remembered and because of it I could not concentrate on what people were telling me half the time. I told him that I would like it if he could tone it all down to a more normal level. For an example, my sense of pleasure was magnified so high that even the touch of my own skin made me sexually aroused. I even told him that peeing felt so good now, that I was afraid to know what would happen when I had a solid poop for the first time.

"That's the way you were designed to be", he said. "I can help you to concentrate a little better but that is all I can do according to the parameters set by your family and your other un-named sponsors." He told me that an uncle from Saudi was to come soon and approve my recovery before my release, and that I should make myself ready for him. "Any other questions about your body or your family duty, should be directed to him," he said. "I would caution you to just agree to his demands. We had to. Since your father's death, this uncle is the one who has claimed owner-ship of you. He is your guardian now." Then he said, "As for the other concerns, I would wear a skirt or some real baggy pants."

And just like that, the interview was over. As I was wheeled back through the check points, I thought about what he had said about my duty and this visiting uncle, and I wondered about these "un-named sponsors" he mentioned. Who were they, and what would they want from me? The one good thing I learned was that I can't get pregnant and that I would never have those associated problematic symptoms that are related with having a period. I actually was quite concerned about that, and I felt so much better knowing that I will never have to deal with it. No bloody clothes, stained sheets, no tampons to carry around, and no cramps. It was some good news on an otherwise bad day.

It was what he didn't say, that was bothering me the most. It seems that the English side of the family had abandoned me. In most cases, an Arab female will not have a say in the life she is forced to live. She is bound to the family and hidden away inside the home. When she does come out, she has no face. Having ba-bies and her rank in the list of the other wives, is the only status she can have. The only thing Faatina would be good for was display. It would be up to the uncle to say who I would be given to for that. I could only assume that it would have to be someone that has at least one wife with children and wants another just for sex and a show piece for family gatherings. I needed a working plan, now!

I never let on but this time the nanomites did a lot more than anyone could have expected. Yes, I was very distracted by all the input but in truth I kind of lied about not being able to concentrate. I only wanted to tone things down to a more manageable level. After this new injection, that disorientation I was feeling was now gone for the most part and I began to feel more like me again. Now, not only was I able to control a lot of the continuous stimuli but I found myself able to vividly recall and review many of my past events as if I were watching a movie. I also had the ability to take all my past knowledge and move it around in my mind. Later my brain began to work much like a good computer program. I learned to cross-reference and recall just about anything I had reviewed, in an instant. But at this early stage, I was toying with the separation of my two lives. I began to practice thinking in levels and layers of thought. It was very tiring at first but later these newly built "programs", for lack of another term, could run continuously even on a subconscious level. If you were watching video from my room and saw me staring up at the ceiling or sitting up in bed with my eyes closed, you would think that I had lost my mind. In truth, I was reviewing and filing my memories.

It was a relearning of my old self. So many things that my old brain had forgotten were now starting to reawaken. I found a lot of dangerously classified and secret information that I wanted to keep hidden. I didn't know how but if these people had the technology to do what I had already seen, I wouldn't put it past them to be able to transfer any valuable information they discovered, out of my mind and into another device of some kind. So, for security reasons, I took those files and hid them far away in my head.

Some days later, the dizziness completely went away and at the same time I was started on solid food. I was now able to walk unhindered to the toilet on my own. That is not to say that I didn't occasionally fall from time to time. It felt so good to be out from under the yoke of the bedpans, so a little fall was still a good trade. The toilet experience in itself, is special and sometimes even magical. I could write another book just on my times in the can. I will however, say that the doctors were out of their collective minds to do that to a person, and that is another part of me that has never changed.

Yes, at first, I hated this body in a way that I find hard to express in words. But, that was before I found out all the new things I could do with it. The nanos helped reorganize my mind but that was just the start. I used them, along with my now enhanced brain, to make more improvements. My reflexes, reaction time, muscle memory, and healing, were also dramatically increased as time went on.

In Her Shoes

Living inside the female body is very different. I always thought that most females walked the way they did to draw attention to themselves. I felt they were just trying hard to look sexy. "She was walking like a slut." "That chick is a whore." I thought all these things and more about a woman, just on account of the way she was walking down the road. But now I have come to understand the real truth of it. Of course, there will always be many women that will put a little extra in the way they move, to tantalize or otherwise distract a man, but the majority of women walk the way they do because they are women.

Women are built altogether differently from a man. If she has any kind of chest, it will sway from left to right. The waist turns to pull her hips around. It acts as a balance or a buffer between the upper and lower body. The hips are wider than a man's are and require more muscles to move them around her pelvis. A girl like Faatina can't just step forward. Her hips have to swing those thick legs around. And with the reduced muscle in the rest of her body, this kid would bounce and jiggle with every movement.

I learned why females are not as strong in the upper body. The capacity to lift and carry is equivalent to the broadness of their shoulders. And the smaller the shoulders are, the weaker the arms will be. On average, the feet can be 1 and a ¼ size smaller than a man of the same height. That makes a great difference in the way she can balance herself. Most men will always run faster and jump higher.

Now, I know that most women may not agree with my findings because none of them have anything to compare this to. Men know that there is a difference, but they cannot know how much. I cannot and will not analyze the way women think and process their information. My mind is trained to think the way I do, and I know nothing else. I will hypothesize that a woman with similar training could do the same.

Everything about this new body was so different. For the longest time I had to keep reminding myself that I could now stand and walk freely without all the mental preparation to overcome the pains I used to have. I don't even want to talk about the incredible flexibility. Other than the fact that it was female, this body was next to perfect.

The old body could walk too, but bending was extremely painful. I had to become comfortable with others bending down for me. It did make me very good at not dropping things on the ground. I had a hip replaced five years before. I wanted to replace the other one, but I just never got around to it. I lost part of the calf muscle on my left leg when our Huey crashed during Project DELTA in '65. Pieces of the blades went everywhere. I considered myself lucky since two other guys died in that crash.

In truth, I had been shot, stabbed, beaten, and blown the fuck up more times than anyone else I knew. My life history was written on my flesh from head to toe. The old injuries of my youth had long since returned to make themselves permanent residents and I had come to feel a sense of pride in my pains. I wore them much like I wore my battle scars and they were the same to me as the many ribbons, medals, and coins I kept in my display case. I was in pain most of the time but that was part of who I was. The body I have now is like new. I see no burns, cuts, or bullet holes. My new flesh is soft, clean, and real easy on the eyes.

In September of '66, I and a few other drunken Rangers, got tattoos next to our favorite whorehouse in a town we were never really at. The other fellas got eagles, snakes, or our unit insignia permanently stenciled into their arms, chest, or on their backs, but I got something a little different.

You see, I was engaged to this girl named Cindy Cain, who at times I would lovingly call "Candy Cain". Candy was a pretty church-going girl out of Cobb County, Georgia, and we were in all kinds of love. Two days before this night I had received a 3-week-old letter stating that not only had she been dating James Stanton, my old football teammate, and not told me, but a week before she wrote the letter they had actually gotten married in the same church that we had planned our wedding in.

Well, I was upset at the world, of course, and I had punched a few guys, but my buddies took care of me and got me out of trouble. I was still pretty angry on that drunken night so, when I sat down in the artist chair knowing that I too, could have had the proud 91st, an eagle, snake or even a big red dragon placed on my chest, I chose hate instead. I hated my ex-friend James and Cindy, but mostly I hated myself for feeling the way I did.

Cindy could never be part of any real team. She knew nothing of that kind of bond. She was no buddy and she was definitely no friend. She was just a girl. So, to remind myself against a girl ever making me feel that way again, I asked that guy to give me a big beautiful red heart with the word "Love' inside of it. After he was through, I told him to put a big black 'X' right on the top of the new tat. I never again let a woman know how I felt about her, even if I did love her. (They divorced in 2 years).

I guess you could say it was the moment I let myself become cold. And yes, I did want it that way. It's true, I may have missed out on a lot of joy, but now, now, I was protected from Love's knife. When I look at myself in the mirror now, Cindy is nowhere to be found. All I can see is a beautiful little girl looking back from the glass. James Stanton was killed behind the wheel some time ago and for all I know Cindy is dead, too. But "Candy Cain" will always be with me. Unlike me, she will never die.

Learning to Cry

I didn't realize it at first, but I was fighting the fact that I was a girl and it was holding me back. Every time I woke up I hoped that yesterday was a bad dream. It took weeks to realize that I had to accept the reflection I was looking at, as the person I now needed to play. Once I did, things became a little easier.

I had graduated from the wheelchair and that walker contraption. I was walking on my own around a small track outside in the courtyard. The concrete walls towered to the sky, but it was a nice little place with grass, flowers, and a few small trees. My senses would go wild and I did feel so much more alive. I always looked forward to enjoying the way the deliciously warm, un-air-conditioned air, and the sun felt on my skin, but each time I was told to walk my mile as fast as I could and get back inside. I'm sure it was for security reasons. Someone of real importance would most likely need that area soon. I did what I was told but I made them have to tell me every time.

The eyebrows and eyelashes were all in now. My light brown head hair was about two inches long and growing fast. The tingles were completely gone, and I was feeling more in control of my body movements. I still had some trouble with my balance, but other than that I felt like I was 60 again. I was steadily growing stronger in my motor skills, my flexibility was off the chart, and my mind would whirl like the wind. I continued to arrange the files in my head, carefully editing and hiding the classified stuff, while at the same time reviewing past events for useable information. I could sit alone all day if they would let me, just facing the walls.

The uncle from Saudi would be coming sometime soon. I was certain he would collect me, ready or not, and force me to become someone's sex slave. After all, it could be the only real purpose for saving my life. I was sure that I would probably be pampered by day, only to be brutally ravaged and abused by night. Arabs don't expect much from their women. All they are good for is to make babies, and this man well knew I would never be able to do that. If all he could do was fuck me, I would have no other real purpose. He, or whoever he chose for me, would treat me like a dog. The other women of the house would surely treat me like dog shit for the same reasons. I've never had sex with a man, nor did I want to. Even now as a woman, I cannot see myself enjoying that position. My body was made to enjoy it, but my head was not. I had to come up with something so repulsive that this man would not want me. I still needed a good idea, and time was running out.

It occurred to me that appealing to the English side of the family might make all the difference in the world. I didn't know if the family would help me, still, Arthur Britten had been a powerful man. The mention of his name to the right ears should mean something. My goal was the British Embassy. All I had to do was get over there and act like a lost girl.

First, I needed to get hold of my IDs. Then I needed some cab fare. There was still no telling where I was, and how far away a government office might be. I could find some clothing around someplace easy enough. The real question was how to get out of the complex. I was not ready, but there was no telling how much time I had. It was now time to put the beginnings of a plan in motion.

The next morning at 0700hrs, Doc Stacy was prompt as always. When she entered the room, she found me in tears. I knew that would be the one thing that would get to her. She had wanted me to cry since the first time I saw her. In her mind, I was dead inside. Up to this point, all her talks and questions gave her no insight on my mental state whatsoever. This was my chance to give her what she wanted.

This wasn't an easy thing for me to do so I set my mental alarm for 0500hrs to give myself time to prepare. I started by trying to recall all the sad things I could think of that would make a normal person break down and cry. Things like losing my men in battle and not being around for my kids, but that didn't work. I had hardened myself to those things long ago. As time went by I began to think about how my life would be if I didn't figure something out. Or more precisely, how it would make me feel?

I thought about how it would feel to be trapped in a room with nothing to do but wait around until someone entered to fuck the hell out of me and then leave, locking the door behind them. If I didn't wish to conform, I would just be raped. I would be left alone again until he, or someone else, returned to abuse me again.

If it did come down to that, I would have to find some way to kill myself. But what if that option were to be taken away? What if that was to be my life? My body was built for just that very thing. It was also made to be flexible and durable. I could conceivably live a lot of years this way. Escape would be impossible, and any resistance would be futile. Even if I could escape, any authorities I ran to would just bring me right back to the house. This I'm sure would drive me into insanity. All I could do about it would be to cry, and I know even that would get me a good beating. You could be visited twice a year or twice in a night. It was totally at his whim.

A young wife is expected to be ready and appealing at all times and it is not uncommon to be taken by every male member of the family, especially when she is viewed as an outsider or unworthy of respect. The other women of the home would jealously scorn her for her selfishness. A frigid wife would be repeatedly raped into submission. After all, in that society a female is still only a piece of flesh.

I had eaten the usual hospital breakfast at 0630hrs as I always do. At 0645hrs, I knew that I was going to throw up. Around 10 minutes later, I did. All I had eaten that morning was now in the bed and over the front of my body. It was a real foul mess, too. I imagined myself doing this very thing again every morning in my lavishly furnished prison and at that moment, I began to truly cry.

I had intended to trick Doc Stacy into believing that I was disturbed and that she now could whip out one of those pre-programmed healing solutions from one of her many books. But on that day and time, I knew with all my heart, that if Uncle Saudi got his way, what I had imagined would be my reality.

Doc Stacy walked into the room and freaked. She tried to get me to tell her what was wrong, but I could not speak. She called for Mama Meg and together they began to use the dirty sheets to wipe me up. I wanted to tell them that I missed my parents and all of that, but I could not get out a word.

I felt so disgusted with the vision of my possible fate that it made me sick. My finely tuned sense of smell made me throw up even more. I must have lost 5 pounds that morning because I puked until I had nothing left inside of me. Even after I had emptied, I dry heaved for a while. It was out of control.

Looking back, I feel sorry for the Doc. She and Meg were working so hard to calm and clean me. They were so concerned that they too, were crying. They undressed me, held me, and we all cried together. Their arms around me were comforting. Their tears mixed with mine were releasing. Their kind words were soothing. It was my first real feminine moment and it was like nothing I could have ever known. They stayed with me as I cried myself to sleep. (What a moment).

When I awoke, I felt hungry but truly cleansed. My throat hurt a little but other than that, I really felt great. Doc Stacy was sitting in a corner reading one of her big books. I was dressed in a new gown and wrapped in clean sheets. (I never knew how they could do that without waking me up).

When she saw I was awake, Doc Stacy walked over and softly asked me if I was feeling better. This was my cue. I told her that I knew that my parents were dead and gone but I still wanted to go home anyway. I said, "I want to wake up in my own bed.", "I want to go back to school.", "I want to have my friends around me.". This one was the kicker. "I want to hold something in my hands that reminds me of who I am." Oh, my nose ran, and I cried again. As far as my acting was concerned, I was beautiful. It was truly my best work up to that date.

I got Faatina's passport, the mother's silver necklace, and a school ID. The passport was British, and the ID said London, England. There was a partly burned "This Is It" ticket for the concert at the O2 Arena in London, and I got one more thing. It was something I didn't expect. It was Arthur Britten's driver's license. It was bubbled and burned around the edges, but his name and photo were clear. They let me hold them for a while but later they wanted to take them back. I refused to let go and cried like a little girl until I was told that I could keep them. I put the necklace on and held the other things in one hand or the other. They never left my touch. The plan was starting to come together.

The ladies told me that I would move to a new home in Saudi. They said that I would make new friends there. I couldn't blame them because they had no idea what they were talking about. I tried to explain to them that things in Saudi were not like the US. Marriage is only a matter of signing a few forms and I was now within that minimum age. Once I was married my life would not be my own. I could never hang out with friends at the mall or go to the movies. And that's when I had an epiphany. Every pretty chick I ever knew could not function without spending someone's money. So, I asked them to take me to the mall, to see other kids and buy something pretty one last time. In Saudi I would only ever be allowed to sport a Burka outside. You may have a few nice things for the home, but I had nothing to wear. "When my Uncle comes, it will be too late!"

After much debate it was agreed that I could go but only under close supervision. I was told that I could have a four hour "hall pass". The mall was about an hour away. That gave me two hours to spend shopping, and two hours travel time. It was a one-shot deal and I had two days to get ready.

That first night I woke myself at 0200hrs. I tiptoed barefoot down the halls and snuck past the unmanned check points. I dodged the rotating cameras and found a lab with big and small bubbling glass tanks of clear liquid that was oily to the touch.

This had to be the place of my rebirth. I saw other tanks with living organs suspended inside them. Computerized machines controlled the flow of blood, oxygen, and who knows what else. A bar code label had been placed on each occupied tank. I was just about to leave when I came across two brains. They too, were coded but they also said, "Identification Unknown."

I knew that I had to do something. One of these had to belong to the little girl. That was the brain that should have been placed into this body. The other one probably should have been mine. It was still possible that someone had made a big mistake. After all, the labels did say, "unknown". No one really wanted to know my secrets. They were just saving the girl.

Then again, these things had wires with sensors all over them. The device that they were wired to was daisy-chained into other devices and those devices were attached to computers. Who's to say that they had not downloaded my mind into this body or into another brain that was placed into this body? This could even be part of a living chain. If I were to destroy these brains, would the mind in this body die?

It seemed to me that whoever these brains did belong to, sooner or later the doctors were planning to reanimate them somehow. But where were their bodies? So far all I'd seen were a few random body parts. Maybe all they were doing was downloading one mind into another. Still, if and when these minds were to awaken they would also begin to speak. It was my guess that one of them would be saying, "Where are my Mom and Dad?"

I couldn't take that chance. I figured I would unplug the bubble making device from the wall. That would kill the brains, but I needed to destroy the computers as well. Then it occurred to me that it's not the computers I needed, it was the memory storage units. I needed to steal or corrupt that memory. Places like this would surely have backups around and I didn't know what was what. Computers and I have always had a mutual dislike for each other.

I didn't understand them, and they couldn't stand being slammed on the floor. This whole room would have to be demolished.

What I do know are chemical explosives. I had seen a cleaning closet not too far away and I was able to find everything I needed to poison the brains and start a nice chemical and electrical fire at the same time. The next night at 0200hrs, MacGyver would have been amazed (He's got nothing on me). I got some of those cleaning products, a pail, and a little bit of water to create a gas that would poison all the living tissues in the lab. I knew the sensors would go off and a Halon Gas would be released in the computer room as soon as the oxygen levels dropped. By SOP the doors would close, and I needed to get the two gases to meet so I had to remove a panel under the raised floor that connected both sides. The resulting explosion will prompt the mains to release a water solution that would not react well with the chemical mix. The lethal, ion-charged, vapor mixture would now corrode everything metal in its path.

The trigger was the metal pail and rubber glove. I stripped some high voltage wires with my teeth, wrapped them around the pail, and placed the first mixture inside. On the cold airconditioned floor, I figured it would take about five hours to heat the pail to the right temperature. The rubber on the glove of water would melt and... Let's just say, woe be it unto anyone in that area. I wrapped it all up at about 0330hrs.

At 0700hrs I was given a T-shirt, sandals, short pants, boxer shorts and a bra. The bra was painfully too small, and the boxers hung lower than the shorts, so I couldn't use either of them. I had to squeeze my hips and butt into the shorts but once I did, the waist was way too big. Except for the bra, everything was too big. Meg fixed me up with some bobby pins and that took care of the pants.

I put the IDs in the pants pockets and tied the large white T-shirt with a knot on my left side. That pulled the shirt closer to my body. This was my very first time wearing clothes of any kind.

The feel of the cloth brushing across my nipples was driving me nuts. The big sandals they gave me fell away from my little feet with every step. I had to shuffle my way out of the building and into the car. I left the scarf on the bed.

We were in Georgia, west of the town of Macon and south of Atlanta, in the USA. We were on Hwy 74 heading north right into Peachtree City. I saw signs for Griffin and La Grange. I was born outside of Birmingham, Alabama. When my Dad died in Korea I was sent to my uncle's place in Newnan. That was 1951 and I was 11 years old. I played football in grade school and high school in Newnan. Peachtree City was only a few miles away.

Peachtree City is the land of the rich. Golf carts are the normal mode of transportation around the neighborhoods. People can play golf through your backyard. When I was last here, there was nothing for a young man to do. From where I sat in the back of the limo, things hadn't changed much at all. We continued north into Atlanta. It was springtime.

The Atlanta traffic was nuts. It was about 0830hrs when we arrived at the Lenox Mall. Two security guards were waiting outside at the main entrance. The shops would open at 0900hrs but Doc Stacy, Sgt James, and I were escorted right into Abercrombie & Fitch.

The guards were a wacky pair. The guy was a big, fat, sloppy Bubba. He had either already spilled today's breakfast onto his uniform, or dinner from last night. I couldn't tell which. The woman was a little, short, fiery, Mexican girl. She looked like she was 19 years old and was as excited as a Chihuahua. A real chatterbox too. The fat boy never said a word.

The Abercrombie ladies treated me like I was a celebrity. They took my sizes and flew around the store like bees working up a sweat. It was really something to see. I learned that I am 34DD, 25, and 39. I'm 5 feet 6 inches tall, and 134lbs. The doctors had mentioned that I had some excess water to lose. (No doubt from spending a lot of time floating in a bubbling pool of fluid). Still, if you want to talk about being well endowed, you were talking about me. I'd never be a runway model but if you saw my body on the cover of a girly magazine, and the body of any super model on the cover of a fashion promo, most guys would rather turn to find my pages and leave that puny runway girl on the shelf. (I know I would).

In truth, I did need something to wear. I didn't even have a pair of panties, for crying out loud. But, all I really wanted to do was to get into that dressing room and sneak out a back door into the city. Unfortunately, the ladies would not leave me alone for a second. Not even in the dressing booth. I don't know what they were told about me or what their instructions were, but I can tell you that it was very strange having someone help you pull up your underwear. I was reasonably certain that the next customer would not get this same treatment. As weird as it was to have these pretty young women put their hands on me, all I could do was just stand there and pretend that it was all normal.

I have to admit, I was a little intrigued with the colors and feels of the fabrics. (More of those little things I never needed to pay attention to before). The other women seemed to believe that these little things made all the difference in the world. Who was I to discount or dispute them?

The ladies were blown away with my ignorance about the items and were all too glad to educate this unfortunate Arab child. They gave me so many complements about how I looked and how my voice sounded. They all wanted me to tell them the names of the items in Arabic. Many of them I didn't know so I'd make up words that I thought they might be. What did I know about women's clothes? They worked so hard to make me smile and when I finally did smile they seemed so overjoyed. By the time the store was open to the public I had started to have fun.

When a guy wants to buy a shirt, it's all business. He won't ask for help and he may not even try it on. When a woman comes into a shop, it's a girl party, and she will have more fun there than she can have at Disney Land. If it isn't that way, that chick may never shop there again.

Sgt James answered his phone. He turned away from the yapping Chihuahua girl and moved out of my sight line. Doc Stacy as usual, was buried in one of her books, and Bubba was nowhere to be seen. What else could it be but a call from the hospital? I asked one of the sales women to take me to the ladies' room. Once in, I asked her to please step away from the door. I told her that it was an Arab thing and she said she understood. I had tried on so many things that hour, but at this time I was wearing a little yellow sun dress with tiny pink flowers and some open-toe cork shoes that looked kind of like sandals to me. I still had the IDs in my hands and the chain on my neck. I had to tell the ladies about my dead parents in order to get them to put the items back into my hands after each changing.

The only way out other than the bathroom door was a small back-flow trap door in the ceiling. It wasn't easy, but I was able to twist open the lock by jamming the tiny links of the necklace into the screw opening and turning it. I couldn't pull myself up, so I had to climb on top of the stall and leap up into the opening. I bumped my head, scratched my hips, and tore the dress a little doing it. I put more scratches on my arms pulling my big ass inside the door. Once inside I closed the hatch, but it wouldn't stay shut, so I tied it off using the necklace.

Right away I began moving in the direction I was facing. It was a tight fit. Traveling on my elbows and knees must have put a hundred more punctures into my skin. When the duct began to grow larger I knew I was going in the right direction. Using the dim light that filtered in from the vents, I travelled upwards quite a ways before heading down. That first exhaust fan scared me. After using a shoe to slow and stop it, I was able to squeeze myself through it. I negotiated two other fans before reaching the main exchange in the cellar of the mall.

It was incredibly loud, and I was now in complete darkness. A great wind whipped me around and tried to suck me into the surrounding vents. It was all I could do to keep from losing my precious paperwork into that thing. After about five minutes of struggling, I found the handle that opened the hatch. It felt like an hour.

I was more tired than I could remember. I felt dizzy and forced myself to sit on the ice cold cellar floor for a while to rest. I lost what was left of the shoes someplace, and my dress was shredded. Blood and sweat dripped from all over. I'm sure I wasn't looking very pretty at that time.

A building engineer found me passed out on the floor. He picked me up and laid me on a couch in his office. It was quiet and a lot warmer in there. He was on the phone with Security when I came to. I had overestimated my endurance level. In the air ducts I could have rested several times, but I didn't. I had to keep going and going, and now I was caught.

"Hey, excuse me mister, I need your help," I said. The old black man may not have been 80 years old, but he looked like it. He was tall, thin, and frail looking. It must have been a real effort for him to lift me and set me on that couch. "Help is on the way," he answered. "I called the medic and I called Security." I sat up too quickly, and my head began to ache. "Are you still trying to run away? You kids now-a-days are just plain crazy. You got money for drugs, games and who knows what else, but you'd rather steal. Now look what you've done to yourself. Now think; wouldn't it had been better to just pay for that stuff? Climbing through the ducts was a real bad idea. Just look at you!"

I told the man that I was running away from kidnappers. I asked him to call the police. I told him that I was rich and even promised a reward. "See, that's the big difference between me and you. I can look in my pocket right now and pull out my wallet. I can open it up and when I count the single dollars in it, every last one of them is one I earned. Unlike you, I don't steal, I don't cheat, and I really hate a liar."

"Then just call the cops, man," I said. "I'm begging you! Security will just hand me back over to those people! You have to call the police. They'll take me home."

The old guy just wasn't having any of it. I tried to get up, but my feet had gone numb. I so wanted to leave that room, but I wasn't going anywhere. Weak and in pain, I resolved to lay back, shiver, and quietly cry.

When I woke again the police were there. They were two big, tall, black men that looked more like football players than cops. I was on a gurney outside in the parking lot next to the car. I heard the Chihuahua saying something about, "That shit ain't fuckin' right." Bless her Hispanic heart. She had talked to the old man and decided to call the police herself. Sgt James was trying to explain to them why I had said that I was kidnapped. The police had my passport and the other items with them and were taking notes. Doc Stacy gave me a shot of something in my arm. I was dazed and in a lot of pain but before I passed out again I was able to say, "My father was Arthur Britten, and I want to go back to my home in England. I don't want to go to Saudi. Don't let them send me to Saudi!"

I didn't see the uncle, but he saw me. He came by Saint Joseph's Hospital in Atlanta later that day and decided that I was too much trouble. He told the staff, "It would have been better if she had died with her mother." I was free to stay in America for now. I was told that the police were able to contact someone in the Britten family somehow and they were sending me to the Sunshine State of Florida, to live. It looked like I was saved. (For now).

As far as the escape plan went, it was successful only because I was no longer going to Saudi. The plan was sound, but I had grossly miscalculated the limitations of this new body. If I had another month to prepare myself I think I could have gotten away on my own. In truth I didn't have much of a choice. Still, I had to do better than this. My confidence was low.

Two days later I flew alone by private jet into Miami. I was still fairly sedated at takeoff and didn't notice that all my items were taken from me, to include the ID cards I wanted to save. In my stupor, I sat looking out the window wearing the same hospital PJ's and slippers I had on in Saint Joe's and covered with a blanket. I don't even remember getting on.

An older white lady met me at the foot of the plane. It seemed to upset her to watch my banister-gripping, slow, one-step-at-a-time descent, but not enough that she would stoop to help me. I could tell that she felt this assignment was beneath her. With the manner of a cop, she looked me up and down. She must have been told that I was flighty because she took me by the arm and roughly pulled me straight into an awaiting car with not so much as a "hello".

Another lady cop was behind the wheel and together we sped off into the city. I had never been in the city of Miami. I sat in the airport a bunch of times, but I had never walked outside the door. I hoped we were not going to another hospital. It took me three months to break out of the first one. I sensed that if I had made any sudden moves these ladies would hold me down and beat the shit out of me. I decided to play it quiet and shy. Besides, Lady Cop #1 was staring a hole into me and it was creeping the hell out of me. I looked at my feet until the car was parked.

It was a beautiful new 15 story condo. We were on Collins Avenue and in the heart of Miami Beach. A Valet took the car away and an old-fashioned bellhop met us at the door. The place was more like a hotel than anything else. I saw gold leaf, slate, and marble all around. Without a word, the man at the counter handed Lady Cop #2 a card key and the hop took us into the glass elevator. We could look down at the lobby all the way to the top.

A young lady by the name of Krystle met us at the doorway. Krystle was a 22 year old part Cuban, part Philippine, and part-time singer for a Miami band called "The Third World". The first thing I noticed about her was that she had a badass brown skin body and an even badder tattoo of a bright red dragon on her back. She had the shape of a model, 5 foot 10, long black hair, and thin. The Cops stopped at the doorway. Lady Cop #1 pushed me inside and #2 gave my new roommate a small package of papers and said, "She's all yours." I never saw them again.

I had stayed in some nice places before and this was no exception. This spacious 3 bedroom condo had a view of the water on every side. We were on the top floor. A glass door opened to a deck with a private pool and spa. The living/dining room was vast, and the three bedrooms were almost as huge. The first bedroom was Krystle's, the second was mine, and the third was in the process of being built into a kind of gym. Flat screens and phones were in every room. Even the window blinds were run from remote. It was like something out of the "In Like Flint" movie, only better because this was real.

The package had my new identity inside. We found an English passport, a Lebanese passport, a birth certificate dated September 3rd (18 going on 17 now), and a Florida Learners License, all with the name Jasmine Aiza Britten. I had the title to the condo, a car, and a credit card. There was also a letter addressed to Krystle.

The place was not completely furnished. The next morning we ordered beds and furnishings by phone, but on that first night I had to lie on the living room floor.

Krystle was no Doc Stacy. The mothering instinct was just not in her. I remembered feeling very cold that night. I was so wiped out from the drugs that I could no longer stand. When I sat down on the carpet it felt like I was falling off the world. Krystle tossed my blanket over me and then sat by the door.

A Red Wave

Like everything else in that package, the car was really only a piece of paper. The next day we went to the Jaguar dealership, presented the form, and drove off in a new blue XKR-S. (Love those British cars). Krystle then drove us to a private shop where I was again fitted for several new outfits and a lot of underwear. We ate lunch on the beach and put our feet in the water. When we returned home, the furniture was set-up and in place.

Krystle treated me like her baby sister. I didn't drive the car and I was never left alone. She told me when to sleep, dress, and eat, and she watched everything I did. She did teach me a lot about hygiene, hair, and makeup. As a form of exercise, we danced to her band's music twice a day and stretched out in the gym. She was real bossy with me, but I let her. I had the dumb-little-girl-act down cold. I could tilt my head to the side and hold my mouth open with the best of them. Perfecting the female mannerisms was a long, tedious, and tough ordeal. I continued with the shy kid role and studied Krystle's every move. (She was hired for a reason). She wanted me to eat, walk, stand, act, and talk in a certain way. I kept the Arab accent and would throw a word or two in from time to time just to get her upset. She was a fiery thing when she was mad. She would swear at me in Spanish. I would put my head down, pout, and pretend to be sad until she apologized. Afterwards she would say something nice and I would pretend to be happy.

I was learning how easy it was to manipulate the emotions of others to get something I wanted. Body language and voice tones gave me some of my best results but throw on the water-works, and the game was over. With the right technique and a lot of time I could win a war without firing a single shot.

This went on for about a month. I became bored with practicing our little game of torment. She figured that I was never going to understand American life, and I figured the same thing about her. Then the sisterhood came to a standstill. The real straw was dropped when I found out that she had been giving me a drug.

One afternoon we had some bad sushi at a beach side restaurant. Krystle threw up out the window while she was driving the car. I had to hand it to her. We nearly crashed but she showed great control of the wheel. I threw up too but only after I got a good whiff of her breath. I couldn't get out of the seatbelt, so I threw up on myself, as usual. When we got back home, I threw up again in the lobby.

My stomach was really turning over and over, so that night I refused to eat anything for dinner. I laid down for a while but around midnight I got up. Krystle was in the gym playing on her portable keyboard with her headphones on. Normally, I would sleep through the night and into late morning. But that night I was wide awake, and my head was clear. I took the keys and went out the door.

The car had been cleaned and I have to say was a real joy to drive. I took it all around Miami Beach. I've always done some of my best thinking on a barstool, so I stopped by a club, but they wouldn't let me in. I couldn't buy a drink any place. So, I got some cash at the ATM and paid a Cuban guy to walk me into a store to buy a bottle of brandy. Afterwards I had to pay him again just to go away. Then I drove to the beach, sat in the sand, and waited for the sun.

I thought about what I should do next. If this was not a trick designed to get me to spill my guts, and if I truly had this chance to start over from 18, then things could be a lot worse. I was young again, healthy and free from all my old problems. I was a girl, but I was rich, pretty, and in Miami. No one was trying to kill me. The only enemy I could think of might be Krystle. What was her role anyway? I figured that she might be my only loose end at the moment. Maybe it was the brandy talking, but I came to the conclusion that she needed to die.

I could chop her into pieces and dissolve her body in the tub with some lye. I had killed women before. Only, her band would miss her. I would have to deal with them later. I knew that I wasn't in the best shape to take on more than one at a time, even with surprise on my side. So, it was time for another plan.

There were a lot of things I could do now. I could go to school and learn about another way of living. I could get out of the "Game", leave security inspections, spies, and government, behind for good. I still couldn't see getting married and having a normal relationship (not with a man anyways). I'd have to be a lesbian. I thought about that for a moment and before I was one-quarter into that bottle, it started to sound pretty good.

A security guard woke me around 0730hrs. I had forgotten that I wasn't myself any more. With this body, it would probably be better not to ever get drunk again. I wasn't built for it. Not to mention the fact that I could have gotten raped out there, or worse.

It was about 0830hrs when I returned to the condo, headache and all. The lobby called when I came in, so Krystle was waiting for me at the door. She was as angry as an Hispanic/Asian could be. She yelled at me in Spanish. She looked really sexy and hot, so I gave her one chance to save her soul.

I pushed past her and sat the half bottle of E & J on the table. "You have been putting something in my food," I told her. "I want to know why, and I want to know who you are working for, or I will break your face open with that bottle." She stopped talking and just looked at me until I picked up the bottle again.

Then she did something I didn't expect; she went into her bedroom. I couldn't believe that she just walked away from me like that. I didn't know what this bitch would do, so I followed her with the bottle in hand. Right then I was in the mind to smack her on the side of the face like I was Hank Aaron swinging for that 755th. The feeling came over me that I should jab the broken bottle into her neck, but that "little voice" told me not to. Her keyboard case was under her bed. She pulled it out and was about to open it when I stopped her by placing my foot on the top.

"If there is a gun in that thing, I'm going to make you eat it." It was a good thing that girl started crying. She showed me the instructions for the drug she was giving me. She also told me that she was given this assignment by her manager. The manager said that he was trying to get her signed to a label and that this job would be a big favor for a very important friend. She didn't know who this friend was. All she knew was that she was supposed to prepare me for school and make sure I didn't make any more trouble.

She had never heard of the British and Saudi names I knew. She didn't know a thing about the two cops that brought me. Her only contact in this assignment was her manager, Bobby Simms. According to her, he was only concerned that I get into this "High Society School."

The rich and famous have a prep school in the area. Krystle's job was to get me ready to attend classes before September. I would fit in with the other rich misfits and be trained to be one of those debutante types. "OK. I'll go to your school," I told her. "But know three things, bitch. First, I'm not eating your cooking. Second, I'll be driving the car from now on. And third, I can speak Spanish fluently."

"OK," I thought. This is an old man in the body of a teenage girl, and I can't tell anyone about it. Any chance in the world of reversing that, or putting me in the body of a man, was gone. I must have destroyed the lab where I was reborn. Besides, it would have been impossible to hold a gun on a man while my brain was being removed, or programmed, or whatever. I was going to have to accept the fact that this was my body now. I could love it, or I could hate it. That was the only real choice after all. I had to start appreciating what I had and find a way to acquire what I didn't. It wasn't beyond all reason to consider that maybe I was reborn to be part of some higher purpose. This was my second chance.

I had done so many things that no sane man would be proud of, or even want to admit for that matter. I could set my soul back on track, I thought. Then again, it was no telling what new and wacky surprise could drop out of the sky, so I would have to be prepared for them all. That meant physically and mentally. I still needed to continue to structure my mind. I had no idea what potential my enhanced brain was really capable of. But getting my body in better shape had to be my next priority.

I said nothing at the time, but I made it a point to meet the Simms fella in the near future. I wanted to be more prepared for the unexpected, so I was willing to wait. Besides, a meeting at this stage of the game might overplay my hand before I was ready to bet my life.

Krystle and I came to kind of an understanding. She would get off my ass a little, and I would try not to do anything that would jeopardize her potential record contract. We ate at restaurants and she schooled me on how girls in America were supposed to act. She still corrected me whenever I gave her the opportunity, but I had the freedom to roam the building and the nearby shops, in the car. After all, I was only 17 on paper.

The next morning, we were supposed to start some speed walking. I didn't know I would need a sports bra and loose shorts for that. Krystle didn't seem to have any trouble with her smaller breasts and flat ass, but I was thrown around from side to side. Later I discovered that stuffing pads in my pants would soak up most of the dampness of the tiny orgasms I got from all the bouncing and my thighs rubbing together. Any wetness that did escape would be hidden by all the sweating I was going to do anyway. It wasn't a choice. Without these precautions I couldn't exercise.

Our fifth floor was pretty much dedicated to food and fitness. It was everything from bagels to bras. I have to say I've never found those things the least bit comfortable. The more weight you carry, the more the straps sink into the skin and leave you with marks. But they are vital when it comes to physical activity.

I was fitted at the fitness center. They had all kinds of classes just for women. I signed up for Cooking, Pilates, Jazzercise, and Self Defense. I was sure I would need a bra for all of them.

In this building the women outnumber the men by 8 to 1. It seems that most of the women are mistresses or trophy wives of rich old guys, drug dealers, and gangsters. These chicks were insane with fashion, lipo, diet, makeup, and Botox. If any of them had a job, it was best not to let any of the other women know about it. While the men were off doing whatever it was they did, the women competed with each other and spent as much money as they could. You had no friends in that place. They were a bunch of conniving and back stabbing bitches. They would sooner seduce your husband then to push the button in the elevator for you when your hands were full. With that in mind, I will now breakdown some of the 5th floor experiences.

I walked out of the cooking class. It was an unorganized mess and a real big waste of my time. The women were just talking about a lot of the other women in the building. The only thing I did was make a salad. I'm sure they talked about me after I left.

The Pilates was interesting. I had to buy an entirely different outfit for this one. I hoped it would be a good physical and mental exercise, but I just couldn't hack the atmosphere. There were a lot of outstanding looking women in that class. I had to focus hard on the workout and try to ignore how horny those spandex clad beauties were making me feel. As it turned out, I was the most flexible one in the room, but I always had to leave early to avoid an accidental eruption. I quit that class after three tries.

Jazzercise turned out to be my best class. I've never been a dancer before but now that I have been able to literally defragment and move files around in my mind, I've opened up vast amounts of new brain space. I was now able to learn timing and execute all the dance moves I was shown. The music was nice, and the instructor was outstanding. I would try to make this class three times a week.

I ran into some trouble in the Self Defense class. I wanted to learn from an expert how a woman should best defend herself. Unfortunately, that was not to be the case. The instructor's name was Rico. He was a Cuban- born American, about 6 foot 1 inch, good-looking, and well built. His Bio listed some Korean styles and it said that he was trained in-country. It didn't list any military history so if that were true, then this man might have an interesting story to tell.

I arrived a little late on my first day. The class start time was posted for 0900hrs, but when I walked in the door wearing my new Korean style uniform, the other ladies looked as if they had been there for quite some time. They were on the mats talking and stretching out, but they were not wearing a uniform of any kind. These 6 women were between 30 and 40 and were all in great shape. They had tiny shorts and tank tops on. None had bras, and three of them were not even wearing panties under those shorts. When my happy face walked in carrying my own bag of pads and gloves, they all laughed.

These girls weren't learning the martial arts. They were just showing out for the instructor. I actually felt a little over dressed so I removed my uniform top and started stretching on the floor. Rico came in with his uniform on, at about 0905hrs. The women and I stood up and bowed to him. I remember thinking this was looking better. He exchanged the normal pleasantries in his Cuban accent and got us lined up. I already knew some of the basic Karate moves, but I was never a real student. I knew the "horse stance", the punches, and some kicks, but the other women in the class acted as if they knew nothing at all.

Each one of them called to Rico for help with their form. He happily moved from one to the other, each time rubbing, caressing, and squeezing their wanting bodies. Rico was quite aroused and boldly displayed the lump in his pants. The ladies loved it. The more they were touched, the more wet their little shorts became. Rico clearly had his pick in this room and the rich ladies greatly enjoyed the attention they were lacking in their lonely apartments. In a way I was proud of him. But this wasn't a defense class. It was something else entirely.

When he saw me in the back of the class he nearly lost all his cool points. I had decided that I probably wasn't going to learn anything healthy there and was just about to pick up my bag and go, when Rico leaped right in front of where I was standing. Moving into me real close, he said "Oh, ooh, damn! You are new in Rico's class. What's your name, baby girl?"

Never in my life had a man said anything like that to me. So, you can imagine how repulsed it made me feel. The old me would have driven his fingers into that man's throat and pulled out his speech cords. But, this was a new me and I needed to start acting the part. So, I took a deep breath and said, "I shouldn't be in here." I picked up my stuff and walked out into the hallway. Rico followed behind.

Before I could leave the Fitness Centre, he caught me at the double doors. He grabbed my right arm and held it with both hands. "I know what you want," he said. "You are a private person, Rico knows this. You want a private lesson with Master Rico, am I right?"

Staying in form, "No Rico, I've changed my mind. This is not for me. I just want to go now."

Rico was a lot stronger than I was. It was too easy for him to spin this kid around and pin both arms against the wall. He put his mouth next to my ear and said, "You are the most sexiest thing Rico has seen in the longest time. I think I have claimed you to be mine."

I could see some of the other ladies peeking out of the classroom. I don't know what they were thinking, but they seemed more curious than concerned. "I know that you think that you're Rico Suave with the ladies and that's great, I'm even happy for you, but you've got to let go of my arms," I replied.

"You are very young and afraid, Rico knows this. Allow Master Rico the honor of turning the little girl into a woman."

A red flash of rage rolled over me like a killer wave on a rocky beach. I don't remember doing any of this, but I was told that Rico was hospitalized later that morning. The word was that I jumped up off the floor and clapped both his ears with the palms of my hands. I would have had to first drop down in order to slip away from his grasp. Then I could see me having to jump up to get to his ears. I guess I could have gone for the balls, but I have never been a believer of that. For me, the "sac" was kind of sacred. They said that he might have some permanent lost hearing in one ear. I had no idea what I had done until Krystle told me the next day. Rico never returned and those 6 ladies from class hated me from that day on. They should have helped me so to hell with them.

After the Rico incident Krystle gave me a wide birth. I still needed her to sign me into school and all the other things that you need an adult for, so it was best not to alienate her completely. Even though I didn't remember that moment, I did learn from it. Rico was a lot bigger than me. The only reason I beat him was because he was distracted. A girl my size would have had no chance against a trained fighter. He could have picked me up and thrown me across the room if he wanted to. I'm sure I could get a little stronger, but I would have to use all kinds of supplements to do it. The failing of supplements is that I would have to take them for the rest of my life. Girls cannot compete with men when it comes to strength. They are not designed for it. I needed a fighting style that took strength out of the picture. It was also time to look for a good weapon.

One Soul... Two Minds...

It took about two weeks of diligent searching, but I found a school I liked that taught some forms of Kung Fu. Before I discovered this place, I went through two weeks of hell. Two weeks of touching, ass grabbing and "come back to my office baby." No one believed that a girl that looked like me wanted to learn fighting. I didn't want to have another Rico incident so soon after the last, so I endured what I needed to in order to get out the doors. Each time I felt like I needed to wash myself afterwards, but I didn't give up.

This place had a small class for women, taught by women. The families that owned the school were real (China) Chinese people. I had to twist Krystle's arm to get her to sign all the forms and come in for the interview. She had a closed-door meeting with one of the Masters and she never told me what went on in there, but I got in and became the only non-Asian student.

The school was about 40 miles southwest of our building in a warehouse district. It took about an hour to get there but it was worth it. On the outside it looked like just another old dilapidated warehouse near the Everglades. Inside, it was as traditional as I have ever seen. It had the look, smell, and feel of a real temple. At least it looked a lot like some of the ones I'd seen on TV.

The building was separated into two halves. The left half was used for making and repairing fishing nets. Some of the old men would work after hours building an old style Chinese Junk. They said that they would use it to sail to China before they died. The other half was a school dedicated to the study of Shaolin Martial Arts, weapons, meditation and philosophy. There were rooms set aside for the different forms of study and a private section for the three families that lived there.

These people lived in a world that was a cross between the old and the new. They had cars, TV and school, but they also caught or grew their own food. They learned about business and engineering, but at the same time they were bowing and placing bowls on their heads. To them, passing the Old World traditions into the New World was just as important as the way they studied their Kung Fu. I found it easy to admire the contrast they lived in and how they were able to balance it all. When I began to know them better, I asked one of my teachers how they were able to switch back and forth so easily and she said, "One soul. Two minds."

They made two traditional uniforms for me and gave me a white sash to tie around my waist. I was forbidden to wear jewelry, make-up, or even perfume. The uniforms I could wash. The sash I could not.

My main motto had always been, "Live it. Love it. Believe it." It didn't matter what the situation was. It could be a life or death conflict or an everyday challenge at your job. If life gives you a curve ball that you just can't step back from and you find yourself having to take that hit, the best thing to do is to embrace it. Make that thing your life. Love the challenge of it. Believe in the process of change. That is how we overcome and learn to reshape our world to a better fit.

I started with the basic stances, blocks, punches, kicks, and falls. I tried to learn as much as possible as quickly as I could, so I would be allowed to train with a weapon. I learned about pressure points and breathing techniques. I also started to pick up little bits of the language here and there.

The meditation part scared me. I saw too many flashes of all the things I was trying so hard to hide. I knew I had to make a whole lot of adjustments in this new life and I was concerned about a clash. An old Special Forces Operator cannot be a high school teenage girl. In this way I liken myself to a refurbished home. The inside and the outside look brand new, but many of those old things are still under the floor boards and between the walls. In other words, I needed to hide all the bones in the closet and under the stairs.

Never had I willfully subjected myself to pain and physical exhaustion like this. The only thing I could compare it to was high school football training and fighting for my life in the hell of 'Nam. The thing that made this worse was that I started out with close to nothing to work with.

I walked into the place as a pretty-faced young girl that had a sex magazine figure and absolutely no physical strength. You could find me by following the trail of sweat. I got beat up and bruised in every class. I felt like the Masters wanted me to quit but I kept on coming back. I learned that my Nanomites could not only speed the healing process, but I was also able to use them to help build some solid endurance muscle by using my force of will. If I had not had that secret advantage I would have not been accepted and the true (true) art of the styles would have never been revealed to me. Try as I might, I couldn't fix the sweating part. (At least it was clean and odorless).

This was when I was made aware that the food I ate, exercise, clean water, sleep, fresh air, sunshine, and some meditation, were really as important as I had always heard. Except for naturally grown fish and chicken, I was a vegetable eating fool and all things carbonated were off the menu. My body improved, and my mind was open to wisdom.

When I made Green Sash rank, I had a ceremony and was made to swear an oath to the school, the Masters and to Shaolin itself. At Yellow Sash, I was introduced to a new teacher. Due to my body size and physical ability, it was decided that I was to be trained in the Snake styles focusing on Viper and Cobra techniques. I could have also chosen another style on my own, but the teachers chose the study of Qigong, or "Chi" as it is also called. I gave no argument. Later, I was shown the White Crane.

I have never had any appreciation for the Oriental race. I considered them all "gooks and zipper heads," but after being with them, studying and learning from them as close as I was, that all changed. Now I could identify with them in many ways. I learned to understand what they believed, and I embraced it.

I fell in total lust with one of the daughters. Her name was Bo, she was 19 years old, and she was very, very kind to me. Never was there a more graceful person under the sun. Her breath smelled like fish, but she looked like a Chinese goddess. She was thin, and a little tall as Oriental girl go, about 5 foot 9 inches and had long muscular cartoon-hero legs. Her shiny black hair was twisted into two long braids and when she wore it down it nearly touched the floor. She held a Black Satin Sash and wore it with respect and pride. The way she stood, sat, ate, and even the way she walked, seemed to be perfection. How could I not fall?

All the Masters and some of the students, had one or more marks on their arms or chest. The branding was an honor given to them when they mastered a particular style. Hers was of the White Crane. She was also a specialist in the Long Staff, which is called "The Grandfather of All Weapons". I would stay over just to sit and watch her work out with it. I was inspired to make it the weapon I chose to master.

In late May of that year I moved into Bo's room. I visited the condo on the weekends but that was it. I was crazy for this girl but was afraid to tell her. I was a new person now and felt that maybe it would be OK to try to show and receive some affection again, but I didn't know how to do it. There were all these wild urges for her and sensations that I couldn't stop and had no idea what to do with.

I did everything she did and followed her around like a puppy. I even helped with the nets and made friends with the Old Ones that worked on the boat. I inhaled the very essence of her. I drew that girl inside of me as if she was what I needed to breathe. I had long since mastered the cute quiet role, so I hoped that Bo would soon see my interest and understand what I really wanted. Besides, she was the older one.

I had come to a point where I could hold my own and I was sparring with some of the older and more experienced students. Bo gave me further instructions on how to channel my energy. Once I relaxed, I stopped trying to rip my arms and legs out of their sockets and became one with my body at last. I gained another rank.

Two weeks later we were at the point where we would hold hands. We stayed up late and told stories about our families and the little adventures we've had so far in our young lives. I told her about my escape from the mall. The rest of mine were all lies of course, but we discussed the philosophical and cosmic ramifications of them just the same. We talked about men and imagined the first time we would make love. Her dreams were simple and uncomplicated. All she wanted in life was to be the best wife and mother she could be, as long as her man understood her family. I knew then that this China Doll could never be in a lesbian relationship. Still, I wished she would and I didn't give up.

It was a long and slow process, but I was able to introduce a game where we would touch each other and pretend we were boyfriend and girlfriend. We took turns in this role-play. We even practiced kissing our husbands with each other. We shared the only bed in her small room and many nights I was so charged by the mere touch of her skin that I quietly held her and came by myself as she slept on. Sometimes it was the only way I could get to sleep. For a Martial Artist, she slept like a rock.

Besides my frustrations in bed I was having the time of my life. Bo and I were inseparable, the Wang family loved me, and I had advanced to Blue Sash with a Stripe. With my flawless memory and the comfort of mastering my body and spirit, I was well on my way to the advance ranks. I was even able to trim one inch of that baby fat from my waist and two from my ass. I gained good endurance muscle and still lost two pounds. Not counting the chest area, my jiggle issue was greatly reduced. Except for the fact that I still had not had sex with that girl, it seemed as if there was nothing I could not do.

In mid-July, Krystle arrived at the school and demanded I return or she would cancel my Kung Fu training altogether. She took me outside and tore into my ass. "You are starting your real school in two weeks! This Kung Fu shit is not going to interfere with our program! You are being a selfish little spoiled slut! This is about me and my ass too!" She was pretty harsh and had obviously rehearsed what she was going to say.

In Spanglish, she told me that my parents would roll over if they knew I was about to throw away an opportunity that only few girls could dream of. I have to admit that I was touched. Every word she said felt like a spear in my chest. If this was my life and if those people were my parents, then I guessed I should have been ashamed. I really did feel bad about what I was doing and what I wanted to do with Bo. Who was I to disrupt two innocent lives in pursuit of a silly fantasy? I started to cry. She made me limit my visits to two hours, three days a week. I hadn't felt like that since I was a little kid. When we arrived at the apartment I was so distraught that I ran to my room, locked the door, and cried myself to sleep like a little girl.

The House of the Second Sons

"Dane Ann's Preparatory School for Girls," said the sign at the gate. The place looked more like a prison with its high fences, brick walls, and armed security. Later I found that the girls had another name for this place. They called it "The House of the Second Sons." The very rich, the famous, the political, and the infamous people in this world, all have children. Some of those children are girls. Only in recent years have any girls been able to rise as leaders in those kinds of families. That spot is reserved for the favorite son. The least favorite son went away to school, usually for his own protection, just as most of the girls do today. Here, they could complete high school and leave with two college years under their belt. They would also be prepared to be a suitable society wife and mother. (The true goal).

All the girls at this school had wealthy sponsors and nearly all of them were pretty. Ages went from 12 to around 21. It didn't matter if you were White, Black, Asian, Stupid, or even a Legal Resident, as long as those first two criteria were met. You were still going to get the best education and training you could handle (or afford). It didn't even matter if you advanced from one grade to the next. The one thing you were definitely going to do was learn how to "be a lady", any other options were solely up to you and your potential.

Krystle took me into the dormitory, dropped my single bag on the bed, shook my hand, and took off in my new car. She would be back on the weekend but right then I felt like an abandoned child. The other new students would have gone through tests and interviews, but I was different. All of that was done with one phone call several months ago. So, I sat on the bed. When I grew tired of that I looked out the window. I found myself thinking about how long my hair was getting and who was going to fix it for me now. When I got tired of that, I poured out my bag and looked at the contents.

We were told that we could only bring underwear, hygiene items and two family photos. I could have taken some small pieces of jewelry, but I only had the gold watch they gave us when we got the car. I didn't have any earrings or piercings to put them in. All I had was underwear for one week, a comb, brush, watch, one 8 x 5 frame of Bo, and the track suit I was wearing. The picture frame was bright jade and showed Bo and I in our uniforms holding our Long Staffs. I remember thinking that I would have to be satisfied with wrapping my arms around a pillow for quite a while.

The next day I met my roommate Sophia. She was a tall girl from Chicago who claimed to be Sicilian-Italian. This 18 year old was a loud mouth, fast talking, rich bitch that knew everything about everything. She knew every important family in New York, Chi Town, Miami, Vegas, and LA. As far as she was concerned those were the only cities in the US that mattered. She had family in Naples, Catania, and Palermo, and she knew all of them too. What she didn't know was how to shut the hell up.

I knew her type. Sophie was very pretty and did have that Italian look on her but what was more interesting was that this high school senior, in many ways was a leader. She just needed to be shaped in the right way. OK, she was an ignorant little rich kid with a big mouth, but Sophie was popular, and she knew how to easily manipulate the other girls. Still, I was so annoyed with her. I hadn't done a good "Mind Fuck" in a while, so I figured I'd have some fun.

At one point Sophie finally asked me where I was from so I told her I had ties in Saudi, Lebanon, England, and around the world. I told her that my father was from an ancient family line and that he was an Ambassador. She asked if we were rich and I told her that my mother was part of the richest clan in all of Arabia. I also told her that they were dead now and that I was the sole heir to both their estates. That last part was a lie, but I knew it would keep Sophie's interest.

She didn't believe any of it, but it did get her to think. She asked me question after question. I told her that I didn't want to say much more about it and that she could be in danger if she knew too much. "People have been known to vanish so completely that even their best friends have forgotten them."

She had no idea what to make of me. I learned from Krystle that women's wars are fought with words. This kid was most likely the child of some mob boss in Chicago, but I felt that someone had to have the guts to put this stupid child in her place. It was also a lot of fun to see the different looks on her face.

Later, I told her that I understood her situation and where she stood in the order of things. I told her that my family had set the course of history for thousands of years, "but like you, I'm just a girl. We will never be heads of our own families however smart girls like you and I can do a whole lot more than they think."

"Like what?"

"I'm planning to do something very big when I leave school, but I can't be tied to it publicly. I may be able to use a person like you in my organization, but I'll need to think about that first." I then retreated into the cute, quiet, shy kid role.

Each time this chick would start talking about money and power I would blow her mind with my vague and evasive world changing plans. I would drop little hints at her like, "One thing leads to another", "Always thinking forward", and my favorite, "People can forget." Once I got her interest going I would stop and say something like, "I don't know if you're ready to know any more." Sometimes in our room I would stare at her until she would turn to me and say, "Why are you looking at me?" I'd look right into her eyes, open my mouth as if I were going to say something important and then say, "Never mind." She thought I was crazy. My intent was just to bring her down a few notches, but it later developed into something wild.

Blame it on the money or the parental neglect. In that place we were all just a little too wild or touched in the head one way or another. It was nothing to see a mad pit bull and a frightened rabbit in the same dorm room. With all the chatter and attitude these rich kids needed a heavy hand to keep them in line. If it were up to me I would have just locked them all in the same closet until the noise stopped.

The biggest issue I had to deal with was that "Rich Bitch Attitude" that most of the kids wore around their shoulders like steel plated armor. At least 70% of the girls in that school suffered from RBA. It was all I could do to keep from punching one of them in the stomach on any given day of the week. If it were not for my breathing and meditation exercises, I would have never been able to make it.

The other real nerve wracking annoyance was that freakish week to week and a half attack of wide spread PMS. This time period was aptly dubbed "Red Week". Imagine 450 teenage girls, mood swinging, crying, and cramping all at the same time. Many of those kids were just beginning their journey into womanhood and had no idea how to handle it, and I did feel sorry for them. The school offered a lot of support in this area, but for me and the other girls that were less affected it was hell just to be around.

The school colors were black and red or as they would say "The Ebony and Scarlet." I had one outfit for class, one for PE, one for special occasions, one for off campus events, and one for just around the school after classes. On an average day I would do at least three costume changes.

Math, Language, Computer Sciences, and World History were the core school classes. Political Science and Business were pre-assigned for me as my main studies. The only choices I had was what art I would take, and a sport. I went with dance because I wanted to learn something new to challenge my body. For the sport, I choose Soccer, and I'll tell you why.

It's still my belief that a sport, a real sport, should not be a contest in fashion. I want to see skill, sweat, and bodies being challenged. I want people to jump out of their seat and say, "Yes!" American men play hard, or contact, sports. The most played sports in the US are ones where something or someone is hit or slammed. Girls typically play games like badminton, volleyball, basketball, and soccer. With the first two you can work up a sweat but unless you fall on the floor, you may not get dirty. If you wanted to, you could even play them in a skirt. As far as girls' sports go, soccer is the most physical, and if you play it right, you can get very dirty.

I was just a junior, a new kid, and I couldn't hide the fact that I looked a little Arabic, so all but a few girls were mean to me. They did things like place nasty notes in my books, stare at me, and stop talking when I came around the corners or down the hall. For me it all seemed silly, girly, and childlike. Then again, if you're a 17 year old high school girl, that kind of silly shit would be real important to you.

I needed to learn how girls socialized and I really wanted to be "lady like" (as they would say), so that meant I had to fit into some kind of a clique or start my own. At this point all I wanted to do was go to school and fit in. I needed to learn how to be the best me I could be, in this new life. Sports had been my ticket before, so I thought "why not?" I would get to work on my body strength, kick ass, and make some friends at the same time.

In truth, I had another reason for getting on the soccer team. Jenny Smith. Jenny was the captain of the losing senior Soccer team. She was a boyish, 19 year old, 5 foot 9 inch, soccer playing fury, that hated anyone who wasn't white and American. Her father happened to be US Army Major General Frank R. Smith. I had met the General on only two occasions. At our first meeting the General expressed to me his extreme dislike at having to report to a man whose highest military rank was Sergeant Major. I was a GS 14, and in charge of a fact finding team that demanded his cooperation. The second and last time I saw him, was just after he was removed from his post for not cooperating with my fact finding team. I passed him on the way out, as I, and his replacement were walking in. I believe he was retired later that month.

My dislike for Jenny had nothing to do with her old man. Jenny was a real good piece of crap on her own. I'm sure she did get a lot of that from her father, like her "my way or the highway" attitude for one thing. In many ways she was a lot like the old me. We both had a low tolerance for people in general. I could see why people hated me so much in my old life, and I felt a little sorry for her. Nobody else liked this kid, either. Her so-called friends feared her. Her teachers tolerated her. It was undeniable that she was the star of the team, but the way she ran it was so disorganized that they all hated her, too. When she heard that I was an Arab, she went out of her way to bump into me in the cafeteria. She spilled my drink on my uniform and I had to leave to clean up and change before class. When I saw her the next time, she asked me if I was going to "blow up the school now." She wanted to be hurtful and got a few laughs doing it.

Real school didn't start that first week. Girls were still filtering in from around the country and around the world. We spent most of this time in briefings, filling out forms, and touring the different departments of the school. Cheer, Sports, Music, and Drama all held competitions for placement.

I tried out for the Junior Soccer Team and made it easily. I have to say that at the beginning of the day, there was great speculation that I would not last more than 15 minutes on the grass. Some figured that a shapely kid would only throw out her back or trip over her own legs, but I proved them wrong. A good sports bra is a powerful thing. Besides, I was re-engineered for endurance and durability.

The other new kids played like girls. I had seen a few games before in my travels and I knew there were rules to it, but nobody on the field seemed to know what they were. I just kicked the ball in the general direction of the other end and ran like crazy. Later, I would learn to pass and kick into the net but on that day, I just screamed, talked junk, and got really dirty. I ran doughnuts around those children. It was sick. Talk about a fun time. It was without contest, the best time I had since day one of my arrival. Then we all went to the showers.

I got into big trouble one time for sneaking into the girls' shower room just before the cheerleaders came in after a basketball game. I was 16 and it was the coolest thing I had done all year. Today, you could go to jail for that, but Dave and I got laps from Coach Jones until I dropped, and Dave puked. Then we cleaned the showers and the puke. At the time, we thought it was worth it. Now I was the one taking the shower but as one of the girls.

Months ago, while staring at myself in the mirror I realized that I was a beautiful and sexy, young 18-pretending-to-be-17-going-on-18-year-old girl. It's kind of strange to think it, but if I had met me when I was young, I would want a piece of this bad. I also remember thinking that even though I was 17 again, other people younger and older also thought that I was beautiful and sexy. I couldn't avoid it. I heard the whistles, the yells, and saw all the looks from the men, boys, and some girls, too. At first it pissed me off a lot. After wrapping my head around it, I realized that kind of shit was not going to stop, so I decided to try to enjoy it, and suddenly things were better. It's odd how complements can bring confidence to a girl.

Inside my head I had the brain of a 70 year old man but the rest of me (excepting the child like face) was only 18. I would more than likely live out the rest of my life all over again starting at this age. Don't get me wrong. Being 17 (on paper) and alive, is better than being 70 and dead, any day of the week. It's just that I have been old a lot longer than I was ever young. I was used to looking past kids as if they didn't exist. I thought about this for a long time and decided that it was now OK to be attracted to young people. In fact, it would be in my best interest, as the alternative would bring me trouble I didn't need. It took a while to sell this idea to myself and I wasn't completely convinced until the day I met Bo.

When I was 17 before, I found girls around my age and a little older, to be very attractive. Now that I was almost 18 again, I had to learn that it was OK to admire them once more. When I first left that hospital, I made up my mind to try and avoid sex at any cost. That's why I thought sending me to an all-girl school was a brilliant idea. The truth of the matter was that this was not to be the case.

The last time I was 18 the girls didn't look like this. We were all around the same age and I guess this is the way things are now but 51 years ago the girls had pretty faces but they only had bumps on their chest. Like the food now-a-days, a lot of things are different. It's public knowledge that there are now more hormones then vitamins in what we eat, and that is what was showing on the bodies of those girls in the shower. Some of these kids had "Playboy" size breasts, hips, and "Player" magazine cover butts. (White girls never had butts before). I never looked at kids long enough to notice when all that changed.

I'll tell you something else, too. Back on the field, every one of the girls was a little nervous at first. Once they got warmed up and started to have fun, I noticed an awful lot of body contact. I let it all go past me because I figured that it was just something girls do, but it picked up quite a bit more in the locker room.

Looking back, I know that most of it was innocent, but some of these girls were soaping each other. One was washing another's hair. Overall, they seemed to be having more fun in the shower than they had on the field. They used a lot of soap, a lot of time, and a whole lot of water. One of the others that made the cut came up to me with shampoo and washed my hair. We were all naked. It was like watching one of those "B" rated late night Cinemax "After Dark" profiles, except for the fact that I was in it.

Just as I did in Abercrombie, I had to suck it up and pretend that it was the normal thing to do. Girls are generally touchier with each other than boys, anyway. And the girls that were on the team considered themselves to be sisters now, so it was OK to become more than friends, but deep inside, I was on fire.

These rich and maladjusted kids were in no way your average girls. At another school I would have been tossed into a room full of hungry animals called "boys". There would have been parties, fights, guns, and drugs. As fresh and insecure as I was, I would have had to pay people to look after me. I may have had to defend myself at some point. I'd be telling this story from prison. It was better to "consider the lilies" as the Good Book says. Dane Ann's was a more controlled environment and I was still lost.

Once I was established as one of the "Sports Girls", I never had to worry about my hair again. I just didn't have the knack for it anyway. It was really growing like crazy and without Krystle to work it every day, it looked wild and was all over the place. With all the sweating from Kung Fu, soccer, and the showering two to three times a day, I really bent towards cutting it way down. The school frowned on the idea of short haired girls and Krystle forbid me to even think about it. But as one of the sports girls, someone was always around to play with it. So as long as it wasn't cut, I didn't much care what they were doing. If they thought it looked nice, I was OK with it. As it turned out, it was one of many ways a girl could show care or admiration for another girl, and one of my first noteworthy lessons in school girl behavior.

My birthday was coming soon. At 18 I should have been a high school senior this year. I guess with the explosion, my death, the rebirth, and the rehabilitation, my last year was cut really short. Besides, Faatina was about as smart as a box of broken rocks. There was no way she was passing her classes. Jasmine on the other hand, would not get straight "A's", but she had to be a whole lot smarter. I was ready to research girls "from the inside" so to speak, so I was a little jazzed about getting this year started.

I knew it was going to be a challenge. The RBA alone was a show stopper. The class work and study would all be new to me. Mostly, I was concerned with trying to somehow fit in with hundreds of misfits. But no matter how it would play out, it was guaranteed to be a weird and wild adventure.

I've observed that as a whole, girls are easier to manage than boys. In most cases, they tend to do what they are told. You may have to motivate them, but they will do it. The ones that don't, are rebels. One dominating force however, can keep all of them in line. And that force at Dane Ann's, was Dean Carmen Hattered. Many of us called her Dean Haggard, but we would look around the corners first, before we did.

From a distance I could see that Dean Hattered was once a beautiful woman in her own right. She might have been 65 or so but when you saw her up close you would swear that she was around 50. She was dedicated to the girls and the principles of the school. So dedicated that she had never married. Her main philosophy was, "the arts, academics and sports make a well-rounded woman, but to be ladylike is everything". This school was her life. Some said that she was Dane Ann herself. They said that she chose to use that name instead of her own, only because she thought it would look better on the sign. There were so many stories about Ms Hattered that there was no telling what was true and what was not. (There was a real good one about her torturing and killing a girl in the Grounds Keeper storage shed). The one thing I did know was that she knew how to act mean.

I also have to note that this lady had style. The way she walked, stood, dressed, and even when she was ripping your tail about chewing gum, she did with class. She was the school, and the school was her. If she had not had such a passion for education, she would have made a great Ambassador.

Dean Hattered watched the soccer tryouts and spoke to me the next day in her office. The room was immaculately arranged. "You have a gift for soccer, I think." This was part of her style. She talked like an American version of Margaret Thatcher. She pulled a large photo album from her shelf. "I was a Striker for my team in college, you know", she said, as she flipped through the pages. "I teach my girls to be lady-like in everything they do. And yet it cannot be denied, that the player that sweats, is the player that is trying to win." After finding the desired page, she placed the book in front of me. It was a cutout page from the Oxford Times, now immortalized within the plastic leaf. Her team had won the

"Women's Nationals" in England. "You will play as a Forward for the senior team this year". I left with a rulebook in my hands and a smile on my face.

On the weekends, Dane Ann's was all but a ghost town. Only a few girls that had no place to go had to stay while the rest of us went home. Krystle would pick me up on Friday afternoons and I would drive (my car) back to the condo. She was gigging again on Friday and Saturday nights and I got to hang out for the shows. I tried to behave myself and I never drank, but so many guys would crowd me and buy all kinds of things for me, that I ended up on stage with the band. I'd dance around and would shake bells or the tambourine. Krystle only sang half the time, so when she wasn't holding the mic, we danced together. We wore the same outfits and had a great routine. It reminded me of "In Living Color" and the old "Solid Gold" TV shows. As a result, more people came to the shows and the band got better paying gigs. Everyone was happy, and I got a lot of flowers, gifts, and love notes (AKA complements). No one would ever know the ecstasy I felt, shaking and sweating on those stages. All I could do was smile.

Sundays were spent with Bo and her family. We would train in the afternoons and talk for the rest of the day. I missed the time we used to spend together, and she wished she could come to my school. Mostly we talked about girly stuff and the wacky people I knew at Dane Ann's.

I was still a relatively quiet person but when I wanted to, I could hold my own in girl-to-girl conversation. I never got it down to a science, but I've found that it's OK if you don't understand what the other person's point really was. The fact is, pretty girls seem even prettier when you can't understand them. But Bo wasn't like that. Everything she did made perfect sense. In my eyes she was still a god.

After a weekend like this, I would be wiped out. I'd sleep in the car that evening on the way back to school. I could stumble past my roommate and fall right into bed without saying a word.

Sometimes it would take me until Tuesday morning to get back on track.

The weekends and soccer were my only real release. I knew some girls who wanted to play around and experiment with lesbian sex, but I held them off. Even though my body was burning every time I saw them touching each other in the shower or in the restrooms, I walked past. I understood that I was going to an all-girl boarding school with confused and frustrated females packed full of oozing hormones. It would have been easy for me to take advantage of so many things in so many ways. But instead of jumping headfirst into what could have been a wild and possibly magical fantasy world that no one but me could know, imagine, or experience, I chose to fight back the cravings my body was giving me. I did choose a few of them and attempted to open their minds but I'll get to that later.

I just couldn't get past the thought that so many of them were kids. Sure, their bodies looked mature all right, but there were children inside of some of them. I wanted to slap their faces and make them do their homework. Besides, at that time the only one I wanted was the one that didn't want me. Bo.

The truth be told, I was in no way prepared for this reality. If I had come to Dane Ann's at 15 or even better, 13, I would have been able to grow into those emotional and physical discoveries as my friends did. The girls my age, were past talking about this stuff. They were now into dealing with it. Being thrown into this complicated "girl world" at 18, cut me out of vital background information. I faked my way through conversations about monthly cycles and emotions that I knew nothing about. The school did have support in these areas but if a kid needed advice from me or wanted to vent, I just hugged her.

This wasn't my only frustration. The rich girls and their silly rivalries had formed themselves into three main groups. There were the very rich, the high society rich, and the political rich. To these girls, the other kids didn't even count. I qualified for membership in two of those groups, but I couldn't see the point in it. Each group had subgroups that were broken into even smaller groups. The whole thing seemed like a big unhealthy competition in popularity. I had to constantly remind myself that I couldn't hit anybody.

The best way I had found to fight off those urges was to practice my Kung Fu. It was nearly a nightly ritual to make my way to the gym after I was through with my studies. At 2100hrs, the gym and shower area would be clear of all the basket and volley ballers. Security wouldn't allow me to bring a weapon like a Bo Staff onto the campus, so I had to use a broom handle or a pole I found later. Until the lights went out, this hall was mine.

I would stuff an oversized T-shirt and some baggy shorts in a bag. I'd pop out of a side door in the dorm and pop back into the west door of the gym. Until I acquired the keys, each afternoon I had to make sure I placed a piece of tape on both doors to keep the locking mechanisms from engaging. I would remove it that night when I was done, so that the Building Super wouldn't find me out.

Once inside, I would change to only the shirt and shorts so that I could breathe and sweat as much as I wanted. I'd workout with dance, some falls, my katas, and the staff. I would do this for an hour or so. I think I would sweat everything out of my mind. After a long day of study and that workout, I'd be more than ready to fall asleep. This was my way of life for my first two months of high school.

My new birthday was on a Friday. Krystle got special permission for me to leave the campus a little early that day. For a surprise, she took me straight to Bo's place. At the time, I thought "this is no surprise", but instead of dropping me off like she did on Sundays, this time she came inside with me. Bo, the families, some of the other students I trained with, and many of the people I knew that worked in the area, were all inside. My teacher handed me my Staff and my uniform and told me to prepare to be tested.

When I returned to the testing room, everyone was sitting on the floor. I was tested on all my new and old forms. This included takedowns, punches, kicks, blocks, and the Staff. It was everything I had learned from day one to the present. After that I had to spar with three higher ranked students and one of the Masters. Then I did it again with a different group using the Staff. The Masters kicked my ass, but I held my own. I fared better with the students and was matched only once. Each time they came at me like I was an enemy but, in the end, I was praised for my courage.

I was presented with my Red Sash in front of Krystle, Bo and most of the people I've known since my rebirth. They all stood up, clapped hands, and congratulated me. In a matter of a few months I had moved from an application form to the first advanced ranking in the Art of Kung Fu. It was a great surprise after all. I was touched to the point of tears. Afterward, I cut a cake and we ate Chinese food.

The Old Ones had another surprise for me. After dinner we all walked into the shop to see the finished Junk. It was a real sight to behold. Complete with paint and trimmings, it was a masterpiece of craftsmanship. We all helped push the Junk into the water for its first time. Bo and I, along with other children, had grape juice while the adults drank champagne. Many of us, to include Bo and I, had our pictures taken on the boat. Then the men loaded it with boxes, bags, and some bed rolls. Seven old men climbed on board, started the outboard motor, and sailed out of sight.

It's possible, in a remote sense of the word, that they did sail all the way to the China shore. It's also possible that they just sailed across the Gulf and got off in Texas. Maybe they were arrested by the Coast Guard or killed by pirates. Personally, I would like to think that all seven men died at sea on their way to the Motherland.

I could see them getting through the Panama Canal, but the Pacific Ocean is worse than treacherous in the winter months. These fellas sailed off to their deaths and they knew exactly what they were doing. Maybe they fought the wind to the last man, or maybe they just went headfirst into oblivion without blinking an eye. The only thing that was certain was that we never saw or heard from them again. I was honored to see them off and it was the best birthday gift I ever had.

Miss Janet (If You're Nasty)

One night while studying in our dorm room, Sophie unexpectedly burst through the door and ran up to me. She yelled, "You will stop treating me like an asshole and talk to me like I am a real person!" The way she startled me almost caused me to stab her with my pen. She saw my body language and the look on my face and backed up. She retreated with, "I'm sorry for that, but I want to be included in this thing of yours. You're right about the plan my family has for me and I'm smarter than that." I told her that I didn't think she was ready, but she wanted none of it. "Bull Shit, let me prove it!" So, I gave her a test. I asked her to find out all the information she could gather on Mrs Janet Wilson. (What the heck).

Janet Wilson was a new teacher that taught Algebra. She came around a few weeks ago as a substitute. She was young, tall and very attractive. The old basketball coach was about to retire and Mrs Wilson was gunning for that spot, so she could stay in a more permanent position. I'd seen her a few times in the hallways and I watched her practicing her jump shots in the gym some nights. I had to stand outside and wait for her to leave before I could sneak in. She was really good.

Sophie took the challenge and in less than a week returned with the following information. Janet Fisher graduated with honors from Dane Ann's and earned a basketball scholarship to the University of Florida. In her first year there, she met and married Mr Harold Wilson, who was in his senior year. Harold also played basketball and graduated with a degree in Criminal Justice. He joined the Army and was now a Captain serving in Afghanistan. Janet stayed in school to play ball and earned a degree in Education. She was 5 feet 11 inches tall, 165 pounds, and had a killer outside shot.

She also told me, "Just to show you how good I am, I'll tell you a secret about her that maybe her own husband doesn't even know. Miss Janet is black. That's right, she looks white, but she's not!"

OK, I thought to myself. The lady is tall, she can jump high, she looks to be a great ball player and for an athlete, she had a really nice butt, but that didn't make her black. "I don't see much black on her," I said.

"Her mother is half black, but she looked white skinned too. I have a picture," she answered, and handed me a copy of an old family Christmas card. Janet was about my age, standing with her folks next to the tree and wearing the "Ebony and Scarlet" uniform in her living room on Christmas Day. In the picture, her Dad looked like your average white guy, but her Mom was more exotic. She had some black facial features, but her skin did look white. Janet's hair was kind of frizzy looking. "Her parents died in a car crash while Miss Janet was in school, right here, at Dane Ann's. Her room was right next to ours! That woman spent four years behind the wall next to your bed!"

I made her my Lieutenant and I tasked her with the job of recruiting other girls of means who believed in our way of thinking, but they would be sworn to secrecy. No one could know that they were in the Club. They were not even allowed to know the other members. She could test them however she wished, to find if they were loyal and could be trusted. I wanted detailed files on these girls and Sophie would have to maintain them. At the time, I was just trying to assign her something that would keep her busy. It was to be her final test before I would make her a real partner, but I did stop fucking with her.

I got to know Miss Janet in a more personal way about a week and a half later. I didn't mean for it to happen, but it did. I could have gotten over this issue I had with teen sex if I really wanted to. Everyone around me was about the same age as the person I found myself within. The truth be told, I was afraid.

I kept that Sex Slave memory I had in a wide-open computer brain file. Looking at it now and again helped to remind me of how things could be. All I had to do was slip up or lose my head for a moment and I would be lost in a never-ending addiction that could make things much more horrible than I could even imagine. This body I've acquired isn't designed for soccer, Kung Fu or even school for that matter, it is designed for sex. But, I refused to accept this fate. I would be so much more than that, if it killed me.

It was an October Wednesday evening when I came into the gym in my usual James Bond type fashion. Miss Janet didn't practice every night, so I had no reason to think that anything was strange when I saw that the coast was clear. I had begun to switch around my workouts depending on the day of the week. Mondays and Tuesdays were my soccer footwork nights. Wednesday nights were all Kung Fu. On Thursdays I worked on my dance. Every night, I would give myself at least 20 minutes with the staff. This particular Wednesday night ended a little different in more ways than one.

I was working on the katas for my next step in rank. I never had an issue with mentally memorizing the forms, it was the physical memory that was still a slight problem at that time. I had been reduced to one 2-hour class a week and I didn't want that to slow my momentum on the way to mastering a style. Then I would workout with the staff. I remember sitting on the mat afterwards with my eyes closed as I do, trying to control my breathing. It was part of my normal cool down routine, when I sensed the presence of someone else on the far side of the gym.

I heard nothing, but the feeling was strong. Someone was trying to sneak up on me. Her breathing was controlled, and her steps were carefully placed. She was an expert in timing and patience. This someone was trained in the art of stealth. But, so was I. The moment I detected her presence, she knew it, and she knew that I knew she did. Still she continued her approach.

I fought back the reflex to run or lash out. As a rule, a soldier who finds himself in an ambush will commit to a straight forward attack. It's his only chance to survive. But, the voice was telling me, "don't do it," so, I remained still.

Everyone and everything has its own unique energy that moves with and around them. People, animals, weapons, hell, even IEDs, send out signals on frequencies that the human mind can be trained to receive. I knew a kid that could somehow just know where bombs were hidden because he said he could "feel them" even a hundred yards away. That guy saved more lives than Superman.

When attacking a prey that is also aware of this energy, it's best to try to mask it with a distraction. If you can't find a good distraction, then a long-ranged attack is a better idea. I had felt this a thousand times in Vietnam, Iraq, and Washington, DC. The difference this time, was that I felt no real danger. This person was only testing me.

There is a science behind this, that is hard to explain. It can be best seen when two or more people who have been together for a while, think the same thing at the same time. Most people believe it's a coincidence, but it's so much more. Your mind is a mass of concentrated energy, and energy has no bounds. Once you understand that, the rest will come to you. I could always detect fear, anger, and peace from a long way off. In my old military life, distance and distraction was my bread and butter. It was one of many things tied to those memories I was trying so hard now to hide.

Eventually, I could feel her hand reaching out to touch my left shoulder from behind me. The warmth of her long fingers moved over me as her hand came closer still. Not knowing who it was, I had to decide how to react. I didn't recognize the energy or her scent, but I knew this person was not an attacker. I didn't want to hurt her, but she had to understand that sneaking up on me was a bad idea.

Miss Janet had some training from her husband, but my advantage at that moment was speed and surprise. I knew that this person's tall body was extended. In one motion, I was able to reach up and back with my right hand to quickly grab and pull her wrist forward to move her body over mine. I pushed myself out of my lotus position and onto my feet. This move put the sneaking sneaker onto my shoulder. I was about to power slam her onto the mat with a thud that would have gotten a thumbs up from Hulk Hogan and no doubt left a permanent scar in this girl's brain, when I suddenly realized that this was no student.

The last time I used this Jujitsu move was on my 55th birthday in Osan, Korea. I ran an Intel Opp. around those parts for a few years and one of our offices was based on the Air Force Base. The guys in the shop secured a bar in the Ville that night for an evening of drinks, food and table top dancing (the works). All was well until a bunch of Squids showed up, fresh off the boat. We were all old Rangers. They were young and stupid. I paid the seven thousand dollar damage bill out of my own pocket but we won that fight. As birthdays go, it turned out to be a good one and one of my better memories of Korea.

I nearly twisted my back in my attempt to let Miss Janet down a little more gently, but she still got slammed on the mat I was sitting on. "You're a lucky lady," I said. "You're lucky you weren't someone else." When she began to stand, it seemed as though she just kept going up. At 5 foot 11 inches, Miss Janet was 8 inches over me and arguably the tallest person at the school. In her "coach voice" she barked at me, "You'll be lucky if I don't have you expelled!"

I could understand that she felt embarrassed, but this was her fault. In the old days, she could have been killed. Then again, she was a teacher and an adult. I didn't want to get kicked out of school for something like this, so I just shut up. She ordered, "Stand up straight when I'm talking to you, young lady!" It was something we girls heard all day long. I quickly complied. "You are not in the proper attire for a Dane Ann student. What is your name, anyway?"

I told her my name and when she asked, I told her my teacher's names, my room number, and everything else she wanted. She told me that she had seen me in the gym at a time that I should have been in my room. She told me that it was against the rules to be there by myself. As I stood there at the position of attention, she talked and walked around me in a circle like I was back in Basic Training.

I started to think about what would happen if I did get kicked out of school. Krystle would no doubt ban me from dancing with the band, Kung Fu would be out, and I wouldn't get to see Bo ever again. Soccer would be no more, and I would be moved to another school just when I was at the point of feeling comfortable.

I started to become nervous. There was no telling what this chick was going to do with me. Was she so much of a hard ass, that she would really get me expelled for something like this? I could feel new sweat forming. It began to gather with the moisture in my clothes that were still damp from the earlier workout. It started to trickle down from my wet hair all the way to my bare feet.

While these thoughts were rolling around in my head, I had somehow missed the part when she transitioned from scolding to complements. Her tone had changed, and she went from kicking me out of school, to telling me that I had "an awesome form". (And she wasn't talking about my Kung Fu). She thought that I was strong and well-endowed for my age. She asked me if I had a boyfriend or a girlfriend, "here at school yet". Now Sophie had put nothing about Miss Janet being AC-DC in her profile, so I was taken aback at this question. I so much wanted to slap Sophie in the face right then, that I couldn't think. "Well, are you looking for a girlfriend, or are you looking to get expelled?"

That lady was too good at this stuff. I knew right then that she had pulled these moves before. She kind of had me pretty good. I was breaking school rules, I had a "weapon", and I had been seen doing this for some time. If I said "no" to her, she could make up any story she wanted and get it into Dean Hattered's mind before

I could even deny it. I lowered my head and said, "Ma'am, I don't want to be expelled."

"That's right! You will do what I want, when I want you to. Do you understand?"

"Yes Ma'am," I meekly replied.

"Now," Miss Janet demanded, "I want to see what I own, so take off that old wet shirt of yours." (Miss Janet was nasty).

I was more than a little confused. I didn't want to be anyone's bitch. But, then again, if a tall, fine, exotically mixed beauty like this wanted to have girl-on-girl sex, somebody would have to play the submissive part in this fantasy, and the look on her face told me it was not going to be her. It wasn't like two guys were having sex or anything. This was going to be me and one of the Amazons Warriors I used to read about when I was a kid. I was going to have to be the little fuck bitch in this story. She would be Xena, and I would be Gabrielle. I thought to myself, "I could do this for a while." Hell, I needed to do this! And it might save some other weak minded kid from getting really fucked up if she was distracted with me. At the time, it all really seemed like a win-win situation.

Unlike most kids, I had a lifetime of experience to understand what was going on. This lovely two-timing teacher had some issues. She, no doubt felt abandoned, lonely, and useless. Her way of taking charge of her life involved taking over the will of innocent young women with a mixture of guilt and good old-fashioned blackmail. I broke some minor school rules, and I knew that. I also knew that even though my 18th birthday had come and gone, legally this is what they call rape in this country. (That's at any age). But I didn't stop her. I was terrified and yet I wanted this.

If I thought I was sweating before, it was nothing compared to the amount of water I was pushing out of my flesh now. She took my chin with those same long fingers and lifted my head to see my eyes. "I hate waiting and right now you are making me mad." I raised my arms and pulled the sweat filled shirt up and over my head. But, before I could get my arms out of the shirt and drop it to the floor, she stopped me by grabbing my wrist. She held my arms up in the air and looked down onto my breasts. "I'm going to suck a pint of milk out of these beauties." She let my arms go. "Now, drop those shorts, but do it nice and slow. No undies", she said. "I knew you were a dirty little girl. It just so happens that I like girls who are dirty. You are the one the others are calling Jessica Rabbit. I'm going to call you Bunny." Her words and her tone gave me mixed messages. Her voice was smooth and sweet, but the way she spoke was raw. Meanwhile, my mind and my body had lost all control of themselves. At this point I was a lump of wet putty in her manipulating hands. Whatever she wanted was exactly what I did, when she said to do it.

She kissed me deeply then laid me on that mat and licked my whole sweaty body clean as if I would be her last meal on this earth. No words can describe the way that woman made me feel. It excited Miss Janet to know how much power she had over my flesh. It pleasured her to pleasure me. It was the kind of thing she and I both prayed for. I exploded first in her face, then on her hands more times than I could count. All the waiting, the frustration, the stress of my sacred secrets, and the worry about my future, burst out from between my legs like Mount Saint Helen's Volcano did in 1980. I don't know how many other women can feel the electrical energy from another's touch the way that I can, but I am glad that I am one of them.

Her touch was a magic thing, but that was only part of it. The smell of sex oozing from our heated pores and the sounds we made (especially mine), were just as exciting as the sight and feel of it all. The whole experience felt so unbelievably wonderful, that I thought this crazy bitch was trying to kill me. I had gone far beyond any known limit for pleasure I had ever reached and had no idea how much more I could stand. I had lost complete control of all body functions, my heart was racing to the point of shut down, and now I couldn't catch my breath. All I could do was hold on and let go. It wasn't like I had a choice. I remember thinking that if I did die that night, it would be worth it to have gone out this way. (I would have left in a bang, so to speak).

Except for a few rare exceptions, when a guy has sex it feels good every time. It can feel really good, and sometimes even great. You can put a lot of energy into it, and a little emotion if you want. But for most guys, that's it. You are not going to cry, and you can maintain your awareness. With girls, it can be a whole lot more.

I'm sure that I am on the extreme end of the curve on these things, but I found it harder and harder to breathe. I was made weak and completely helpless as I flopped around on the mat in slow motion. My will was so far away from my body that I could not control my own thoughts. Miss Janet had to move me around, which she happily did by toying with my flexibility. I could feel drool running off the side of my face, but I didn't have the strength to wipe it off. I was so completely overwhelmed that I started to cry like a little girl. Then, I just couldn't breathe anymore and all I could do was let myself go into a place I had no idea ever existed.

All I can say is that I was gone! It was a place with no sound or smell. The light was everywhere but I could not see. I felt as if I were submerged and floating in a vat of warm water. There was no care, no fear, and no time that passed. It was "the place with no name". Once I knew I could get there, it would be a place I would often return.

It would not be the last time I hyperventilated and blacked-out for a while, but this was the first. She gently woke me. "Drink this," she said. She filled her mouth with water from a bottle she had gotten and softly took me by the back of the neck to pull me into a kiss. The water slowly flowed from her mouth to mine and I drank it in. I felt like a baby bird in her nest. She wanted to make sure that I knew I belonged to her and it was true. I would find that lady was full of all kinds of mind blowing tricks and stunts.

We finished the entire bottle that way and it was the most refreshing drink I'd ever had.

She gave me some rules. I would be free to use her gym when I wanted, but to wear perfumes, sprays, creams, and even soap was forbidden. She said that she would be putting me on the mat a minimum of two to three times a week and hated the taste and smell of those chemicals. She preferred if I didn't use them at all, but she knew that the other girls would single me out if I went that far. (I needed to shower before I worked out).

I needed to rest, but she had me wipe up the body fluids on the mat with some gym towels and watched me take a shower before she told me to go to my room. Before I did, she gave me another bottle and said, "You want to make me happy, don't you?"

"Yes Ma'am" I answered.

"Then keep drinking water. I like the way your cum tastes." (I've been a water drinking fool ever since).

The whole next day I was useless. Sophie woke me three times. The first time was when she left the room to go to the shower. The second was when she was on her way to class. The third was when she heard I had not gone to my first class. I told her that I was feeling sick, but the truth was that I was still in heaven. In the nurse's office, they had me pee in a cup. They gave me aspirin, vitamin B, a day pass, and another bottle of water. I wasn't sick. I was just lost in a hex that Miss Janet had put on me.

My head began to reset later that afternoon. I wasn't allowed to play soccer with the others due to my "illness", so I sat on the ground and watched. Jenny was back to her old self and the girls sucked as a whole, without me. (I desperately needed to take over that team). Looking at them allowed me to take a good look at myself. Even though I would have eaten all the grass while crawling across the playground like a snake if Miss Janet asked me to, I knew that I had to find control before things got too far.

Miss Janet on the other hand, had no plans to make it easy for me to shake her. That nasty chick had my mind and body both flipped and twisted. Every time I saw her I was too nervous to speak. She'd call me "Bunny" in a crowded hallway and I would nearly drop my books when some girl would giggle. Also, in public she secretly referred to my overflowing ejaculations in a code by saying things like "someone was playing in the water last night", "I found a crack in those pipes", or, "I'm going on that wild water ride again". She used this to keep me from regaining my balance and it worked. I was lost inside of her and I hated her for it. (What a dream she was).

I knew from that one experience, I would always get lost when it came to making love. If this was what a person could do to me with just her tongue, those full lips, two long fingers and the feel of her skin on mine, then I shuddered to think of what would happen if Miss Janet were a hermaphrodite.

That is not to say that I couldn't regain my composure sooner with practice. I just knew I didn't want to be a slave to it. Somehow, I would have to learn to use this to my advantage. I decided that I was not going to be able to avoid sex, so I would just have to find a way to master it. I would live long enough to find that this decision was much easier said than done.

The first time I had sex, I was 14 and she was 16. I was in 8th grade and she was the high school sister of one of my football teammates. She was a wild girl named Jan Parker, with reddish blond hair and big blue eyes. She drove her mother's old 1940 DeSoto Custom (the one with the collapsed roof look) to our games each week because her mom was afraid to drive.

You see this car in a lot of '50s movies. People made these into Hot Rods and painted them with stripes or flames. Not this one. That girl had run this thing into the ground. Her father drove it for 10 years before he passed it to his son, who drove for another 5. It was Jan's turn now and its future wasn't bright.

Dan and I used to say, "There is nothing Jan has not hit." If you saw it at night or out in the distance, it was a cool looking car. When you got near it, you wished you had kept your eyes closed.

I don't think you could find a spot that did not have a scratch on it. The sound it made as it came down the road was like a crash landing. It smoked so bad, that you might have thought it ran on wood fuel. But, the back seat felt like the clouds of heaven after she dropped her little brother off before she took me home.

As I said, she was my first. The feeling was awesome, but after it was all over, I moved on to other thoughts. Sure, it was good enough to talk about, and I did. I know you've heard about that guy who would "hit it and quit it." It's the same guy that could get sex whenever he wanted, even though it seemed not to mean anything to him. Well, that guy was me. It was never more than a physical thing. The mental part was something that women and tree huggers dealt with.

Well, for the first time, I knew what the other side was talking about. It felt like part of Miss Janet's power and passion was still deep inside of me. It filled me up, knocked me back, and drained me out each time we made love. I wanted to wrap my arms around that feeling and hold onto it for as long as I could, or at least until I could get my fill of her again. Still, it wasn't love. It was just lust and I knew that too.

I spoke to Sophie later one night in our room. I questioned her about her progress with our new recruits she had been researching. As it turned out, one of her top candidates was a student in the IT department. She convinced me to get this girl to secretly install several hidden remote cameras around the gym. These cameras would pan, tilt, and zoom, and could be controlled with a mini console stashed in our room chest lockers. The images were recorded and placed on a coded drive hidden in the Media Centre. At 2100hrs, Sophie would work the controller and record the times Miss Janet returned for me in the gym. Don't get me wrong, I was both terrified and embarrassed knowing I was being filmed, but it wasn't enough to make me stop. I just figured that if I had to, I would one day use her in the same way she was using me.

Each time Miss Janet would visit me, she would wait until I was through with my routines. I would always be genuinely shy, nervous, and ever obedient. As the recordings show, I was helpless as she would joyfully pleasure me to the point of torture and each time she took me to that "place". I totally enjoyed it, but I was careful to never initiate a thing. Our new society was not yet complete, and we already had one heavy weapon in our arsenal to be used in the case of an emergency.

I had taken a big step on my way to becoming a real woman. I had learned to use sex as a weapon and I learned it from my teacher. We also found that Miss Janet was fond of three other older girls from the basketball team. I pretended not to be angry about that, but it was obvious to Sophie that I was. She assured me that Miss Janet seemed to give me a lot more attention than the others, but she was pissed too. We also caught them on our cameras.

The Society of the Princesses

Sophie and I now had three other girls fully initiated into our society. We called ourselves "The Society of the Princesses." Our motto was "One day we will be Queens". The first rule was to never do your own hair.

Kendra was the IT girl that installed the network of cameras in the main gym, shower area, and in Coach Janet's office. She came from a small white-bread town in Nebraska. She, like most of the others, was a pretty girl but you would only ever know that on an occasion when she was forced to get cleaned up. At 15, she was what you might call a Tech Nerd. No nail polish or jewelry for this kid. Oil, Math, Paint, Computers, and Robots were her loves. She would work from project to project without food, drink or even sleep. This was the kind of person that you had to physically pull away from what she was doing in order to get her into her bed, no matter how tired she might be.

Olivia was another sports player. She was one of the basketball girls that Miss Janet was seducing. From a privileged black Georgia family near Macon, she was studying politics. She was a 5 foot 11 inch, dark chocolate, 18 year old, big booty HS Senior, and the star of the team. She had discovered that she was a "Chapstick" lesbian a few years ago. Miss Janet told her that she reminded her of herself when she was younger, but of course she was wrong. Olivia was not in hiding from whom and what she was. She still had her frizzy hair.

She was very pretty and had no trouble attracting boys, it's just that she would rather be one of them. She introduced me to a few other party girls and showed me how to spot the signals that the others like us put out. Unlike Miss Janet, Olivia taught me that when it comes to sex, all women are a little different. That was when I began to understand sex as more of an art. The funny part was how much I used to hate black people. Now there I was, exploring the most intimate things imaginable, with two of them.

Her test was to tell Miss Janet that she had to stop sexing the other girls on the team. One day she threatened to quit playing if Miss Janet didn't make her the exclusive lover on her program. Miss Janet was forced to agree if she wanted the team to win, and a winning team was the push she needed to secure that permanent position. Unlike me, Olivia was in charge of that relationship. She knew about the camera in the office and made that her favorite spot for her encounters with the coach. She had a good mind for politics and was well on her way to becoming a Governor one day. (Miss Janet left me alone).

Natalie was from India. She was supposed to prepare for Medicine, but she had decided to defy her family's orders and study Finance instead. She was as dark skinned as Olivia, 5 foot 7 inches tall, and thin. Her straight black hair hung to the bottom of her butt and she had that flat runway shape going.

Nat was a junior, 17, and had been a student at Dane Ann's going on three years. She worked in the office after hours for extra credits. At the end of this year she would have enough credit to skip right into college. In her downtime, she took to the challenge of mathematical theories and their application to the deck of Poker cards. She gave the girls love predictions and was able to make a small bit of change which she used to pick penny stocks under an assumed name. I gave Sophie some money and the two of them started a Poker Night. It became much more lucrative then fortune telling ever was.

They also began a pool to predict the times and frequency of the public (PA) announcements. Normally, there would be a "netwide" announcement before the first class and at the end of the day. But, a kid could bet on the announcements done between classes. How many different subjects were mentioned between those periods or throughout the entire day? You could try to guess how many different speakers came across each break or through the day. You could do one single bet or do a spread of averages if you wanted. We had other investors, and anytime a girl brought a new player to the pool, she would get credit towards one free bet. We took in cash but paid out credits. Enough credits could get you a cell phone or minutes for the phone you earned. It is no surprise to know that many girls are eager to throw away their parent's money on the silliest of things, but a phone is a whole other story.

The cash was used to bribe one of the Security Guards to buy and bring in cheap phones. Kendra was able to clone the phone cards and found a way to steal time from different carriers in the area. This turned out to be our top grossing operation and everyone involved had to sign a release form to get the cash credits for phones and the minutes. The whole thing was Sophie's idea and she ran it.

Weeks later, others joined our team, like Arleen the Debater. She was a 16 year old senior from Texas. She planned to become a lawyer so that someday she would replace her father who was a judge in that state. Arleen was 50% white, 50% Mexican, and 100% American girl. She was the smartest kid in the school and the Captain of the Debate Team. She wanted to join the Princesses because her father had told her "the only thing better than powerful friends are powerful friends that were made before they became powerful." Her test was to make an extra Public Announcement between each period one Friday. It threw the weekly spread completely off and allowed us to retain all the credits for that popular line of betting.

Mariko was a Japanese girl all the way from the Big Island. She too was a martial artist. Her father was some kind of crime boss in Tokyo and was killed by members of a rival faction. Mariko and her mother escaped to the US just this year. If she were a boy, honor would demand that she avenge her father's murder. If she survived, she could try to take her father's place as a leader in the crime world. Then again, the other Yakuza heads would not have let a boy survive, much less leave the country. The fact that she was a girl was the only reason she made it there at all.

Mariko had just turned 19 and like me, was just a HS junior. But one look at her grades would tell you that she might never graduate high school at all. Her English was bad and what little she did know of it was very hard to understand. She was basically lying low until the right time to take her revenge on the Kyokuto-Kai family or die trying. She was full of hate, anger, and paranoia. This was a short but very pretty girl with long hair and a wildly colored tattooed back. When we first met, she had a small tat on one arm and one larger one on her back. The last time I saw her, she was a complete work of art.

Iko carried a pad with her all the time and would write notes when she wanted to say something. With the money her father left behind, her plan was to learn the American ways before she returned with enough money and power to buy a small army. She was such a cute moon-faced girl, but the way she would walk, talk, stand, and act were all so boyish. With her long, well-groomed black hair and strong body build, she was a walking contradiction. One day she told me why she kept herself so unbalanced. "The day I cut hair is same day I go to confront my enemies. Even if I do return, Mariko will still be no more." (And that was the re-translated version).

Sophie and I took the school bus to support the basketball team and to see Olivia play against St. Mary, our main school rival. During the half, she and I went to the restroom and found Iko fighting two boys in the hallway. We heard her yelling and the guys crying out in pain as we came around a corner. We saw her as she kicked one of them through a classroom door and crushed the other by pulling a big display case on top of him as he helplessly lay on the floor.

When she saw us, she stopped. She took the money from their wallets, fixed her hair and straightened her skirt before walking past us on the way back to the stands. I didn't know what else she would have done if we had not come around when we did, but I knew right then and there that we had to have her. As for her test, I figured that she had just passed it.

Sandra Donaldson blackmailed her way into the group. She and the other spies she led, found out that we were the ones running the cell phone caper in the school. It was not a real big secret. Everyone knew how to get their hands on an unlocked cell phone. From time to time a girl would leave one lying around or just get busted with one in her hand. We tried to cover ourselves pretty good. As I said, all the kids signed a release. For that and the exchange of their credits, they received a phone and a receipt from one of the local stores for the purchase of that phone. No money (per se) was ever exchanged. So, when a kid was discovered with one of our products, the paper trail came right back to her. We didn't need that unnecessary heat.

Sandra was a daughter of a famous musician turned actor. She was a 16 year old, boy crazy sophomore, about 5 feet 6 inches tall. She was a white Californian from LA. She looked the part, but her father's talents did not pass to her. The poor kid couldn't sing, dance, act, or anything. What she did have was a nose for a story and a burning desire to tell it. There was a time when a person with this gift would have made a great investigative reporter. That was before they called them "un-American" for telling the truth. Now-a-days, people just want to hear fluff. The truth is too boring and underrated.

I have to admit, I liked the feeling of building and running a team again. I didn't mean for this whole underground gambling, phone smuggling thing to get too extreme, so I thought about ending it. Iko wanted the girl killed and Sophie agreed but Sandra was too much of a public figure for me to even think about that. Besides, she was just a stupid kid. She didn't want the money. All she really wanted was to be included in our club.

We refused to accept her crew of nosy back-stabbers, so it was decided that she, as well as the other seven core members, could have their own crew of members. The leaders would be allowed to recruit, assign duties, and function on their own independently. The recruits would answer to their leaders and not interfere or conflict with the other leaders' affairs. These subset members would not have a say in the core, nor would they ever know the names or meet with the other core members. With that understanding, we core members cut our fingers and made a lifetime blood oath to support each other in all things for as long as we lived. They also swore an oath to me as the supreme boss. I retained the power to assign and approve all activities. With this move, I became a Godfather (or Godmother). It was the first time we eight met as a group.

We were just a group of school girls. I started out looking at this whole rebirth deal as a weird alternate reality. I had been learning new and exciting things to do with my mind and body but as I began to closely study these other girls, my thinking started to change. Let's face it; the average life of a smart girl is limited and boring at best when it is compared to a simple boy that is looking for a little adventure. I was more than both of those and I wanted to do much more with these gifts I had assembled.

Before, when I would try to listen to women talk about the things that were happening in their lives, most times I would think to myself, "I wouldn't have done that", or "why didn't you go through with it", or "what were you waiting for", and my favorite, "what were you hoping to gain with that action?" It was one of the things that made talking to females so trying for me. It seemed to me that there was something in the chromosomes that prevented a pure and clear line of thinking. This is generally speaking of course, but it cannot be denied that the nature of what defines a forward-thinking plan is lost on most women. It's not that they can't do it, it's just harder and usually not required. I felt quested. These kids were getting reformatted. From then on, every idea was discussed in detail to include all its possible effects.

I was still going to push this rich girl world as far as I could roll it. I knew that something interesting was going to happen out of it and the exciting potential overwhelmed me. The Society was building itself. This phone caper was just the first of many tests to train the minds of the other girls. Maybe a new kind of power could spark into existence. Historically, it was about time.

We continued to meet separately but we were now also holding weekly meetings together. We met at different locations and at different times around the school. At these times I was a Boss, a Leader, and the Queen. But in the eyes of the public I remained meek, quiet, humble, and an innocent child. I was getting a "B" average, kicking ass on the soccer field, and becoming increasingly respected.

We began to expand the operation by making contacts in the other private schools. Their "Credit for Bets" operation had to be setup the same way as ours. Phones and minutes were awarded to the winners through that school's contact. Daily records were sent via email and reviewed. Monies were exchanged and a small profit of 30% of that school's take was given back to the contact. They also would receive store receipts in exchange for their release forms signed by the students. The planned exchanges were made at sporting events and other joint school gatherings.

Sophie and Iko ran the handovers. Natalie and Arleen kept the books. Olivia and Sandra made the contacts. Kendra cranked out the chips and acquired the phone time. The girls also began to plan ways to build their unique corner of the Society that would aid in the world changing plan I had devised.

Sophie aimed to build a large underworld organization that moved high dollar products into places they would not normally be acquired. Inspired by the phone caper, she was making moves to trade automotive parts for cigars in the country of Cuba.

Kendra would focus on developing the technical expertise needed to support the Society as a whole. Engineering School was in her sights. She didn't mind reinventing someone else's ideas and combining them with hers to accomplish this goal.

Olivia's plan was to recruit other sports players and fans to support or promote our future services. We had t-shirts and hats made off-campus. Olivia and my jerseys were sold in the stands by our "fans".

Natalie was researching ideas to invest our funds as we moved to manipulate our small and large markets in our small community.

Arleen planned to build her legal contacts into her own powerful network. They would be available to support the Society in all matters involving the law. This would make it easier to make the moves we wanted later on down the line.

Mariko would be our Enforcer until she could gather a worthy crew of her own. Later, she would build a strong enough force to reclaim her honor.

It was decided that Sandra would be best suited in some type of investigative role. She could be good as a police officer but an FBI agent or even something in Homeland Security would be better. When I suggested this to her, she looked at me like I was shooting the words into her head with a gun. She began to come around when I told her, "Think of the information you and your network could bring to us. Think of the pool of information the Society could provide for you."

I told them all, "The more one grows, the more we all grow together. The real keys in this plan are Trust and Loyalty. I don't give a shit about your mothers, your brothers or any of the other people in your operation. Your and my greatest concern, is the Society of the Princesses. That's who I care about! One day we will all be Queens!"

The Cost of Doing Business

In Florida, a lot of high school sports like soccer can be played all year round. In October, I was formally awarded the position as Forward or "Striker" as Dean Hattered liked to say. This spot is usually held by the team leader, so Jenny was outraged. She threatened to quit the team and yelled at me in the locker room about stealing her spot. "You can't be me! You will never be me!" Then she called me a Sand Nigger in front of the six other girls that were there at the time. Two of them laughed.

It was only after she walked away that I realized what she had done. First, it took a moment to wrap my head around the fact that I was being insulted. Then I had to think about the words themselves and what they meant. Once I did, the hurt feelings it gave me put a shock through my system. I had to sit down on the bench. The laughing ones were two of her lackeys, so I didn't expect sympathy coming from them, but the other four came to me.

Sand Nigger, she said to me. I was built from parts of many nationalities, so this derogatory term now applied to me. This is the kind of term that white Americans will use to put Arabs at the same level as we forced the blacks into. These are wicked words used to suppress our prospective and provoke a hatred based on ignorance. Arabs are not as dark as black people, but to more than a few whites, they are just as low. (At least she didn't call me fat).

I knew what stock she came from, still that kind of comment was unexpected and quite uncalled for. It was the first time I had ever heard those words spoken in my direction. They hit me like a good stomach punch. I must have used them myself countless times over the years. I do admit however, that I had to die before I learned that people are people. The only real differences between them are personality, sex, and opportunity. That doesn't mean that I have love for everyone. It just means that it's possible for anyone to become better than they were.

She was angry, and I know that she felt that she was losing her powerbase. So, I wasn't going to have her stuffed into the food processors or something like that. But, word got out that she had threatened me. (Girls talk). That wasn't the case but that was the word. Everyone knew that her father was a General. They also knew that I was half Arab. People were beginning to take sides in a matter that they were blowing way out of proportion.

I was called to the counsellor's office to discuss it. I told Mrs Billings that it was nothing and "all I want to do is play soccer." The Princesses wanted to meet too. Sophie told me that if something was not done about this girl soon, we would lose control of the Society. It was her Chicago way of thinking, but I knew she was right. I had to find a way to eliminate her without damaging my status.

I put it out through the grapevine that I challenged Jenny to a one-on-one, no penalty, no time clock, match in the gym. It would be a contest between me, her, the soccer ball and the scoreboard. Whoever made three points first in the other's net would be the winner. The loser would have to leave the team. This challenge would take place on Friday, twenty minutes after the last class ended. If she didn't show up, she was not only a loser, but a coward as well. I gave her two days to prepare.

As anticipated, that Friday brought more than the usual electric twinge that the weekend normally brings. By late afternoon the air itself was static with anticipation of the upcoming event. All day long I had heard that I was either going to get my ass kicked or that I was stupid for challenging someone for a job I had already won. A few people did say "good luck" but, they were just being nice.

I'm sure that half those girls wanted me to stomp a puddle into that little shit but were afraid to say. I understood their trepidation. It was more a political choice then a logical one. She was popular, a white American girl, and even though they had not won a trophy, this was her team. On the other hand, I was new, a foreigner, a Muslim, and a Sand Nigger. They were just being safe. Bets were made, and spreads were put into place.

After the last class, Sophie went ahead to setup the gym, while Iko and Olivia escorted me to my room to change. I put on my knee highs, the team skirt, and the sports bra too, but instead of the old number 7 team jersey, I wore a new, freshly printed t-shirt that had my face on the front and the name "Jasmine" with #1 on the back. It was a black shirt with white and red lettering that worked really well with the red and black skirt. My new sneakers were also red and black.

In the gym the kids were stomping their feet and yelling. The racket could be heard in every direction. Walking the halls on the way to the match reminded me of my old high school football days. It's got to be the same feeling "the Rock" would get on the way down to the ring, or Elvis walking from his dressing room on the way to the stage. I met Miss Janet, Miss Hattered, Sophie, and the other Princesses in the halls. By the time I stepped into the gym, I was so pumped that I jogged a lap around the floor like I was "Rocky Balboa" and the kids loved it. It was a high unlike any I'd had in previous memory.

Arleen used her influence with the faculty to legitimize this match. Olivia used her wiles to acquire the setup in the gym. Soccer Coach Hogue happily chose to ref the event hoping it would end a feud that had begun the day I walked out on the field. Then again, if Jenny were removed from the team, that lady might be able to really coach again. Kendra was taking pictures for the Year Book.

Except for the two small net goalposts set in the middle of the floor 100 feet apart, the place looked like a Pep Rally. Nearly 300 girls, most of the staff, and half the security force were either sitting on the bleachers or standing around the court. Everyone I knew at school was there, except for Jenny. The big clock on the wall read 4:15pm. She had 5 minutes to show her white ass.

As I bounced and kicked the ball around, the crowd counted down the minutes. We were all aware that if Jenny didn't show before Mickey's big hand got to the 4, she would not only lose her place on the team, she would also be branded a scary-cat.

At one minute to go, Jenny and her small entourage stepped through the double doors. Again, the place went into an uproar. Wearing her standard team uniform with white sneakers, she too felt the rush as she came trotting in. But, that all changed when she saw the number one (1), her number, on my back. The chick flipped all the way out. She pointed her finger right in my face. "You are not me! You can never be me!!" The crowd went into a hush. "Fuck you, you camel riding bitch!!" she yelled. Then she threw her hand back to slap me.

It was not the first time that a one second period slowed to what would seem to be more than a minute long. There were a few ways I could have handled that situation. These are some of the ones I considered during that adrenalin charged rush.

I could have blocked the blow with my left arm and countered with a right uppercut to the chin. I also could have taken her arm to pull her into me and toss her over my shoulder onto the wooden floor. Either of these two options would have effectively taken her out but they could have also gotten me banned from school at the very least. I actually considered letting her hit me. I thought about turning my head with the slap and falling on the ground. I could have held the hurt part of my face and cried. That move would have gotten her kicked out of school for fighting. I could have taken over the team and effectively beaten the Smith family once again, without raising a hand. However, I would have lost total face with a sorority that I had helped to build. It would have fallen in on itself and onto me.

There was another option. The whole point of this exhibition was to embarrass her to the point of leaving the team. Beating her ass and getting expelled was not part of that plan. I would have to block and dodge her swings until one of the faculty stepped in.

This was the hardest of all the options. I didn't want to get hit and I couldn't hit her back. I hadn't forgotten what happened with Rico that time and was afraid that if I got too angry, I could have another 'Red Wave' episode.

I deflected that first swing with my left arm. At the same time, I turned left, and cross stepped a little to the right. This put me behind her back. There were so many things I could have done to her at that point that it made me smile. "Stop!" I yelled. "I don't want to hurt you!" She came at me again but this time with a high right punch meant for my head. I ducked low and stepped forward this time. I threw my open hands onto her boyish chest and used my chi to push her as hard as I could. The girl went back on her ass. "I said STOP!!"

The athletic Jenny jumped to her feet, but Coach Hogue moved to stand between us followed by Miss Hattered and Mrs Billings. Mrs Billings motioned for the security guards to respond. As they did, Miss Hattered said, "Jenny Smith, this is most unlady like!" To the guards she said, "Take her to her room for now. I shall want to see her in my office later." Once Jenny and Security were out of the gym, Miss Hattered addressed the group. "Two roads stretch before your young lives. The high road is a constant challenge, but the rewards are dignity and respect. The low road is a fast and easy slide that will leave you permanently stained in the end. Let it not be said that Dane Ann's School for Girls is a collection of common street trash!" To me she said, "I will speak with you another time." We were dismissed for the weekend.

As we all made our ways back to our rooms, I was amazed with the number of handshakes, hugs, "good job" and even the "thank you for this" I received from people I saw along the way. Jenny on the other hand, was instantly expelled when Security saw the 15 cell phones (without the Sims) in a clear plastic bag lying on her bed. They also found the store sales receipts for not only those phones but all the receipts for the ones that had been found by the staff so far.

Natalie and Sandra handled the 'bag job' and Kendra saw that some snap shots of the gym fight were blown up and posted on You-Tube. We all, to include myself, had passed our first real test in team work. This operation put us in a bind with our next few phone deliveries and we had to lay low for a short time. It was hell to catchup but, worth it in the end. We chalked it up to the cost of doing business.

My Soccer Name is Score

The sports bra I was using in my Kung Fu studies was just not at all up to this new challenge. Besides, Kung Fu is all about centering and controlled movements. Soccer on the other hand, is a lot of running, jumping, bouncing, falling, and faking out the opposition. Which for me, is an ordeal of self-gratification gained through torturing my new body. Yes, there can be pain and bruising doing something that any man takes for granted.

I love these great breasts, so don't get me wrong. I love looking at them in the mirror and the way they feel when I, or someone else, is touching them. However, their mass does carry weight. This weight effects my balance when moving and the uncontrolled bouncing about can be very painful on my skin and surrounding muscles. In other words, there are no big tittied track stars. None! If she is a star, it's not because she wins the races.

Knowing that people are watching my big bouncing boobs and hearing those things flopping against my wet skin can be more than a little embarrassing. Especially when they should be watching and hearing the game. I never wanted to be that kind of star.

Now that you have that picture in your head, think of my big butt bouncing and damp cheeks slapping and clapping against themselves at the same time as the breasts are doing their thing. Now, try being the girl that is out there on the field in front of families, players, and fans alike causing all of that distraction. Not at all good for the rep. (Being a girl can be complicated sometimes).

From this experience, I can now advise all other well-endowed ladies that want to play some kind of sport, with three quick tips. The first is rhythm. Once you've learned how your body moves and sways, practice that with the timing it takes to get all of the parts in motion. If you don't, you end up fighting yourself and looking real stupid doing it. Second: a strong back. Mid and lower back exercise will make holding your breast weight easier and make you look a lot less like Quasimodo at the gym. I was designed with a reinforced back, so it was easy for me to make that adjustment. You other ladies will need to baby step this one, so a good plan is essential. The third and best word is gear. If you're going to be a serious player, then get some serious gear. High-support elements built into the bra is a must. Things like molded cups, underwire, and good old padded straps. The goal is to stop as much of the bouncing as you can while still being comfortable. If you can get your boobs and torso to move together, you have solved the problem. Now, all you have to do is get your ass on the field. Speaking of ass, I found running shorts with built-in panties worked the best for me. (Again, think comfort and flexibility).

After much discomfort, deeply personal but informative chat room advice, and more return shopping trips to the same places than I want to talk about, I was left with only one last issue. And that's only because I'm not talking about footwear. Sweat! I was already the sweat champion of the world. Now, I had to drag a uniform over this extra stuff. Dirt sticks to sweat better then two teenagers when parents are out of town. In this body, I could make mud on a sunny day. No way around being the last to suit-up. Getting undressed once I was wet, took so long that I was assigned somebody to help me after each practice and match. Still, we found a way to have fun with it when we weren't rushed.

After a few games, I got the idea to build the uniform colors and design into the shorts and top. It took a few weeks to get it right but it payed off by giving me a more breathable and less bulky outfit. I even looked slimmer. Nothing could ever stop me from sweating, but I felt much cooler and it marked the end of my passing-out phase. This got me thinking about one day designing my own clothing line.

I kept telling myself that sweat was why I chose the sport in the first place. In the end it was tougher than high school football. I was so hot that I fell out more times than even I can remember. But, we won games. The crowds got bigger and louder. So, I had fun. It was all worth it.

I won a nickname. I drove in a lot of goals, so I wanted to be called something like "Slam", "Dam", or "Sting", but I was told that those were guys names. Some of our rivals used to say I was one of the "Wonder Twins" (the wet one). They called me "Sweaty Girl" and giggled when they saw me dripping. As it turned out, at my fourth game some fans started yelling "Score, score, score" each time I would get the ball, and it stuck with me. It put a halt to that "Wonder" shit fast. "Score" turned out to be a real cool name for this overheated player. After that I was the one laughing.

I also started talking a little trash about that time. It was unladylike, and I was made to stop, but before I did, I made more than a few people cry. Truth be told, I was on the edge of falling back into that same habit of treating females like garbage. Most times it wasn't intentional, but other times it really was. I had to be placed into another body to understand any of that.

So, I changed into this super nice encouraging girl. Yes, I did. It was a true 180-degree turn. I told the other players that they were "putting out good effort" even if they sucked. Now, even our worst rivals started to like me. I would whip the opposition's ass on the field and at the same time I'd put sweat and dirt on their clean uniforms with my wet hugs and slapped a good handful of ass cheek for encouragement. Some of us were technically still in our teens so I admit, it did take a little bit to get used to that part, but a lot of the girls had already been doing this to me since day one.

I learned that this is not a new tradition in female sports. It is well known that among the best players you will find some lesbians, bisexual, and bi-curious ladies and girls. Those chicks were slapping, grabbing and some were confidently groping my ass for weeks. Sometimes I would not see it coming. One second, I'd be drinking a bottle of water or talking with another player and the next, someone would have come up from behind, whisper in my ear, put her hands all over my butt and trot off in the other direction. (Some of them were real sneaky that way). Now, I'd be left standing with even damper panties and no idea what the hell I was talking about.

It was shocking at first and even though I was clothed with extra padding, it did feel good to be handled by another female. Later, I thought "what the hell". It turned from strange to another fun part of the game, and I became used to, and even enjoyed it, as those girls obviously did. I took it as a kind of training for the real-life lesbian I wanted to become. All and all, soccer was berry, berry good to me. (Taken partly from Minnie Minoso of the Chicago White Socks and Saturday Night Live by Garrett Morris. Later Billy Crystal with Sammy Sosa of the Chicago Cubs).

All Hail the New Kid in Town

When I returned from my weekend, I was worshiped like a god. No longer did I hear the nasty comments I had heard in the past. The hateful looks were all gone too. Everyone smiled and wanted to find a reason just to talk to me. I was constantly asked to run for student leadership or be involved in one wacky program after another. I had gone from "the back-room boss", to one of the most popular girls in school, almost overnight. Even the Princesses now started to call me "Queen". Unfortunately, I now felt like a red Corvette at a stop light. This was truly an unexpected turn of events and it was not what I wanted at all. I needed to find a good way to use this or lose it altogether. I now had to pay to have my hair done professionally. (Anything less wouldn't be civilized).

Requests for my T-shirt went through the roof. There was no way we could have handled the orders we had and kept the operation on the "down low." Deals and contracts had to be made legitimately with the school taking the lion's share of the profit. They in turn, gave the money away to a shelter for homeless people or something. However, we were able to make a little on the markup from the printer we arranged. Also, our new company had legal rights on the design. The school's name was added to the front but when it was all said and done, we sat on our asses and made $3 from each $18 shirt sold, and we got the school to buy them. Not too shabby.

Like it or not, I was popular now. The coolest girls in the world, it seemed, wanted to buy the same kind of underwear and wear my perfume. They wanted to hook me up with their brothers and invite me to all the high-class events that the rest of the world never even hears about. Before, these girls would have nothing to do with my kind. Only after that win over the General's daughter, did the question of who I really was, demand an answer. Now suddenly, I was cool enough for the girls of the upper crust. These

"Super High Society" chicks were more than eager to extend their arms and legs just to be seen with me.

After meeting some of these people, I invited Arleen on a research assignment that amazed us both. We found that this crazy idea I initially had (to fuck with my roommate) was already a real breathing entity of sorts in many places around the US. It had no leaders, direction or purpose but the network of powerful women was sound. This organization was loose and unorganized but as I saw before, it was possible to create a sub-group of go-getters that believed in a change of direction.

This was a world of another kind of people altogether. They are above all law and government. These were beings living in the same kind of world that Faatina was so violently snatched away from. As dim witted as she was, a person of her rank would have still functioned quite nicely here. You could say that these were the American equivalents to the European aristocrats that in one way or another, served people like Faatina's father. Their world of famous family names and extravagant living was missing only one small thing, me. I wanted in.

I already knew that most of the older ladies in this group were not going to want to hear about planning, strategy, loyalty, or anything related to the word "work". They were too good for that. I also knew that most of the younger ones only wanted to travel, shop, and marry well, so that they could continue to maintain that life style. After all, what use is life if you can't live well? Still, there had to be some in this gaggle that had their own ideas about the course this world was taking. Some of them may have been interested in hearing even more good ideas. We just needed to find one respected member to support us in our cause, to get it started.

Glendale was a descendant from a family that fled to America from Europe after selling weapons and ammo to the wrong side of France just before the 1800s. They continued to deal in arms and explosives for over a hundred years. It seemed that every war fought anyplace in the world was supplied partly by this family in some form or fashion. Long before moving into synthetics in the 1920s, this clan had become something that no one had ever before heard of, "millionaires". For the same reasons I mentioned at the beginning of this story, they too, disappeared behind the wall of secrecy.

Glendale had mentioned my name to her grandmother and she badly wanted to meet me. During a November 4-day weekend, she and I flew by private jet into a cold and rainy Washington, DC. We spent one day there and one day in Philadelphia. The next day we took a boat on the Delaware River that docked right in the back yard of the old family homestead.

This was when my first real lessons in my family history began. That old lady showed me, Glen, and two of her cousins, how to visually identify the untold succession of power and government from one part of my family to another, over the centuries. It was all right there in the public and private pictures, paintings, and drawings of the history making faces in this world. "Facial markings and bone structure are the keys to look for," she told us. Her great line could be tracked back over 400 years to some minor European nobles. She said that my line, "the First Line", had been recorded for over 2400 years and showed me proof that Philip and Alexander of Macedon had the same ears and nose then, as I do today.

These facial features were also immortalized in the coins and stone carving of Greece, Mesopotamia, Rome, Egypt, and all over Europe. They were Emperors, Kings, Explorers, Builders, and Merchants of great renown. At first the Line was eager to travel about the known world. They intended to conquer as much as their great ancestors did, but soon discovered that the cost to life and resources were much too great. Their focus was later reevaluated to put wealth and power as its main focus. Paid armies could do this kind of dangerous stuff in the King's name.

These people were the ones that began the practice of intermarriage in order to keep the bloodline and those prized identifying features separate and distinct from the common man. However, this was not a healthy practice. Before too long, babies were born dead and many had other deficiencies like retardation and hemophilia, just for starters. They became so afraid of getting hurt or sick that they would live most of their lives indoors. It became very uncommon for a noble to know the feeling of dirt or sunlight on their flesh. People could see the blood vessels beneath the pale skin and the blood appeared blue. They began to see the ones with the palest skin as the ones with the noblest blood. Hence the true origin of the coined term "Blue Blood".

Later, when husbands and wives, brothers and sisters, fathers and daughters, mothers and sons, could no longer produce normal offspring, the practice of sending the children off to marry a cousin that ruled in another land was put into place. In no time at all, most of the truly noble families were related in many, many ways. The clans stayed small, but they still retained all the wealth and power between them.

As did their ancestors, power of all types was gathered, collected, studied by scholars, and stored in fortresses to include the knowledge of medicine, science, and art. These riches were not offered to the public masses. The Nobles owned everything and everyone in the area and the people began to hate them for that. As time went on, many old governments were overthrown by religion and new ideas about humanism and free will. The old demigods collectively decided that the only real key to their survival was to step back and rule from behind the scenes. This relatively new practice continues to this day.

Today, most of the pure strain of Ancient Noble Blood, this "First Line", is nearly extinct. No amount of wealth or science has been able to stop the natural degradation of DNA. Doctors have found ways to extend life for a while, but the same cells cannot be copied indefinitely and be expected to thrive. That is just how this planet works. The air we breathe today is altogether different than it was 2000 years ago. Microbes that thrived in those days were all but replaced by new ones now. When your environment changes, you too have to change and adapt, or you will die. In the old days, children were killed because they were born without enough of the required Noble traits. Now, it's nearly impossible to have a healthy First Line baby at all.

There are members of Faatina's father's family that are 100 years and older, but only a few in these last generations were able to have healthy children. Of the entire clan, the last generation produced only five boys. Boys are not only important because they are boys, they are also the ones that replicate most of the family gene cells. Of these last five men, only one was able to have children (Arthur).

We know the stories of monarchs dying and leaving no heir to the throne. It was not because the King or Queen wasn't getting enough sex, it was because the babies died, or he or she couldn't get, or get anyone, pregnant.

It's the answer to the question of the frozen caveman. A caveman gets frozen in an avalanche. One million years later, he's thawed in a laboratory. The man lives again, but can he ever adapt in today's modern society? Will he be able to master our language? Does he even possess the mental capacity to learn a trade? The answer is no. He gets a simple infection and he dies before he can leave the laboratory. (Today, most modern organisms can't survive without an occasional dose of unhealthy bacteria).

There was talk about allowing the First Line to gracefully die off. After all, it would be only fair to let the other lesser branches of the tree rule now. Arthur's father disagreed. He wanted the privilege of his son to be the father of this new and improved line of Noble Borne that their scientists were working on. With one or two good infusions of this new traceless DNA, the First Line could silently rule for another 200 years. Surely medical science would have a real cure by then. In the meantime, Arthur's children would be partly Arab, but their blood and features would still be just as "Royal Blue".

You would think that the DNA fusing was something that the First Line would want to keep locked behind closed doors. But Granny Joe explained that the other lines needed to know that the First Line had no intentions of going "gentle into the night" (to quote Dylan Thomas). The Second and Third Lines needed to be told to stand down and step back. The First Line needed to let them know why. That anointment was made when Arthur was born. He would rebirth the Line.

That's why Faatina's mother was so widely sought after. She was designed to birth babies that showed little to no trace of her own family traits. She was to be the one to help restart the process by producing at least one healthy boy. Girl babies in her clan were rare at best. When one did happen along she would be a lot less than bright, but she would be beautiful, and historically she was guaranteed to have a boy child.

The wait for this process to naturally come to pass was a long one. When Faatina's parents were married, her father was 56, but her mother was 17. It took her mother three years to become pregnant with her first child and it was a half Arab looking girl. They were disappointed, but 15 years later, while accompanying her husband on a trip to Baghdad, she discovered that she was pregnant again. They didn't want to take any chances with this one. It was the reason they were in such a hurry to get back to England in the first place.

If the baby was a boy, all the bells in London would simultaneously ring on his birth. If it was another girl, she and her older sister would be married off at the earliest age to an older cousin some place, and the world would just have to wait a little longer. Faatina was 16 at the time. If this new baby did turn out to be another girl, then the teenager would have been up for bidding before she turned another year older.

I thought about these facts for a while and they troubled me. Knowing that everyone has their enemies, it stood to reason that Arthur must have had his too. I could see how some members of the lesser lines might have felt badly about being denied their chance to lead. It was also possible that even another member of his own family thought that this new process was a stain on the ancestry. That line of thinking could still be a factor now. So, could there be an unknown enemy out there someplace? This thought alone echoed in my mind in the form of a faraway scream.

The fact that it was now impossible for me to have any children at all should have been enough to keep me safe. Any continuing conflicts about power, changes in power, and blood lines should not involve the likes of me (at least not any more). I was just a stupid girl that no one really wanted. Then again, Faatina was born with a pocket full of bad luck. Someone may feel that I might intend to seek some sort of vengeance at some point in the future. I still had the potential to be a threat to someone. Only time would really tell if I was in the clear.

Her parents had just found out that the mother was pregnant again. I'm sure they made some happy phone calls, but they were trying to get out of Iraq so fast that there really wasn't enough time for someone to plan and put to action an effective hit like that. It was too quick. Yes, it would have been the perfect place and time to kill them all off but that almost seems too perfect.

And what of this grandmother? She had some gaps in this tale, but then again, she knew so much. Was her line so far down the chain that it could not profit from my demise? Would her family name not ascend if the First Line was effectively wiped out? Did she honestly want me here to teach and protect me or did she really want to finish the job? (I put those thoughts in one of my active files).

What Glendale's grandmother didn't know, was that it cost millions to try to save something out of that blown-up piece of trash that was once an armored SUV. In the end, all they got for their money was a junior version of the "Bride of Frankenstein." With what they had to work with, those doctors performed a miracle. But, they couldn't save her. All they really did was save what she looked like in the face. All their earlier planning and hoping was nothing more than wasted time. Someone else would have to be the mother or father of the next Noble Borne. That's why Faatina was rebuilt as a sex model for trade and for fun. If Granny knew that part of the story, she would have never spoken to me in the first place. Still, I wondered how it was that she didn't know.

This was by far the most interesting weekend of both my lives. To find that you are part of a history that civilized the world is incredible. To find that you are part of a family who is so rich that they own nearly the entire planet, is incredible again. To be a member of the secret society that began most of the other secret societies that at the same time holds all the real secrets ever kept in the last 2000 years, is amazing. The flip side was learning all of this and knowing that the family heads had no real use for me other than something to trade, was greatly depressing.

It is very possible that Glendale and I are related. Her grandmother believed in the connection, but I didn't tell her that I did not. The missing gaps were just too great to ignore. Her family has completely different traits, but it is conceivable that she is part of a branch that dropped from the main tree many hundreds of years before she or I were born (or, reborn in my case).

Her roots come from a minor Nobel through marriage. They came to the US at a time when the family business was needed. It was the story of "the right place at the right time." They could in a way, qualify for aristocracy in America (such thinking is extremely unpopular in the US), but their wealth and power are young when compared to the European blood. In these circles, "old money" always rules over the new, no matter how much more the "new" may actually have.

In an attempt to try and appease her, I used my sweet shy voice and said, "The paths we have taken are truly legendary. It's too bad that for security reasons these things are kept hidden from the rest of the world." Then I asked her if she, or any or the other ladies, "had any ideas about a new Noble vision for this new time?"

She thought for a few seconds then said, "Being a lady of Noble Birth is the best possible life anyone could imagine. No lady would choose to change that. The men have always held enough vision for us all." I asked her if she had ever felt that she could be an equal with her brothers. I also asked if she ever thought that she would do things a little differently if she held the power as well as she held her name. In her shaky voice, she answered "no" to both. "I am a woman and my place is a woman's place. We are what we are and that is all we can be," she said. "You are young, so I can forgive you for having your own dreams. That is natural after all. You are also smart. Maybe you're a little too smart. You've gotten much more from your father then I had realized, but there is little place for a smart woman in our world. Believe me, I should know. In time, you will learn as did I, to hide it. It will make you of much more desirable interest to our men." She got up from her chair. "We will talk more on this at your next visit."

After the 90 year old heiress had left the room, Glendale and her two cousins wanted to know what I was talking about, but I didn't want to blow it completely with their grandmother so at that time, I didn't say. Later, Glendale told me that her grandmother was impressed with me. She thought that I was very wise for my age. So much so, that she believed that I may possess part of the living soul of my Great Macedon ancestors. She volunteered to be my new grandmother and train me properly in the ways of a person of my station.

She demanded that Glen, her cousins Windy and Lisa, and I, spend every other weekend with her, and this was not put in an offer that could be refused. There are no rogue princesses running loose in this world. Every princess from the beginning of time has always belonged to, or in, a Great House of some kind. The only ones that have tried to be free have lost their titles or lost their lives.

When I returned to Miami Airport, I had to call Krystle as per our agreement. In secret, I told her about the Delaware family in more detail then I am allowed to state in this book. The girl hungup on me. Glen, Arleen, and I were in the limo on the way back to the school when she called back. "You will do like that old woman ask you," she said.

Frankly, I was hoping she was going to forbid me from doing anything like that. In fact, I was planning on it. At the time I was thinking, "This is going to the cramp the shit out of my style." Her answer was so far out of the norm that I hadn't even considered what would happen if she did say yes.

It would cut my time with Bo down to just two times a month. That meant even less time working on my Kung Fu. I wouldn't get to hang out with the band every Friday and Saturday night. I loved that shit too. I ended up hanging up on her, so I could think about it for a while.

It was a hard fight, but we agreed that in exchange for my tutoring weekends in Delaware, I could spend both days of the other weekends with Bo. It cut me completely out of the band nights, but on the other hand, I was no longer trapped in the condo with Krystle anymore. It was a kind of lose/win alternative.

A Class Within a Class

When George Bush the 1st spoke about the 1,000 points of light, this Delaware family was part of the network he was actually referring to. The first time I heard him say that, I thought it was a strange thing to say, mostly because I had no idea what he was talking about. I thought it stranger still that none of the news media who seemed to enjoy twisting every little word that any President would say, never commented on it. (Especially since he mentioned it in more than a few speeches).

This Katharine Hepburn-sounding Matriarch called herself Granny Jo. Jo was short for Jocelyn. She told me the reason she wanted to be called that was because, "When I was young, I was a very beautiful girl. I had a wonderful life and my pick of any of the eligible men in the country. When I became a mother, my name became 'Mommy.' When I became a grandmother, my name was changed again to 'Granny.' The name Jocelyn is no longer spoken in the house. I am old, tired, and I no longer see that beautiful girl in the looking glass, but I remember a time when I did. I am the oldest living woman in the family now. By tradition, it is my duty to teach and pass on my memories and the memories of all the other Grannies before me. Those other Grannies had their own special names too. It's how we remember them. Mine is Granny Jo, and I also do not intend to be forgotten."

Granny Jo was one of those people that had a switch. When she was off, she was off to the world, but when she was on, she was on all the way. Half of the time, she would sit in her favorite chair, locked away in her room with her books and her thoughts. The other half of the time, she was in our ass.

Dropping the Arab accent was the first thing I was made to do. It was the fourth time I was made to learn how to walk, talk, stand, sit, dress, and eat, all over again. Nothing I did was right. Every time I would visit Granny Jo, was like going to football and soccer practice at the same time, but without any of the fun. I was not alone in this feeling. Glendale, Windy, and Lisa were there too. Their company was the only reason I never smothered that lady with a pillow in her sleep (Just kidding). I did love that lady.

Granny Jo was planning a big New Year's Eve Ball. "Just like in the old days", she said. It would also be an official "Coming Out" for the four of us. She kept the details secret, but I had imagined a Cinderella type experience. A tailor came to fit us with gowns and she hired a trainer to teach me Ballroom Dancing. I slept with an I-Pod to learn Classical music to the point where I knew the composers and the variations that noted directors made to each piece. I messed up from time to time because I didn't want the others to know how easy it was for me to memorize everything, but Granny Jo somehow knew.

This was going to be a real big affair. Family names that I had read about in school were invited. Presidential names too, ranging from our distant past to our distant future (so I was told). There would be other dignitaries and some of the owners of the top 20 companies in the United States were expected to attend. We would meet movie stars, recording artists, writers, musicians and Nobel Peace Prize holders. All and all, we were expecting over 800 guests. It was time for a whole new hair style.

Granny Jo lived in a big house, but there was no way she could squeeze in more than 100 people at a time. But, as we moved into December, construction began on an outrageously lavish temporary hall. It stood on the grounds and partly out over the water. Boats could even dock there. It had some guest rooms just in case someone needed to stay over (or whatever). There were halls within halls and yes, you guessed it, the Great Ballroom complete with a bandstand. The fireworks on the water could be viewed outside of course, but we would also see them through giant windows behind the bandstand. It promised to be more than spectacular.

The Davenports (just a name) had done things like this before. In another month the estate would return to normal and no one would be able to tell that a massive structure was once there.

I got permission to add a few friends to the list, so I submitted Bo and the names of the girls in the Society, and Sophia, Olivia, and Arleen were able to make the final cut. Not even Krystle was allowed to come. Bo understandably, could not attend do to family reasons. At first, Sophie, above all others, did not meet the security requirements, but a minute before the final list was presented, she and her brother did appear on it. Mariko told us that her mother did not want their names to be mentioned at all. We understood.

I added Glendale into the Society, but not to the core. I explained the concept to her and placed her in my personal crew along with Sophie. Her head was full of a lifetime of privileged living. She would never want for anything and would not understand why she needed to work or even think, for as long as she lived. However, she, unlike any of the rest of us, she was somebody. Her name in the US High Society Crowd got an ear. It reminded me of those old E. F. Hutton ads, "People Listen." I knew she would be useful in the future and right now, she was listening to me.

She and her two cousins were pretty enough to capture the attention of any boy with eyes in his head. The weird thing was that they were all exactly the same. They looked about the same, talked the same, acted the same, and they were all the same height and size. They were all around the same age, too. They told me that they often had sex with each other and with the same boys. The three of them with one boy or girl, was their favorite past time. They had their preferences but, in a pinch, they could pick anyone. Apart, they were responsible, alert, outgoing, and in control. Together, they were a pack of silly little clones, each one just as silly as the other. I think their minds were even connected, because when they spoke in their half sentence giggly language, the others already knew what they were about to say. That is why they were farmed out to different schools around the United States.

Glendale attended Dane Ann's with me in Florida. She was 19 and a first-year college student. She was in all the right clubs but did not play a sport.

Lisa and Windy were sisters. One of the older male cousins (Franklin) told me that all three had the same father. "My uncles are all playboys," he said one day. "And they like to share the same women sometimes. It's a game we play." He said that among the family circle, they were known as 'The Triplets.' "Everyone knows that they have a strange bond between them, but every man still wishes they could cut one out of the pack." He himself was into young men I discovered, but he liked talking to me.

Windy was the oldest, but only by a year. She was 20 and went to school in California. She played tennis and was engaged to one of the Winchester boys. She was a second-year college kid, and a good student.

Lisa went to school in New York City. She was 18 and a high school junior with very bad grades, even though she was very smart. She, like her cousin, was a big club member.

Besides sex, the second thing they loved was ballet. When they were kids, they were taught by the same instructor. They all still danced at their schools and performed Drama.

The family also had a stable of horses. There must have been at least 30 of them. The girls loved to ride those smelly things for hours at a time. I learned to ride too, but just sitting on that giant quivering beast made me so horny that I couldn't stand it. Riding would cause me to have an orgasm before I could get partway down the path. Everyone could smell me over the horse and I would end up with soaking wet pants, no matter what I tried. In the end, I just had to lie and say that I was afraid of horses.

It only took a few weekends before the girls sniffed out all my other sensitivities. Like spoiled little kids, normally they would get something new, play with it for a while, and then leave it lying on the floor. But playing with me never seemed to bore them. They were fascinated by the way I would lose all control. My explosive orgasms were met with wonder and surprise every single time. I tried to return the pleasure, but I could never make it past the petting and kissing part. I would be overwhelmed in minutes. I felt a little guilty about it, but they not only understood, they thought it was great. Between them and their grandmother, I almost looked forward to some rest back at school. I could have said "no" to them but why would I? I knew it would end much too soon.

It's Beginning to Look
a Lot Like… Fire

There were five Fridays in this December. On the second one, the school was a ghost town. By the third Friday, the doors were locked tight. Any girl that had at least one loving family member someplace in the world, was shipped out. This year, the five girls that didn't have a place to go, spent their month off with Dean Hattered at her home outside of Miami.

These were the same girls that never went away for the weekend. They were as rich as all the others, it's just that no one wanted them around. Maybe it wasn't safe for them at home. Maybe their families were full of bad people or maybe that girl had done something so horrible that she was banned from ever returning home again. Miss Hattered treated them as if they were her children. She made them feel like they mattered. She called them "My Girls." They went shopping for gifts, had a big tree, and took trips around Florida. It wasn't like flying around the world or going to a Cinderella Ball, but she gave them a real nice time.

That's where some of that project money, to include my T-shirt profits, went. That lady kept notes, the receipts, and all the pictures she took, in a scrap book in her office. She had been doing this for over twenty years before I heard about it. Many of the girls kept in contact with her long after school. From time to time, some of those girls would come by to visit her during the holiday season. They brought their husbands and children with them and she knew all their names. As always, after the holidays things were back to business but that lady made such an impression that she would be invited to their weddings, baby showers, and funerals. Those unfortunate ones were her girls and they always would be. Dean Hattered was truly a righteous woman. It was the kind of thing you could really admire and respect.

Krystle and her band were gigging their ass off. They hired two hot girls to take my place and changed the act. It was her band now and they were packing in the crowds and making money hand over fist. She was booked solid but never too busy to take my call.

Bo, her family, and all the others in her Everglade home, had a quiet and spiritual holiday. That was of course before they started the fireworks. It was a mix of a little American and a lot of Chinese. (One soul- two minds). On Christmas she was told that she was engaged to a 28 year old Chinese American businessman. He had a degree in Marketing and owned four charter fishing boats. In her family's eyes, he was a "good catch." She now had a chance to stand behind a good man and he was getting a wife that was more traditional than anything he had known. Everyone was happy about it but me. Still, who was I to hold her back from her dream? I didn't see her much after that engagement.

I was in Delaware. "The Davenport Trio" had a lot of other cousins and almost all the men were so far in my ass that I could smell my shit on their breath. It was the craziest and creepiest experience and I have nothing to compare it to. I was supposed to enjoy all the attention but instead I wanted to hurt every last one of them. All I could see, hear, and smell, was a guy scheming some way to try to fuck me. I couldn't get a moment of peace. Still, I was determined that they wouldn't either.

That's when I learned that the true meaning of 'coming out' was "Jasmine Hunting Season." Oh yeah, it's an old European tradition that dates back hundreds of years. When a promising girl becomes of marrying age, she is publicly presented (mostly at a party of some kind) to only the most eligible bachelors. It can be a real big celebration that could involve many physical activities too. Sometimes, the men would take turns chasing and grabbing her until she ran out of breath and could no longer fight them off. And then there's the "Old Surprise Attack". I was a deer, and this was a no limit gun season.

They followed me around the house and grounds. They wanted to bump into me and touch me (mostly on my ass) at every opportunity. I tried to hide out in the bedroom, but someone was always knocking on the door or standing next to it just in case I wanted to come out. I had to lock the door on account of guys were accidentally coming in the "wrong room". I'd sneak to the bathroom and some guy would have to get inside right away. Once the door was opened, he didn't have to pee, throw-up, or whatever lie it was to get me to open it. He just wanted to talk to me. I had to start peeing in a pail that the maid had to place in my room. She called it a chamber pot. I called it medieval.

One guy tried to jump me in the barn. I was on the second level just looking out the window onto the grounds. It was cold, but I had a coat, scarf, and a long thick skirt on. I was listening with headphones to Wagner's "Ride of the Valkyries" from the opera "Die Walkure" on my iPhone when I was attacked from behind.

In my mind I could see the first four sisters on the mountain top as they were met by the second set of four. As they began to sing their battle cry songs, I closed my eyes, so I could have a better view in my mind. It's one of Wagner's most popular pieces and in my opinion, it's his best. That's also why the volume was up so loud that I didn't hear that guy climbing the stairs.

The sisters were preparing to take all the "Fallen Heroes to Valhalla" when one of them grabbed me and slung me to the loft floor. Roland Davenport was about 35. He was a tall, strong man that was married and had two children in Boston. The move knocked the wind out of me and before I could catch my breath, he had gotten my coat all the way off and was working on my skirt.

Instead of my training and reflexes kicking in, I felt shock, surprise, and panic. There I was, lying on straw and wood, with this big man on top of me and unable to breathe. His left hand held both my arms over my head. His right hand was pulling off that skirt.

I had only been on the floor for a few seconds but it seemed more like an hour. Unable to settle in one direction, my mind was wild with thoughts. "I fucked up", and "How did I let this happen", were among the many repeats. At the same time my burning lungs were fighting for air, the music in my ears was rising in intensity. Before I could even begin to fight this guy off, I would have to be able to take a breath. At this point, all I could do was lay there and twitch.

That's when it hit me. I was about to be raped and it was already starting to look brutal. At the ancestral home of one of the most prominent families in all of the Americas, I would be raped in a barn one week before Christmas Day. Taking into consideration the way my body was designed, I was pretty certain that after the initial penetration, I would no longer be thinking about fighting him off. That meant that once I relaxed, I might not get too beat up in the long run. I loved the fun of experimenting with the girls, but I was in no way ready to have sex with any man at this point. I was afraid (with good reason) of going to Saudi for just this very thing. My Chinese friends might call this, "The Hell of Hating Love".

I tried not to draw this kind of attention to myself but there is nothing I can do about what I am and how I was designed. Still, I thought that what was happening to me now, and everything that would happen as a result, was all my fault. There was something I still wasn't doing right. Was this supposed to happen to me? Am I in hell right now? Was this my penitence for a life time of bad deeds? Shouldn't I just let this happen, so it could be over with? But if I did, he would talk. It would almost be inviting the next guys to take me whenever they wanted, however they wanted to. Thinking about allowing it to just happen, made that old sour feeling in my stomach return. It quickly began to walk its way up the path.

"I know you been on fire girl," he said in a voice that reminded me of JFK. "Hell, everybody knows it. I'm just gonna hose you down a little for your own protection. If you're real quiet, Great Granddaddy's barn won't have to go up in flames," he laughed.

With my first good breath, I pulled in half a lung of air and pushed out most of my breakfast. Partly digested egg, tomato, cheese, milk, and orange juice reached out from my lips to travel up into the air, before landing on the back of his head and neck. Before he could get in a position to push himself off of me, my next volley was a double pump that blew the rest of breakfast onto his face, his red shirt, and that blue blazer they were all wearing. A lot of it fell back onto me as well, but Roland kept most of the sticky stuff on him.

I slid myself back to the wall where I was standing just moments before. I wanted to get to my feet so that I could yell out the window. This guy was too big for a close-in fight anyway. The only real option was to get some help. I had seen a couple of Secret Service guys the day before and I figured one of them might be within ear shot. But before I could push myself off the floor, he used one of his long arms to grab my right foot and snatched me back across the loft.

I tried to kick my foot loose, but he wouldn't let go. He had gotten to his feet and was beginning to pull me back into a dark corner and further away from the window when I remembered something. It sounds crazy but for one quick moment, everything I had ever seen about a girl being dragged, kicking across the floor, flashed before my eyes. I had nothing from personal experience, so I accessed crime footage, written reports I reviewed as an investigator, and even some horror films I had seen. In just about every incident I could remember, when the girl survived it was because someone heard her screaming her head off and they came to investigate.

What the fuck! I thought. I'm a chick, I should be screaming like I'm about to be raped! So, I just let it rip. I'd never screamed before, so I tried to go with a sound as loud and as high pitched as my voice could make. It seemed to me that the better thing would be to yell out, "I'M IN THE BARN WITH A BIG BASTARD TRYING TO RAPE AND POSSIBLY EVEN KILL ME!!!" Then again, none of the successful rescues ever noted any directions given by the victims. It was the noise alone that saved them.

He was angry now and there was nothing I could do to stop him from whipping me around from wall to corner like a rag doll. That corner spot was covered with cobwebs, old horse blankets, bird shit, and a lot of dust. I tried my best to grab onto anything I could use as a weapon but everything I touched was yanked out of my grasp as I slid by. The cracks in the floor were too small to get my hands into. The rope on the ceiling was a mile away. Even the straws of hay passed through my fingers without a care.

He twisted my leg until I had no choice but to roll over onto my stomach. Once around the corner, one quick jerk was all that was needed to slide me back underneath him. He rested his heavy knees on my back and waist to smash me flat against the wooden floor, effectively putting an end to my attempt to scream. I was pinned now.

He shifted to work on my skirt again. The way he had me made it impossible to get it off, but he could reverse it and pull it up. I could breathe, but it wasn't very easy. My specially designed back and chest could take the weight, but my lungs and my bladder couldn't. I pushed my elbows into the wood to raise myself up enough to get something in my chest but every attempt to scream was met with another weight shift that would force my exhalation into nothing more than a small cloud of dust.

At the same time, I could feel one of his hands on my skin sliding between my panties and my butt. I could also feel tears rolling down my face and off onto the dusty straw covered floor only inches below. A wave of heat rolled through my soul and all the colors of the world turned to a shade of red.

I had always been lucky in the face of death and danger. It gave me the power of confidence and that made me a god on the field of men. That was another lifetime ago. On this day and at this time, I was truly terrified. The shifting weight of his body was so great that it actually began forcing the pee out of mine. Then again, maybe it was my fear that drove it out. In any case, Roland was about to get his fingers wet. If the 100 year old wooden boards that supported this loft hadn't begun to snap and break when they did, I may not have mentally survived this event.

As our section of the floor gave way, I remember dangling from a 2x4. Roland struggled to hold onto a piece of sturdy foundation, but everything seemed to disintegrate at his touch. It was a 15 foot drop onto some buckets and a wooden bench. He rolled off my back and into the air below me and landed on his back. I dropped too but I don't remember the impact.

I woke to my screams late that night. I was back in my room at the Davenport Manor. Granny Jo and a tall nurse lady, stood over me. I wanted to reach out to grab something or someone, but I couldn't move my arms. The look on their faces was as frightening as the way I felt. I was on the bed, wrapped in blankets, dressed in a long white nightgown, and covered in sweat. The room was washed in the same red that I had seen in the barn, and it felt like my skin was on fire.

Early that next morning when I woke again, the two were still there. The thick blanket was gone, and I felt a whole lot better. Both my hands were wrapped in a loose gauze and as I looked at them I felt a mild pain as they began to tingle.

I looked up at Granny Jo and asked her if I was OK. I tried to tell her that Roland had attacked me in the barn and I couldn't remember if I was able to get away before he raped me. I tried to tell her that it felt like I was on fire, but I didn't remember being in a fire. I wanted to tell her everything about the incident, from the "Cry of the Valkyries", to the fall into that fluffy bed, but my head was moving faster than my mouth could pronounce any of the words. "It's good that you don't remember," she said in her shaky Granny voice.

"You have got to tell me what happened next!" I demanded. "I can't remember if I got away!"

I was pretty excited, and the nurse knew it. She was about to give me a shot when Granny Jo stopped her and asked her to stand outside. "Roland was not able to rape you," she answered. "And yes, you did get away, so don't think about that anymore."

"Are you sure?"

"Yes, the nurse gave you a complete examination. He did try as you say, but you fought him and were able to prevent it. You really did get away. You ran to the river."

"I ran to the river?"

"God knows why, but that's what you did. You got hypothermia in that water. I thought that was what would kill you. You were so wet and cold that it almost killed me."

She told me that I had hurt my hands on the wood. I had bruises and some splinters that had to be removed. After that, she told me that she was going to get some sleep and that I should do the same.

Two minutes later, the Triplets were at the door. They didn't know how to express themselves. Their emotions ranged from shame and embarrassment about Roland, to excitement and pride at how I had been able to fight him off. They claimed to know nothing more about the incident than I did.

As it turned out, Roland was a hound. He had made moves on others before but never towards his nieces. He, like many of the Davenport men, had several mistresses that were well taken care of. These women were sometimes frequented by other Davenport men (which has always been the custom). But, the Davenport family women themselves, were off limits. They were always a cut above the average lady. I was not a Davenport.

Later, I was told that Roland was drunk and was not briefed on who I was. He was under the impression that I was just another school friend of the girls and that I had no real status. I was to be offered some form of adequate compensation for forgiveness in this matter, and that if I did not choose something soon, the family would make the choice on my behalf. Like it or not, I was to be paid off.

Any and all offers were on the table, to include excommunicating Roland from his own family. In respect to my partial Arab background, he would be made to divorce his current wife and marry me if I felt that I was violated beyond the point that I could no more find myself respectable. Money was no object and I was also assured that I could live a hundred years and never see him again, if that's what I wanted. The field was wide open. They went as far to include his ties as a "super DC insider" over military operations.

The first thing that popped into my head was to be made back into a man. Ultimately, I had to throw this one out. No matter how I ran this idea, I could not shake the fact that what had been done to rebuild me could only be performed by just one handful of scientists. I was still the legal property of entities in Saudi and England, and they would have something to say about a sex change. Way too many questions would have had to come into the light. I was already said to be too much trouble by the Saudi side. It would have been too simple to just erase me all together when my secrets started to come out.

However, it did give me an idea for another request. This one was a lot less risky, but just as radical. I told Granny Jo and her oldest son Raymond the 4th, that I wanted out. I spoke to Arleen on the phone. Her and her father's team came up with an idea. They emailed a draft that loosely went like this: I wanted to be released free and clear of my ties to the two Great Houses of England and of Saudi Arabia. I didn't mention the details about my recovery, but I did say that I was incapable of having children and that neither house would find me of any use. I considered myself a burden and for the sake of any further issues with me, I would give up all claims to the families including my previous and current names. I agreed to keep Roland's military connection open. I also felt that Roland did owe me something, so I asked for a simple five million dollars in US currency from his personal account to start my new life on my own.

Other than that, I just wanted to be allowed to live without restrictions. I knew I could never run for public office or serve as a high-ranking officer in the military, (standard for people that know too much) but if I wanted to be a business woman or a movie star, I should be left alone to pursue it. I wanted the Davenports to do whatever it took to arrange this offer, and my release into the world. If they could not do this for me, I would endeavor to create a vacuum in the place the Davenports once filled. I would, of course start with Roland and his part of the family. (The last was not in the document).

I wanted to leave the estate, but they would have none of it. Lawyers studied the form and made changes in the writing, but in the end the final form meant the same thing. Granny Jo loved Roland because he was a part of her family. She knew that the First Line did have the power to wipe a small thing like the Davenports off the globe, but she did not believe that such a thing would happen over me. However, it could create a rift that might never be repaired. We had a deal. After all, it was just business.

Christmas for me was quiet. By choice, I spent a lot of time in my room. I talked to Granny Jo, the maid, and the girls, but no one else. They wanted me to come outside, but they didn't push me to do so. Plans for the Big Ball continued and more and more Secret Service and Private Security people began to fill the empty spaces in the landscape outside my window. The day before New Year's Eve, I did come out.

Everyone was nice without being too nice. They were ice skating, playing hockey, and kids were being pulled by horses as they sat on sleds. There were snowball fights, snowmen, and a fortress build out of snow. Real live reindeer walked around to freely mingle with anyone who looked like they had a morsel of reindeer food (AKA Scooby snacks) in their hand. It was Norman Rockwell in every direction. Men could shoot skeet and the women could laugh. The staff was busy bringing everyone something hot to drink. Even Granny Jo was outside.

When Sophia, Olivia, and Arleen found me, I was sitting in a gazebo listening to an Elf tell a bunch of little kids about the First Christmas Flight. I was glad to see them skate towards me. My smile was enough to alert my personal female Security Guard that she could fall back for a while.

The girls were to share a room, but I insisted that they all sleep with me. The bed was big enough for the four of us and I hoped the familiar sound of their breathing and the smell of their skin would keep me from the strange dreams I had been having lately. In my dreams, I was being attacked, but not by the rapist. This was another man. As always, it's really dark and I can never see the man's face, but I know he is tall. The only colors I can see are shades of red and black. I watch and see myself from outside of my body as if I were a spectator at an event. I think that I am dreaming that I'm watching myself have this dream. But, even though I am outside of myself, I can hear what the other me is thinking and feel the things she feels.

The first time I saw him was the night I thought I was on fire. I heard explosions way off in the distance. As I looked, I noticed that the smoke and fire were moving in a big pattern that would eventually encircle me. Just in front of this slow-moving trail of destruction, was a man. It looked as if a plague was following him or that he himself was the source of the plague. The ground vibrated with each of his steps and I was made to brace myself against gusts of hot air from unpredictable directions.

I had two of these dreams, and the second was more intense then the first. I didn't know what to make of them except that in some way it all felt familiar. It may or may not have been related to the incident in the barn, but at the time it seemed a reasonable explanation. I told no one.

Believe me, I know a little something about wild and crazy dreams. I had been dreaming about arguing, running, fighting, or killing people on and off, for fifty years before this. Each one felt just as real as the other and was a hell of a challenge to wake up from.

My worst and most sleepless nights starred those dreams, featuring the faces of the dead. A few were people I had known, but the rest were lives that I had taken in some bloody fashion, now made even more gruesome in my helpless sleep state. And there were always those dreams that would continue right where they left you, when you tore yourself awake. But those are what guys like me call "warriors dreams". Monsters, now that's another story altogether. It was now one more thing I could never tell a soul.

With my friends' arms around me, I felt safer than I had in a week. I didn't have any more dreams, but that didn't stop me from lying awake with my thoughts.

The Big Ball was just as it was advertised to be, fantastic. The Triplets were beautiful as they walked down a long flight of steps into the Main Ballroom and were presented to the crowd. Things went just as we rehearsed, with the exception that I was not one of them. With all the things that were going through my head, I thought it was best to let this moment go without me. I felt real happy for them and they seemed to have the time of their lives. I was later told that negotiations to marry Glendale and Lisa started as they made their first steps onto the staircase.

Sophia, Olivia, Arleen, and I, had fun too. We saw famous people everywhere we turned. You couldn't ask for autographs, but everyone was nice to us. No pictures were taken in the ballroom, but people took private shots in the smaller areas away from the other guests. The overall atmosphere was lively and festive. The fireworks at midnight were impossible to describe, except to say that for one hour every star in the galaxy appeared to fall someplace on the Davenport Manor. I could only compare it to every fireworks display I had ever seen, all rolled into one.

At 0900hrs the next morning, I was called into the office of Raymond the 4th. With him were three very old men that I had spotted at the party. I wasn't told which, but one was supposed to be my father's uncle. In some ways, they welcomed the idea of letting me out of the family. They said that this had happened only twice before in recorded history. In both of these cases, the person in question was unable to have children, but I was the only woman ever considered. They wanted me to know the gravity of my decision and understand that something like this could never be discussed in public. And once this was done, it could never be reversed. I still had the choice to stay.

I assured them that I did understand what I was doing, and that the accident and the rape attempt had nothing, and at the same time everything, to do with my request. I told them the experiment that was me, had failed. The child they wanted, died in Iraq.

They said that I had been the focus of much discussion since the day I tried to escape from the mall in Atlanta. Later, I showed high levels of mental and physical skills at Dane Ann's. They admitted to being impressed that I was able to build a smuggling ring under the noses of my school leaders and were curious to know how far I would go with it and how long it would be before I was exposed.

Because of this ingenuity, they would now offer to train me in the family business. I would be a liaison of sorts between the real power, and the power that the world thinks they know. Like my father, I would make no real decisions or suggestions. I would only counsel world leaders on the path they were taking and remind them on the ramifications of veering from our plan. I would receive all my instructions from the Body of the Counsel and their staff. This position was known as the Breath of the Counsel, or the Breath.

I may never stand in front of the Counsel, sit on the Counsel, or know who the members on the Counsel are, but I would live like a Queen and my power would be near absolute, as long as I did and said only what the Body told me to. My life would be a gilded cage existence, but I would be able to take full advantage of technology, science, history and information in its purest form.

Since my stunt in Atlanta, there was always the question of what to do with me. This new offer and the act of removing me from the family however had not come up in conversation until now.

The offer sounded really interesting. On one hand, I would know and understand things that no one but a few other people in the world could know. (Very tempting). On the other hand, I'd never been a fan of automation. I've always been allowed to think on my own, and right or wrong, do what I thought needed to be done. So, I equated this to the same as having more money and power than I could possibly imagine and having absolutely no choice in what to do with it. This time the voice inside my head was yelling "Just Say No!" So, I did.

I was asked to step back into the outer office and was met by a woman who looked to be in her mid-20's. She set a paper before me on a small table near a roaring fireplace and said, "This is your last chance. Are you sure you really want to be one of the Commons?"

Thinking this to be a test I answered, "Like you, the blood of Alexander the Great still flows in my veins. No matter what I am called, I will never be common."

The lady looked into my eyes and said, "Thank you. I will assume the position that you just refused. Being the Breath is the kind of thing that people like us only wish for, but never dare to hope. It's a unique responsibility that is usually only filled by one man per generation. You could have been the first woman to do it. Now, the honor will be mine." She paused before continuing, "We all had our doubts about you, but it is now obvious to me that the spirits of the great adventurous ones still live within your soul. Some of the Counsel sees this too. It is your gift as well as your curse, my sister." She handed me a pen and asked me to sign the form.

It was a simple form. I was signing my name to a list of rules and relinquishing all ties to the clan of the First Line. There were three other signatures on the form and their names were all

Britten. She took a picture of the form with her cell phone and then placed the paper in the fireplace to burn.

I asked about Krystle, the Lady Cops and this Bobby Simms guy. She told me that Krystle knew nothing, and I should leave Simms and the Cops alone for my own good. It seemed like sound advice.

Before I left, she placed a small phone SIM chip in my hand. "I'm sorry but no one is ever completely free. We all have one of these things. This device can be placed in a phone or placed underneath your skin. The one in your forehead was activated in that Georgia hospital before you opened your eyes. Because of who you are and how much you already know, you can never be allowed to be out of our sight. You may also be called from time to time, to perform certain tasks for the Body. If you choose to complete that task, you will be well paid for your efforts. If placed in a phone, this will give you free calls to anywhere, from anyplace in the world, and it cannot be tracked. I would suggest you do that now." Then she hugged me and whispered, "I want you to know that I have some big plans for us. Because of what you are doing for me, I am giving you a onetime favor. My number is on that chip. Only call me if your life depends on it. Do you understand?"

"Yes," I answered.

"No, I want you to say it back to me."

So, I did. "I will only call you if my life depends on it." With that, she showed me the door.

I'm Going to Disney Land

I walked out the front door of the Manor and for the first time since my rebirth, I felt as though the air was without taste, the breeze was silent, and that today the sun drew back from my gaze. I felt like I had just flushed 10 unwanted pounds down the toilet. I spun around in a circle with my coat open and I walked across the snow without making a print. It was euphoric.

I had a vision of Julie Andrews taking a breath before singing "The hills are alive with the sound of Music", when I suddenly felt the cold of that January day penetrate my sensitive skin and it brought me back to what I had just done. I came to a realization that I was now a little frightened to have no plan, direction, or support, but that is what freedom can sometimes be like. (And it cost me everything to understand that).

I wondered why no one had directly mentioned the Society of the Princesses. Was it because they didn't know about it or was it because they didn't care? I knew they would be keeping tabs on me so maybe they wanted to see how far I could go with it. Maybe they thought I would abandon the idea now that I had some money of my own. Or maybe they thought it was something that they could one day use. After all, I was only "kind of" free. They also failed to mention the damage I did to that hospital in Georgia.

It was nearly a year since my rebirth and in that time, I had grown one inch taller and six months younger. July 3rd was Faatina's original birthday. It was pushed back to September 3rd and was now being pushed again to November 3rd. It was not a question of memorizing it. It was just a question of rehearsing it for when I would be asked. As I looked at the photo on my driver's license that they took, I still looked a lot like a little kid in the face.

My new name was Jasmine Aiza Davis. I was half white American and half Lebanese. Born in Lebanon, I had a US and a Lebanese Passport. My driver's license was from the state of

California, and I had a new birthday. I was still 18 but would now turn 19 in November. 10 million US dollars were deposited in my name with Bank of America, and another five in a safety deposit box in LA.

The Britten's were never going to completely let me go, but so what. That was when I came to the conclusion that Robert Blake was really dead. I was wrong this whole time. This was not a trick. No one wanted my old secrets anymore. The guy that died in June of 2009, was gone and had been for some time. With limited restrictions, I was free to go and do what I wanted. The "64-thousand-dollar question" now was, what do I do next?

I remembered an old advertisement that used to answer that very question. The most famous and best remembered was the one after Super Bowl XXI. New York Giants quarterback Phil Simms had just led his team to a 39-20 victory over the Denver Broncos. He set a record for the highest completion percentage and was named MVP. When he was asked on camera, "Hey, Phil Simms, what's next?" He answered, "I'm going to Disney Land." It was the first thing that popped into my head, so I went with it.

I had two more weeks of vacation left and the state of Delaware had become just too damn cold (in more ways than one). It was easy to convince the Triplets to join Sophia, Olivia, Arleen, and I, to take the Davenport plane straight into LAX that very afternoon.

Natalie and Kendra couldn't make it, but we met Mariko and Sandra in the airport and together the nine of us got into a stretched limo that drove deep into Hollywood. Sandra had set us up with a three bedroom suite at the Four Diamond Disneyland Hotel. We would sleep three together in three big king-size beds. The plan was to have the "Greatest Week Long High School Slumber Party of All Time". We were going to play music, laugh, cry, take pictures, and jump on the beds in our underwear, all night like a bunch of wild silly teenage girls loose on the 12th floor. But first, we had to meet Sandra's father.

Deak Mandrake was a product of Arista and the brain child of Clive Larkin. Before moving to Elektra Records to pursue a failed solo career, he was the fourth member of a briefly successful "Boy Band".

In 1990 Clive held talent contests around the state of California to find the right mix of kids for a new pop sensation he would call "Smooth Boys". Mark was the shy looking one that wore bright shirts and shorts and had an incredibly high falsetto voice that was the real trademark of the group. Pete and Garry wore jackets and ties, sang the sweet harmonies, and danced. Deak held the "bad boy" image with his ripped jeans, sleeveless t-shirt, and broken heart tattoo on his shoulder. Singing the lower tenor and bass parts, he would never smile but was the most popular with all the teenage girls. He was number one in poster sales from '91 to '93 in three states.

Deak was 15 when he was signed to Clive, and "Smooth" did well around the west coast for about five years. But, a Boy Band is not a Boy Band when they are no longer boys. At 20, Deak had turned from 'bad boy' to a 'tough guy'. He had hair on his face and muscles on his body. The other fellas were no longer motivated and had become disillusioned due to the lack of worldwide fame that they were promised. Sales dropped, and Arista was forced to drop them from the label in the spring of 1995.

Elektra Records elected to pick them up but Deak was the only one who took the bait. They changed his name to just Mandrake and strapped him with a bunch of pretty lingerie-clad stage dancers. The company wrote him a lot of Hip Hop and dressed him up in Bling. To me, it looked like what would happen if Billy Idol, Madonna, and MC Hammer could have a baby. He got a few new hardcore Rap fans, but his old teen girl fans rejected him when gangs would clash at his concerts.

Fortunately, Deak had saved enough to buy his contract, and his name, in '97 and shopped himself to MGM as an actor. They were able to make two low budget action films before going chapter 11 in 2010, but Deak was a hit. He saved them hundreds of thousands by doing his own stunts, but he couldn't save the company. At this moment, he was seeking a part that starred a troubled but red-hot Rapper that used the sale of drugs to finance his studio time. It was the old 'out of the gutter and into glory' story. It was perfect for him and he all but had the part.

Deak was a real ladies' man, but had not married, still, somewhere along the way Sandra was born. Her mother died of alcohol poisoning, which is another way of saying that she drank herself to death, at 21. Sandra was one year old at the time. No one ever knew that Deak Mandrake even had a child, until he mentioned it during an interview on the Letterman Show.

Knowing that Deak had injured himself a few times on the set, David laughingly asked him why he did his own stunts when others were trained to do that kind of thing. Deak answered, "So that one day I can live next door to Bruce Willis." The audience laughed, but Deak wasn't joking. Sandra told me that about six months prior to that interview, he had met Willis in an LA night club and told his superstar hero that he would do just that very thing.

Sandra and her dad lived in a beautiful Hollywood condo. It was a lot like the one I was staying in, but bigger. It had five bedrooms that were made into small apartments of their own. Each one had a bathroom and sitting room. One was for rehearsing dance, another was for rehearsing and recording music. The other three were rooms with actual beds in them. The living room/dining room/kitchen was "party central"', and this day was no exception. When we entered, the clock showed 1015hrs but last night's party was still rolling.

Two women were lying on a couch together, two more were on the carpet, and three were sitting in lounge chairs. Most of them looked like models and all of them were passed-out or asleep. Their hair, makeup and most of their clothes, were in all the wrong places. Including Sandra's dad, four men sat drinking and smoking while a big screen TV blared music videos from the center of the room.

It was obvious that Deak had mistaken what day his daughter was to arrive in town. She had spent one week with her grandmother in Hawaii and another skiing in Washington with some LA friends. These next two weeks she was to spend with her dad, before heading back to school.

Sandra and her dad were on a first name basis and spoke to each other like equals. So, to hear her angry voice was no surprise for this Hollywood father. She told him that he was irresponsible and an embarrassment to her. He apologized but then reminded her that she had known him to be like this for all of her 16 years and could have called to tip him off. Sandra stormed back to the limo and we all followed.

I couldn't blame the girl for being upset, but like me, Deak was the man he was created to be, and no amount of arguing was going to make any difference. They loved each other in their own Hollywood way and even if Sandra couldn't see that, I did. After all, Deak Mandrake was not a caricature from some magazine or a page from a movie script. Deak was himself. On the way to the hotel, the girls couldn't shut up about how hot and sexy he was. Sandra, on the other hand, was unusually quiet.

We unpacked before we went out to lunch. We all wanted to get into one of the parks but had previously agreed to chill on this first day. Besides, Sandra was sad and the rest of us were tired from the trip. It was bugging me that I hadn't worked-out in over a week, so I convinced Olivia to go with me to the gym for an hour. When we returned, the others were already in bed and asleep.

At 2120hrs, I woke to the sound of a man's voice in the place. Deak was talking to his daughter in the lounge and all the girls were peeking and listening to the conversation. Most of them were fantasizing about what it would be like to be married to him.

I wondered if any of them had taken into account that if they did, they would then be Sandra's step-mom.

Deak was a handsome man for sure, but instead of being married to him, my fantasy was that if I ever got blown up again, I wanted to wake up as Deak. I'd be young, good looking, and on my way to being a movie star. Then I could marry one of these girls just to make everyone happy. My fantasy was complete. I just couldn't say this to any of the girls.

By the time I came out of the shower more people had arrived. As soon as Deak stepped out of the door, Sandra got on the phone with some friends. Now, boys were all over the place and they brought alcohol and weed. As I dressed, I felt real dumb to have not thought this would happen. I would have kicked them all out sooner, but Sophie and the Triplets were starting to have a great time. Arleen, on the other hand, was horrified with the sudden change of atmosphere.

I was on my way to speak with Sandra about taking these half-lit surfers, bike jumpers, and suicide skateboarders someplace else, when I lost sight of her. I had no interest in talking to a 17 year old boy, or any boy for that matter. Still, I couldn't make two steps without a guy stopping me and telling me his nickname. Despite the difficulty, I remained calm right up until this one guy put his hands on my chest as I was trying to move past him.

His name was Buggy Boy and he was a Surfer/Rapper. That's what he told me, just before he placed both of his long-fingered hands on top of both of my only partly exposed breasts. "Am I tripping or are these things real?" You can say what you want about Californian's, but there is one thing that I know to be true. When it comes to girls, these boys don't waste time.

At first, I guess I was more surprised than anything. It had not been one week since I was previously touched by unwanted hands. The pure shock of this new attack caused me to freeze up. Visions darted across my mind, but I wasn't in an old barn this time. This time, I was on vacation and in Disney Land for crying out loud! I thought to myself, what the fuck is going on! This dude is handling my breasts like they belong to him. What was I doing wrong this time?

Let it be understood, drunk, high, or sober, if a man thinks he can do this to a woman that he doesn't even know, then he is also likely to think that he can do anything he wants, any time he wants to do it. His risk-taking personality demanded that he should grab me before I tried to take off again, and I remember desperately needing to get away. When he wrapped his arms around me and pulled my body into his, I flipped out.

Something came over me. I wanted to move away from him, but I couldn't. I was suddenly afraid that I was being attacked again, but I didn't want to find myself in a river this time. (The pool was a long way down). I could feel heat filling my body like water fills up a jar. A red smoke-like haze began to flood the air around me and I felt that I needed to scream. My biggest fear was not of being raped, but of blacking out again. I didn't want to wake-up and not remember what happened this time.

I was told that I did scream once. They described it as a glass shattering force that burst from my lungs as if it, too, needed to escape (kind of like that "Alien" movie). The rest of the story was varied depending on who was doing the telling. The quick version was that after the scream, I dropped my weight to fall out of his grasp and short punched him in the crotch a few times. As he bent over and made an effort to turn, I leaped up and axe kicked him between his shoulders to put him hard onto the tiled floor.

That, in itself, would have been good enough to set me free and end the party at the same time. But, that's not how it ended. After he was down, I picked up a brass lamp from a nearby end table and proceeded to bash him in the head until I was made to stop. And even that was no easy task. Some thinking person got a blanket from one of the beds and had to throw it over me. He and another guy wrapped me up, threw me to the floor and sat on me until I stopped struggling.

The guy said that he had to do the same thing with his little brother who would have violent outbursts when he was a little kid. Except for that one time he almost went OD at a beach party, the kid has been fine now for years. Eventually he was able to control his anger and is now studying Engineering at Berkeley. He is currently working on a new type of wheel for skateboards.

The hotel detective brought the police and the paramedics. I didn't become lucent until they were on their way out the door. Except for Trever, AKA T Dog, (Sandra's boyfriend and surfer jock), all the boys were gone. The girls did a great job of cleaning up the drugs before the hotel dick came in the door.

Sandra called her dad, who showed up with a doctor friend. He had given me a shot earlier and it was just now starting to kick in. Things were in slow motion and I felt sleepy as hell. The cops wanted to take me to the station for questioning, but Arleen made a call and got that taken care of. Mariko acted as my bodyguard protector for the rest of the night.

I found myself sweating and wrapped in a blanket for the second time in only one week. As I looked around the room at all the wide-eyed faces that were just starting to come into focus, I thought to myself, "not again." Like before, I tried to tell them all that I was just minding my own business when a guy I didn't even know started to handle my body. "I wasn't doing anything wrong?" I said in an asking way.

Everyone assured me that Buggy Boy was way out of line. They told me that he was high. And they told me that he was fucked-up real bad. Most everyone agreed that I had lost my mind (or something had taken it over). They said that if they hadn't stopped me when they did, I would have killed him in front of everyone in the room. The kid was trying to get some magazine endorsements, but now that he'd have scars on his face, he could pretty much write that off. I was told that he may try to sue me in court later.

When I woke at noon I had a slight headache, but I felt a lot better. The cops had called all the parents and the school, so except for Iko, Sandra, and T Dog, the rest had gone home. So much for that "Greatest Week Long High School Slumber Party of All Time", plan.

We spent the rest of that day and most of the night talking and relaxing. T Dog surprised me with his intellect. He was a smart guy and I don't mean 'for a surfer'. Not only did he know what to do with that blanket, but he knew a lot about business and marketing. From the hot tub, we talked about colors and images within an image. It was more like a discussion on the philosophy of the visual arts.

The next morning, Deak picked us up and took us to a movie set that was in the process of making a film. The producer was the same guy that would be working on the Rapper movie. He knew some of the stunt people too and was hoping they would let him be part of the fight scene they were shooting in an outdoor bar on Long Beach this day.

His aim was clear. Deak wanted that Rap part bad. He didn't really want to act; he just wanted to be seen. This was just a way of getting noticed by that producer. He also thought that it would make his daughter happy if he was able to show her friends a "Hollywood good time".

As it worked out, Iko and I were filmed sitting at the bar just before the fight starts. Sandra played the girl that gets all the drinks spilled on her, and Deak got to fight. It was really fun, and the director said that we handled directions well. They liked T Dog too, but he had to refuse on account of a prior contract stipulation he was obligated to uphold.

Later, Iko had a confrontation with a guy that was following us around. She couldn't understand him and there was no way he was going to understand her. We were walking around the set during a break when she suddenly pushed this "Steve Urkel" looking guy and was about to kick him into a nearby wall when I told her to stop. I wasn't mentally ready for another blackout yet, so I asked Sandra to tell him to leave us alone. During the lunch break he showed up again at our table.

The guy said that he had seen me dance with a band once and wanted to know if I could sing. He remembered me as the girl that looked like Roger Rabbit's wife with a cute smile. I explained to him that I didn't know or want to know, any of the new songs I heard on the radio today, but I did know Carly Simon, Carole King, Joni Mitchell, Dusty Springfield, and Sade. The guy seemed a little shocked at first. He was silent for a moment then he said, "I hope you're not pulling my chain, 'cause I've always wondered what would happen if someone had the guts to redo some of that golden classic stuff in a smooth Jazz format." He thought for another moment, "Can you imagine what the right woman, in the right clothes, with the right voice, could do with that? No, don't answer that. I'm sure you're too young to know what I am talking about."

In another life, I would have expressed my thoughts about what Bob Seger did with "Night Moves", Ray Charles on "Georgia", James Brown on "It's a Man's World", the Cars with "Drive", or my all-time favorite working-class man's rocker, Bruce Springsteen on "Born to Run", but those would not be chick songs. As far as female singers go, I've always admired the ones with class. In my opinion those songs done by these people were perfect and should never be touched. But he didn't look like the type that would even recognize the names I knew. (I was wrong).

The guy sat down. He opened a notebook and started writing down some notes. "I'm always looking for something, that's how I survive. But today, you have to believe me when I say that I felt something when I came through these doors. You know what I mean? No, don't answer that." He took out his cell phone and said, "Sing a little Sade for me."

"Right now?"

"Yes! Right now! It's important."

So, I went, "Your love is king... crown you with my heart..."

He stopped me. "No, no," he said. "That is not it." The guy put his hands over his eyes and said, "I like this song. Do you like this song?"

"Mister," I said. "I love this song. And just for the record, you're starting to bug me!"

Mariko added, "She no like being bug!"

"She's right," said Sandra. "The girl don't like it."

T Dog stood up from his chair. "O.K., O.K, but I want to make a point first and then you will never have to see me again," said the man.

"Then mister," I answered, "make that point."

"You love this song you say. But, do you believe this song? Do the lyrics pull on you at all? If they don't, then don't sing it. If they do, then make me feel what the song does for you," he explained. "Tell me in your own words, what you think Sade is trying to say in this song." He looked at us all and said, "Can anyone tell me?"

Surprisingly, it was T Dog that said, "She is not afraid to say out loud that she is completely in love with someone. It's out in the open for him to know and understand. No games, hints, or questions are in this tune. She is too in love to care what can happen next. It makes me think that she is telling the truth." Sandra stood up and kissed her boyfriend.

"That's what I'm talking about," said the guy. He looked at me and said, "Do you understand what I mean, because I think they do."

I had to lower my head and admit, "Yes, I think I do."

"Then stand up this time and try it again," he ordered as he stood up and reset his phone to record. So, I did.

In front of everyone in the lunch room, I stood and without any music, sang the first verse of "Your Love is King". The guy stopped me again and asked T Dog to walk with him for a minute. When T Dog returned to the table he handed me a business card. It read, 'Dave Ellis, Vocal Coach'. "It's not his card. This is a guy he wants you to call," he said.

"Very funny," I said. "He thinks my singing sucks."

"No, he doesn't," T replied. "I think you should call him. Actually, he really wanted me to call him for you but, that's up to you, I guess."

T Dog called him a little later at the hotel and the vocal coach said to come by on Tuesday afternoon. He said that the Urkel guy (whose name is James Willis) would cover the cost for any training he would give me. He had heard the recording from the phone and thought that I might be able to fit in with a Jazz sound. Up until then, I only thought that my voice was good for screaming. (Who knew?).

By Tuesday, Sandra had moved to her dad's place. Mariko and I moved to the Blvd Hotel and Spa in central Studio City. It was closer to Dave Ellis' home/studio and a good place to see some of the sites.

We met Dave as we were pulling into his driveway. He was wearing a half buttoned white long-sleeved shirt, white T- shirt, black belt, and white long pants that were tucked neatly into tall black boots. He wore dark black sunglasses and was smoking a long-stemmed pipe.

He reminded me a lot of Mick Fleetwood with his white beard and long ponytail. He was a very tall slender man with a kind face and a soft voice. Like Mick, he too, was in his 60's, a singer, a song writer and a musician on several different instruments.

For the time being they were considering T Dog as my manager, so he was only allowed to shake Dave's hand and introduce himself before he had to leave Mariko and I behind.

It was a really nice two story three-bedroom home. The two bedrooms on the lower level were real bedrooms, but the big one on the upper level used to be two rooms before it was turned into a music studio complete with a sound booth for recording. The entire house was dedicated to the appreciation of music, to include the decorations themselves. In many ways, it looked more like a museum than a home.

Dave took the time to show us anything and everything we wanted to see in the house. He talked about many of the items and when he got them. A lot of things were given to him directly from the hands of famous people themselves. He told us that he showed his house to every would-be student that came by, for two reasons. "First, I want to show them that music is a whole lot more than one guy at the microphone. Second, I want to get them in the mood to sing." Pictures and paintings of singers, musicians, and producers, hung next to autographed musical instruments and even microphones on the walls. Books about music, records, CDs, and awards were framed, mounted, or placed on shelves. They were signed, and some had notes written on them from the previous owners. In the back there was a pool, Jacuzzi, and a sauna. The garage had two sports cars and three motorcycles. One would have never known all these treasures existed behind the unassuming palm tree, grass, and flowers you saw in the front yard.

After showing us around the lower level, we were introduced to his 23 year old girlfriend, Bambi, who was built more like the real Jessica Rabbit than any other living person. (She had me beat). Don't get me wrong, as far as really dumb blond, 5 foot 9 inch, long leg, tiny waist, wide hip, 40 DD boob job, girls are concerned, she was a winner. The work on her alone, must have set Dave back a pretty penny. The girl didn't just look like a dumb blond, she absolutely was.

When we first saw her, she was coming out of the dining room with a silver tray and gold rimmed glasses of water. She was wearing nothing but a skimpy white bathrobe. I asked her if she too was a singer or performer, and she paused for a moment before saying, "I don't think so." But, we were sure that in some way, she was. One thing that was certain, the girl didn't get out much.

Before Dave took me upstairs to the studio, we left Mariko and Bambi in the game room to play a video game. Bambi didn't understand how to play the game or even how to work the controls, so she was going to watch Iko shoot all the bad guys and Bambi would just point them out. As we were walking up the steps to the loft I heard Iko ask the girl, "Why you dressing this way?" Bambi answered, "I can take it off, but I was told to put something on." Iko then said, "You go get more water."

The first thing Dave did was to give me an examination on my ears, nose, and my throat. He said he wanted to better understand where the sound was coming from. I was asked to blow into a machine that would calculate the force of my lungs. Then he gave me some headphones and performed a hearing test. All the while he was stopping to type notes on his laptop. Only then was he ready to test my voice.

I did that 'Do Ray Me' thing as he played the notes from his keyboard. Then he would play only the first note and I was made to sing the rest from memory, in different keys. Next, he sang a simple little song and had me sing it back to him. After that we talked about music styles and singers that he thought were best examples in those categories. Later, he played a song by Tracy Chapman called "Baby Can I Hold You." The way he sang it brought a tear to my eye.

I told him that I didn't know if I could sing it like that, and he said, "The computer says you can. All you have to do is do it. Mr Willis told you about thinking and feeling the music. I'm asking you to be the music." I was told to have it ready for him by noon Friday.

When we came downstairs, we could hear Mariko and Bambi outside in the backyard, yelling. Mariko had the garden hose and was spraying Bambi with the cold water and yelling something in Japanese. It was the first time I had ever seen or heard her laugh. Bambi was holding her big boobs as she ran around the yard, screaming. I never found out how it all got started, but it seemed that between the yelling and laughter, they were actually having fun. Dave didn't say a word, but he did smile.

We called T Dog for our ride and left with Billy Holiday, Bonnie Raitt, Lena Horne, Dionne Warwick, Nina Simone, Basia Trzetrzelewska, Erykah Badu, and Cindy Lauper, on DVD. Studying these ladies in detail changed everything I thought I knew about female singers.

I had two disturbing dreams since this new incident with Buggy Boy, before I met Dave. I had been attacked three times and had three 'red outs' in the last 10 months. Now I was sure all of this was related somehow.

On the Buggy Boy night, I slept in bed with Olivia and Sophia again, hoping they would keep the demon at bay the way they did at the Davenport's, but I still saw him. I know that the tall man was still slowly circling me, but the drug I was given prevented me from understanding what I saw. A couple days later I had another visit.

As it turns out, the man was not just making a circle, but a circle that was slowly collapsing around me. When the man came to the point where he had initially started his first revolution, I could see that he was actually tightening the perimeter. He would appear to move at a faster rate from now on. I still could not see enough of him to recognize any features.

School's Out Forever

The next morning, T Dog and Sandra arrived at the hotel at 0900hrs. James Willis (AKA Urkel), had called T Dog late last night asking to meet with him by noon this day. James wanted to discuss some things about signing me to some contracts that would include modeling, singing and some dancing. T Dog needed a lot of information about my background and my legal guardians. James also gave him a list of recommended entertainment lawyers and the name of a new hair stylist.

I talked with Sandra and Arleen, and we came to an agreement that Deak Mandrake would act as my guardian, James Willis would be my manager, T Dog would be my agent, and Mariko would be my bodyguard. Arleen's dad knew an old friend in LA that was not on James' list but was eventually accepted as my entertainment lawyer. Sandra would work with T Dog as my press agent.

Mariko and I were now going to stay in LA. I had learned everything I thought I could from the all-girl school in Florida and had earned the freedom to go and do as I please. Mariko felt that she wasn't going to graduate and like me, had decided that she could learn more outside the confines of the "House of the Second Sons" then she could ever learn from inside their stony walls. Besides, watching my back was important to her and as a member of my staff she would not only be earning money, she would be gaining some experience.

I planned to continue to cultivate the idea of the Society in whatever I was going to do. But to be honest, the question of what to do with myself had been in the forefront of all my thoughts for some time.

I had always liked music but before my rebirth I was never any good at it. I used to be so bad at dancing that I would refuse to even try, and my singing was more than horrible. But the new me it seems, is not only good at both, but good enough to get signed to a deal. I'm not stupid. If I was an ugly fat kid, no one would have given me two shits and a handshake. Still, I was convinced that this would surely be a learning experience that I could build some kind of life around. I figured, what the heck.

I saw Dave twice a week and studied everything from how to hold a microphone to how to "sell a note". James reintroduced me to wardrobe and spent a lot of time helping me with my onstage persona. Deak schooled me in the business of "show". He called a friend that was more than happy to sell a rich 18 year old a new car (the same XKR-S, in silver) and Iko and I drove around the city in my free time seeing the sights and looking for her recruits.

Another interesting thing happened. While working with the music I discovered that I had the ability to think on multiple levels. I found a way to concentrate on four completely different things at the same time. I don't know why it stopped at four and I don't know why music woke this ability. I do know that it started just after I began singing.

Until it became a habit, I had to think about the constant adjustments needed to work the mic when hitting certain notes. I had to think about the sounds I was making and how I looked while I was making them. I had to think about the words themselves and how I was to put my whole being into each one of them. And lastly, I had to put it all together and judge how the audience might perceive the performance and adjust for it.

Later, I found that performing in that way became automatic; I used my thinking for planning strategies and alternatives to those strategies. It's another secret I was forced to hide but it has made an indescribable difference in every part of my life.

The singing style and persona we chose was a conflicting one. It was discovered that I had a strong three and half octave range. I can push out a four, but Jazz singers never really need more than two. Sade has two, Erykah Badu can go over three, and Billie Holiday had a little over one. On the other hand, Rickie Lee Jones has a solid four octave range. Her dramatic vocal style was a mix of many things and was hard to place into any one category. I too, chose a dramatic form of phrasing. I settled someplace around Rickie Lee and Erykah Badu. I tried not to imitate them, but they became very influential to me.

Like Deak Mandrake, I had to portray a character. Mine would be the character of a sexy but shy, sad, and lonely girl that sings her feelings in a clear and distinct voice. Every song was done in a way to make the listener believe that I was in some kind of pain. I dressed in classy gowns that showed a lot of skin. Some were backless or split but I always wore a lot of jewelry. I sang alongside the keyboard, synth strings, acoustic guitar, and the drums but the music was driven by the bass (a mix of Badu and Basia).

The key was to learn not just to feel the music but to be the music in every way. I had to breathe it in and let the sound beat my heart for me. During a performance the audience is a major part of this complicated process. The emotions they released fed into the energy of the 'vibe'. Now, the vibe had a consciousness of its own and together we became one, again and again.

It was easy to become addicted to that kind of feeling. The power of the vibe felt like living in another dimension. I kept reminding myself that I was just acting and not to be consumed by the passion of it all. That's the reason I kept training with my staff and working on my fighting skills. But it wasn't an easy battle and I found it impossible not to fall in love with it. (Live it. Love it. Believe it.).

James enrolled me in a school of the arts to study Music Theory and Piano. It was a lot easier to pick-up the piano (literally) then it was to nail down the theory part. I kept thinking of it as a math or a science but there was more to it. It had to have a feel. I went twice a week for four hours.

By the springtime I was more active than I had ever been in my entire life. Miami and school were nothing compared to LA and music. Not only was I still having classes with the arts school and Dave, I found another Kung Fu school and had started to perform at some small venues out of state in Seattle and Vancouver. James wanted to open with something big in LA but needed me to work on my ability to feel comfortable with any audience. It also gave him time to come up with some original songs.

I sang old covers of songs like "Fever" and "My Funny Valentine" but I also could do a real good job on "Sailing", "Still", and "Mercy, Mercy Me". During that song, we showed a picture of Marvin Gaye in the background and some people actually cried. After that, it gave us the idea to use more video in our show. Mostly it was closeups of me, but other pictures and video were inserted to help control the mood.

Deak travelled with us like a real tour manager at that time. He videoed every show and got us to the point where we could critique ourselves. He also taught me how to control the atmosphere without making it too obvious. "If the crowd isn't where you want them, then you have to go get them and bring them back", he told me. "Mood and the order of the songs can help you. Sometimes, you may have to talk to them. Try telling them a short story that can lead them into your next song. Make them hungry for what comes next." So, I did. And that was basically the act.

As head of my security, Mariko now needed to recruit a small staff. It would be the beginning of her training as a leader in the army she would one day build. Mariko was not what you might call a bright kid, but she did have learning potential. I would have to use my lifetime of experience to train her about security, strategy, tactics and how to lead. She did have one good idea. The way she figured it, if they couldn't fight, she didn't want them. There are many martial arts schools in California and recruiting some local students would not only get us someone that had a little discipline, it would also give us a person that was still willing to learn. Then again, it's a well-known fact that the toughest warriors are always found on the battlefield or on the streets, in this case. It was time to look for a fight.

Keeping in mind that a celebrity has to have beautiful people around them, we first searched for some girl fighters. This proved to be a challenge. We went to school after school finding nothing but a lot of RBA at every turn. Iko would challenge them only to have them back down. (The few that didn't got beat up).

We got a real good break (so to speak) in China Town early one evening. Iko and I were eating and talking to the staff at a very nice Japanese restaurant. We thought it would be fun to look the part and were wearing our little silk, low-lined, sleeveless, long dresses, and high leather boots. She was in her favorite red and I was in all white. On the way back to the car, we were passed by a small group of Japanese tattooed biker kids. The gang of two boys and three girls had come on three bikes and one of them had parked too close to our passenger door which made it impossible to open without moving the bikes. Mariko said something insulting in Japanese about the Suzuki GSX-R1000 that made all five of them turn around.

The bike in question belonged to a girl who called herself Fuu. As it turned out, Fuu was a junior leader on the girls' side of a larger part of her organization and had somewhat of a name for herself as a fighter and skilled bike rider. In broken English, the girl told us that she was a Yakuza and that we should run away. She said some other things too, but I didn't get any of that. Mariko called her a "Baby Boryokudan" which I learned later roughly means 'violent one', and the girl took real offense to it.

These kids had their leather jackets, boots, gloves, and I could see a few knifes and nunchakus dangling as well. All we had was what we were wearing. Still, that didn't keep Mariko from asking that girl to step around the corner out of respect for the owners of the restaurant. This was a loud and heated exchange of words that quickly began to draw some attention. By the time the seven of us walked into the ally, fifteen other young people followed behind to watch.

The fight took about a good minute and a half. Blows were exchanged on both sides but ultimately Mariko ended as the winner by way of an arm break. Mariko had torn her dress but was celebrated while Fuu faced a hard humiliation from her friends. On the way back to the car we found the other riders and all of the bikes, gone.

We took Fuu to a hospital to get her arm set and plastered. The 17 year old cried and confessed that she now had no place to go. "I may have to kill myself," she told us. "If I don't do it myself, my cousin may choose to kill me later. He is real Yakuza." With my permission, Mariko offered a place to stay and a job. That girl became the first of Mariko's posse and later one of the main lieutenants in her army. That night, we dyed her hair a bright purple to hide her appearance, and her name was changed to Battle Angel.

Instead of removing her markings, Battle Angel decided to cover most of them with more. Like me, she too became a walking work of art. At that time the coverings had no real meaning. Later, it would transform into a hero that comes to life right out of a comic book.

Mariko took this opportunity to get a few more tats. She knew her mother would have something to say about it and that was the real reason she didn't go all out at that time. Eventually, you would be able to read the story of her life in the pictures on her body.

I had found a way to sync my reflexes directly to my memory. My new Kung Fu school was so impressed with my skills that they quickly allowed me to advance through the Red and Brown levels in no time. I could now learn new combinations by just thinking about them. Later, I no longer needed to think. However, before I could get my first Black Sash, I was put through a gauntlet of testing that was judged by Masters and Grandmasters who travelled from every corner of the West Coast to test me. I was no Bruce

Lee and there are other female Masters in the Art, so I didn't understand why.

Even after I passed, a major board meeting that included the Head Masters of all the affiliated schools thought another meeting had to be held to discuss the implications of a Black Sash rating to a person such as me. (Whatever that meant). It finally took a letter from my original Master in Florida to seal the deal.

I was later branded Master in a ceremony that took place in a secret location high in the Sierra Nevada Mountains. The temple was again something that I had never seen the like. It had all the trimmings to include real Monks walking around. The three Masters that took me, assured me this kind of thing was not only highly irregular, but it was an honor so high that it would be unworthy to even try to describe its magnitude. (Especially for a person "such as me").

There, I spent another week testing and discussing cosmic philosophies. I told them about the story of the Old Ones that sailed off into oblivion and answered question after question of what that moment really meant. They asked me if I had come to them seeking knowledge. I answered them by saying that I don't know enough to ask the right questions.

None of the other Masters of my school ever had to go through this kind of ritual audience with the Supreme Grandmasters. And it was hard to understand why I couldn't have been presented with a certificate and just let go. They did tell me that my ability and wisdom overshadowed my age, but it was my inner soul that outshined the rest of it.

I was made to swear that I would not disgrace the Masters and was told that gods would be sent to capture and torture my soul if I did. (And they weren't fooling around). It didn't matter if I believed it or not, they believed it, and it mattered to them.

After all of that, I was made to place my arms onto an urn filled with burning coals that permanently marked the images I see on my flesh today. On my left forearm was placed a small

Green Bamboo Viper and a King Cobra. (That was two brands on one arm). On the right arm I have a small White Crane. Due to the fact that I was a female and soon to be a celebrity, it was decided that the smaller brands were appropriate (I don't think that it hurt any less). I was sick with a fever for a day.

As a Master, I was now authorized to start my own school if I wanted or continue more study as I saw fit. No one in the Martial Art world would be able to dispute my training and rank. (My branded forearms would be my resume). That is not to say that I would not be tested and challenged in combat for the rest of my life. On any given day, someone might notice my markings and want to see if his Kung Fu was better than mine.

I was told that no one does this kind of thing anymore. Then again, all the other Masters in the temple had brands. Like all the other Masters, the marks show that a great honor had been placed upon you but that comes with a price. As a member of this esteemed society, I was tasked to seek out frauds, strip them of their rank, and disgrace them everywhere I saw them, anyplace in the world.

The power of the Shaolin authority is limited to the small Martial Arts community, but it is absolute, none the less. Those bestowed with honor from these Supreme Grandmasters not only had the mandate to strip ranks, they also were empowered with the authority to kill in the name of the Temple. It is an ancient code that has no borders and is subject to no written law. With that being said, my chief mandate was to promote peace, justice, and honor for my great house. Most of the rest is secret and cannot be mentioned in this paper. I can only say that as far as secret societies went in this world, my plate had gotten pretty full.

On the way down from the Temple I was told that the real reason I was made to endure the interviews and the battery of test after test, was because the Grandmasters had seen some kind of light. They tried to explain it to me like this: Every living thing in this world and possibly the universe, has a light. To a trained eye or to one that is in tune with his spirit, these lights are visible. Some lights can be clear or mild and some are colored in shades of yellows. Every so often, you may see some darker colors like blues, reds, and brown. The colors have a lot to do with your motives and your personality but not to the extent that one color is better or worse than another. The interesting thing about me was that I had two.

Normally they said I would show shades of blue but when I was fighting and testing, they could see a fiery reddish-orange pulsating light. The second light would consume the first and become more intense. It was as if I had two spirits and one was fighting the other. This puzzled the first Grandmaster so much that he was compelled to consult his colleagues on the meaning of this phenomenon. As he went higher up the chain, the path led him to the Supreme Grandmasters, taking me along for the ride.

I was never told the meaning of the pulsating flashes, or of the great shifts in color. I was not a freak, per se. I was told others could do this. But they were Priests and Monks who studied this "way" for a lifetime. I could have had the branding ceremony in any of the local gyms in town, but our Grandmaster wanted this phenomenon verified and documented.

"Bust a Deal... And Face the Wheel..."

One Friday night after a small show in Tacoma, I got a phone call. The man on the other end asked me if I remembered the Breath. He told me that there was a gap missing in the Arm and the Hand of the Counsel.

The Hand of the Counsel is the worst thing known to those who oppose the Counsel's will. They may be mercenaries, police, or a single sniper or bomber. The Hand will kill or destroy any target at the behest of the Arm. And they will do it in exactly the way the Arm told them.

The Arm receives its orders from the Breath and is mainly used to lean on individuals that are not following the Counsel's will. The Arm also has the ability to erase people from existence using bribes, threats, or legal means, to help accomplish this. That is to say, that they have the ability to make a person appear to have never been born, even to their friends. (People can forget).

The Arm is normally called to make an impression on someone. They have the authority to set time limits and can threaten an individual as the Counsel wills. After building a strong legal and militant force around them, they can dispatch the Will of the Counsel when called upon. The Arm can also be ordered to have a target destroyed without hesitation. People who have discounted the Arm's power have run away from home, fallen down stairs, been lost at sea, had a drug overdose, been hit by a car, and/ or were killed in a hunting accident. Building fires was also very popular. One can be made to vanish into thin air.

I was ordered to fill this gap in the Arm. He knew that I was already exercising my legal connections within the Society and was now recruiting fighters. I didn't have to ask him how he knew those things or why he was giving an 18 year old this kind of responsibility. I'm sure that I would not have gotten the answer I was looking for, so I didn't ask.

If needed, one of the other Arms could assist me with the use of one or more of their assets. That agreement would not only greatly reduce the payment received but it could cost me a lot more in status. The Breath would have less use for my services in the long run. Of course, there are some cases where asking for help would be considered a wise decision.

This would be a test for Mariko as well as my ability to control her. Just as it is with the Body, the other branches in my Society were considered extensions of myself. We would be paid a handsome sum for our efforts and the idea of a refusal or failure, along with the compensation, were things that would never be discussed. This first test would judge us all.

Mark "Stink Fingers" Johnson, was an up-and-coming 23 year old Gangster Rapper living in Tacoma. When he was a kid growing up in Compton, he wanted to be a professional Rapper but had to join a gang to protect himself and his family. He joined the gang mostly out of obligation after his older brother was killed in a shootout with another crew.

Five years ago, he won a talent contest and collected $5,000.00 dollars. Instead of spending it on a car, clothing, or drugs, he used the money to take his mother and baby sister with him to Washington state. He put a down payment on a small house and changed his handle from Mr Mark to Stink Fingers. His mom got a new job and he continued to rap and record, using some second-hand equipment he setup in the downstairs portion of the house.

Mark made a 'devil deal' a little while back with an organization that promised to not only get him a one-shot record deal but would also pay off his old gang so that he could be removed from their hit list once and for all. Even I know that it is always easier to join than it is to quit. With this agreement in effect, the future, as they say, was wide open. Mark would repay this debt by relinquishing all profits from his first release and performing one small service.

A group of individuals from Florida and Nevada were seeking permission to claim what they believed to be their heritage in Chicago. Unknowingly, Mark was to deny them the permission that they had been looking forward to for over two generations by saying the line, "the Sons of Snorky are not yet welcome in this city," at some point during his concert in Chicago. However, on the day of this concert, Stink Fingers did not show. It was a real deal breaker and it affected a whole lot of powerful people.

That was a week ago. Many people in the know, believed that the Chi Town ban for the forgotten Sons had finally lifted. Many others did not. The balance of power was disrupted, and a clarification was in order. Stink Finger's life was forfeit, and it was only a matter of time before someone would collect.

My orders were to make sure that Stink Fingers made himself available to perform in Chicago this coming Friday night at the Hideout. Not only was he to be prepared to deliver his message, he also had to be properly motivated to rock the house. This would ensure that the word went out. The arrangements were already made. Mark was the only one not yet advised.

On Sunday we began surveillance on Mark's house. The little kids in the neighborhood told us that Mark's mother and sister had moved to Seattle. Mark rarely left the place and was only visited by his pregnant girlfriend. She would enter quietly but would nearly always leave in a loud tirade about money or something. Although they had not seen her in a few days, they were sure that she would soon return.

Disguised as a homeless person, Battle Angel set herself up on the second floor of an abandoned two story building down the street that had a good view of the front of Mark's house. She noted that Mark's mother made two short visits on Monday and again on Wednesday.

Mariko also stayed in the building at night. She used an old bicycle to ride around the area bringing supplies to the building. She confirmed that Mark had been inside the house by asking him to buy Girl Scout Cookies one afternoon, using a uniform she stole from someone's clothes line. She found Miss Johnson's house by following her home one night, using the bike. (They both claimed to not have any extra money at the time).

Stink Fingers not only had to be healthy enough to perform but he had to be motivated as well. He needed to make the audience feel that he was worth a two week wait. I had planned to speak to him on Thursday morning and show some pictures of his mother's house but when the three of us entered the ground level window that night at 0100hrs, I saw something else. It was the reason why we had seen Miss Johnson four times and had not seen Laquisha once.

We found Mark asleep with his headphones on in front of his computer and two empty 40oz bottles in the lower room of the house. A newborn baby girl lay asleep on the nearby couch next to her bottle of mother's milk. Laquisha was asleep in the upstairs bedroom lying next to a bottle of pain killers. All three were out cold. We could have moved a baby grand piano in and out of there unchallenged.

Laquisha had given birth on the Thursday before last and that was the reason for Mark missing his performance in Chicago. The reason was understandable, but he could have called someone. Besides, a deal is a deal. We took the child and left a note in her place.

It was 0200hrs when his sister finally answered the door. We paid an old crackhead guy that called himself Willy the Wino, to bang on the door for $20 bucks and a possible tip. Mariko wrapped the baby in one of the blankets she had been using, along with the bottle of milk, some new diapers, and a note.

All of this talk about breaking the deal reminded me over and over about a scene from one of my favorite movies. Mad Max (Beyond Thunderdome) starring Mel Gibson and Tina Turner, was in my opinion, the best of that franchise of films. The turning point for Max was when he had to face this giant Wheel of

Fortune looking thing, that would determine his fate as a punishment for breaking the deal. The Thunderdome was surrounded by hundreds of people. They wanted Max to be able to leave unharmed and began to chant "the law". He had just won a fight against a champion called Blaster. Max chose not to kill Blaster and Blaster had to be killed by Barter Town Security. The law of the Thunderdome was that two men enter, one man leaves. Max broke that deal. Tina's character pointed out the only other law in town, which was bust a deal and face the wheel. That last line was what I wrote on that note.

I was almost certain that none of the Johnson's had even seen this movie. Still, breaking a deal is a very serious matter. I figured that note along with a traveling baby, should have an eye-opening conclusion. On the back of that note I put, 'rock the Hideout this Friday and say the words you were told'.

The movie had a lot of other great quotes in it and they made me think about where I was going with my life. I had overcome a lot but somehow, I had fallen back into the same life that caused me to get killed the first time. So many things were different but so many were still the same. This wasn't the first time I transported a body from one place to another. This was however, the first time one of them was a baby, and the first time nobody died.

Everything I had done so far, from my first escape attempt to starting the Society and now becoming a singer, I did to carve my way out of my situation and into freedom, but some blades have two edges. At the same time I was carving my way out, I was really carving my way deeper into a captivity from which I can never escape. Instead of making myself useless to the First Line, I had made myself invaluable. Not only had I now become the Arm of the Council but I was developing a great cover as a Jazz singer to mask it.

I got another call from one of the Breath's aides, early on Saturday morning. He told me that not only did Stink Fingers deliver the message he was supposed to, he put on the best act ever seen in Hideout history. He was so inspired that the crowd wouldn't let him off the floor. The follow-on act was not allowed to go on and became so outraged that they charged the stage and started a scene. Security came in and helped Stink Fingers put a beatdown on the other crew. It was bloody, equipment was destroyed, police and ambulance were called but Stink Fingers was allowed to keep Rapping through it all. He was on fucking fire.

The performance was broadcast worldwide via internet later that night. The host of the website said that Stink Fingers "put some Stank" on a punch that busted J. P's nose (another Rapper) wide open. He asked if Stink's name should be changed to Stank. The answer was an overwhelming yes.

Armed with another new handle and worldwide attention, Stank Fingers could at the very least renegotiate his current contract. Later, I heard that he moved his family to Chicago and started to make a lot of money. If you are in the mood for a happy ending, we can end the Stank saga now. If you want to know the whole truth, you can check the internet.

The aide sent me a bonus that he said was for the entertainment value of the event. He wanted me to continue to build a young team but suggested that I add some older experts into my arsenal. $300,000.00 dollars was added to my LA account. Now it was time to start Mariko's training.

Mariko never asked me about the Stank Fingers job or who had paid us to do it. She knew that I was working many deals and accepted all that I asked her to do. As far as she was concerned, it was a means to seeing her dream come true. She continued to recruit the best disciplined young fighters she could find, and craft her own body. I began her tactic course of study and she wanted to learn everything.

With the help of Deak, we bought an old abandoned warehouse near the water on the outside of LA. We contracted workers to build a large studio apartment, a rehearsal room (complete with stage), dojo, conference room, shooting range, and a small changeable Hogan's Alley style training area (complete with cameras and score boards). It cost about half a million dollars and took a month to rebuild. When it was ready we threw a party and moved in.

At first, Deak was opposed to the location. When I told him that we needed that location to build the range and tactics area, he flipped his lid. Only after I gave him exclusive rights to use the area to train for his roles as an actor, did he agree. He knew some discreet advisers that would love to train my crew for a fee. Later, the advisers themselves became part of our organization.

It was Spring Break at Dane Ann's, so I insisted that the core members of the Society attend a private meeting at what we called the Factory, the day of the party. I told them that I was initially overseeing the training of our security force. If they needed someone for any reason at all, they could make a request through Sophie. Sophie would get my permission to authorize Mariko to send one or more handpicked units as needed. We discussed current business and touched on the progress of some of the old. We decided that several markets could be made to spin off my musical endeavors. Then we were held hostage.

Mariko told them in advance that they were going to participate in a live demonstration. Four hours later, six masked men burst into the meeting room with Uzi machine pistols. They yelled at us, broke the table, smashed my laptop, threw things around the room, pushed us on the floor, and zip tied our hands in front of our bodies. Anyone who gave lip, got their mouth taped. One by one (in seemingly no particular order), two of the men took us out of the conference room and tossed us into the storage area where we would wait for an interrogation by one of the leaders. It was intense.

There were six men in the room with plastic Looney Tunes masks on. They all wore blue jumpsuits like the kind your mechanic might wear. We knew that there was at least one leader walking around someplace in the building. Whoever was outside the building would call in to the Porky Pig guy in the room whenever someone came near. When he was told, Porky would point at one of us, and Daffy and Tweety, would drag one girl across the floor and out of the room never to return.

The other three sat around bullshitting about their part of the money and the different ways they intended to fuck each girl as soon as they got the go ahead to do so. One of them might say something like, "That girl reminds me of this chick in high school named Cynthia Paterson. That stuck-up bitch walked around like she had something huge jammed deep inside her ass. I always wanted to fuck the shit out of her just to see if I could make whatever it was pop the fuck out."

The leader was a muscular white woman that looked like Zap from the old American Gladiators show. She told us that she was going to kill two of us. She planned to ransom most of us but didn't have room for everyone in her van and couldn't risk leaving two people behind to talk to the cops. She wanted to know which one of us we could do without, and why. She said it was a test. If you were one of the ones that didn't want to cooperate, you got finger jabbed in some pressure points or got put in a wrist lock until you did. She also had a habit of smacking us on the top of the head, with her hand. She told us that she wanted us to look good for the picture and didn't want to show any scars, just yet.

The girls thought it was a big joke at first. But, a 20 minute interview, a bruised head, and eyes full of tears took away all hint of a smile. After the interrogation, the woman took a picture before having us moved downstairs to the living area. As we were each dragged by the same two men into the downstairs apartment, the leader left us with the impression that this may not be part of the demonstration that was earlier mentioned. If that were true, the fact that she was the only one not wearing a mask might mean that she planned to eventually kill all of us. That, coupled with the less than gentle way we were being treated, prompted the girls to ask me what was going on. But, there was no way to answer with tape over my mouth.

Sandra was the second to be taken from the conference room, and Mariko was the last. They, along with the Amazon woman and Bugs Bunny, were unaccounted for in the great room of the apartment. We laid on the floor waiting on the order to move outside, when we heard two gunshots from upstairs. At once, all the girls began to cry.

Porky's phone rang, and he was just about to answer it when the power in the entire building suddenly went out. I made noises to the other girls. I wanted them to stay on the floor and crawl to my voice. At the same time, we heard crashing and yelling, followed by lots of shooting upstairs. Nearer to us, we saw great flashes of light cutting into the very fabric of the darkness and the heart stopping thunder of shotguns blasting all around us as we tried to huddle together. Then as suddenly as it all began, there was silence.

From someplace in the distance, we heard someone on a walkie talkie call out, "Status check", and from different parts of the building we could hear, "Alpha clear, Bravo clear, Charlie clear, Delta clear" and "Team Leader clear." The team leader asked for the power to be restored and all the lights came on.

As we looked around the room, we saw five bloody perpetrators lying dead on the floor. Five other people walked toward us. Their uniforms, bullet proof armor, shielded helmets, and shotguns were all in black. We were piled on top of each other near a couch in the center of the room. One of the rescuers began to cut the tie straps off and help us to our feet. They moved us away from the bodies and asked if we were O.K. One of them went to the fridge for some water.

The girls told them that two of our friends were missing. The leader took off his helmet and asked, "What were their names?" The girls told them that Sandra and Mariko were some place upstairs dead or dying. The guy answered, "No, no, Sandra's not dead and neither is Mariko". The girls started going nuts. The guy obviously didn't know what he was talking about. They were all in an uproar until I yelled out, "Hey you! Weren't you supposed to be getting some water?"

The woman that went to the fridge was returning with two bottles of Carlsberg. We all watched as she walked over to the bloodied Porky Pig guy and said, "Why drink water when you can have a beer?" Porky stood up, took the drink, pulled off his mask and said, "Thanks, baby girl."

It was Deak and she was Sandra. Then the other kidnappers took off their masks and without so much as a word, walked with the rescuers into the dining area and began to drink beer out of the fridge. The rest of the girls just looked at me. They were understandably confused and wanted to know if this was a test, and if it was over now, and if this was over, where was Mariko?

Mariko appeared with the Gladiator on the steps to the upstairs office and said, "Thank you for participation very much, arigato except for NATALIE!"

"Why me?" Natalie asked.

"You never like me! You want me die!"

"No, I love you Mariko."

"Bull shit! You love only you. Everybody pick self to die. Only you pick me! That very bad shit girlfriend", said Iko.

"This was just a demonstration, right," Nat tried to explain.

"Next time you get purse took. I no help you. I tell them she got money in her shoe. Check both socks!" It was a good tension breaker to say the least, and the demonstration was a success.

I wanted to be straight up with the girls, but I knew adding a trained hit team would be a hard sell. They had to understand the need for a private security force. This "in your face" demonstration gave me the ability to shake them up before I could bring them completely in. They had to feel that something like this was needed even if they would never know the whole truth of it. It also re-energized my leadership.

I knew that the girls were thinking that my leaving school and getting into music would be distracting. I was sure they felt I was planning to leave them and the dream of the Society, by the way-side. This gave us all that we needed to refresh and refocus on our goals.

The girls met our trainers and Mariko's security force (after they changed their underwear). We ate pizza, drank some beer and played with the weapons, the rest of the night. We watched the hidden camera video of the demonstration and discussed other scenarios. We also played music, danced, and watched video from some of the small shows I had done. It was almost the kind of party I was looking for on that first night in Disneyland. (No underwear bed jumping). I still had fun.

Playing Twister

This was the day that the Society as a whole were formerly introduced to my new girlfriend. Tandy (AKA Twister) was a 5 foot 7 inch, 165 pound body builder, part time professional wrestler, and Martial Artist. The 21 year old blonde haired, blue eyed, pretty faced girl of Austrian descent, played in the school band and used to wrestle for Oklahoma City University until she was kicked off the team for steroid use. She was top ranked in the nation at the 155 pound level in the WCWA at the time she lost her scholarship. That was two years ago.

Since then she had been modelling mostly and performing in demonstrations around the country. She never gave up her addiction to the way that steroids made her look or that feeling of power it gave her, so she could never perform in any legitimate competitions. She boxed women, wrestled men, and fought animals, between the bad movie parts and cheap calendar shoots she got from time to time.

We first saw her at a sporting goods convention in Santa Ana. Wearing a leopard skinned outfit and holding a rubber club, she was supposed to be an angry cave woman. She was in a boxing ring challenging people to fight her for T-shirts and other prizes. Mariko and I had come to find items for our gym, so I didn't notice her at first. Iko was the one that pointed out how massive she was but at the same time, sexy. It was just for show, but she used some Jujitsu moves that were surprisingly effective.

We saw her again at an all styles Martial Arts competition later that week in San Diego. Like us, she arrived as a spectator but ended up winning the women's board-breaking challenge. A cocky Chinese girl named Kiki, broke three boards and challenged any woman in the building to beat it. The girl had a big mouth. Twister walked up out of the audience and broke four. She was also the only woman to break bricks that day.

I had never before seen 16 inch biceps on a person with exceptionally beautiful breast implants. The almost freakish mix of sweet feminine sex appeal and rock-hard brawn, was mind boggling. I had overheard some guy comment that they knew for a fact that she was a muff diver and didn't like men.

Anyone who would dedicate that much time and effort to craft themselves into the body of an Amazon Warrior, that was pretty, strong, and sexy, was worth noticing. She was also someone I had to meet. The voice in my head told me that I needed to speak to this girl immediately. Hearing that she might be a lesbian put my feet in motion.

We went to the women's dressing room only to find her fighting in the hallway. The prize money was a lot less than promised and Twister knew she was being wronged. We came into the hall after she had already punched out the promoter and was holding his body over her head. She was just about to toss him onto Kiki and two of the other female winners, who also wanted that money for themselves.

The hallway was beginning to fill with other fighters responding to all the noise. I knew that she would need an exit and decided to keep everyone back. Mariko and I rehearsed this move before so at the same time we split our skirts and kicked into the crowd that was forming behind us. I yelled to Twister, "I need a bodyguard. It's for good pay and a 6 month minimum contract. Do you want the job?"

"Sure, just let me put this down and I'll be right with you."

I thought that she was going to push that guy into the girls ahead of her but instead, she turned in our direction. She took several body blows from the three that were now at her back and was still able to throw that man into the air over our heads and onto those people we were kicking. They all fell down like bowling pins after a strike. It was something out of WWF. All that remained was to push the other three girls (who were in a state of shock), out of the way as we made for the exit. There was no time to think. We just moved. It was the most fun I had had in a long time.

After we barred the door behind us with a garden hose, we quickly made our way to the car. On the way, Mariko asked me why I wanted this girl. "You can't spend all your time protecting me," I said to her. "I've asked each of the Society members to build their own teams. It's time I started. I trust you to fight for me but it's wrong to keep you away from your training. I'll start with a bodyguard first."

"I know you all the time like pretty girls but this one throw people in air like She Hulk cartoon! One day we blast her with gamma rays I think", she warned me.

"Let's give her a chance. You remember the first time Sophie and I met you," I reminded.

It was mostly true. She was the only one in LA I could call a friend and we had learned to work and fight so well together. Still, Mariko had her own mission. Before she could complete that mission, she needed to be trained. While she was training, she could faithfully perform missions for me. It has always been my style to build a soldier so that he is well trained to make it on his own. Then, when the time was right, I would let him go. I could call on him later if I really needed to. His sense of loyalty and training would make him honor bound to return but I rarely ever asked.

I did need to start building a personal staff. These had to be people I could trust with secrets. They would not be invited into the core of the Society and they could never know about my work as the Hand. As a business woman and an artist, I needed an assistant, a chef, a maid, a driver and yes, a sexy She Hulk looking bodyguard of Austrian descent.

After touring her around the Factory, I showed her where I slept. That's when she backed me into a wall and told me that she knew I wanted her to kiss me. She heard the earlier conversation between Mariko and I and said, "You want me to lick you dry.

You can't fool me. I see the way you're looking at me and your desire has a very strong scent. I don't do porn films and I am very picky about who I'm with. So, my question is, do you really need a bodyguard, or did you just want to rent me for the night?"

What could I say? She had me cold. With stumbling words, I told her that she was right. It had been months without a lover, but I needed a bodyguard too. I told her that I could fight a little but, "I'm starting a high profile singing act and I need someone to watch my back, so I can relax and perform." I told her that the kissing choice was hers and that I would still hire her if she wanted the job. "As for the scent, it happens when I'm turned on. It's a kind of love it or leave it thing." I was trying to be funny.

In a surprise move, she kissed me so deeply that it actually sucked the breath out of my lungs. Then she asked, "Will this be a 24hr job, or just a part time gig?" Her power caused me to tremble. I squeaked out, "You stay with me 24-7." I offered her a thousand dollars a week to start and told her that she was almost guaranteed to be in a fight once a week when we hit the road. She countered with meals, the use of the gym and all the fight training my team could provide her. I, of course, agreed.

Twister made it clear to me that she wanted to someday have her own T.V. show. If being with me could help put her in the public eye, then she was in. Then she offered her advice for free. She thought that my success would be good for her as well. I admired the honesty in her words. She sealed the deal with another kiss. This time she grabbed me and pulled me into her. She squeezed and rubbed her hands all over me like she was checking every crevasse for a small weapon or a listening device. My mouth felt like she was looking for cavities using her tongue as the dental tool. At the time I thought maybe she just wanted to see if I was real. When she let me go I almost fell to the floor.

"OK," she said. "I like you. You taste good and you're not too soft. For one thousand bucks a week (cash), I'll stay with you, protect you, I can massage you and help you with your upper body weakness too. I like to fight so that's no problem, but I think I'm going to sex you for free. Don't worry, it will be good for both of us." Later that evening, she showed me another way the game of Twister can be played.

Twister was not only an aggressive hunk of athletic female flesh, she also knew a lot about performing and show. She knew acting, faction, presentation, and how to wear a mean Xena the Warrior Princess outfit. From leather to lace, if it wasn't tight or too small, it was strappy. From time to time, she would put on a suit but never a dress or skirt.

She dressed me too. I liked the feel of boots but everywhere we went she would point out some kind of high heel shoe that she wanted me to wear. In Delaware I was made to wear a long nightgown but now in LA, I had to wear lingerie to bed or Twister would get upset. It's not that she would yell or become abusive, she would just refuse to come to bed until I did.

Twister's training method was just as brash as she was. There was no half stepping about it. Instead of slowly stripping away the old man out of the young girl, she just demolished and replaced him. I was shocked and overwhelmed by her continuing challenges. This girl went to extremes to teach me that it was very important for me to learn to be submissive. This was her chosen path to train me to look, feel and be sexy. Which was something I was greatly lacking in. Example: She would always have me slowly take off those new bedclothes, but there were times when she would get excited and tear or rip them off me while I stood. As a note, if you haven't tried this, you're missing something.

Another way she blew my mind was that she also liked to watch me pee. At first it was weird and took a lot of getting used to just to even do it. I could see on her face that it did give Twister a good measure of joy to see my embarrassment and watch me go through the sensations my overly sensitive body would put me through each time. But chiefly, it was used as part of my training. She would take that embarrassment and turn it into bashfulness and that would become the shy and sexy person I needed to be. Besides, it seemed to make her so happy that I thought, what the heck.

She showed me how to make every movement I could possibly make, look and feel sexy. She insisted that I use this skill in every aspect of my being. "Every breath you make should be like a little lap dance", she instructed. "You already have the body. I will teach you to use it." It was something that the iconic Marilyn Monroe had perfected on screen and in her life. With the exception of fighting and training, (where I was another creature altogether), I too, now walked, talked, ate, drank and even went to the bathroom with sensuality. I used it in my act and it worked famously. I really felt it. I would even do it when no one was watching, and it became a natural part of me. (Live it. Love it. Believe it.).

In the time we were together, I easily allowed myself to become emotionally attached to her. Not only was she an aggressive (sometimes rough) lover, she also became an equally powerful teacher and friend. I began to become more and more dependent on her strength and affection. We had a connection like nothing I had experienced before. She really gave a shit about me and that in itself was mind expanding and at the same time, overwhelmingly addictive. She helped define my look and style. She even joined the band as an outstanding saxophone player. For a time, things seemed to be wildly perfect (in an alternative kind of way). And I finally knew what it was to feel happy. (Although, I would never have imagined this).

Once I mastered the shoes, the lipstick, and the sexiness, I became what they call a 'High Femme' or a 'Girly Girl', if you will. Outside of the Factory, you could not be more girly looking or acting than I was. Behind closed doors however, I was still fighting and training. I hired a live-in chef named Jane, a housekeeper named Gabrielle, and Annette was my assistant, courtesy of

James Willis, (who was also very good at hair). I was now able to concentrate more on my stage performances and just relax.

The only bad thing about Twister was that she, like Mariko, loved to fight. Mariko was learning to control her anger and could now consider the larger picture most of the time, while on the other hand, Twister lived the life of a Wild West gunslinger. People would see how big she was and sometimes they would give her shit about it. Maybe it had something to do with the extreme mix of natural hormones and man-made steroids, but Twister would challenge them to a fight, nine times out of ten.

Hollywood and Vine

The Society was slowly beginning to make some expansions. Mariko's team of 20 had completed a few strong-arm jobs in Miami and in the open door we made in Chicago. This paved the way for even better paying jobs outside of our own interests. She was upset when one of the team got killed in a fire fight but that just meant more training for the team as a whole. Those moves did make it possible for Sophie's crew to take over some of the smaller textile operations in those towns. We were now able to produce T-shirts, hats, and shorts for the teenage market for next to nothing, due to the sudden surplus in material. We were also able to jump in and fill the void in contracts when the competition mysteriously disappeared, simultaneously slightly raising our profits. Glendale was passed a deal involving a small toy manufacturer that was going out of business. They had gotten stuck pouring all their assets into a breakthrough toy that they couldn't get to work. Kendra was able to solve the problem and sold the solution for the exchange of 32% of their whole company.

While Natalie and Arleen made everything legal and balanced, Olivia continued to whip ass in the basketball arena. She was a walking promotion for all our sports products and fan wear. I knew she could have gone pro, but she had bigger dreams. Sandra and her team, as always, were the eyes and ears of the company. Her network kept a constant look-out for the talk around certain circles and was the first to investigate a potential lead in any direction.

My slowly growing entourage and I were gearing up for our big debut show off Hollywood and Vine. I was now comfortable with the realization that I had become a living part of our music. Another singer could have taken James' sounds and done the same as I, but it wouldn't have been the same. My voice and my feel were now woven into this creation and it was just as much a part of me, as I was a part of it. The whole thing gave me a mix of confidence and fear.

Believe it or not, at first music intimidated me more than anything I had ever experienced in both my lives. What started out as an embarrassing dare, turned into something like a complete emotional exposure. Each time I took the stage, I felt naked in a crowded room. But with the help of Deak, Twister, James, and Dave, I had learned to project my feelings across that room in a way that made everyone within the sound of my voice and the edge of my sight, feel naked too.

The 1,021 seat, Fantasy Island Theatre is surrounded by some of the most famous streets in all America. There is Hollywood Blvd., Vine St. and Sunset Blvd all in one place. James had been working on this deal for a while. This classic looking theatre needed a classic looking act to re-establish itself in the community. However, James needed to be able to prove to the owners that he could fill the place before he could swing that deal.

In the months since I'd met him, James had me playing small venues up and down the West Coast. He called it his Jazz injection into the west. I had built a small following of my own but with the ads, fashion promo's, and internet traffic he had me on, the feedback was very positive. I did some radio interviews and our remake of "I Can't Make You Love Me" (in our sad girl Jazz arrangement), was getting some airtime.

James had a gimmick in mind. He felt that he could reintroduce Jazz music to America by disguising it in older Pop songs that they already knew and loved. He called that his Jazz Distraction. My young but clear sounding voice, was mixed with one part shyness, two parts mystery, three parts sexiness, and four parts passion. I continued to use the Deak-taught technique of changing and shifting the moods of the crowd. That, mixed with video, lights, smooth sounding tones, and fashion, made the guts of our show.

My initial impression about James Willis was wrong. He didn't want to steal or bastardize those great old songs. He had a unique respect for them. He wanted only to pay homage to the tunes and bring the best parts of them into the present from out of the past. He called them "eternal pieces of sound and time." He told me, "It's not only sound that's captured on a recording, it's also the time you heard it and what it meant to you when you did. That sound lives forever." I asked him why he chose Jazz as a platform and he said, "My dad convinced me that it was worth saving. I've never argued with the man."

The act became a showcase of all that was great about Jazz. I was now adding some Billie Holiday, Etta James, and Shirley Basey, into the routine and it gave it a more legitimately classical feel. The strong bass, Funk rhythms, symphonic keyboard and powerful saxophone sounds, washed over the audience like a smooth warm wave of audio pleasure. It had shaped into a great act.

Normally, I would let the band start off with one or two instrumentals and I would stay offstage and judge the crowd. All the band members had their own mic so when cued, anyone of them could introduce me. Sometimes, when it all felt right, I would just walk on singing. After two or more songs I might talk about the next song or tell a story that would take us into a tune that changed the mood. For faster songs, I might do some simple dance moves, otherwise I would just stand. On the sad songs I could stand or sit on a nearby stool. If the song was really sad, you would see me wipe away some tears.

It was our style to have me appear to look down towards the floor half the time. I needed to look shy and a little bit nervous. I would always get soaked in sweat, so I'd change outfits at least once during a full show. People in the audience started to give me tissues or something to wipe the tears or the sweat from my face. I could have carried my own towel out with me, but this was a way of interacting with the fans and some people wanted the wet cloth right back. I never shook hands or did interviews afterwards. The fans were told that I was too shy, too tired, or too sad to come out of the dressing room and that made me even more mysterious.

When I first walked onto the stage at Fantasy Island, something felt different. We went through our sound check and everything seemed strangely new. It was like I was seeing the music through different eyes. I felt heat, chills, and my old friends 'the tingles', again. At the time, I couldn't explain it at all but Deak knew exactly what I meant. He hugged me and said, "It gets even better." He told me not to be afraid. I had earned this feeling and he was happy for me.

On the night of the show, I went into a trance. As soon as the music began to play, I felt the vibe flowing out of the speakers and into the crowd. I could almost see the connection as I walked onto the stage. My first note was so pure, so clean, and so real that it felt for the first time that part of me had flowed out of my soul and into the song. Now the vibe changed. Now the energy from the music was part of a chain that went from us into the speakers, from the speakers into the audience, and from the audience back into us. Whatever I pushed out, I got back in a different way. That was when I left myself.

I remember everything going into slow motion. Then I remember Annette taking me to the dressing room to change outfits. She told me that I was doing the best show I had ever done, she gave me some water, and led me back out again. I started talking about how much I loved them all and moved into the next song on the list and it happened again.

When Annette took me backstage once more, I knew that the show was over. I was so tired that I drank a bottle of water, closed my eyes, and leaned back in the chair. It was not until T Dog burst into the room yelling about going back on for two more songs that I knew what was happening.

I don't remember hearing the applause or seeing any of their faces. I don't remember the standing ovation or even the flowers that were brought to the stage. I do remember the joy and ecstasy

I received through the exchanged flow of energy that filled my soul but ultimately left my body completely drained. I had to be helped to the car later.

The performance was recorded in sound and video from many angles. It would be remixed later and released as "Jasmine-Hollywood and Vine". The next day I woke late in the afternoon. I still felt drained but after I ate, Twister let me watch one of the disks. She had a hard night too and was almost as beat as I was. We sat on the couch together and drank one of her wacky vegetable drinks while the disk played.

Everywhere I've gone my name has always been spelled 'Jasmine'. I've been sometimes called "Jazz" but when spoken, it is to be pronounced as "Yazz-mean". I never enforced this pronunciation at school but when I moved to LA and started singing, I insisted on it. As the singer, I had no last name, so I was referred to as "Yazzmean" only. DJs were required to say it that way on the radio and that was the way it was heard on the stage. Hearing it this way on video that afternoon and watching my little self walk out onto that stage, made me finally believe it.

I did all that I had rehearsed so I had to be in some kind of control, but the fact that I didn't remember doing it felt strange. I told the stories. I thanked the audience and the band. I was sad and shy. I cried and took the tissues, cloths, and T- shirts to wipe with. I changed outfits twice, and again for the encore. I did all the things I was told to do. And I sang better than I had ever sung at any other time. It was better than the studio recordings. I didn't understand it. It was as if I was on some kind of automatic mode. I felt like I missed the whole concert.

I was later told that I was in what musicians, athletes, and race car drivers call 'the Zone'. The Zone is a place partly outside of normal reality. All time is slowed and nothing you do is wrong. You feel the power over others' emotions, and it is as addictive to the performer as any drug you can take. But unlike a drug, this feeling can only be obtained when you re-enter the Zone and is the reason why athletes and musicians never really want to retire. Dying on the stage or behind the wheel is always preferred over dying of old age in your bed.

I used to hear these stories and I did feel a little bit of it from time to time in my football days long ago in Georgia. I felt it again in Miami while playing soccer for the Ebony and Scarlet and on many battlefield encounters. But that was still small when compared to this feeling. Maybe it was sparked by the sound of the acoustics. Or maybe it was something that I had to earn through the baring of my soul. The end result was that I was hooked.

Annette came in with my messages. She told me that T Dog and James were upstairs in the conference room making deals on the phone. The two of them had begged a lot of the media to come down to the concert. Only one local TV station and one sports magazine had showed. However, a few of the Jazz Radio DJ's were seated in the first rows. They were all on the phone asking for interviews and tour information.

Ultimately, it was agreed that I could only do an interview over the phone. I was instructed to be sweet, grateful, bashful, and vague. I could not agree to anything. When asked about dates and times I should refer them to my managers but there was a hint of a live DVD in the works. I was no longer acting for free.

The Society saw a potential in investing in James' company. He would get the cash he needed to bring his operation under one roof. That would end the need to outsource jobs to experts from other companies. One staffed company would only have to share its profits with the owners, meaning James and us. As it turned out, James had two original partners (front men) that were not ready to deal just yet.

Before the entertainment gangsters stepped in, things were real good for us. I worked hard to capture that same sound and enthusiasm in my recordings and my performances that I had at Fantasy Island. James was now able to make contacts with the best song writers and music producers in the business. The magazine people followed me around and many well known recording artists wanted to meet me.

Three weeks later, T Dog, Twister, Annette, Jacky (one of our security guards) and I, were at a private party in Vegas. A few big behind the scenes players in the music industry were there. I acted the shy and innocent girl so that T Dog could do all the talking. A few other up and coming musicians were with us as well as a few well known and respected music stars. It was one of those parties that you never hear about. The food and service were great, and the drinks were greater. (I myself did not imbibe).

The name of the place cannot be mentioned but it looked as lavish as Saddam's Palaces once did. Marble walls, gold leaf on the ceiling and crystal chandeliers were all around. This was just a hall in the hotel, but I had met Kings that would have sold their souls to live here.

I was prepared to sing one of our new songs and had rehearsed with the band earlier that day. Three of the other acts were called up before me. After each of their performances, the high rollers would congratulate them. Many of the performers spent their time mingling or jamming on the stage. At random, a few of their managers were invited to sit with one of these important guys, to drink and chat.

When they called me up, I did "Wild Horses" by the Cranberries (originally by the Rolling Stones), "How Can You Mend a Broken Heart" written by the Bee Gees but perfected by Al Green, and a song I co-wrote called "Momma Can't Know". Later, T Dog was sitting with the big wigs when I sang" Inner City Blues" ("Make Me Wanna Holler") by Marvin Gaye, as a jam. Twister played the sax on that one and she chewed it up and spit it out.

The girls and I went to our suites and were all asleep when we got a phone call from Sandra in LA. T Dog was badly beaten and was in the intensive care unit of a nearby Las Vegas hospital. When we arrived, the police told us that he would have died if someone had not noticed that there was a body in one of the dumpsters of our hotel.

When the police arrived, they took his cell phone and called the first number on the list. That, of course was Sandra, and she called me. It was three days before we could move him back to LA, so we were forced to rent an exclusive part of the hospital and secure it with our own people until he could be flown out by private jet. Jacky broke her hand fighting some guy that was giving us trouble on the helipad.

When he could talk, T told us that he was offered $100,000.00 to sign over management to a man named Martin Goldstein who refused to take 'no' for an answer. Goldstein was an 86 year old music promoter and old school gangster. During our research we discovered that Goldstein was the behind-the-scenes Boss that controlled nearly everything musical on the West Coast. If he didn't own it outright, then he owned part of someone that had a part of it. He was mostly retired but there was something about me that interested him, and he wanted it. Upon hearing this, T signed management over to Deak.

Martin already controlled the music scene in most of California, Oregon, and Washington. He had a good piece of Nevada and was well respected in New York City. In that three day time period, Deak was told that his movie was put on hold. James's studio was set on fire and my songs stopped playing on the radio. It was time to go to war but before I did, that little voice inside my head told me that I had better make a phone call.

We speculated that if Goldstein died (accidentally), it would create a small vacuum in the industry. His assets would have to be divided amongst his heirs and his partners. I made my call and had to wait until I received another call with my instructions. It was a very long two more days. However, it didn't stop us from planning and putting the man's offices and home under surveillance.

Mariko was recalled, and Sophia was advised of the situation. It was argued that we could attempt to fill Goldstein's gap with our organization. To the naked eye, nothing in the world would change except who was getting paid. We had absolutely no standing in Vegas or New York, so we would have to make some big deals. If we worked it right, a few of the small players could profit and we could end up holding a minor piece of the industry. In order to do this however, some people would have to die. (The girls were not easily persuaded).

I received a call from a man named Ian, who introduced himself as "your other arm". Ian told me that he was asked to meet Mr. Goldstein. He spoke to him about the incident with T Dog and my music but did not reveal who or what I really was. Mr. Goldstein considered it a matter of pride and disrespect that T refused to accept his most generous offer. He believed that he was forced to take T Dog out and blackball any Jasmine related projects for the sake of his reputation. Not only could he not be dissuaded from this position, he fully intended to carry on with this course of action until we either gave up or gave into his demands.

In the total scheme of world events, Goldstein was a small fish in a tiny river. However, he had big friends that held a greater purpose. My 'other arm' told me that a war with this part of organized crime was too closely attached to the media and had the remote possibility of exposing the Line and its influence. I was advised that if I could not negotiate a truce with this man, I should either allow Goldstein to run my music career or to get out of the business for my own good.

While on the phone I had an epiphany. I proposed that it was possible that someone else might want to replace Mr. Goldstein's rule. "It would of course, have to be someone that was known by all the players. That way bloodshed would be at a minimum. This should be someone that needs to feel they are still useful. I suggest somebody we already have a personal relationship with. I am positive this someone would be very grateful for that opportunity."

"If you're speaking about the Sons of Snorky," he asked, "it's not a bad idea. In fact, the more I think about it, the more brilliant it sounds. Many of the players would have to except this change but there must be a justification in it for the peace to hold within their separate organizations. This is something that needs to be approved from the top. If it does get approved, I would love to work with you on this one."

If it was of any benefit to the Body, then the Breath herself would call us back. Meanwhile, I had a hard time putting Sandra on hold until we were advised. James decided to leave town for a while.

Smoke on the Water

"'OGs" (Original Gangsters) are painfully predicable. In many ways they are like the movies that depict them. The only problem with that was that they had no idea who they were dealing with. We knew where Goldstein and his henchmen were at all times. I also had a man that worked on his yacht, one that worked maintenance at the airfield he used, and a lady that filled some of his prescriptions. We could have made a frontal attack whenever we wanted, or we could have just had something blow the fuck up. Unfortunately, my hands were tied. I forced everyone in the Factory to disburse until our plans could be approved.

A week went by and in that time, it was reported that Goldstein had used his yacht twice, he flew to New Jersey for the weekend on his private plane, and his favorite asshole grandson picked up two of his prescriptions. All missed opportunities.

The grandson's name was the same as his. He was the 'chip that fell off the old block'. He and his granddad had a reputation for treating women badly. He was 27 and thought that he was tougher than his granddad was when he was young. The kid got his way at just about everything and was a sure thing to take over the business as soon as the older Martin would let him do so. The only thing was that the old man wouldn't let him. Old Martin would rather die before he gave anything away. It was true that he was not as active as he once was, but he was still very much in charge. Young Marty had ideas, but he was forced to run small jobs on the side, just to feel like he was doing something.

Sophie's older brother was in town. He agreed to work with his sister (unofficially) for 20% of whatever we could make. Pauly and Marty met at a downtown club (as chance would have it) and discovered that they knew some of the same people. Marty mentioned that he had some ideas for a new direction just waiting to be put into action. Pauly decided to invest as a partner. They would hook up again later in a week or so and show each other their money and their sincerity.

As I said earlier, old Martin couldn't take "no" or any other word that wasn't "yes" for an answer. In an attempt to burn down the Factory, two of his men were badly injured and one died. Against my orders, Mariko had decided to protect our building by posting three guards. The would-be arsonists were spotted driving into the parking lot and caught as they attempted to douse the place with gasoline. Battle Angel, Jacky, and Joy beat the two men holding the gas cans with sticks. The other man was burned alive in his car. It was the same man that broke Jacky's hand on the roof of the Vegas hospital.

The man drove around to the side of the building to act as a lookout and to wait for the other guys to meet him. When they delayed, he drove back around the lot to find them. As soon as he saw his fellows getting the shit kicked out of them by three little Oriental girls, he drove the car right into the fight. Joy was hit in the leg and knocked into the wall. The man and Jacky instantly recognized each other. He had taken her before and surely thought he could take her again. He may have been right, but Jacky and Battle Angel were so angry, together they beat that man near to death. Afterwards they took his wallet, cell phone, and the radio from the car. They scratched gang symbols on the vehicle then pushed it into a ditch and set the car on fire with him in it, using his own gasoline. They then took the other wallets, mounted their bikes and took Joy to the hospital before the cops came.

At the time, the only thing they could think to call themselves was "Fucking Little Cunts". It was something the man had said when he first came out of the car. He kept saying it over and over. That is, until he started screaming. The girls carved it into the car in several places.

I didn't dare to think that a man like Goldstein would believe that a rogue gang of Chinese do-gooder biker girls happened to be defending warehouses in my neighborhood that day. In a way, I felt good that we had one-upped him, but we were now in a real war. I had not yet been given the go-ahead and now was in violation of my agreement with Ian and the Breath. So, I was a little pissed.

I called Ian and explained to him that the girls were just defending themselves. He said that while he could understand the action, he could not condone it and was not able to help me. He unofficially suggested that I finish the job before Goldstein made the next move. "You could at least have a leg to stand on, if you could somehow make this work." He also hinted negotiation should not be ruled out.

From the names found on their driver's licenses and an internet search, I sent Mariko and her youngest girls to write gang signs on the homes of all three of the men. They rode their bikes through the yards, threw fire bombs and bashed anything that was standing outside, with sticks and pipes.

The three attacks were synchronized at 0300hrs. Shots were fired but no one was hurt. All the families ever saw was a bunch of Oriental girls on motorcycles. The letters "FLC" were marked all over the place. The cops blamed it on a new gang in town and went into Chinatown looking for clues.

At this same time, Sandra got word that two heavy hitters from the Sons of Snorky were seen at LAX. I knew that they knew something about a possible deal brewing. There was no telling how much they did know or what their intentions were. I had no idea what Ian had arranged with them at this point. It would have been in true gangster style to jump the gun on something like this. Their part of the agreement was not yet sealed. It was the only real unknown factor. All we could do was try to monitor their actions.

Nathaniel Goldstein was old Martin's first child and young Marty's uncle. He was unhappy that he had been passed over in the family business just because his mother was Puerto Rican born. His sister's mother was a New York Jew, and her son Marty was Martin's favorite child. Her marriage to a Hollywood Jewish family connected part of the country and most of the entertainment industry, in one way or another. When she named her son after their father, Nathan knew that there was nothing he could ever do to please his dad, so he left town in shame.

Nathan owned some clubs in Ponce, Caguas and San Juan, Puerto Rico. From time to time he would travel to LA on his boat to see his dad, but he and young Marty never got along. In fact, the word was that they hated each other. It was said that at more than one occasion, they were overheard threatening each other's lives. We knew calling him might be a good idea and Sandra's people had been trying to make contact with him for over a week, but he had still not returned our calls.

The next morning, I put on my skimpiest outfit, took Twister and picked up Deak on the way to Goldstein's office. I knew he wouldn't want to speak to me. He was all old-school business. He would only speak to the management and never with the talent. That's why I asked Deak to tell him that I had other talents, and that he would have me do something extra special just for him. All he had to do was listen to our offer. It was a 70% deal, so the man was very interested over the phone. The $20,000 we brought in a briefcase was a small offering of respect. Negotiation was the 'A' in our 'A-B-C' plan.

When we arrived at his West Hollywood office, we were all patted down at the door by two big men waiting for us outside. Once inside the office, we were given an extremely thorough search by two other men. They were all wearing shoulder holstered weapons under their jackets (two Berettas and one CZ 75B). Even the money was checked. When it was discovered that I wasn't wearing any underwear under my cutoff white T-shirt and Daisy Duke blue jean shorts, I was sent right in to see the Boss. At this point, it looked as if my diversion was working.

We saw young Marty leaving as we came in. I knew that he had been to the pharmacy that morning. As soon as he returned to the office, he received a phone call from his new partner asking him to meet him with his papers and some good-faith money at his granddad's yacht on Marina Del Rey. His granddad told him to take one of the men with him for security, but young Marty refused. The meeting was urgent, and he had no time to wait for "this fat ass to get into the car". He left angry, with a folded paper bag in his hand.

A man named David told Deak that he would be discussing the matter with him before it was brought to Mr Goldstein. Twister was told to have a seat and keep quiet. The man named Mathew led me into Goldstein's office. The other two guys stayed outside in the parking lot.

The plan was to distract the guards. The FLC would arrive to throw more firebombs but I didn't want the old man to get hurt in the process. I had not yet decided if I wanted him to die. What I wanted was for him to suffer for what he did to T Dog and stopping Deak's dream. He had hurt me too. I had spent a lot more money in this little war than I was taking in, and my credibility within the Body was damaged.

I really did have my heart set on singing. It was my big ticket to putting a positive spin to my past and present existence. I could still run the Society and work the Arm as my side jobs, but I thought I could focus on music and fashion as my main careers. We were supposed to negotiate, but I had secretly planned to kill as many people in that building as I possibly could and let the chips fall where they may. I'd take the blame for what might be a nuclear explosion, so that my girls would survive most of the radiation fallout. Unless he said something I liked, Mr. Goldstein was to be the first casualty. (That was plan B).

It was a big office with bookshelves and a large desk in the center. Except for the dim chandelier above us, everything else was made from oak. In between the Gold Records and mounted newspaper and magazine covers of famous recording artists, were the heads of the many animals Goldstein had killed in his hunting days. He had been to South America and Africa, according to the little placards underneath each head. There were also lots of pictures of him standing next to some famous politicians and gangsters during their heyday. They too, were now just as dead as all the other things in this room.

From these pictures I could see that Martin was just a kid when the Mob took over the West Coast. Like the other kids, he started at the bottom, but he knew and worked with some of the most noted names at one time or another. Armed with his law degree, he helped to change the way they conducted their business. Thanks to men like him, most of what they did now, looked legit.

With the exception of his desk, the place was clean and neat. The old man must not have liked computers. He had been working on some papers and had piles of receipts and a calculator on the desk. His medication bottles were lined in a row and he was in the process of popping some of the pills when I was pulled through the door.

Mathew said, "Jazz Mean, Boss", as he placed me in the center of the room. Goldstein asked him to turn me around so that he could see how I looked. As he did, Martin asked, "Checked her out and she's clean right?"

"Yes, Boss but, not for long I think", he laughed before leaving and closing the door.

Although dressed like a slut, I tried to appear as shy and as nervous as an 18 year old could make herself look. He needed to think that I was forced into doing something that I didn't want to do. I wanted him to think that we were desperate, and I wanted him to feel like he was safe.

The truth was that I really was nervous. I had not personally killed anyone in a long, long, time as Robert. Jasmine had never killed at all. I'd been trying so hard to block those thoughts from my mind so that I could become this other person, that I was now blocking the person I most needed to be.

The man before me looked older than he did in the surveillance pictures I had seen. Liver spots covered his hands, arms, and a few were on his face. He was a heavy man for his height and must have been over 270 pounds at least. His white hair loosely stuck around the sides of his head and his glasses were as old-fashioned as his blue pin-striped jacket and tie. With his shaky free hand, he waved me forward while saying, "My eyes ain't so good." It seemed odd to me that after spending all this time in Southern California, he could still maintain that thick New York accent.

I kept my head down and moved up about a few inches. I was ordered to move closer, so I slowly crept up a few more so that he could ask me again. I needed to kill some time, so I did it once again before he finally said, "get the fuck over hear before I slap your fuckin' face." Only then did I move to the front of the desk.

He gave me the rundown. "Just so's you know, I don't usually talk to the performer. To me, you're just a product. Like a piece of meat or a pair of shoes, your only real worth to me is how much money I can make from working you or selling you off. Any real businessman, to include your manager, knows that. I mean no offense in saying that but now that you know this, you can understand that there ain't nothing you're going to be able to say or do, to change that fact. The only reason you're in here is so's I could get a better look at the little girl the boys are calling Jessica Rabbit." He also told me that the West Coast runs the whole entertainment world and that he ran the West Coast. There was no way that I was going to sing, dance, or have a juggling act in his world without going through him. "That other piece of shit you had working for you didn't know his head from his asshole and that's why he got fucked up! Now, this actor guy here has got a little moxy, and he shows me the respect a man like me deserves. He wants to make things right and I can see that. The only question is why I should change my mind."

"Mr Deak has some money for you," I shyly whispered.

"$20,000?" he said. "I can shit more than that in one day. That kind of money means nothing to me! Kid, don't you know's nuttin'? That was a gift for my time!" He put a long cigar in his mouth and painfully came to his feet. "What did you bring to the table?" He moved from behind the desk to stand beside me.

"I don't know," I answered.

He looked me up and down again. "I've seen a lot of real pretty girls before you, but you are something special. You're like something I've already seen and at the same time, you're completely different. Why did he dress you like that? It's low class. I don't like it."

"It's so I can dance," I said. "I'm a real good dancer Mr. Goldstein."

"Dancer," he laughed. "You really are dense kid. You think I want to see you dance? All right, all right, get on top of this desk and try to impress me... I warn you, it won't be easy."

I learned how to dance on stage from Krystle. Together, we were able to draw a bigger crowd and boost the band's popularity. With Miss Janet, I learned to dance for an audience of one. She wanted to see me sweat and would have me belly dance just because she knew that I was half Arabic. She wanted to humiliate me so that I would remain humble. She was also a fan of the old Shimmy and the Twist, believe it or not. With Twister, things were even more different and sometimes a little on the bizarre side, (like the whole peeing thing). For her, she wanted hard core Lap Dances and it thrilled her to no end to have me do it.

I figured I'd get a rise out of Goldstein. Get him as excited as I had the others, and he would be (to quote Blazing Saddles), "like wet sauerkraut in my hands". I'd charm him, he'd agree to reason, and that would save his life. (Plan A in a nutshell).

I didn't hear anything from the outside rooms or beyond, so I still needed to kill some time. I really had no other choice but to slide my big butt up on the side of that desk, stand over his papers and start shaking. It was all part of our plan of distraction, but it still made me feel like a piece of trash.

After about a minute or so, he told me that my dancing was nice, but that it wasn't doing anything for him. "That's the same crap I see in my clubs. Take that shirt off and try it again." When I hesitated, he slapped me on the leg with his open hand. "When I say take it off, I mean right fucking now!"

The slap stuck to me like glue even after his hand left my skin and no amount of rubbing would wipe the sting away. I did what he asked and removed the shirt. I started dancing again but about a minute later he asked me to remove my shorts.

I was about to tell him that I didn't want to do it but before I could say a word, he quickly removed his belt. "That's not fast enough," he said as he raised his hand to swing. This man was actually about to whip me as if I were his newly acquired slave. I tried to unbutton the shorts and drop them before he hit me, but my sweaty fingers couldn't work the buttons fast enough.

I couldn't believe this was happening. The pain of that first strike on my thigh seemed to go all the way through me. It felt like I had been burned. This body had never experienced that feeling and it brought me down to the desktop on one knee and pulled tears from my eyes. I stood up but since I still had the pants on, he hit me again.

If you have never been whipped, you may not know that it not only hurts, it weakens you as well. Each time the belt hit me, it brought with it a fiery explosion of pain. And every time it left me, it ripped energy and strength away from my ultra-sensitive flesh. I couldn't help screaming.

Pain and memory are closely related. In the Old South, it was discovered that the pain of the whip would cause mental as well as physical scars on a slave. Pain can trigger the memory and that memory can trigger productivity. After a slave was beaten that first time, the master may only need to threaten him with the fear of another to get him to produce more work. Martin was not trying to destroy his newly acquired money maker with permanent scars, he was merely attempting to destroy my will through the fear of more pain to come.

I quickly learned that sex appeal does not work on everyone. Some people are able to get off on the thrill of power. It didn't matter that I was trying to take the pants off. If it was not that, it would just have been something else. He wanted to make a point and he would do it by beating me. This was his way of establishing the fact that he was now my boss. He had already told me in so many words that I was worth only what he could get out of me. It seemed that his expectations were low. Now, he'd make me understand that fact. He would do the same thing later to Deak's pockets.

I couldn't imagine what had happen to the FLC. I wondered why it was so quiet in the other rooms and why no one had come in to see what was going on. I began to feel the Red Wave building after the third hit but after the fourth, I was too weak to use it. All I could do was lie down on the desk and cover up as he continued to beat me. (So much for the 'A' plan).

I woke hours later on the floor of Goldstein's large office bathroom. It was dark, quiet, and an old but familiar odor was thick in the air. After fumbling around for a moment, I was able to find the light switch. There were two doors. From the sounds I heard, the locked door led to someplace outside the building. The other led back inside. When I adjusted to the light I discovered T Dog's bloody naked body hanging in the shower.

His hands were tied to a pipe that had been installed to run the length of the shower. Hanging by his arms with his mouth taped, he had cuts all over his body. Even his penis was cut off. By the looks of things, he had been very badly abused before he bled to death. Old blood was on the wall, the floor and on me. It really didn't look like him anymore, but for the tattoos. It could have been no one else.

No blood was dripping from his body, so he had died long before I was ever placed in that room. I guessed that he had been hanging there for no more than a day. It was a horrible thing to see and smell. I could not stop myself from throwing-up on the body, the floor, and myself on my way out of the room.

I found myself back in Goldstein's private office. The lights were off, but his door was open. With the light from the hallway and the bathroom light, I could see part of my shirt and flip flops on the floor under the bloody body of Martin Goldstein. He had been shot several times in the chest.

I was still wearing the partly buttoned short pants. I reached inside to remove the small folding blade that I had hidden inside my vagina. I'd planned to use it to cut Martin's throat at the fall of Plan A. It was the only way I could think of to get it into the room. If I would have taken off my pants, it would have certainly fallen to the floor before I began to dance. I checked Martin's body and began to look around for something else to defend myself with.

Goldstein had a safe under his desk. I found it open and empty. I also found a snub-nosed Smith 38, loaded with 6 hollow point rounds, in the desk drawer. It was old and used but in good condition. The papers and the pills were now inside the desk. I put the shirt on, stuffed the blade in my pocket, and put the gun in my hand. My legs were killing me.

In the outer office, I found the bodies of the two men that were assigned to the inside. Mathew and David were both shot in the back. They lay on the floor where they once stood. Someone would have had to get in real close to do this. It could only be someone they knew and trusted. My friends were nowhere to be found. Neither were the other two guys that had been posted outside.

I remember worrying about Twister and Deak. It filled my head with all kinds of scenarios. The best of which was the idea that it was possible that one trained guy with a pistol could have done all of this.

I figured that Deak and Twister had to have been taken away as soon as I went into Goldstein's office. It would have been hard to convince Twister to leave without me, so it was reasonable to think that the two outside guys had to remove her by gunpoint.

Martin beat me and later had me placed in the bathroom for transport but was interrupted by a visitor they all knew but did not expect. The visitor was able to get them to relax enough to turn their backs. Once they did, this guy shot both the guards then emptied the rest of the weapon into Martin's chest before he could arm himself. I no longer needed to complete plan B. Someone had done it for me. The question was, who?

More than one person might have come in the door, but one guy did all the shooting from the same gun. The spent 9mm shell casings told the story. Whoever it was had no idea that I was unconscious on the floor of the bathroom or he might have killed me as well.

Goldstein wasn't tortured, he was just shot (a lot). That said that his killer made it personal. I guessed that whoever it was, knew what was in the safe and how to open it. Goldstein was not the type to leave it open. That assumption alone, narrowed the field. What it didn't tell me, was where my friends were.

I needed to make some calls fast. From the window I could see that my car was still parked in the same place it was four hours ago. My phone was in there. I didn't want to walk outside looking the way I did. Someone would remember a half-naked, bruised girl with blood and puke all over her. Instead, I used one of the laptops in the office to send an email out.

I told Sophia that we were going to war. She informed me that Mariko and the FLC girls were arrested but could be out by 1600hrs, but Twister and Deak had not checked in. I told her that she needed to send a crew to collect me and bring transport for T Dog's body. She then had the sad task of telling Sandra that her boyfriend was dead. The time was 1330hrs and I was initiating the plan C option, to kill them all. (The other girls agreed).

At 1415hrs, my cleanup crew arrived. The group of two policemen and one X SF guy dressed as cleaners, wrapped up T Dog's body. Then they cleaned the bathroom, dressed and cleaned me, in all of 20 minutes. One of them drove my car to Deak's place while the rest of us left through the alley door in the bathroom. They loaded T and I in a van and headed to the scrap yard.

While the crew burned T Dog's belongings, the laptop I used, and placed the gun and the body in a junk car to be crushed and shredded, I made some calls from my phone that was recovered from the car. I knew that this was Standard Operations, but I really liked T Dog. He was a fair guy and my ticket to a more normal future. I felt nothing but hate for Goldstein but he, of course was already dead.

The old text message on the phone was from an unknown number. It showed only three words, "Green to go." I knew that it had to be from Ian. He was letting me know that I was approved to take down Goldstein and his crew. The text was three hours old.

At some point in everyone's life they must be made aware that there are consequences for their actions. I have lived almost all my adult life by a simple philosophy of five little ideals, laws or rules, if you will. I don't expect others to follow or even understand what I stood for, and I never gave a damn what drove them to do what they did. But in this new life I was honestly trying to be a different person. Yet, there I was.

It was time to step out of the box and implement Rules 2 and 5. Rule #2 describes the use of war and the mental state required to win at it. Rule #5 states that "Payback is a Mother Fucker". (you don't break the rules).

Pauly told us that Marty wanted to meet him later, to celebrate. He mentioned that he had to "teach garbage to swim first." Pauly volunteered to help him and it was agreed that they should meet again on his granddad's boat at 1900hrs. He told Pauly that "this is a good opportunity for me to show you how I can deal with people who stand in our way."

At 1700hrs, the FLC girls were out of jail and in hiding at a biker club in Escondido. I was wrapping a bandage around my legs in a safe house near Oceanside. I had spoken to Ian earlier and he said that Nathaniel Goldstein was in town. I told him that someone else had killed Martin, two of his men, and robbed the safe. Ian was now calling me back to say that Nathaniel knew it had to be his nephew and wanted him "as dead as dead can be" which was good, because I had just arranged an Air/Sea Operation with the help of my new Marine friends from Camp Pendleton. I had to call in my option from Roland Davenport to make it all happen.

I called Granny Jo and had her call me back on a secured line. I gave her the particulars, and Roland called me back in less than 20 minutes. He knew that I had been recruited as a direct Arm of the Body and didn't question my request. He made it clear to me that he would be honored to work with one of the Arms and offered his insight and position as a DC Insider freely and without condition.

It had always been the family's plan to put its children into positions that would make them more attractive to the First Line. To Granny Jo it was a lifelong dream but for Raymond the 4th and his sons, it had been a quest. Now they all had their chance. It was at that point that I formally brought Roland into my organization and considered this mission to be his test of loyalty.

At 1830hrs the SF guy and I met our pick-up at Oceanside Municipal Airport wearing my new black jumpsuit, headphones and helmet. The MH-60L DAP and the two MH-60H Seahawk Helicopters were already on the deck. I was introduced as a Special Agent (no name) before we boarded our Seahawk. It was what we could get at short notice. I said nothing and kept the glass shade over my face, so they wouldn't see how young I looked.

After all I had been through, I was also wearing my new favorite pistol strapped on my right thigh. I never thought I would go for a gun that was made partly of plastic, but I found that the Glock 19 fit perfectly into my now smaller hands. I had some issues with the ejection port, but our gunsmith fixed all of that.

I really wanted to go back to the Colt 45 but due to the incredible recoil, I could never put two rapid shots on the target paper. Besides, due to my stubbornness I hit myself in the forehead twice before giving it up. On the other hand, the Glock would hardly move.

The Navy Pilots and Marines were not new to government sponsored operations. These men were used to reacting to any threat at any time. They had been told that the man they were looking for was above the local law. Their orders were to eliminate this International Terrorist and rescue two hostages that may be on the boat. They were also told that another member of our team may be undercover on that boat. The Special Strike Force didn't want, or need to know, anything more than that.

No names were mentioned, and no one would ever speak of this incident. As far as they were all concerned, no one gave these orders and the equipment never left the compound. All that they were really concerned with was that I personally identify the targets. These men would not shoot unless I was sure.

It was 1915hrs when we spotted the moving craft five miles west of Marina Del Rey. The locator on one of the $100 bills, confirmed it. As we approached out of the sun from the west, one of the snipers reported that one of the men had just shot someone and that the body had fallen into the water. At that time, we were still too far out for me to positively ID our mark.

A minute later, the same Marine reported that he could see four men and one woman standing on the boat. With the aid of binoculars, I was able to ID Marty, and gave the Green Light to terminate him. But, before we could get close enough for a clear and clean shot, Marty shot another man.

As we moved closer, I could clearly see that Deak and Twister had their hands tied with rope. Marty and Pauly both had guns in their hands but seemed to be arguing with each other. Marty pointed his weapon at Pauly and Pauly did the same to him. It was a real Mexican standoff type situation.

I gave that same Marine an order to shoot, but Deak's head was in his way. Due to the way the people on the boat were standing and the angle of our approach, no one had a good shot. At that time the Marines had to refuse the order claiming the risk to the hostages was too great.

Both the men on the boat fired at close range but neither was hit. A brawl began and Pauly was knocked down on the deck losing his weapon in the process. Marty raised his weapon to fire again and before the snipers could take him out, Deak, having broken loose from his ropes, charged into Marty. They wrestled on the deck until Deak was finally shot and fell over the side into the water. Marty came to his feet and again pointed his gun on Pauly who was still attempting to reach his weapon at the time.

Suddenly a great space about the size of a softball opened in Marty's chest and his body collapsed on the deck. We were about 50 yards away when the shot from the AW50 (a heavy battlefield rifle) was taken. Within seconds, two men dropped out of the sky and into the water to look for Deak. Another Marine lowered himself onto the boat. He cut the engine, cut Twister free, and prepared her for extraction. Only after he dropped the Springfield 1911, Pauly was allowed to gather the important documents he needed before he too, was lifted into one of the Seahawks.

Deak was recovered and pulled into my Chopper. The flesh wound to the chest was not as bad as the fact that he had nearly drowned. When he began to breathe on his own, I was as relieved as a girl could be. Sandra had just found out that she lost her boyfriend. The news of losing her father on the same day would have been more than even I could stand. The Strike Force used a Sidewinder rocket to blow that boat to bits before we took off for the hospital in Santa Monica. Plan C had been completed.

In my former life, I was never what you would call an emotional guy. I knew a little about fear and anger and I knew a lot about hate. Since my rebirth, I had taught myself to cry and look sad, but I was only acting. I did it at school and I performed it on the stage. I tried to study the emotions of females and when would be the most appropriate time to use them, but I couldn't find a solid test case to pattern myself behind. I found it best to wait for clues from the other girls before I would fake my own response.

The thing I had found most confusing was the way some women cry when they are happy. I know that it doesn't have to, but it would help if that one made a little more sense. It was not until I saw Sandra run to her father in that hospital room, that I truly understood that feeling.

The documents Pauly recovered were agreements between himself and young Marty to share several small to medium percentages in many of the venues on the West Coast. He had vending contracts that worked those venues as well. There were contracts on a percentage of ownership in Radio and TV stations all up and down the West Coast. The deal even included the build site for a new amphitheater near Malibu. Most of the other agreements were in the name of Marty's grandfather.

According to a signed agreement, Pauly would own 30% of the entire operation once he made a cash deposit of $200,000 US. In my briefcase, Marty had stashed the $20,000 I gave to Deak, the $20,000 I gave to Pauly, and $260,000 he had stolen from his grandfather's safe. Even though my management had been signed to Deak, we also found a letter signing over management of "The Artist Known as Jasmine" from T Dog to Mr Martin Goldstein. There was blood on that piece of paper.

After speaking with Twister, Pauly, Ian and the rest, I was able to piece together the following sequence of events:

Our FLC gang was detained by the LAPD. When they found knives and sticks on the girls, they were arrested and taken in for questioning. Mariko called Arleen from the police station and she started working her magic. Arleen notified Sophie and Sophie took command when I could not be contacted.

As soon as I was pushed into Goldstein's inner office, the two guys from the outside came back in. The four gangsters moved my friends out the door by gunpoint and placed them into a van that the outside guys drove to a second office about a mile away. Mathew and David stayed behind.

The other office was in a bar that the Goldstein's were turning into a night club. Peter and Frank were instructed to show Deak around the place. They told him that if he released all ties to T Dog, James, and I, Mr Goldstein would let him run the place. He could refuse the deal but that would mean that per Mr Goldstein's instructions, they were to kill them both and place their bodies inside one of the walls wrapped in a plastic bag. Deak had little choice but to agree. After all, he too, was stalling for time.

At that same time, young Marty was meeting with Pauly near his Marina hotel. Marty was angry with his granddad. He told Pauly that he didn't trust the LA crew and insisted that Pauly call some of his people down from Chicago, today. They both signed some forms and Pauly promised the rest of the required $200,000 within a week. After the meeting, Pauly called his sister.

Marty returned to the main office around 1030hrs. He used a small 9mm handgun to kill everyone he saw before he opened the safe. He made calls to most of the LA crew on his cell phone and noted the numbers of the men that called back to the office for confirmation on Marty's story. Everyone he had called, made an attempt to call his granddad.

It was 1045hrs when Marty called Pete and Frank about his grandfather being killed. This time he said that he thought it was a robbery gone bad. Marty had assumed control of all operations. He wanted to hold an emergency meeting and said that everyone should stay put until he called them back. Pete tried to call Goldstein's office, but no one answered the phone. The two men never liked young Marty and were vocal about signing their allegiance over to him. Since Twister worked for Deak and Deak now worked for Marty, they too had to stand by for instructions. They were all understandably on edge.

If you include Deak and Marty, old Martin had nine men that directly worked for him. The rest were just people he owned or owned a piece of. One of the men was killed by the FLC gang and two others now lay dead near the body of their boss. Marty thought he had Pauly in his pocket, so he planned to kill at least four more of the original crew before the end of the day. He was up in the air on Deak.

It was about 1230hrs when Twister hit Frank with a bottle of Rum. She was worried about me and tired of Frank fucking with her about her muscles. Pete was ready to shoot her, but Frank convinced him to let the two of them fight it out. They did, and she lost. Frank hurt his hand and she broke her rib. Deak couldn't find a way to overtake Pete without getting shot so he had to end the fight before Twister became permanently damaged.

We discovered later that Marty killed the next two men he had called at their homes, one at a time. Then he setup a meeting with Frank and Pete at the boat. He knew that Deak was with them and demanded that he and Twister be taken along. On his way to the marina he called Pauly for backup.

Deak told the guys that his deal was with old Martin. He had no desire to work with Marty and insisted that he and Twister be allowed to go on their way. The gangsters refused and were forced to tie both of them up to avoid another fight. They left the building at 1800hrs.

After speaking with me, Sophie told her brother to play along with Marty. He needed to delay him. His mission was to get the boat as far out to sea as possible before Marty started shooting any more people. He was to try and find out what happened to Deak and Twister, then call us back.

At 1845hrs, Sophie tried to call me. She wanted me to know that her brother had arrived early and found Deak and Twister already on the boat. He told her that the two were tied up and that he would do his best to set them free. I was in the air and never got that call.

Frank wanted to keep the prisoners tied until Marty said otherwise. He was tired and didn't feel like fighting Twister again. Besides, he and Pete didn't know Pauly from Adam. They called Marty when Pauly drove up but had no reason to trust him yet.

When Marty arrived at 1855hrs, the gangsters shook hands and quickly boarded. As Pauly drove, Frank and Pete asked if Marty had recruited a hit man. They had made some calls too and knew that their friends were dead. Those were men they had known all their lives. Frank wanted to know why he brought down a "Wop" from Chicago to do the dirty work. Pete wanted everyone to calm down.

Pauly looked as much as a Sicilian as his sister did. He also walked, talked, and dressed in the Chicago way. It was understandable that the men felt that he was part of some outside muscle Marty was using to take over his granddad's operation. As Pauly stood beside him, Marty corrected their thinking.

He admitted that he had gone outside LA and that he was taking over the business. He surprised them by saying that he alone had taken out the others to include his granddad. He said that he would give them the same opportunity that he gave the rest of them. Johnny and Dan were old friends of the family and they were with him. "You guys can either choose to support me too or take a swim."

The two older men were angry. Pete told Marty that he was crazy and that was the real reason why his granddad didn't think he was ready. Frank went for his CZ75B and was shot by Pauly. The body fell into the water. Marty supported Pauly by drawing his gun and pointing it at Frank. Frank began to swear and dared Marty to kill him. Marty obliged him, and Frank fell over the side.

Now that Pete and Frank were gone, Marty asked Pauly to shoot Deak and Twister as a final show of loyalty. Pauly tried to convince him otherwise. Marty accused Pauly of trying to take over his operation and the two young men began to fight.

To close it all out, Pauly did not get his 20% because the Society was not given control of the Goldstein operations. To keep peace between all the heads of the families involved, control was given to an off- branch of the Sons of Snorky, with Nathaniel Goldstein as its boss. However, I got to control my own music contracts and my songs began to play again on the radio. Pauly was given $50,000 for his efforts. I recouped the $90,000 I paid out and kept $160,000. Nathaniel gave me a gesture of $500,000 for my pain and suffering. Why not, we had won the Battle of the Bands and deserved some compensation. It was all a part of doing business. Back East was satisfied, and the Counsel saw no fault in my actions. Later I sent Pauly another 100 grand and built a small open skating park in T Dog's name.

The truth be told, young Marty would have been killed one way or another, in less than a week. The syndicate back east frowns on this type of regime change. If his Boss was murdered, he should have informed the Big Bosses before acting. That, in itself, looked like he was involved. But then to go on to eliminate the rest of the old boss's organization and at the same time making deals with another house, was an obvious sign of guilt. His uncle was obligated to kill him and set things right or the guys from back east would come in and assume control. But before I learned all of this, I fell sick.

The beating and the exhaustion of that day put me into a fever later that same night. I was tired and in pain while I was attempting some self-healing. I remember sitting in the bathtub soaking my legs when I suddenly became very dizzy and passed out. While I was out, I had the strangest experience. When I woke again, I was in another part of the world.

There's No Place Like Home

I was the centerpiece in a medieval type ritual. It was a dream-like experience and at the same time it was much more than real. I felt, heard, and smelled a lot of strange things but the things I perceived the clearest were the ones I saw when my eyes were closed.

I remember being led into a dim, candle lit room, by two women wearing white robes. The robes had hoods that went over their heads and their eyes were covered by a white blindfold. I too, wore a white robe but unlike them, I could partly see. Smoke filled this area and I could smell smoldering leaves or herbs nearby. I could not speak and had no real control over my body movements. I was in a trance and went where I was led but I had no fear.

They took me to something that looked like a sunken tub, where I was made to sit on my knees with my head down. The robe was removed, and I sat naked while a thick dark liquid was poured or dumped onto me from an opening in the ceiling above, until the small pool was filled. I was covered in the stuff.

I was then made to lie in the pool face up and let my body float in the warm red liquid for a moment. Suddenly, the floor began to move in an upward motion. The white-hooded women stepped back as the center of the floor rose through the open ceiling above.

As I ascended, a long pillar formed below me and pushed me into an upper hall. The tub fell away from me in pieces and I now lay on top of an altar. The fluid rolled off my body and I heard the voices of men chanting words in Latin. There were 12 men wearing black-hooded robes with gold trim. With hidden faces, each one took his turn starting a new verse of the chant. They stood below me arranged like numbers on the face of a clock. They all had true English accents.

When the monolith completed its ascension, flames shot up from all sides around me. The top of the structure was cold, and I could not feel the fire's heat. The flames continued until the structure was lowered to about three feet above the floor of the main hall. A great wind seemed to blow the fire away. Then everything stopped, and the men went silent. There was more, but I can't begin to describe it.

One by one, the men walked up to the altar. They spoke strange words and poured a large cup of what may have been water on parts of my body until the red stuff was washed away. The last man told me in English to, "Arise you child of Alexander, now reborn." I stood up and a black-trimmed robe was placed around me.

He told me, "You see before you the very heart of the body of Alexander the Great. Like us, you too were once cold, but your heart was rekindled with the breath of the gods. Your body was empty, but it has now been refilled by the blood of the men who were your enemies. Your eyes were once blind, but they will soon be made to see the truth. Your head was numb, but through death, intellect was bestowed upon you. Your arms were weak, but you have shown the ability to command an army that still shouts your name. The Spirit of the Conqueror lives within you, and you have been found worthy to lead!" He placed a ring on my finger and kissed it. "I place upon your finger the symbol of the Outer Body of the Counsel." Then he said, "Take your place once more, you child of Alexander, as a god among men." That last line was repeated around the room by each man. Then they chanted, "You have been Reborn! You have been Reborn! You have been Reborn!" One by one the men came to kneel before me and kiss the ring.

When I awoke again, I was lying on a great 17th century type four post bed (canopy, curtains and all) wearing a long white nightgown and a big jeweled ring. Obviously, part of the experience was real, and could not all have been a dream. I removed the blanket and half expected to see a pair of ruby slippers on my feet. My legs felt fine, so I ran to the nearby window to discover that I wasn't in Kansas anymore.

It was raining outside. The window opened to a large outdoor balcony. Beyond that, a long flat yard of green grass and trees stretched out before me as far as I could see. I had to be in England. "I've got to get to a phone," I thought to myself. Just then, there was a knock on the door. I recognized the voice on the other side as one of the men I met in the office of Raymond the 4th. "May we come in please," he asked. I said yes. The man slowly opened the door and said, "I have brought someone who really wants to meet you. We have told him all about you and he could not be made to wait any longer." As soon as the door was fully opened a little boy flew past him and into the room. The child ran to me and jumped up into my arms as fast as his little legs could carry him. I knew in my heart exactly who this was. It was the only person it could be. As the boy hugged me I looked deep into his face. "Jasmine Aiza Britten, I am happy to present young Master Arthur James Alexander Britten the 3rd"." He was right. It was my brother.

All that morning the child clung to me like an extra append-age. Clearly there was an attachment that I could not understand. He was well behaved and didn't cry or whine. He seemed to be in-telligent for a two year old, (if that is what he truly was) but the kid never spoke no matter what I did. I tried asking him questions and did things to try and trick a vocal response out of him but all I ever got was smiles and simple body language. I even tried mak-ing faces and singing to him. (Nothing).

The boy was in the process of being potty trained and pulled me into the adjoining toilet with him four times before I was finally relieved for a moment by the nanny who brought in his snack and more water. After he ate, he wanted me to lie down with him on the bed for a nap. I noticed that the boy had one blue eye and the other was brown. His father's IDs had two blue eyes. At the time I chalked it up to a side effect of the accident. It was not until much later that I discovered how wrong that assump-tion was. Don't get me wrong. I found him to be a handsome and affectionate little boy and it fascinated me to no end that he could be alive in the first place. Still, what did I know about children?

After a while, it was hard to pretend that I was not bored. I did get the impression that the kid needed me or needed something he thought I could provide. As he lay sleeping, I got up from the bed and walked out of the room.

The door opened into a hallway. I stood in a 'T' intersection. I saw other rooms going down on the left and to the right, but the servant in the hall bent before me and motioned that I should go straight towards an opened door to a large dining room.

On the way, I passed other doors on both sides and saw art and paintings of what must have been family members on the walls. I recognized Arthur and Lamees in a wedding portrait and figured that it was a hall dedicated to my part of the family. In the large dining hall, I saw that same man that had let my brother into the room. His face was also in the hall, but I didn't see mine and neither did I see young Master Arthur the third.

The horned-rim, glasses-wearing man, introduced himself as Lloyd and invited me to sit and have lunch with him. His ring was a little different from mine, but the style was the same. I saw three other unopened doors in this room and I suspected that at least two of them led to other hallways like the one I had just come out from. The man told me that he was my father's uncle which meant that he was my great uncle and besides my brother, was my closest living English family member. "I will be straight forward with you and say that I have been studying your progress from long before your birth. I know that you have no memory of your life before your mind was awakened by the accident, so you do not need to pretend that you do. Your face is young, but I am under no illusion that you have a child's mind. I came to this understanding when you told me yourself, that our project had failed. The fact that you could speak with such certainty on something that should have been beyond your comprehension, meant that the test had actually succeeded. You may ask me any question and I will answer within the scope of my authority, but first we need to talk about you and your brother."

As we ate salad he told me that Arthur's grandfather, father, and Arthur himself had been born in one of those rooms down the hall. I had been born here too and although I had scarcely spent more than a week here, this place was my real home. I asked, "Did it have something to do with the fact that I looked a little too much like my mother?" as I held up my arm and pointed at my olive colored skin.

"You have to understand" he answered, "that your grandfather was completely devastated by the failure. He had such hopes for this project. Your father was upset as well but he had grown to love your mother more than we had anticipated. When the offer was given to release your mother and marry her younger cousin, he refused and moved you both that very day into the Old Priory home outside of Oxford."

He was calm at first, but now his mood had changed. "Your grandfather gave up his hope to rebuild the family and died within a fortnight. Your mother blamed herself and cried incessantly. I admit that I was angry with your father. Arthur the 1st was my brother after all. In those days, I considered myself part of the project. I was never going to produce a child, so I too allowed myself to be consumed by the power and the arrogance involved in recreating a living god. The others in our clan were either too old, or like me, unable to even try this experiment. Your father was our last real hope to extend the family line."

"But there's a little Arthur now," I prompted. "Why would you go through all the trouble to rebuild the older sister that no one wanted from the start?"

He seemed a little shocked with the bluntness of that question and took a moment to recover before quietly saying, "I am older than I look. Who would take charge of him after I am gone? Make no mistake about it, your unborn brother saved your life. At first it was argued that you were too dense for even that job, so I was forced to trade you off for some minor favors. But from the moment you opened your mouth, I knew that you had been changed. As you continued to develop, it occurred to me that you could be an asset. Your lifestyle is less than conventional but it works well for this new age. Even the Heart of the Counsel has decided that you may be the perfect embodiment of the very spirit of Alexander himself. With the proper training you could be allowed to help lead our clan into the next era. Your brother would have a protector. You will be able to enforce his right to rule and his progeny will continue to dominate the Earth and beyond, for all time. That was, and must continue, to be our plan."

I felt like I really needed a glass of wine and asked one of the servants to bring me something, but Lloyd cancelled my order. (I was only going to drink one). "Uncle," I began, "It is possible that one of our own may have had a part in my father's death. If, and I say again if, that is true, they will surely now have to kill little Arthur for those same reasons, whatever they were. To do that, they would have to get rid of me and they may think it necessary to kill you as well."

He looked up at me strangely. He asked the servants to bring two glasses of wine, then told them to leave the room and guard the doors. "You will have to forgive me," he said. "I shouldn't find it so strange that you can know my thoughts. It's too much to hope that your brother could ever grow to be this wise. That will not be his destiny." He savored a sip of the wine before saying, "I am told that those tiny machines that travel through your body help to duplicate and replace the living cells they cannot repair. Your intellect is a far cry from what it used to be, and it may continue to grow. The spark may have come from your father, but this was truly a one in a million shot in the dark for us. You are smarter at 18, than he ever was. On the other hand, your long-lasting youth will be a side effect from some of those added machines, that you requested. We will all just have to get used to the fact that you will be looking young for a very long time."

"You're right," I said. "I've gotten a little taller and my body has adapted to my needs to become stronger in what would seem to be a short period of time, but I don't seem to be getting any older. I think that being young is good and all, but I can see how that could cause some talk later on. Then again, I could live a lifetime as a child before I would consent to seeing any of those Frankenstein doctors again. How long did they think I will stay this way?"

"Well," he began, "the electrostatic charge corrupted most of the records in the facility where you were reborn. That cannot be changed. So, without further examinations, all we know is that many of your brain functions have been raised by a factor of 10 to 20 points above what is normal, especially when it comes to healing. It may please you to know that Doctor Mujawar believes your aging is slowed by a factor of 12. So, by the time you've aged one year, the rest of us would have aged about 12. Unless you're re-examined, there is no telling how long you can live. But this is not the question you really wanted to ask me."

I knew I could have been taking the risk of my life, but I had to ask. "I need to ask you a question Uncle. And I want you to understand that this is in no way an accusation. But it is a question that has to be considered as valid, and a valid question demands an answer." As he took a bite of pudding, he gave a motion with his hand that I should continue. "When my father found that my mother was pregnant, who else in the world would he call other than you? Now, that's not the question. The way I see it, my father was killed for the reasons of hate or jealousy. Hate for this experiment and the possibility of its success, or jealousy that he was the only one that had the slimmest of chances to complete it. So, the question is this... who did YOU call?"

He removed his glasses and said, "Revenge is it?"

Maybe I did mean to shock the man. He could have been my only ally or my greatest enemy. I had to know which one he was.

"You are completely discounting the possibility that it was an accident?"

"I am," I answered.

He took a long breath and said, "I assume that you not only suspect the lesser lines but perhaps the Council members as well. If this, as you say, is not the powerful accusation it sounds like, then I have to ask you a question before I can give you your answer." I knew that I was on thin ice, but it was possible that his answer would either lead me to a path or the destination itself. "If I tell you what you want to know, will you promise to clear your mind of this?"

"You would have to convince me," I replied.

He told me that when his brother first came up with the radical idea to extend the First Line using this print-less DNA, he was the only one that supported the plan. "The Line must not die," his brother told the Counsel, but they felt that the Holy Spirit of the Conqueror that had forged the Line was dead. "We were merely hanging on to the ashes that were left behind. They felt that tampering with the blood would defile our claim to Nobility. We forged ahead without their support. But you have proven them wrong. If there were still a saboteur in the family, you would have never gotten the required unanimous decision to become an active member of the Body. The Counsel is the most powerful force ever devised by man. It would be impossible to try to fight it. The name you seek can no longer be considered our enemy. The proof is sitting before me now."

I was not so easily satisfied, so I pressed him by saying, "So the murders of my mother and your nephew are to go unanswered!"

"Yes unanswered..." he said as he stood up from the table. "For now, and perhaps for all of eternity. I can't afford to just throw you away. And if you have any love for your brother or gratitude to me for saving your life, you will never mention this again! There is a lot to be said about breeding, but you have talents that no one could have predicted. I wish I could take credit for them but in good conscience I cannot. What I can do is take advantage of them in a way that complements Council strategies. The way you live and act make you perfect for the task, and with my guidance, you will become even better." He told me that I should spend some time with my brother in Oxford to bond and reflect on our conversation. "You will need your wits about you in the coming weeks," he said. Before exiting the door that led into our hallway he turned and said, "Don't let your brashness be your undoing, as it was in the time of Alexander the Great himself."

I sat alone realizing that I could have played that a little differently. It was part of the old me. Reaching for the meat before eating the vegetables. I knew he would now never willingly tell me the name of who I thought the killers might be.

I wanted to talk more about my brain. I wanted to ask if it was removed at any time, or if my consciousness was somehow transferred from one mind to another. I wanted to ask about the other brain I was not supposed to see in that basin. Was it from some other person in that convoy (namely me)? Could it have been Arthur's, or was it someone else? The only problem was that I would have had no real reason for asking that kind of question. It would not have been my concern. The question would have made him suspicious. That suspicion would have led to a deeper investigation that would surely have been my doom. For all I knew, that brain could have been Arthur the 1st. I had taken enough chances for one lunch with one of the most powerful men alive. Instead, I wrapped my lips on those two small wine glasses and let Uncle Lloyd and those questions, walk down the hall.

What he didn't say, was that I was the reusable wild card in the deck. First, he used me as a trade when he thought I had no other function. He used me again to test the waters when he confirmed that I was alive in Florida, without bothering to tell the clans that I was infertile. (No one took the bait). Then he tested my abilities to prove my worth to the Council. I was more than just something stuffed up his sleeve, I was a decoy and a distraction. The Counsel would focus its eyes on me and not him.

Uncle Lloyd had some kind of hidden agenda. Whatever it was, was beyond me at this point. If I became the world's next puppet master, there was no telling what I would do, given the chance. Little Arthur was Lloyd's prize and perhaps his greatest accomplishment, but he was also a hostage in this game. The Counsel would use him to keep me in check and I knew it. I would have to bend or conform in order to protect him. It would be a win/win situation for all of the players (that is, until Lloyd was ready to lay down his hand). That had to be the real reason why we were being forced to bond.

The Priory was dated before 1176AD, when it belonged to Benedictine nuns. It's been a family manor for several different Lords, a sanatorium for the Royal Air Force and most recently a hotel. This rustic Oxfordshire Manor home, and its grounds, have been filmed and written about for almost one thousand years, and by the looks of it, you could squeeze a few more hundred out of it before you would need to rebuild. The caretakers (the Parker family) were raising champion dogs. They had full use of the ten-acre spread and had done so for about 50 years now. They were quite renowned in many circles.

I took Little Arthur and the nanny (Freda a 35 year old Irish lady), and had Annette flown over (my hair was a mess without her). I was told that my father had planned to rename the place but never came up with a name that stuck. Being his oldest child, I now had the right to do the same and make any changes I wanted. Except for some decorations and bedroom furniture, I didn't set out to change much, if anything, but I did re-name the place, Jasmine on the Green. I ordered those same flowers planted around the buildings and it all seemed to fit.

I didn't feel that I had the right to throw any of our family's things away. Except for a few pictures, I had the personal things stored in one of the extra rooms. It would be Little Arthur's choice what to do with them when he became older. I also claimed our parents' bedroom as mine and put Little Arthur in what I was told was my old room. Annette had a room next to mine and Freda stayed in the room that my old nanny used to use.

The Parker family was shocked that I didn't know them or this place. They were all briefed that I had lost my memory when I almost died in Iraq, but they could just not get over the fact that I could look so much like both my parents and not remember a thing about them. They accepted Little Arthur right away. He looked like a color copy of his father. But it took them some time to feel comfortable around me. The change was just too much for them.

I couldn't blame them really. The tales they told were of a child that was as dense as a stone. No one would admit to this, but it sounded like she was (a lot) on the retarded side. I saw pictures of her mother wiping what looked like drool from her face (my face) at 11 years old. In fact, this kid seemed to always have her mouth open and staring off in the wrong direction. Even so, she was beyond pretty. And the family had a plan for her.

The grandson, Peter Parker (no relation), told me that he thought that I was smart, self-sufficient, responsible, and dangerously sexy. He was a tall, good looking (or strapping as they say), 20 year old that loved girls as much as he loved his dogs. He honestly admitted that he was once afraid of what would happen me. But now he was thrilled to see how far I had come. He also made it clear that he would break all protocol if given the opportunity. I of course gave him no play, but it was entertaining to watch him try. He was never too forward and the fact that I already knew that nothing would ever happen between us, made it O.K. Besides, I needed to practice being in close proximity to men.

A week later Uncle Lloyd told me that he wanted me to prepare to sing in Cairo. Muhammad Hosni Mubarak had been forced to step down from the Egyptian Presidency. I needed to feel-out the situation and remind our friends how far they could really go. Egypt has one of the last standing cities founded by Alexander the Great that kept his name and is more of a symbol of the beginning of the First Line than it is real estate. Going into the country as a singer would be my cover on this mission.

Personally, I never liked Mr Mubarak. I know that he was behind the assassination of Anwar Sadat. For a very brief time I worked with Sadat and felt proud when he won the Nobel Peace Prize in '78. But, when Egypt lost its membership in the Arab League, things went downhill for him. At present, the country is losing billions in the way of tourism.

A few days later Uncle Lloyd told me that I was needed in Tripoli as soon as I could be ready to go. Muammar Al Gaddafi was finally being overthrown by an armed intervention that included help from the US and NATO of all things. (What a shock). I had been ignoring the world news. That had to change.

It's common knowledge that the so called "King of Kings" made the most wanted list when he shut down the US and British military bases, expelled the Italians and Jews from his country, and renegotiated his oil shares from 50 to 79 percent in the '70s. In doing so, he raised Libya's living standard to the highest in all of Africa and remained debt free.

The British took strong offense with his affiliation with the IRA and the Pan Am 103 incidents. His World Revolutionary Centre produced leaders that seized power in Ethiopia, Chad, Sierra Leone, and the Central African Empire. Gaddafi aligned himself with the FARC and Slobodan Milosevic, all the while campaigning to unite Africa into a single state. He used the term "Pan-Africanism" as a rally cry.

We had always hated Mr Gaddafi still, except for the Lockerbie bombing in '88, he had kept out of most Western affairs. It was not until he began relationships in South America that the US began to look hard at opportunities to legitimately rid the world of him, once and for all. Now was that time.

It made no real difference to Lloyd and the family. Oil would still be bought and sold around the world no matter whose name was on the barrel. It did however; make a big difference to the figurehead leaders of the Western World. If money was the stuff that "makes the world go 'round", then oil is Black Gold. With the

Colonel out of the picture, Libya's wealth could be split and balance, in time, could be restored. But, there is another darker story.

At the very beginning of my duties as a "glorified bag girl", I insisted on some kind of briefing on the who, what and why. Uncle Lloyd was overjoyed with the idea and saw to it that I was briefed with as much relative information as he thought was adequate to share with me at that time. Sometimes, I would get a file that I would have to immediately destroy. Other times, I'd get a formal briefing by an Outer Council Member who might have pictures, audio, video, and maps. (I liked those). Then there were times when I was told to "Just deliver the package".

I had begun to piece together small snippets of real history. For this mission I learned that, like Saddam Hussein, Muammar Gaddafi was amassing gold. He planned among other things, to back his country currency on the Gold Standard System to give it a solid value. I asked my uncle the question, "Isn't the US Dollar based on a great mass of gold bricks stored someplace in Fort Knox, Kentucky?" The answer I received was, no, not for quite some time now.

The US Dollar, the British Pound, the Euro, and many of the other major currencies are now based on an agreed upon worth called Fiat Currency which is controlled by the Great World Banks. A Fiat holds no real value, but precious metals like gold and silver do, and always will. A currency backed by something of value will always be worth more than something that is not worth the expense of the ink it takes to print it.

Even on this very day I am not yet allowed to peruse the family archives to discover who knows what as far as all of the details, but what I did learn, is that my family is the World Bank and the World Bank is my family. Also, to defy the Bank is to risk utter destruction. We have seen this in the form of wars (large and small) and the assassinations of high profile leaders. I will not give more than the two names I have already provided. I will say however, that the list of leader names are ones you would recognize. This rabbit hole runs deep. (Feel free to look into this for yourself).

So, now that Europe and the Americas have been painfully tamed, this leaves Africa and the Mid-East. Saddam could have brought the Mid-East together under one supreme leader. Africa is divided and will be divided for some time. The only men in recent history who could have changed that would have been the man that in 2008, 200 African leaders called King of Kings of Africa. Gaddafi would have passed this title to his sons and they too, would have stood against the Banks.

If nothing else, my fact-finding nature will be my doom. As I learned of these things, I was taken aback and at the same time compelled to learn more. Barring any other pertinent facts, I must conclude that this is not one war after another about power, politics, religion, or conquest. This is just one war about who controls all the money. It has been fought for many generations now and will continue to be fought until the whole world submits or is destroyed.

Because these two leaders refused to "play ball" their countries will now have to suffer at least one generation of chaos as a punishment. (Sounds almost Biblical). You'll never see this part of the story in a movie, TV, or on the internet, so almost none of the world's citizens will ever know about it.

Until as recently as a few months ago, I thought it was all about those bad Muslim people. In truth, for them to exchange goods and services for something that is worth nothing is "haram" meaning anti-Islamic, so they will likely never agree. This is the real reason we are being taught to hate and fear them. Imagine my surprise when I realized that I was partly responsible for reinforcing that hoax. But again, I am getting way ahead of myself.

Meanwhile, back at home, the Society was able to buyout James' other partners. The Goldstein incident made them afraid for the safety of their families and the 200 thousand US dollar buyout seemed to be more than fair. We owned 50% of what was now called James Town Productions, but James was completely free to create and promote in any manner he chose.

With two million US dollars at his disposal, he was able to move his operations into a new facility, staff it with his choice of experts, and make contracts and promotions for new groups. The company was primed for success and profit. All he needed was a good track record and some publicity. Touring would help.

Uncle Lloyd put a chopper on call for me and I used it to fly back and forth into London where I rehearsed part of the show and was tutored in a few Arab standards. I was introduced to real string instruments and it was going very well. Little Arthur was starting to talk to me a little bit. Twister arrived bringing her saxophone, two new back-up singers (The Sisters), Tito, Battle Angel, Joy, and the rest of the band, a few days before we were to depart, and I felt on top of the world.

Peter and Twister didn't get along well. It didn't stop her from kissing and touching me in front of him. He would counter by getting real close and bumping into me at every opportunity when Twist could see it. They were like two dogs after the same piece of meat. The unfriendly rivalry became heated one afternoon and I was forced to intervene. They eventually came to an understanding where they would just avoid each other. (She Hulk verses Spiderman). She would have killed him.

Twist told me that she had met someone that was talking about doing a show for women body builders. She would show and critique new and old techniques, diets, and other issues from the female perspective. She might have sealed the deal when she told the producers that she would be traveling with me around the world. She could interview other women that were well known athletes along the way. She could do the same thing while traveling with other groups. It could be the beginnings of a new network and a new product line with her name on it. I gave my blessing, support, and Society funding for a percentage of the gross, and a change to the format.

Instead of focusing on just women's athletics, she could interview and travel with any famous or up-and-coming persons that were into body building. That person could be an actor, politician, musician, model, dentist, or whatever happened to be the theme of that show. We could show what they would do to keep in shape while at the same time pushing the products (and music) we thought that person would most benefit from. Twist might revisit that same person from time to time. The Producers would consider this offer.

The Sisters were two 18 year old identical twin black girls from LA that had amazing pipes. One was named Lila and the other one was Twyla. (Never knew which was which). They were two beautiful, long legged, light brown skinned, 5 foot 7 inch ladies that sang like the Sirens of myth. They were alike in every way and had the ability to know what the other was thinking. Their specialty was vocal sound effects and the ability to seemingly hold a note continually by means of passing it off from one to the other. They were also good dancers.

When they were not singing, they were very quiet. They had no real need to talk to each other but when they would speak to someone else it was kind of strange. They would either say the same words at the same time or one would say a word or two then the other would do the same to complete the sentence. It was as if you were really speaking to one person that lived in two separate bodies. You got used to it.

They both liked the same guy. His name was Jonathan Walker, but he hated to be called that. Because of the reference to the popular liquor, he disliked the name Johnny as well. Many years ago, while in an LA club spinning and scratching records, someone thought he looked a little like one of Michael Jackson's brothers. He has been called Tito ever since.

Tito was a 45 year old DJ/Sound Engineer, that took the study of engineering sound to another level. For the first 20 years of his career, Tito dedicated himself to producing and recording the best live sounds in the LA area. During that time, he helped invent a device that was sold and later modified without his permission. Disillusioned, Tito went underground. He divorced his wife and didn't perform for years.

He was working the sound board for a gospel quartet at a small LA Baptist Church one evening, when the Sisters went up to the sound booth to ask him a question. The three of them worked together for one year before James heard one of the demos the girls were handing out to local producers. James remembered seeing Tito all those years ago and signed all three of them. He used Tito to mix my sound for the first CD and the Hollywood and Vine projects. Tito thought that the girls could enhance my sound in a unique way, but James did not agree. It was not until Tito played him a remixed version of my "Inner City Blues" he and the girls had put together that James was convinced. Tito would now be the leader of my band.

I began to work on James' new arrangements with the Sisters. Battle Angel and Joy stayed near to provide my security, but the rest of the band members took full advantage of the London Music Scene. They left their bags at the manor but unless I saw them in the studio, I didn't see them at all. They quickly made friends and spent all their time playing music and having fun. The day before we were to leave for Tripoli, Uncle Lloyd cancelled the trip. Instead, we were sent to Beirut a few days later. We would spend a week there before heading to Dubai. Little Arthur, Freda, and Joy had to stay at the manor.

I decided that I would learn a few phrases in the local tongues for the stage and speak only English in private. Arabic, as you may know, is a little different every place you go. I could compare it to walking into a bar and meeting a guy from Liverpool, Chicago, and Sydney. They all will be speaking the same language, but it will be hard for one to know what the other is saying. They can recognize the words but the way they are used and the accents they have will be very confusing. When a man speaks in Arabic, he gives up his country and his tribe. Being part Lebanese, I would be expected to say something at some time to someone in the local dialect.

Give Me Shelter

Before 2006, Beirut was called the Paris of the Middle East. That was before the Lebanon War, the Israel-Hezbollah War, the July War or the Second Lebanon War, depending where you were from and whose side you were on. The place has seen many wars and conflicts in its 5000 year history. But the 2006 War hurt the tourism industry very badly. It was not until 2009 that they were able to recover. It did not however, hurt their ability to play and enjoy live music.

I needed to have my game face on. Many of Arabia's greatest singers and musicians were discovered in this town. The giants of the industry have walked these streets since the ending of World War II. It's the kind of place that draws the best of the best in the music world. So, the phrase "go big or stay home" came to mind as I stepped down from the private plane on that Sunday morning. I knew that I was not going to beat these people at their own game. I had to do something completely different.

If you have ever seen any of the musical performances out of Lebanon, you would have noticed that the shows are grand, to say the least. From Pop to Traditional, the artist will overwhelm the audience with a lot of flash, color, and flair. Anything less than that would be disappointing. That is not to say that these people don't appreciate good classic Jazz, Blues, Rap, and Rock-and-Roll shows too, but a slamming show in Beirut could set you up for the rest of your life. Your fan base would expand one hundred fold. So, I had to really "bring it on".

The first thing I did after checking into our hotel and booking a city tour, was to give a respectful phone call to the managers of local sensations Nancy Ajgram (Goodwill Ambassador for UNICEF), Fadl Shaker (Palestinian/Lebanon Super Star), and Nabeelah El Nejem (The Darling of the Stage). We were booked at the "Strange Fruit" on Tuesday and the "Blue Note" on Saturday night. They didn't compare to the size of Fantasy Island but both places catered to a Jazz audience and were highly respected, so I was hoping that I could convince one of those three to come watch our show. I also sent them my live DVD that was, as they say, hot off the press. Then I called my little brother.

We added a little fire, glitter (not at the same time), lights, and more video screens to the first show. The screens that were placed around the hall flashed cool colors and pictures that made patterns. They mostly magnified me as I moved about but the Sisters, Twister, and any soloist, also got plenty of camera time. I thought they were best used in my story time. Pictures of people and places would appear as I spoke. I would point in a direction and an image would appear on the wall of my choosing.

The fire was used to convey the emotions of the songs. An intensely sung word would make them erupt a little. A high note would make the flame blaze high in the air. The flame could also change colors depending on the feel of that song. It was a nice effect, but we didn't want to overdo it. After all, the singing and the music were the main focus of the show.

The colored spotlights and cameras were linked with the video screens and helped make the real visual effects. Sometimes they would simply light up the stage. At other times they would focus just on me to give the illusion that I was the only one in the room. At three times during the show, the lights would come up and reveal a complete set change.

A true visionary, James had proved his Jazz Distraction method and created a new Neo sound with a sexy image to deliver it. Now, with the use of lights, pictures, tech, and this new vocal background sound, the dynamics of the show had sweetened even more. Although it was not what you would call "in Jazz forte", we could almost compete with any of the big Rock-n-Roll, Rap, and the Arabic shows.

The Tuesday evening show at the Strange Fruit was great. It began at 2000hrs and ended just after 2200hrs. The sound was good, the lights and cameras were effective, the video screens and even the fire, all worked well. The band vibed, the Sisters shrilled, and I sang my ass off. The audience stood up from their chairs, threw flowers and gave me cloths to wipe myself. In almost every considerable way, that show went as good or better than my last show, except for the fact that I was not in 'the Zone'.

It was hard to work the crowd. I couldn't tell why. Some of the people were clearly into the sound. Some others seemed to just be into me. I think they all liked the pictures on the screen and my stories but only a few appreciated the flames. I was able to move and shift them to where they needed to be, but it took a lot of effort. I didn't have a strong connection and I had to work hard to make it a good show.

Maybe it was too early in the evening or maybe these people didn't understand the way we were portraying the music, or it could have just been my arrogance to stand in the path of legends. After all, there is a mile of distance between Billie Holiday and myself. This club was named in her honor. Billie may have lacked good management and self-discipline, but she didn't lack style. On the other hand, my style was a working mix of a lot of things (just like me). On the way back to the hotel I considered that, except for the two new songs and the vocal arrangements I was preparing with the Sisters, I was just another fake. I felt completely bummed.

I'm not saying that faking it and having no real talent can't get you famous. Just look at Madonna for example. I admit that I liked her in the beginning when she was cute and kind of sexy. She never had a good voice and it became painfully obvious that she wasn't the innocent virgin she sang about. She learned to dance and changed the act, but she used other peoples' trademark dance routines to do it. Moves from Fred Astaire and Michael Jackson kept up her popularity and for a time it worked. Now she has a good old fashion Burlesque Show and her old fans are not invited to attend. None of it was new or artistic but she made a whole lot of money and set her mark on the industry.

In the car I started to feel real sad about my contribution to Jazz and music in general. The girls saw that I was troubled and didn't know what to think of me. In their mind, we just had a great show. "How could you be so disappointed?" I later discovered that many artists feel this same way after a show.

At the hotel we discussed the matter and came up with an idea. The Sisters would work with me and use their talents to enhance our sound. Using my voice as the anchor they would sing above, below, and around me. The Sisters knew a lot about the gospel style and they began to work with me on a few Acapella exercises, when the phone rang.

It was after midnight and we were all dead tired but when Annette handed me the phone, something inside me told me to say, "hello." Nabeelah El Nejem wanted to have coffee with me at 1100hrs in the restaurant of our hotel. That night I found it hard to stay asleep.

I had to consider it an honor to have coffee with the Darling of the Stage. I didn't know what to expect or what she wanted. I wondered if I should bring a gift but what could I possibly give her. I talked it over with the girls and they voted to give her my hat.

Twister brought over a hat I wore at the beach once. I am not a hat person, but Twister loved that thing and bugged me about putting it on when we would lay out in the sun. She thought that for a girl, the next best thing to high heel shoes was a big floppy hat. Twister had planned to get a board and hit the waves at some point and wanted nothing more than to see me waving at her, wearing my hat. She was funny that way.

The hat was a beige colored, medium soft, extra-large 7 inch wide brim. It was packable, crushable and could pop back to shape with no effort. With my hair down and the hat on, it gave me a Southern feel and looked real nice around the contours of my face. The only reason that Twister allowed us to give it away was because I promised to wear the next one she gave me.

Annette and I arrived in the lobby at about 1030hrs. We saw some media people on the way to the restaurant, but they didn't seem to notice us as we walked past. Battle Angel stayed in the lobby, but Twister stopped just inside the entrance. Inside, we found the place to be about half full of people. The door man walked us straight over to a table that was reserved. Ten minutes later, the lady herself came in. It was a good thing we were early.

There were three times as many media following her than we saw earlier. She too, had an assistant and we four lightly hugged each other and did the two-cheek kiss as the photographers snapped away. She gave me a shiny emerald gown, some auto-graphed photos, and DVDs. I gave her my autographed photo and the hat.

I told her that the best place to wear that hat was at Muscle Beach, Santa Monica, and I invited her to come and visit LA. In Arabic, she told me that she had the gown made from the hour-glass body measurements listed on my web site. In Arabic I shyly answered, "I didn't know that I had a web site." Everyone laughed.

In front of the cameras she told me that she wanted me to wear the gown tomorrow night when I sang with her newly discovered prodigy Aleaha Al Hajjar at the Sky Bar. She had me hold the dress in front of my body as the men took their snaps before she asked them all to leave us alone.

After they had gone she spoke to me in English. "As a sister I must tell you that you have to choose a direction. I see your show and I am confused as to what you are doing." She was very frank. "You are not Rock. You are not Disco. What are you?"

"I am Jazz with a funk beat," I answered. "But you can slow dance with it."

She sighed, "I can hear the Jazz and the Funk, but I see Rock-n-Roll. You have fire and glitter. What is that? I can say that I love your outfits and I think that the video screen works well for you. I would have you change into Pop. If you like Jazz so much you can come back to it. Pop is short-lived and for the young, but it makes a lot of money for you. Jazz will never completely die so you can always fall back to it later in life." I told her that I was going to stay with Jazz but as far as the act was concerned, she was dead on the money. She continued with, "Your web site also said that you don't drink alcohol or take drugs. Is that right?"

"I could drink one beer every now and again, but I have bad reactions to that stuff. I will never be a drug user like some of the other entertainers."

"That is good to know if we are going to be friends, yes?" And then, more directly, "Are you a Lesbian, no?" I told her yes, and that the big girl in the corner was my lover, friend, and protector. "Have you ever been with a man?" I told her no, and I also told her that I had no intentions to ever try it. Then she said, "I understand that you are missing your parents and that is why they say you are always very sad." I said nothing. "It's OK, I understand that feeling, but at some point, it must pass, or it will kill your prettiness."

She talked about her young niece, Aleaha. She was an 18 year old, beautiful and talented girl, that would one day be a great star. She had a five octave range and could sing multiple styles. With perfect pitch, she could solo, harmonize, and back, to most any song. The girl could dance, play piano, flute, and the harp. Her only problem was that she was uncontrollably wild and had a tendency to break into a tantrum from time to time. (Sounded like she needed to be spanked and put to bed, but I didn't say that).

At 14, she was drinking, smoking, having sex with two different boys, and she had been caught using some drugs. For that reason, her famous aunt delayed exposing her talents for as long as she could. Now the girl was threatening to file a suit for the control of her career. The press would have been bad for the Darling of the Stage, so she agreed to set her up, but only if she behaved.

This little notice promo tomorrow night was to be her big test. If the girl could pull off an incident free performance, she would send her with me to Dubai for another promo. On the other hand, if the girl screwed it up, I got the impression that the Super Star would be forced to dispose of her in some sad way that the press could turn in the Darling's favor. For my services, I would be widely promoted throughout the Arabic Jazz community. I found that I had already been obligated and there was no use opting to even think about this deal before agreeing. I felt shanghaied.

The Darling had recently been in contact with one of my Lebanese family elders that had already agreed to this plan. He and I would split a small percentage of Aleaha's first two record sales. It wasn't a bad deal, but I didn't like doing business that way. Nabeelah suggested that I see the man and discuss the details, but I was so disgusted that I never did. It was typical Middle Eastern thinking on his part. Later, I had Annette call and tell him that if anyone ever made another deal without my permission again, I would not sue them in court, I would just make them disappear. The family was greatly offended but they never did that again.

Nabeelah told me, "Tomorrow, you will do some pop for me. If you don't like it, you will never have to do it again." We had to open and close with a duet. She gave me a notebook of songs and asked me to choose two of Aleaha's repertoire. We would only do a total of six tunes. After that first song, she would walk off and I would sing, then we would switch and end together. It would be like tag teaming the crowd. The two solo songs could be of our own choosing as long as they were considered a Pop arrangement.

I knew right away that this kid I'd be dealing with would consider this to be a contest of some kind. Her aunt may have been thinking the very same thing. I already knew that the kid could out-do me talent wise. I had to be smarter. Surprisingly, I saw the greatest Stones song ever recorded, "Gimme Shelter" on the list. We would open with that one. To close I chose "Alone" by Heart.

Nabeelah told me that she was fed up with her niece. She could live with the girl falling flat on her face on stage but if I were to motivate her to do well, she would be grateful. Getting the kid straightened out was a fantasy. The kid getting pregnant and hooked on drugs was closer to reality. If I could somehow steer her away from that, Nabeelah would be in my debt.

She questioned why I was not staying with my family in Lebanon and spoke of a man she knew that would be perfect for me if I was interested. I was not, on both accounts.

As we stood to go, I gave her a warning. "If this kid gets in my face, my friend may have to hurt her."

"Beat her!" she laughed. "I give you the permission. It's something that should have been done when she was little. It may be too late now, and her friends will most likely kill her before her drugs can. I feel, how do you say, I should wash my hands from her. So long as she can sing, do what you must."

I gathered the girls and the band at a studio Nabeelah had set up about a kilometer from the Sky Bar. I set up the meet with Aleaha at 1800hrs. We were to go over our duets and get to know each other, so when the girl walked in with her entourage at 1925hrs, I was pissed. They were talking loudly and had beers in their hands. Except for the hair colors, they were dressed like someone had broken into the wardrobe locker from the 1979 movie "The Warriors". And all of them wore the outfits two sizes too small. If I weren't so angry, I would have laughed.

The Sisters and I were working on a vocal arrangement when the five of them came crashing through the door. The three men were in their early 30s and the other girl must have been about 16. Standing by the door in their outfits, smoking cigarettes, they looked just like the kind of people that Nabeelah was telling me about. However, it was hard to tell which one was the more corrupting influence on the other. They were just as loud as they were arrogant. The girls and I were forced to stop what we were doing on account of their racket.

The little drunken girl dropped her bottle. Then she began to crush the broken pieces beneath her boots as she loudly talked to one of the long-haired guys. The other two guys were almost yelling at each other and physically acting out some fight scene from a movie. Aleaha was probably the most drunk of them all. She made her way to the middle of the room and started calling my name. She wanted to know who I thought I was, to try and run her show. "Tomorrow night will be my time to shine not yours." The little tramp was calling me out. She was trying to punk me in front of my own crew.

After a moment or two of shock and disgust, I walked up to Aleaha. I introduced myself and told her that I had something very special for her in the dressing room. I told her that it was something she had never seen before and that I had brought it all the way from London, England. I had to take her by the wrist in order to lead her away from her friends. As I passed Battle Angel, I used a hidden hand signal ordering her to throw the others out.

On the way to the dressing room, the girl kept asking what I had for her. She said that she doubted I would be able to show her anything that she had not already seen. The kid knew something was up. She pulled her hand away and stated, "Whatever it is, I just don't want it!" I informed her that she was going to get it anyway and pushed her inside the changing room. You can imagine how shocked she was as she went tripping into the lockers.

I took a handful of her bleached blonde and pink striped hair in one hand and slapped her three times in the face with the other. She tried to hit me back but a tighter grip of that rat's nest put a stop to that. She cried and cursed me in English, Arabic, and French. I slapped her again and told her to stop. I told her, "you are late", and I slapped her again. I told her, "you were drinking before a rehearsal", and I slapped her one more time. I told her, "you will not see those tight pants people ever again", and I slapped her some more.

I explained that as long as she would know me, she was going to do what I said, or I would be slapping her face again. For starters, she was going to stay away from boys, drugs, and alcohol. I broke the news that the only thing between her and a shallow grave, was me. I warned, "If you blow this show for us, I will beat you slowly to death." I then demanded that she wipe her sorry face and be on that platform singing our first song in five minutes or she would see the other side of my hand. (Not lady like, I admit).

When I returned to the hall, Aleaha's fan club was in the final stages of getting their psychopathic asses kicked. Battle Angel and two of the band members, (Freddy B and Tom Tom) were kicking the three men in their butts while they were crawling along the floor on the way to the door. Twister had just tossed the female out by grabbing her by her leather jacket and flinging her outside into the alley. As the three others made their way close to the door, they too, were snatched up and tossed out near some trash cans and a dumpster.

Aleaha came around the corner just as the last man was being thrown out. Someone made the comment, "Any more trash?" and everyone turned to look in her direction. I pointed to my watch and the kid moved quickly to the stage. The child's face was already starting to bruise a little, but it didn't stop her from singing.

Aleaha had a flawless CD mix of all the songs she was prepared to sing. She handed it to Tito for inspection. He decided that the arrangements the band had been working on were better, so we went with ours. Besides, Stanley "the Guitar" Smith was dying to work that solo part on "Gimme Shelter".

On that one, the Sisters did the backings and all of the "Ooh" stuff. Aleaha and I went with a tag team approach to the verses. We all sang together on the chorus and I let Aleaha hit all the high parts. Tomorrow we would do this with lights flashing, a bunch of war sound effects, and smoke. It was to be the eye opener to start the show. On "Alone" we sang in unison while the Sisters backed us with a dramatic choir-like sound. It was powerful.

I figured the girl would want to keep her other songs a secret. She was going to sing them right off the CD anyway, so there was no need to waste anymore of our time. I went over "Blue Bayou" and "Natural Woman", with the Sisters and the band. I told Aleaha to pick a single color for her hair and made her promise to meet me at the club at 1700hrs for a sound check, and again at 2100hrs to get ready for our show. I left the studio at around 2300hrs that night, but Tito let her go early. (She needed to fix her face).

We had booked a tour of the city for Wednesday morning that included a lunch. I normally try to relax on the day of a show but at the time I had no idea that I would have to perform this night. I had never been to Lebanon and I really wanted to see some of the 5000 years of history, so I decided to go anyway. It's not like Twister, Battle Angel, and I, would be climbing a mountain or anything and we'd be back in time to take a nap before I was needed at the club. Besides, I had promised all the girls that they could shop on this day, so everybody was doing something.

The three of us met the limo driver and our guide in the lobby just after 0900hrs. We drove around the city and had visited a couple museums before we decided to opt for the quick version and take in an early lunch. We sat outside in the warm breezy air and looked out onto the Mediterranean Sea. We had a good view of the famous Roche Sea Rock also known as Lover's Rock, or Suicide Rock.

The rocky cliffs around the shore give the appearance that at some point a great bit of the land was snatched away and pulled into the water. I thought about the amazing feats of history that took place in this part of the world and how the blood in my veins tied me to those events closer than anyone currently living in this town. I had come home, in a sense. I could live here inside the footprint of Alexander if I had the chance.

The others saw that I was in thought and talked amongst themselves. In their view, I was zoning out again and they were used to seeing me do that from time to time. Most of those times, I was shuffling and reviewing files back and forth, but on that day, I was just fantasizing.

I got up to go to the restroom. I never did get used to the fact that women in general need to pee a lot more than men. By design, I have a tendency to release a lot of fluid and that includes perspiration. I can easily drink a gallon of water before the end of the day, just to compensate. Don't get me wrong, my enhancements make the experience an enjoyable one, still, it annoys me that I have to stop what I'm doing, walk around the corner, pull up my skirt, and sit on the potty umpteen times every doggone day.

When I emerged from the stall, I expected to see people in that restroom. I did hear them talking and moving about. What I didn't expect was to have someone toss a white tablecloth over me and a needle stuck in my hip. I would have liked to see the look on my face. I woke a short time later still wrapped in the cloth with my wrist and ankles tied, lying on what seemed to be a stone floor.

I knew this feeling of disorientation all too well. I wanted to rest for a while to gather myself, but the one-way cell phone conversation I could hear in the distance, was motivation enough to get me moving.

In English, the Lebanese man in the front of the cave was trying to work a deal for 100,000 Euros. The other person was attempting to talk him down to 60,000 but this guy was a hard negotiator. He talked about my age, hair, face, teeth, and body type, like he was selling a horse.

The only light in this dimly lit cave came from one direction, and that was where the voice was coming from. Behind me was a void. My left leg was still quite numb from the shot, so hopping past him was out of the question. I thought it best to crawl.

My wrists were tied tight in the front of me. It hurt quite a bit to do it, but once I found a rough enough piece of stone, I was able to saw through the rope in less than 30 seconds. After I got my legs free, I crawled deeper into the darkness. I saved the cut pieces of rope and tied them together. This would be my first weapon. (SERE Training). Except for that, I had nothing else to work with. My shoes were missing, and I wasn't wearing a bra that day, so all I had was my white cut off top, cream panties, and a short skirt of purple and red flowers.

The darkness enveloped me. I could hear moving water someplace close by, my feet were wet, and I could smell the salty sea in the air. I would hate to fall into a hole that took me into an underground stream or something. I moved as far back as I dared to and waited to start feeling better.

As I expected, the phone guy saw that I had moved and was now using his cell phone light to track me. I didn't go past him, so this was the only other place I could have gone. As he came closer, I saw that I was wrong about the water. Behind me, was a great bubbling pool that was slowly filling the area. It answered the question of why the cold water had so suddenly risen over my ankles. "High tide", I thought to myself. I couldn't stay there much longer. I barely felt 60%, but I was out of time.

The man nervously waved the phone around in the air. The light gave him a short distance but while he was outside in the daylight, my eyes had adjusted to the dark. To me, that tiny light was more like a lighthouse beacon. The flip phone timed out every 30 seconds. He was forced to flip it closed and open it again every time. All I had to do was stay far enough away from him until the light went out one more time.

I moved when he moved, and the bubbling water also helped to mask my steps. At knee level the water was starting to push my body and I found the opening to the underground river with my toes. The phone went dead, and I reached out to him with my readymade garrote when the phone lit up on its own. It was an incoming call.

It was too late to retreat. When the phone rang I was almost on top of him and he saw a part of me. I dashed up as fast as I could, in a sidestep motion. I lifted one arm over his head so that I could twist the rope across his neck and got behind him. The man was bigger than me, but I had surprise on my side.

It was understandable. In a crises situation, most men will run or fight. It's that simple. Most women, on the other hand, will run, cry, or freeze. Untrained and frightened females rarely ever attack and if they do it's mostly just a reflex and never anything with deadly force. The majority of girls would have never gotten out of the rope. My captor knew all of this, and that knowledge lead to his undoing.

Once the rope was on him, I fell forward and pushed him into the water to take away his strength and height advantage. With me behind him, his strong arms were all but useless. He needed both hands to try to keep his head out of the water, but he also needed those same hands to try and free himself from the choke hold. As he fought me to take a breath, all he could get was water. I put my knees into his back, crossed the rope, and pulled until he stopped kicking. It took about a minute.

It wasn't the first time I killed a man in hand-to-hand combat. Other men may have other feelings about it, but I never felt that I was Gods' gift to war. I would be lying if I said that I never felt a hint of euphoria in the heat of a battle. I had a knack for survival and each time I killed, I chalked it up to training and experience. But this time was different.

I felt powerful. An 18 year old girl in a flowered skirt had just killed her would-be kidnapper and slaver by strangling him with the rope she was bound with. I was exhausted, but my mind and body were back to 100%.

The phone had disappeared and with it, the light. I checked the body for money or papers before feeling my way back to a dryer spot, but the water followed me. After bumping into the walls and falling a few times, I was able to find my way back to where I left the tablecloth. It was even darker now. The buyer was certainly on his way, and there was no telling how far the water was going to rise.

As I emerged from the cave, I saw headlights coming down the hill. The setting sun was in his eyes, so it was easy to move from the entrance unseen. I got behind a large stone and watched as the very big man popped the trunk and honked the horn before getting out of the black Bentley Continental Super Sport. I could have tried to sneak past the man, but I had no idea where I was. I needed that key.

This European man was way too big to wrestle to the ground. It was better to hit him in the head with a stone. He was already out of breath as he walked past me yelling for his contact to come out of the cave, so he could see what he was paying for. I found it too easy to get behind him with a good-sized rock as my second weapon.

I lifted the rock over my head and I ran up to him. Using a slanted stone on the way, I launched myself into the air for the extra force of gravity and came down on the back of his unsuspecting head. The popping sound preceded a splash of clear liquid. The man went down in front of me but was trying to crawl into the cave to get away. I was forced to hit him four more times before he was finally dead. "And that's the name of that tune", I felt moved to say out loud. I checked his body for money and papers and found a gun, before the smell of his blood and cranial fluids caused me to throw-up on him.

It was the second time in less than a month that I had someone else's blood all over me, but it was only the first time that I ever killed anybody with a rock. I was also 2 for 2 when it came to throwing-up on dead bodies and I found it kind of funny that I was leaving a trail of puke with them across the globe.

I checked the car and found a blanket, more rope, what looked like a dog collar attached to a leash, a red ball mouth gag, and a leather bag of 50,000 Euros. I also found other notes and papers. My Arabic reading was never any good but from what I could piece together, the big man already had me sold to some guy in Greece, but the trail led back to Aleaha. She was to get a finder's fee of 50,000. The guy in the cave was trying to alter the deal. I think the big guy was going to kill him.

The time was 2035hrs and according to the onboard navigator, I could still make the show with time to spare. I put the gun, the gag, and the collar in the bag, wrapped my shivering self in the blanket, and took the car for a drive. It took about five minutes to discover how to adjust the seat, but after that I was good to go.

On the way back into town I thought about the incident and tried to convince myself that I didn't enjoy it. A girl, an artist, an aristocrat, should not have these "power rush" feelings. Then again, I used what was available and I adapted my past training to the situation. I doubt your average debutante would have been able to get away with only a busted lip. Still, I needed to clear the blood and carnage out of my head as best I could. I wasn't that same old person anymore. I was Jasmine now. A good shower would clear my mind and my body. At least, that's what I thought.

I ditched the car a few miles from the hotel and jumped into a taxi. It was only then that I discovered that my top and skirt were torn in several places. There was still the question of what to do with Aleaha. I didn't want to kill her. No, I take that back. I did want to kill her but decided that it would be a bad idea. That kid needed to be taught a lesson and I was just the one that could take her back to Grammar School 101.

I met Annette in the room and had her call Sophie to cancel whatever she was working on to find me. Uncle Lloyd demanded to hear my voice and know that I was OK. After speaking with him, I called Twister and told her not to let Aleaha out of her sight. Our backup plan has always been: work for resolution of the situation but continue normal operations unless otherwise instructed. The band would be at the club. I took a quick shower and hurried out.

All the shower did was get my body clean. Just as the taste of my own blood was in my mouth, the feel of the slaver's blood was still on my skin. Worse than that, I couldn't shake the rage. I thought that I was controlling it quite well, but everyone that knew me could sense that I might explode at any second.

By the time I got into the club it was 2213hrs. Aleaha was ending her first song, "Piece of my Heart" by Joplin, and the kid was tearing it up. As she started "You Ought a Know" by Alanis

Morissette, Twister marked me and helped me get backstage where I got the band ready for the Rolling Stones. I changed in a flash and walked out into the smoke, lightning, fire, and thunder of one of many Vietnam memories.

She had told the audience that I was delayed and that she would be performing alone tonight. Naturally, the girl was surprised when, instead of her next song, "Zombie" by the Cranberries, the lights dropped, and the unmistakable guitar intro of "Gimme Shelter" started up. The kid wanted to run past me, but I grabbed her arm and started to sing. As the lights flashed and the gun sounds cracked, we sang the tune like an argument and the crowd went into a frenzy. We were both on fire.

At the end of the song I pulled Aleaha behind the curtain. I signaled Tito to stall with an introduction and an invitation to our Jazz show on Saturday night. Twister grabbed our little friend and held her still. I couldn't resist punching her one good time in the guts before I was cued to go back on.

I was supposed to do "Blue Bayou" by Ronstadt, but after that last song, I knew that it wouldn't click. So, I went with my tried and tested method. I calmed things down by talking about the singer of the next song. I told them all that "I'm really a Jazz singer, but when it comes to Pop music I only ever had one hero." I told them that my parents were planning to surprise me with a stage front ticket but before they could give it to me they were killed in the vehicle accident. A month later, the singer himself died and my tears were shared around the world. So, when the anniversary of that hurtful time came around each year, I thought of this song and how comforting it was to know that I was not the only one crying.

The folks did buy the ticket, so it was at least partly true. The girls and I had planned to use this as a backup after hearing the remixed version Aleaha had stored on her flash drive. As soon as I sang the first words of "Cry" by Michael Jackson, I knew I had successfully sold the idea to the crowd. We posted the King of Pop photos on the screens and people that knew the song began to sing it with me. The men held their lighters in the air while all the women cried. (It was the first time I have ever had that happen).

The vibe was with us, and I was back into 'the Zone'. Without a setup I went right into "Natural Woman" by Franklin, with just the Sisters and Jarvis on the synthesized horns and strings as we had rehearsed. The Sisters were fantastic and for that moment I felt like I was Ms Aretha herself. The feeling was so intense that we all cried at some point in that song. A man reached up and handed me a box of tissues that I shared with Lila, Twyla, and Jarvis. He too, was crying.

Aleaha was shoved back out for the finale, "Alone", and I have to say she floated right into the flow. Twister had her in an arm-lock for two songs and my setup, and I knew that my punch to the stomach hurt her a lot. But when it came time for her to sing, the kid was awesome. She was a truly gifted girl.

The crowd was screaming and on its feet. We hugged and gave each other a kiss on the cheek before slowly making our way to the back of the set. We had pulled off a very successful show even though it did not go precisely as either of us had planned. Nabeelah would be pleased. The kid's CD would have a fan base and I would be formally introduced to the Arab music scene. It was now time to give this girl the full attention she deserved.

As I mentioned once before, everyone must be made aware that there are consequences for their actions. (You are responsible for what you do). That's part of life and an undeniable truth in this world. Maybe this kid wanted to get me back for slapping her around and having her friends beat up, and I can understand that. The reason she was slapped in the first place was because she broke the rules of professional behavior that James taught me. I tried to tell her something about that in her own lingo but for my efforts she unsuccessfully sold me to a slaver. I had no choice but to invoke the rule of law upon her.

When I was a young jeep (know-nothing-new-guy), a wise man took me under his wing and taught me a philosophy he called the Five Rules of Life. He told me that once I fully understood them, I would have the power to control my own destiny. The Rules were passed to him many years ago and it was only then that he felt a need to pass them to someone else. Before he could tell me the Rules, I had to swear not to forget that they were sacred and that I should only share them with others who were worthy to use them wisely and for the greater good of all mankind.

At the time I thought he was a little crazy, but he was my Sergeant and the most trusted individual I had found, so I gave my oath. Two days later he was killed by a sniper, while on patrol. I never forgot him or the Five Rules. Since there is a good possibility that I will be dead before I can pass them on the way he would have wished, I am opting for that "greater good of all mankind" now, so here goes.

(1) Life is a bitch. It's a cold fact but it doesn't have to stop you if you have the guts to deal with it.

(2) War is hell. If it's not, then it's the next best thing. It just may take everything to survive it. Maybe your mind and your soul.

(3) People are unfair. Expect to be fucked over at some point by everyone for no particular reason.

(4) East is East, West is West, and pussy ain't got no face. (Or, it is what it is). Knowing this fact could save you a lot of money, trouble, and time. You may have to settle for what you can get, and you may find that it's not so bad after all.

(5) Payback is a motherfucker! Expect the worse possible outcome when you screw with someone. Bring the worse possible outcome when someone screws with you or suffer the consequences of giving them the opportunity to make it even more painful the next time.

That was the short and less philosophical version. At first it sounded silly and stupid. But the guy assured me that if I thought about them and applied them appropriately and generously only when needed, I would see the truth in them just as he and the men before him had seen. The man had never steered me wrong.

In my book, this little chick had fucked up twice. First for fucking with me, and second for fucking with ME! Not to mention the fact that I liked that cute little skirt. I told Battle Angel to stuff that piece of trash in the car and bring her unnoticed into my hotel room.

The hotel lobby was full of media. Pictures were taken, autographs had to be signed, and all kinds of questions were asked. I shyly told them that I was tired but that I loved the people of Beirut. "Please come and see me sing Jazz at the Blue Note on Saturday night", I said as we hurried through.

I was in the shower when Annette brought me the phone. Nabeelah was on the line and needed to speak to me right away. She thanked me for a great performance and said she would now honor her end. I told her about her niece's friends and the 50,000 Euro deal. (I said nothing about the killings or the location). "Aleaha has been very bad, and I need to teach her how to behave like a professional," I told her.

"She is of my blood," the lady told me. "So, I must insist that she will not be damaged to the point that she cannot sing. Keep her and train her if you can. It will be good to have peace in my home for a time, but I must have her back in two months to record. If you still need her, you can always have her. That will be her debt to you. Do this for me and I will, how you say, sweeten the deal." She gave me 30% managing rights for my trouble and arranged to send Aleaha's bags to our hotel.

An hour later, a courier arrived with a contract that, among other things, stated that the deal would be off if the girl was hooked on drugs or pregnant, under my watch. I signed it. A half hour later, Battle Angel arrived disguised as a cleaner with our other package stuffed inside a laundry cart.

You Got Your Mind Right?

Battle Angel wanted her dead. She was as pissed off as I was. And I had a feeling that Twister would beat her to death one day when I wasn't around to stop her. It took some doing but I convinced the ladies that the kid just needed to be reprogrammed. I told them that Aleaha was just too full of herself and that "a full glass can hold no more". I decided that we would break this kid down by way of abuse. I told my friends that we would treat her like a dog until we felt that she somehow earned the right to be treated a little better. It wasn't as satisfying as pushing her off the building might have been, but it was the best idea at the time.

What I didn't say was that I planned to use a regiment of extended, nonlethal, psychological breakdown techniques designed to strip away any mental defenses. This is a long studied and practiced art, used by militaries for extracting information from your most dangerous enemies. This part of the information gathering phase can last for weeks or even years before the first real question is asked and may continue long after all usefulness is obtained. The subject will at some point realize that everything is lost to them and that this is now their new hopeless reality. After this, you now have the option of reprograming. (Remember Abu Ghraib).

That night, I started by showing Battle Angel and Twister why waterboarding is "officially" deemed illegal by the US government. She quickly blamed the kidnapping on one of her friends who had a connection to the slaver. His name matched the credentials I had taken off the first man in the cave. That was all the information I needed to fill the gaps in the plot, but I continued to board her in the bathtub for a while longer. I told her that she needed to be punished for her behavior and she actually agreed with me.

We then tore her clothes off and turned them into strips of cloth. With the strips, we hogtied her. After that, we colored her hair bright red, jammed the ball gag in her mouth, and locked her in the closet wet and naked for the rest of the night.

This gag was a waffle gag. It's so easy to justify my learning these things from the internet, so I was able to show the girls that this type of gag is used to keep your slave from choking to death. The little holes in it ensure that the person can breathe even if her nose is blocked with snot from crying. This gag's main purpose is for humiliation and not silence. A person can still make noises, but they will be completely unintelligible.

The ball must be stuffed or jammed into the mouth. It's too big to be swallowed and it's held in place by a strap that wraps tightly around the head to prevent removal by the wearer. The wearer's jaws are now forced wide open and the subject will drool uncontrollably, especially when she attempts to speak. When hands are tied out of reach, this person will not be able to wipe their face and will drool over themselves and anything that is below the mouth.

For the humiliation to be the most effective, the person must be made to see the drool run off their face onto a floor, table or a mirror. You may also find success with the feel of it dripping on their own body. Being forced to watch themselves this way in the mirror is one of the best breaking methods for new slaves according to many websites the girls found.

They also discovered that the ball and ring gags are used as a training device. It forces the person to get used to holding their mouth open wide for an extended period of time. This is a plus when training your slaves to perform oral sex with multiple partners. The average person could get lockjaw after a while causing her muscles to stiffen and clamp shut. But a trained slave could keep her mouth open all night. I knew that if I had not escaped, I would have been enrolled in that training program before I ever got out of the slaver's car.

At around 1000hrs I let the girl out for a bowl of water. The ladies didn't want her to dehydrate. I kept the gag on her, so she had to put her face in the bowl to suck the water into her mouth through the holes in the ball. She choked a lot, but she learned how to do it. I kept her hands behind her back with those same pieces of torn cloth.

We all called her a dog and renamed her Little Bit. She was not allowed to stand up but could walk on her knees and lay down on the carpet. She was not allowed to use the toilet like a person either. Instead, she had to go out on the terrace to pee and poop on a newspaper. We took turns training her by making her come when called, sit, and roll over. If she was slow, cried, or flat out refused to do the tricks, she was swatted in the face with a newspaper or one of my flip flops. When she was good, we patted her on the head and called her a "good dog". When she was bad, I got Twister to pull her over her lap and spank her bare ass with her hands.

We did other humiliating things to her. Since her hands were kept behind her back, she could not crawl or balance herself. So, Angel had a lot of fun pushing her and laughing when she flopped over. The worst thing may have been the way we made her come over to one of us and rub her head on our arms or hands to let us know that she needed to be let outside to go to the bathroom. Whichever one of us felt mercy for her would have to get the leash, some plastic and newspaper so we could walk her out and watch her do her business, then clean it up. For us, this was the worst part of the dog training, so we would often make her hold it for a long time. If she couldn't hold it and was forced to go on the carpet, she was called a "bad dog" and got spanked again.

The kid was pretty tough in the beginning. We slapped and spanked her for a long time before she decided to behave. At about 1600hrs she broke down and cried for the first time. She needed to pee and refused to go through the routine of asking permission to be let outside. After holding it for hours she got the idea that we were not going to give into her grunts and noises, so she finally went to a corner and proceeded to relieve herself on the carpet and the wall. In a flash, Twister snatched her up by her hair and spanked what was left of the piss, out of her.

We were going to relax this day, but we spent it torturing the kid instead. We took a lot of pictures of everything she did. And I mean everything. She was a heavy drooler, so we let her drink a lot of water, but we didn't wash her or feed her at all, that first day. At night, she went back in the closet with a sheet to cover herself. She would sleep in the dark.

It was hard to get used to a naked dribbling girl slinking around on her knees. I kept reminding myself about what she tried to do to me and after a while the sight became more comfortable. Twister on the other hand was highly aroused by it. She took me to the bed four times that day and wiped me out completely. That, in the end, helped to make a crack in the stress and I was able to focus a lot better.

Nabeelah was already beginning to fulfill her end of the bargain. The media raved about the first show like it was a smash even though it was not. The promo show was so much better, but they compared it to the likes of U2 when they were in town (Bullshit). They were already predicting that Saturday's show would need to be moved to a bigger venue due to the turn out. I knew that it was all just spin, but it was working. The band had to move to another hotel, so they could get out and see the city without being mobbed. Angel, Twister, Annette, me, and our dog, were moved to the penthouse for better security.

We got quite a lot of phone calls and messages that day and the staff slipped all kinds of notes under the doors of all our rooms. I only took one call from a TV station that said that they would play the pirated video of the MJ song all day or until I called to say hello. I told them that I loved them all and to come see me at the Blue Note. I also said, "This is only for people that really love Jazz." They did ask about Aleaha and they thought that she was great, but no one asked to speak to her.

That night I dreamed of the man that brings destruction. If everything has a name, then his must be the Destroyer. I don't remember much about the last time I saw him. I had a bad fever and was drugged for a few days, but I was told that I did have a wild dream. The one I had this night was very clear and a little different.

Things started out pretty much as they always have except for the unmistakable feeling that I had missed some small but important detail. It was like missing the season ending episode of a series of TV shows. I think that in the earlier dream the Destroyer was beginning to get too close to me and I had decided to move, because in this dream I was now walking away from him. The pace was faster than I normally walk.

As I mentioned before, the man had formed a couple of rings of fire around me, so I had no choice but to head towards the flames. Seeing this, the man changed his path too and was now in a direct line behind me. I jumped into and through the first ring and found to my surprise, scenes of some of the places I have been since my rebirth.

I saw myself tiptoeing down the halls of the Georgia hospital and then crawling in the airducts of the mall and more. As I moved from one scene to the next, I looked behind to see the last scene burn up as soon as I left. I woke thinking that at some point I would have to confront this man, but I had no idea what would happen if I did. I soaked the sheets and the mattress that night, with sweat.

The next day we had a show to do but I was determined to get Little Bit's training underway. The plan was to retrain her on how to behave by first identifying what she had been doing wrong. I used the mirror technique I had read about online and forced her to look at herself while we berated and spanked her. We gave her no food this day either, but she did get milk, juice, and more water to drink. She could have used a bath too, but we decided to wait until she was riper.

The drugs, drinking, smoking, and the sex with all the boys were proof that she had no respect for herself or her body. We told her that she had strained the relationship with her family and was on the brink of being put to death. The way she was wasting her talents and the disrespect she had for the spirit of music, was most unacceptable. For those reasons we had stripped her of her dignity. But trying to have me enslaved was something personal. She now owed me more than she could ever repay. More than one rule applied in this case, but Rule # 5 was highlighted.

We left Angel with the "dog" while the rest of us went to the club for a 1700hrs sound check and some preparations. There were many people that had come early. They were standing, talking, and sitting on the walkway looking for tickets. Annette and Twister ran interference for me, so I could hurry inside.

We made some adjustments to the stage setup and basically scaled back to the way the show was in LA. That meant that the fire and glitter was out. I would however do more wardrobe changes and the Sisters' talents would be used a lot more. We also agreed to add more solos from the band members. Afterwards, we all snuck back to the hotel one at a time.

That night the place was packed over the capacity limit. To fill the demand for tickets the promoters rented a few smaller clubs in the area in order to stream the show. One thousand more people would now be able to enjoy the concert live via the internet. This was not the first time people paid money for a show that they didn't physically attend, but it would be the first time I would have an audience this large.

The band arrived at 2100hrs and was escorted through a side entrance. The media had every corner of the place staked out. In order to keep with the shy and mysterious image, I was made to delay my arrival until 2130hrs so that I could be snuck in while in disguise. This was made possible by the use of a planned distraction. We hired a local model to arrive by limo at the front entrance of the club. As the mob hurried to her, I slipped inside and was ushered backstage unnoticed.

The show took me to heaven and cannot be described in written words. I can say that the vibe was already present before I entered the building. It filled the club like smoke fills a room. The band and the Sisters took the crowd to new heights with a powerful mellow mood until I stepped out. Seconds before I did, the sound and lights were cut abruptly.

The next thing they heard was the first two words from the old Johnny Mathis standard in acapella, "Chances Are", before the piano, synth strings, and the band joined in one by one. A dim light spotted me. As it grew brighter it made me look as if I were materializing on stage. The long white backless gown was split and full of sequins. It made me look like a shining angel on the screens. The reflected lights shot off me to spray the darkened hall with a shower of sparkles. As the music continued to climb we all went instantly into the Zone. The rest of it was a blur.

The next thing I knew, I was headed for the car. The band was still vamping the last song as I was wrapped in a long coat and a wide floppy hat was placed on my head. Sweating like mad, I must have left a trail of water from the stage to the road. I know Annette was with me and Nabeelah had gifted some of her big bruisers to protect me, but I don't remember even seeing their faces. As I was practically carried to the roadway, the stretched limo slid into place.

I heard hands clapping and people yelling all around me. I saw flashes from cameras and the security guards pushing people out of the way. Another diversion was staged, but some of the people were wise to it this time and I lost my hat to a souvenir seeking fan. Once inside the car, I passed out and didn't wake until morning. (Someone obviously had to carry me). When I did wake, we packed everything and moved to another hotel for security reasons.

The media had gone Jasmine nuts. People surrounded our old hotel like an attacking army. The TV showed pictures of me on stage. I saw pictures of me getting in and out of the cars. They even had a picture of the girl that swiped my hat. I was starting to have some idea of what Elvis and MJ felt like. Before we left, we stuffed Little Bit in an oversized bag, wheeled her to the car, and snuck out through the service area.

On the way, Uncle Lloyd called me. He said that the Prime Minister would give me a message at dinner that needed to be passed directly to him. Whatever it was, I could not look at it and I needed to hand carry it to him after three days. I was supposed to await his call. In other words, whenever I did get the package, I needed to hold on to it. After three days' time I could then leave and head to London, not before, and not a moment after.

We could have left to go over to Dubai, but I still wanted to see this country. Besides, we had a week and a half to kill, a package to pick up, and a dog to train. Not to mention, I was wiped out.

This new lavish hotel was another one of those places that was secret to the public. The security alone was out of this world. In a well-guarded and exclusive part of the town, this monument to luxury housed diplomats and Kings. They were not happy about the girl in a bag, but all our IDs checked out, so we were allowed to proceed. This could not have been the first time that a guest brought in their own prisoner.

This was day three for Miss Little Bit. On this day we added a mush made of protein powder mixed with smashed fruit that she had to suck through the waffle ball. We continued with her mirror training and it seemed to be having some effect. We also gave her a bath. Every so often, we were untying her and massaging her arms and wrists, but the gag always stayed in place.

We had read that slavers would keep that thing in a girl's mouth sometimes for up to one month, for punishment. Once the ball was removed however the girl's first instinct is to close her mouth right away. In those first times when the jaws are relaxed they stiffen and become very painful to open again. For first timers, a few hours were all it took for her jaws to lock closed. That girl wouldn't be giving any blow jobs, but she would be quiet for the rest of that day. If she ever spoke out of turn, you just needed to point at that gag in your hand and the girl would zip it quick.

To complete her training, you would stuff the gag in her mouth many times if you wanted her to keep it open all the time.

Several hours every day over a period of time, using larger balls or rings would do the trick. To her, it would feel better to hold it open and drool, then to close it and feel the discomfort. But, that is exactly what her master wants.

But, our Little Bit was not a whore, she was an entertainer. The kid would need to be able to work the microphone in Dubai. That's why I made the removal of the gag her first reward for good behavior. What the heck. She was hitting the paper right and coming when she was called. I needed help to remove it due to the fact that it was jammed in really tight for her size mouth.

She was starting to understand what she had done to her family and herself. She knew the price of disrespecting me and what I was capable of. If it were totally up to me, I would have left her in the closet until she dehydrated on day one, but Twister convinced me to put some kind of effort into training her. She still stayed on her knees, slept in the closet and ate from a dish, her arms stayed tied behind her and she still went on the paper while wearing the dog leash. The plan was that each day she was good would be another day she came closer to becoming human again. I was far from trusting her, so I kept her closet door locked at bedtime.

The girl was crazy to begin with and the training we were giving her wasn't making her any saner. Still, the girl would do what you told her, in a flash. She was quiet, and we were teaching her to be polite. When she could talk again, she called her friends and told them that she was changing her life and that she didn't want to see them again. That act alone earned her the right to stand up straight. She had a ways to go before I would let her use the furniture, put on clothes, and go to the toilet, but it was an accomplishment. That was her day six.

We all got a chance to see the best parts of Lebanon and have some fun. Tito kept discipline by having the band meet every day for a two hour session at one place or another. We jammed at clubs and even did the U2 thing on top of a bank one night. Sometimes, we would just walk into a joint and start playing. I even did the Arab standards I had prepared. The media loved the way I showed up unannounced in and out of town.

On Tuesday night I was summoned to a meeting in one of the extra special parts of the hotel. I was told to wear light clothing and bring nothing but a plain standard briefcase. In the hallway the case and I were scanned, then searched and scanned again before I was met by CIA (US), DGSE (France), NIS (Greece), and SO 15 (British), agents. (One each). They were all business, polite, and each checked my IDs before handing me an envelope. I was told to put the four items in the briefcase before we all walked into a satellite office for the Prime Minister at the end of the hall.

The man was kind enough to ask me to sit and offer me a drink before telling me that he needed to see the case. He took out the same envelopes that the agents had given me and had his aide place them in a safe. He handed the agents another stack of forms for review that needed stamps placed on them, before passing them back to the Minister so he could put them into a thicker envelope. Once that was all done, the now sealed package was set inside another briefcase that one of the aides locked and clamped to my left wrist. The Minister then shook all our hands and let us out the door. I got the impression that he wanted this done and us out. It all took less than 10 minutes. And to think, I came hungry just for that.

This was not your normal handcuff. Looking at it, I knew I wasn't going to be able to pick or squeeze my hand out of it no matter what I tried, so I didn't even bother. I would have had to torch the short bicycle looking chain links to get it off. Of course, that would have burned my wrist in the process. I felt it was better to suffer through it.

The three days with that thing cramped my style like I didn't think possible. For starters, I had to cut that dress off my arm. The case was waterproof, but it was too cumbersome to take into the shower. The best thing I could do was set it on a table while I sat in the tub. I had to hang my arm out the whole time. I bought new outfits that would allow for stretching around the case or button up under the arm. Twister enjoyed bathing me, but the extra shows and sightseeing were out. On day four, Annette, Battle Angel, and I flew to London.

Uncle Lloyd met me at the family's private strip on Friday night. He introduced me to one of the advisors to the British Prime Minister who also happened to be one of the Counsel. He removed the case and I was free to go spend the weekend with my brother.

Mariko was in country and arranged to meet me at the Priory. She had a request that needed to be spoken in her own special way. In the hall that was at one time the Most Holy Place hundreds of years ago, Iko got down on her hands and knees and begged to be released from my service. She had the place decked out with candles and incense. She wore the robes of the ancient style and carried her blades. She started by reminding me of our first meeting, her recruitment, the jobs I entrusted her with, and the extra training I pushed her through. Then she asked, "Have I served you well?" With a tear in my eye, I had to say yes.

She had helped build and network a diversified and talented force of fighters, strike teams, and security agents. In our time together, she had learned a great deal and earned a lot of money. Her first quest was always to build a personal army that could avenge her father's death and reclaim her family honor. She swore to do this or die trying, at his funeral years ago. She had recently come across some information that was critical to that quest. "The time for revenge calls me." The killers had no idea that what they thought was the weakest about her, was just the thing she needed to make her strong. She wasn't just a girl anymore, she was a dangerous and well-respected woman.

In the role of the Lord, I could have denied her. No one is ever perfect. I knew I could have brought up a failure or a technicality that would have made her have to stay longer, but true honor acknowledges the honor in others. As she honored me, I was bound to do the same. This had always been the arrangement, and she had fulfilled her part of the deal. I had no choice but to bless her and let her go.

True to her words, while still on her knees she used her waki- zashi blade to hack at her long and beautiful hair until her head was a patchy mess of strings and stubs. She stood, bowed low be- fore me, turned and left my sight. Above any of the others in the Society, she was my friend, all that was left of our time and fellow- ship was in a pile of hair on the stone floor. I felt sure that I would never see her face again. As she went through that door, a part of me tore itself away and went with her.

She took with her the majority of the Oriental fighters. They and the others, to include some admin and logistics people, add- ed up to one quarter of the entire staff element. Each one was a volunteer and believer in Mariko's leadership. Each one was ready to die for her quest. Each one had my leave to go and return if they wanted, at any time. All they had to do was survive.

As a charter member of the Society of the Princesses, we kept her on the books but frozen at the rate she was when she left. A lot of adjustments had to be made. Nick Parker was the SF guy that helped us with a lot of our training. He was also the man that flew with me on the evening Marty Goldstein was taken out. I recom- mended him to head all security matters but arguments that the job should be given to a woman that would take Mariko's place in the Society, broke out.

Via computer teleconference, I put forward that Mariko was still on the books, so she was still in charge. Nick and Battle Angel would share the job until her return. The Princesses all voted in favor of the motion. Angel was moved back to the Factory in LA, and I asked for Joy and Jacky to replace her as my security.

I took a lot of meetings on the phone and on the computer at all hours of the day, but I made time to play and talk with Little Arthur. He was doing better with people and I think the change of faces and atmosphere was helping to awaken his mind. He was still working on the potty training part, but it was all in normal parameters, or so I was told.

Incidentally, Joy had changed her name to Joy Bird Song. She was considering starting a comic book featuring herself as the main character and superhero. Jacky would be a side character that would later spin off on her own, so she needed a new name too. She changed hers to Jacky O.

In their defense I have to point out the fact that today, cartoons and comics are just as much a part of being Oriental as you would think martial arts used to be. If you have never met a Chinese or Japanese fighter with a wacky cartoon type name, you have not been to LA China Town after dark. That Monday we flew to Dubai to meet the band. Little Arthur cried his eyes out.

The Devil Made Me Do It

What can you not say about Dubai? We were all going to stay at the World Trade Centre Residence in two four-bedroom duplex apartments and one three-bedroom for the 11 of us in the original group. This was a very high-end place and one of the most luxurious hotels in Dubai, but Nabeelah wanted Aleaha and I to experience the absolute best Dubai could offer. She sprung for a week in the Diplomatic Suite at the Burj Al Arab Hotel. (Also known as the Sail on the Water).

As I said, the World Trade Centre was a nice place with a lot of nicer perks, but it couldn't hold a candle to the only seven star hotel in the world. At the feet of the airplane, the three of us were taken by a Rolls Royce to another side of the airport and put into a chopper. The daytime flight gave us a fantastic view of the city before it landed on the 28th level of the hotel. (Nicest helicopter I have ever been in). And I didn't have to dive, duck, jump, tuck, or roll to get off it.

The Diplomatic Suite rivaled many of the palaces I'd seen and looked similar to the way modern Arab Royalty lives. The place had three spacious bedrooms and a large entertainment area that was separate and soundproofed from the sleeping areas. This way you could be having a party while your mother was sleeping in the next room. Once we were settled in, I called Tito and Twister to gather everyone at our suite for a meeting and dinner.

When I last saw Little Bit, she had worked herself up in the food chain to the point that she was allowed to wear clothing and be talked to like a human. When I saw her again that night, I was told that she had been caught smoking and drinking. As soon as I heard this, I ordered her clothes removed and her hands tied. (This time in the front). She could only speak when spoken to and had to ask permission to do anything. That included sleeping, eating, going to the bathroom, standing, and sitting. That night,

I had her stand in the corner without touching the walls for five hours. The only time I let her sit was when she used the toilet (and those were five minute breaks).

Later I had her tell me how she got the smokes and the tiny bottles of Jack and she said that she slipped the Bellman a note asking for it, on Friday night. The note offered sex in exchange for items the Bellman knew were already in the room. She told me that Twister had counted the bottles earlier so she made a plan to open the door one time when Twist was in the bathroom.

The kid could have given the man a note addressed to her friends or shown him her rope marks and asked him to call the police. She could also have just run down the hall and left the building. If she really wanted to have sex with this guy she could have done that someplace on her way out.

The guy happened to have four bottles that he had planned to take home for himself. He gave her his smokes and the lighter he had in his pocket. She really did intend to have sex with the man when she got the chance. But later that night, the girl was busted smoking and drinking while she was locked in the closet.

I said to her, "Why didn't you run away?" She told me, "If I got caught, you would have beaten me up really bad and turned me into a dog again. If I would have gotten away, my aunt would have had me killed. I would rather be a dog that sings than a freed girl floating in the sea." I told her that she wouldn't have to go through this if she just acted in the right way. She started crying and said, "I can't do it. I need the sex and the drinks to distract all the voices." I know a little something about voices, so I had to ask, "What voices?" "The ones that tell me things", she answered.

As it turned out, the kid was sicker than I thought. Apparently, the child believed that she was troubled by the spirit of a woman that lived in ancient times. (We are talking way, way back). She too, was talented in singing, dancing, playing instruments, and in pleasing men. She said that the woman was the perfect mix of beauty and talent, but she went insane. Because of these talents, she was worshiped by a great many people including the King of a large city-state. A war was fought, and hundreds of men died so that this King could have her for himself.

The story goes like this: A famous and rich merchant who was the son of a Prince, once owned her as a young girl and used her to entertain his most favorite customers. She loved her role. Knowing that it would be impossible for the wild girl to be a wife and mother, he refused to sell her off at any price. Besides, she brought in the best and most loyal customers. They came to expect her entertainment and were obligated to buy something.

One day this merchant was selling weapons in the Great City. The King, who was at that time known to be a good ruler, was allowed to use the now older girl as a reward for spending a lot of money. The King instantly fell overwhelmingly in love with her and her talents. Unable to come to terms, he very uncharacteristically seized the girl from the merchant and threw him out of town. Then he put her on display for all to see and admire. Through her gifts, many others were also inspired to create, and the young woman reveled in the glory.

The merchant appealed to his father for help with this 'good deal gone bad'. After a time, the two rulers were able to come to a monetary settlement. The King thought that he could domesticate her wild nature with love and gifts, but the girl thrived only for the attentions of others (many others). She had long been habituated to the attention and could not live one more moment without it.

She could not be stopped from her crowd gathering performances and her multiple encounters, so the King was forced to use an addictive drug that made her docile but half asleep most of the time. She hated the fact that she could not dance and sing and began to hate the King and herself. When in her waking moments, she would throw wild tantrums before falling back into a numbing trance. The King himself grew tired of the ordeal and sought to alter the agreed settlement in his disappointment.

Word had gotten back to the merchant that the girl was now ruined and would never be of any use to him or anyone ever again. He refused the altered deal and demanded his payment, plus an extra-large tribute for the horrible deeds done to the girl and his reputation as a businessman. The Prince let it be known that the King was a cheat and a man not to be trusted. This started a small war. When the girl heard about all the fighting and dying, she took her own life by overdosing.

That is of course, where the story would end, except to say that Aleaha questioned if the temptress was actually dead when she was buried. She said that there was a long and painful period of quiet and darkness after the last visual and audio memories. So, it is possible that the girl took only enough of the drug to make her catatonic. She may have slowly suffocated or died of thirst in her underground tomb.

The kid claimed that she felt that she had always heard the voices and had never been alone. She believed that the spirit may have attached itself to her at the age of seven when she visited some ancient ruins during a school trip. The only time she had any peace was when she was either entertaining or indulging in one of her obsessions; in other words, doing what the spirit wanted her to do. She said that sometimes, when in a state of heighten pleasure, "I can hear what normal might sound like."

It was a good story. She could have been telling the truth. Then again, the kid could have come up with it during a moment of inspiration while locked in the closet one of those many nights. So, I sat her down and asked her what the woman's name was. She said, "Euterpe." She told me that she looked up the meaning of the name and found that it referred to the Muse of song, poetry and the flute. She felt that this woman may have been the first person to have ever been called by this name. The spirit told her that the name was taken and used in the story of the Muses sometime after her death. Then I asked if Euterpe had a favorite song and she began to passionately sing a song that I recorded, and later analyzed as something in very ancient pre-Greek. (It was wonderful).

I thought to myself, "I am sitting in the presence of a god and I have been treating her like a dog." I asked her if Euterpe wanted anything in particular that might convince her to leave her body or to just behave. The only thing that she could tell me that made any sense was that the spirit had taken other girls before. Those kids did not have the beauty or potential that Aleaha had. She was waiting for this opportunity for thousands of years and had every intention of keeping what she had claimed.

I hadn't begun to believe her yet, but as a leader I needed to at least investigate the situation. I could see why the spirit of a Muse would want the dancing, singing, playing instruments, and for that matter, even the sex. What I couldn't understand was why she had a craving for alcohol and drugs especially when considering her manner of demise. The kid explained that Euterpe hates drugs and alcohol and has a low tolerance for it in general. Aleaha did it to defy her. The higher she got, the quieter Euterpe became. "She goes into a kind of sleep." Of course, by this time, Aleaha herself is wasted and useless.

I asked her if she knew whatever became of the other girls the spirit possessed. "In a short time, they all killed themselves. One woman was too old to be an entertainer. Another was a slave to a cruel master who locked her up most of the time. One girl was lame and could not dance. Most of them were not able to do the things that the spirit wanted them to do, and it turned them violent and crazy."

Apparently, the spirit returns to the old burial place when the host is dead. There she will wait for some unsuspecting female to happen along. It lives the existence of a parasite. Since the first life was so short lived, its desires to live a wider and fuller version is insatiable.

The spirit is wiser now and knows how to better choose its prey by waiting for the right girl. If it chooses badly it will have to begin the long process of driving that person crazy enough to want to die. She will torment them with her voice, her visions, her desires, and her death, until they do. (The sooner the better).

"At seven years old I was the youngest of them all. It was nothing for me to let her take control of my body and mind. For a long time, it was fun. She made me do things that I had no idea were even possible. The music and dance came easy to me. I was finally the perfect vessel for her return," she said.

"But you outgrew her," I prodded.

"Yes", she answered. "And I am not afraid to think for myself. It's just hard to focus my mind away from all of her noise. The drugs help a lot."

Even though she is thousands of years old, Euterpe is at best only eighteen in her thinking. She has to contend with reading, writing, math, history, TV, cell phones, computers, and video games. Never in known history has the mind had a need to multitask so much information just to function normally. The spirit is truly overwhelmed and cannot understand the modern way of thinking and thus lacks the ability to make any good judgments. She doesn't care about what she doesn't understand. All she ever wanted was fame, glory and the attention of the masses. Her bold and confident nature cares nothing for money, power or things. It is the passion of the art that drives her. She offers to share the ecstasy of the lime light with her host in exchange for the use of their bodies, and until now, they had little choice but to except or fight a long losing battle.

But with Aleaha, and for the first time, things are different. She truly has the best hope of achieving her goals now more than with any other soul the spirit has encountered. Euterpe wants to keep this body for as long as she can and as a compromise, she has given up quite a lot of control in order for the girl to pass as a modern child. Still, the kid hates the fact that everyone loves her talents, but they hate the hell out of her. Her recent willingness to change has made the kid a little stronger and the spirit weaker.

They both want to be a superstar, but at the same time they also fear that one cannot do it without the other. (Damned if you do and damned if you don't). It's the perfect trap.

If that wasn't enough to think about, she told me that the spirit was telling her that it knew me in another time. She said, "It's not the person you remember or the person you are trying to be, it was the person you once were long ago."

That's when I started to believe her. Within an instant I replied with, "Then you can tell her that I am the stronger. I am the soul of the great collector. If she does not make herself smaller, I will cast a net to capture her very being and wear it as a trophy around my neck." (Ghosts and spirits, you got to nip them in the bud). The interview was over but now I had two demons to fight.

I was more than a little prepared for her to say something about the real me. I just had no idea what it would be. It did remind me a lot of what the Grandmasters were trying to tell me at the temple not long ago. It now seemed clear to me that just as Aleaha carried two separate souls, so did I. The Masters mentioned that I had more than one light. I had thought they could somehow see the essence of what was left of young Faatina still lingering inside the body that was once solely hers. Now I began to entertain the idea that it must be at least some part of Alexander the Great himself. (What were they all seeing that I was not?). Aleaha knew the presence of the other. I still did not. I did what I could to appear brave but in truth I was really petrified.

Had Lloyd really done the impossible? Had he and his father somehow reincarnated enough of the things that made Alexander great and shoved them into an egg at the moment of fertilization? If Faatina was born a boy, his name would not have been Arthur after his father. It would have been Alexander, after his destiny.

The person I am now was an accident on many levels, but Little Arthur should be closer to what they all wanted. If that's true, then the question must be, why would you want a guy like Alexander the Great born in 2009? I can see wanting to continue and strengthen the family line, but you wouldn't bring back Alexander unless you really needed him for something. I considered his qualities.

If Alexander's father were not a warrior and a conqueror, his son would have focused that same drive on something else. This leader of that multinational, multicultural army of explorers, cartographers, and soldiers forged his way beyond the mental restrictions of the known world and travelled far beyond what he knew to be true. Imagine how he could reshape the world of today as a politician, a priest, or a scientist. As an added benefit, I am poised to bring the media to wherever I go and to whatever I am doing. As brother and sister, we would promote each other without appearing to do so. I knew that my current situation could not have been close to the way Lloyd and his father originally planned. Still, this very scenario must certainly now be included amongst the many options on the table someplace in that big English mansion.

Before our first show, a discreet and highly recommended hypnotist was paid to help me convince Euterpe to go into hiding. She was permitted to feed on the crowd's affections only. She promised to sleep the majority of the time and come out only when she was needed. She could have the glory of the stage and Aleaha would know what it felt like to be a teenager on her own.

The problem with that was when the spirit was asleep she took her confidence and sense of adventure to bed with her. Aleaha was now like a scared little mouse. The kid was afraid to look her food in the eye, but her thoughts were clear. Euterpe would have complete control during rehearsals and the performances, but she missed the fun and sex she craved. On the other hand, Aleaha missed the stage. Neither was truly happy. I had to have another plan. I called her aunt and we decided we would all have to wait for a better time to solve this dilemma. She would have to make a few calls.

Not counting the promo, we were originally booked for just one show in a medium sized hall. Now, the hall was changed to a larger venue. We were requested to hit a few other locations around the UAE before returning to play Dubai one more time. We met with an agent the next afternoon at one of the fabulous restaurants in the hotel. A schedule was set that included three promo shows for Little Bit and myself. Boxes of CDs and DVDs arrived in a warehouse and we prepared ourselves for a workout.

We did the first show in Dubai and moved to Abu Dhabi before hitting Qatar and then Kuwait. We got requests from Baghdad, but I was flat-out afraid to go. Just the thought of it gave me a bad vibe so instead we went to Muscat before doing the second show in Dubai. From there we travelled to Alexandria where we did one show and a three-day rest. Altogether, we did 10 shows in two weeks' time.

I visited all the museums and saw all the sights I could see before I laid out on the beach. All the girls hung out together, but the guys went to the four winds. Twister bought me a new hat and this time we took Aleaha every place we went. She was shy and well behaved for the most part. There were a few times she had to be stopped from sneaking a drink or trying to seduce some European boy on her way to the toilet. She claimed the spirit made her do it, but she was spanked just the same.

I felt a great flow of spiritual energy in and around that city. Even the smell of the sea gave me a peaceful strength. It was as if all the old souls were welcoming me home. The day before we flew to Casablanca, an Army General who claimed to be a cousin, presented me with a package to hand carry into Spain. We would now have to do a show in Madrid before jumping over to Istanbul on our way back to Beirut.

Our cousin took me on a private tour of the ancient artifacts that the masses never see. Most of the first collection founded by Ptolemy 1st (Alexander's half-brother and direct ancestor to Cleopatra), and Ptolemy 2nd between 323-246 BC was inspired by Alexander himself but was destroyed when Julius Caesar ordered the port and his own ships set ablaze in 48 BC. The fire spread to the museum and only a portion of the most prized items could be saved. Caesar considered himself a reincarnation of Alexander and regretted the destruction of the priceless collections.

I saw items and read reports that proved beyond a doubt that at one time someone on this earth was more advanced than we are now, but the technology was worlds apart. Many of those things have been watered down to the everyday devices we live with today. And there are some that were only recently found to have a use. Most of these items were ancient at the time they were discovered, so none of the artifacts worked.

What they found most interesting were some small devices that when placed on the body would give the wearer the ability to move large items. This would also give that person the ability to push himself off the ground or in other words, fly. Such abilities would give the impression that this person had god-like powers. People with these tools would be worshiped.

I tried on one of the retrofitted headsets. It needed a massive amount of power to run it and had to be suspended in the air, so the weight of the cables and transformers wouldn't have to be placed on my head. I was told to point at a large concrete block and move it across the room with my mind. Not only was I able to move it, I was able to place it gently on the floor where I wanted. Afterwards, the bulky device was lowered into a hydrogen vat to cool it down.

The biggest problem to application for most of the original pieces was the power. It was surmised that the energy used to run these devices came from the brain. This means that humans (or another advanced race) once had the ability to easily focus on a particular item and the device would power up to perform the action. This included weapons, medical tools, and entertainment items such as musical instruments. I was also shown strange writings on metal that dated back to before people would have walked the earth.

I was shown some items that were stored in a secured vault. The lead engineer removed a locked case that had several smaller locked boxes inside it. He opened one box and revealed what looked like a thick tube of solid highly polished crystal. I was told it was confirmed to be solid diamond rod worth millions of dollars. (One of many).

He sat down at a desk, turned on the small lamp and said, "Look at the shadow you see on the desk. Notice that the shadow the cylinder makes is just as dark as the one made from my hand. Normally, glass, crystals, and even diamonds will allow nearly all light to pass through it. This one stores it." He switched off the lamp and showed my cousin and I that the tube was holding about as much light as was put into it by the lamp. To me, it looked like a swirling white liquid trapped in a vacuum. "We think that at one time this cell could hold enough power to run all the functions of this facility," he said.

"For how long?" I asked.

"A year or a lifetime, who can say," he replied. "One day we may find that this single item had the ability to power one of your aircraft carriers or the internal function of a starship meant to travel from one solar system to another."

The man condescendingly chuckled when I said, "It sounds like a super powerful battery of some kind."

"Battery? It's a little more complicated than that but I can understand why you said what you did."

I knew that he was a brilliant man but there was no need to act as if I were a stupid child. So as the man stood and prepared to place the diamond back into its box I said, "I just meant that if it were a battery, maybe it's the rechargeable kind."

The man froze for a moment. He looked at the tube and then looked at me. The silent moment was so uncomfortable that I decided to walk away before it got any stranger.

I learned a few things about Alexander the Great that were chronicled and collaborated by a few of his famous Somatophylakes. The way it was explained to me, the word Somatophylakes is translated as meaning bodyguards. But the men that Alexander designated with this title were his generals and principal advisers. He used them on special missions and they were his emissaries.

One thing in particular stood out to me. Three of them mentioned the fact that Alexander had one odd facial feature. One eye was blue and the other was brown. Just like my little brother.

Play it Again Sam

That evening we all left for Morocco. The first thing I wanted to do was ask if there really was a Rick's Place, or Rick's Cafe American, from the movie "Casablanca". The answer was no, and from what I was told, there never was. What they do have is a Rick's Cafe Casablanca.

The 1930's-built mansion opened its doors as a restaurant and piano bar in 2004. It was redesigned to simulate the feel of the old Bogart and Bergman film made in 1942. The film was used as a propaganda attempt to prepare the US for the involvement in a war that was already raging in Africa, the Middle East and throughout Europe. The combination of famous actors and famous quotes made the US ask the question, "What is going on over there?" It was listed as one of the greatest films of all time and one of my favorites. Of course, not one of my crew knew what I was talking about. I insisted that we all go.

I must have been the silliest person they had ever seen. I wished that at least one of the other 13 of us had seen the movie just once before we walked into the place straight from the airport. I looked all around the joint and hoped that Bogy would walk down the stairs. Hell yes, I asked the guy at the piano to "Play it again Sam" and he did. ("As Time Goes By"). He even sang the song for me as I sat next to him on the bench. After I took a bunch of pictures, the crew had to drag me out of that place. I felt like I was going to miss something exciting. I wanted somebody to say, "Here's looking at you kid."

Morocco and the US have a long-standing relationship. They were the first country to publicly recognize the American republic. The consulate in Tangier was the first piece of property ever owned abroad. The Sultan of Morocco offered his personal protection of US merchant ships from Barbary Coast Raiders during the US revolution. As thanks for that and other gifts of aid, the US promised that no African of Moroccan decent would be a slave in the country of America. (I guess a few slaves were never told).

I added "As Time Goes By" to our repertoire. Tito sent James the video and sound recordings from all the performances via the internet. When James heard that one, he demanded that special attention needed to be made. He thought that it was the perfect song for bringing the 50 and older market into our fold. We played the tune several times before James chose a variation that he said was "just right."

Except for some minor changes here and there, the shows were basically the same. I had a long set list of 35 songs that we had perfected, and depending on the city, we could pick the ones that best fit the mood of that town. Deak taught me that it was always a good idea to scout out the town by reading the paper, watching the TV, or going to the mall before a show.

We continued to experiment with the lights, curtains, screens, and camera angles. The goal was to try and make the show as dramatic and aesthetically pleasing as possible. Like the piano bar feel for the new song, a greater emphasis was placed on the texture. When a Jazz lover came to our show, they not only got some great music, they went into another time and place. It set us apart and got us noticed.

In Casablanca, the show took on a change. The venues grew from small to medium, then medium to large. Local acts were billed to setup the audience for our show and we held the ability to pick the acts we wanted via the internet. As always, we recorded everything to include the locals.

Aleaha joined the Sisters and sang backup. My obligation to her aunt ended in Morocco but I knew that there was no way this kid was going to stand by and just watch me sing. To keep her busy, she became the direct connection between our crew, the agent, and the venue management. Her job was to tell them what we needed and insist that it was done to her satisfaction. It went a long way with her social skills and it forced her to learn the business from all sides. It was a real job, too. After reviewing the diagram of a forthcoming venue, she and I would discuss what theme or stage effect we wanted. She would then send those requests over ahead of time and get the management to arrange it. It was mostly things like curtains, lights, and prop positioning, (like the piano bar theme) but it was a very important part of the act. She was the go-between for the Set Director. In Madrid she got billed as the first opening act of the night.

She hired a local band that did four of the eight Pop songs she sang. No one knew of her in Spain, so the crowd was not at capacity in that first hour of the night. However, that didn't stop her from rocking the house. Three days later she was booked separately across town and the place was packed. The very next night she sang again behind me.

I passed the documents I received in Egypt to the Spanish Prime Minister and had dinner in the palace of King Juan Carlos 1st. It was fabulous and so was the food. We took pictures and he explained his connection to my family. He belonged to a close branch and showed me paintings and drawings that proved his line, but he regretted being so far from pure blood.

The genetic degradation was hard to combat. The main line of his family completely died off mostly due to war from without and within the line itself. Like the Monarchy in England, Spain's Royal family is a copy of a copy of what once was. He knew about my brother and insisted that I show him his pictures from my phone.

Uncle Lloyd was still working on a meeting in Libya. The main part of the tour was over and there were no documents to pick up this time. It was suggested that I hang around, so the crew was given a week off to rest and play. I sent Joy Birdsong to escort Aleaha back to her aunt. She had plans for her and the spirit of Euterpe. Twister found some interview opportunities. The rest of the crew stayed in and around Madrid. I did not.

In Madrid, I was treated like a Queen. While the rest of the crew, to include Twister, kept busy in town, I was obligated to stay in the Palace. After I stopped insulting them by saying "No thank you," I was given priceless gowns and jewelry to wear. They told me that these things were mine long before I was born and that I needed them for the Ball. I didn't know what to make about it, so I called Uncle Lloyd.

Lloyd sent a handmaiden (Jessica 21), and a gentlewoman (Monica 40), to be my helpers for this shindig. They were to be my Ladies in Waiting. They dressed, bathed, served, and schooled me in all the royal things I should know. I needed to know who was who, and the proper title and greeting for that person. I had to learn a little about their family history (the real history). There were so many things that I could not say. The good thing was that they were all coming to honor me and not the other way around.

This time, I got the full Cinderella experience I passed up in Delaware. I was mesmerized by the pomp and ceremony of it all. The Royal European version of the Ball and the wealthy American version were leagues apart. The US version had some rules, some tradition, and a lot of fun. It was more of a fancy business gathering than anything else. (Real fancy). The Royal version on the other hand, had the "rule of tradition" and was hardly any fun. Everything had to be perfect and making the right impression was paramount. Of course, you got your business in too, but that was later on.

I had seen ass kissing before and I thought that I understood the concept. I was wholly mistaken! Those folks kowtowed more than the servants did. It was nuts. I could have snorted and spit in the center of the Ballroom floor and the Blue Bloods would have clapped their hands and praised my name. I was thinking about making them all sing "Da Do Ron Ron" just to prove a point. (I fought the feeling back).

I met one of the candidates I was supposed to marry. If I were Faatina, I would have turned 19 earlier this year. If I were still Robert, I would be 71. As Jasmine, I was 18 going on 19 and still the perfect age for courting in any well-bred society. The old plan was to marry Faatina off right after her 17th birthday. She would have gone to one of the close members of the family in another attempt to extend the line, but that all changed after the accident.

All these people were now fully aware that I could not get pregnant. I had come to the understanding that being reborn barren made me useless to Lloyd and his father's plan, so I was reconstructed to be a sex toy and traded away. What I didn't know was that my unborn brother surviving the incident made me even more obsolete than I already was. As it turned out (and I'm not excluding the medical science), it was the Robert in me that made me useful again, and as it seemed, still eligible to marry.

The 43 year old Duke was the youngest male in the second line of our clan, and more of a true Blue Blood than most. A son born of us would have changed his status and generated a rewrite to bring the Second Line into the First but knowing this could never be, he was no longer interested in me. His two nephews on the other hand, were.

They were not the only ones, but they were amongst the most eligible of all the young nobles in attendance. Sure, I was a pretty enough lure to land them, but the real prize was an inside seat someplace outside the Counsel. Most men knowing this would be willing to make love to a barracuda just to get that opportunity. Then again, there were other reasons. The Duke's deceased wife had two deadbeat brothers that had sons. They were his adopted heirs now and the closest thing to the children he himself was denied. They were fierce competitors with each other, but they were also cousins, family, and now brothers. It has been said, "If those two were on the same battlefield, there would be no other competitors worth watching." They were alike in more ways than could be counted. They were raised together and were of the same age. They went to the same schools and at 22 they were both now Captains in the Army. However, one was serving in Italy while the other served in Spain.

According to Monica, a girl that they were both seeing in college was put into a position that forced her to choose between the two. "Doggy", as the rumor went. And it was the chief reason for her great misfortune. She knew that it was more than pure lust that attracted them to her, so she aborted the child. Being Catholic, the cousins were outraged. They broke with her and each other. Neither was ever informed who the real father was, and the girl was never heard from again.

The brothers did not have the most medals. And as Captains, they held one of the lowest ranks of all the military attendees. What they did have was charm, poise, and style. They excelled in these and it was plain for all to see. The women's eyes followed them on and off the ballroom floor and men envied that.

They later told me that they agreed to flip a coin for who would be the first to invite me to the floor. I felt like a kid in the fairgrounds. I went back and forth, up and down, and around and around. It was my first time dancing with a man and those fellas worked me until my tight shoes began to dig into my feet. Other than smiling and laughing I scarcely said a word but it was fun. Everyone watched as they pulled me from one to the other without missing a beat. Like the rest, they too, were perfect gentlemen. I had no illusion that it was not a competition between them, but I continued to graciously hang on for the ride.

I had begun to sweat through everything, so I removed myself for a quick change of clothing and shoes. When I and my ladies returned, it was time to present tributes. I presented the King with a Scepter commissioned by Henry VIII. It was one of the Crown Jewels of England. Lloyd had dug deep to revive one of the oldest royal traditions. Everyone was genuinely impressed, and the King was unable to speak.

I too, received gifts from many would-be suitors and others seeking favor. Diamonds, pearls, platinum, and gold items in beautiful boxes were placed into my gloved hands. Every item was labeled so that I could later identify who gave me what. When the brothers addressed me, they came together.

The room was called to attention and space was cleared in front of where the King and I sat. In a bold move the two men marched right up to us in a way that they had obviously rehearsed. They halted only two feet before me, drew their swords, and held them in the air. They both pledged their loyalty and love if I would choose one of them to be my Knight Champion. They claimed to refuse to lower themselves by trying to buy my affection with trifles. What they offered was themselves. They took a knee, laid their swords across the palms of their hands, bowed, and presented the blades up for me to choose.

They were magnificent specimens. The guys were impressive, too. The King and I were equally taken aback by the spectacle and the sentiment of the gesture. The uniform, the swords, and the speech were a lot to take in at one time. It was like something out of an Errol Flynn film. Now, I was at a loss for words. If I were a normal girl in this situation, I could easily have wet myself. And I'm not going to lie and say that I didn't feel a tingle from the greatest personal compliment I had ever received.

I guess I was in a mild state of shock because the old man had to bump me to knock me out of the slow-motion trance. I kept reminding myself that they were actually speaking to me. The King steadied my arm and stood with me as I rose. He whispered some words to me until I could flow on my own. "You are indeed gentlemen of the highest caliber. I am humbled by the honor and the privilege of standing before two splendid Knights." Then I took over. "To me, you are both champions. To choose one brother would be saying that this one is better than the other and that I cannot and will not do. Such a decision would follow my every thought." I had an idea. "If you would meet with me later, I will have a counter proposal for you both." The ballroom was a hush.

Later, Monica, the King, and I, sat in a conference room and listened to 37 peoples' issues that they wanted the Council to consider. This one thought he was due more authority than the other. That one wanted a blessing to undertake a certain venture. Mostly, it was a lot of very polite whining followed by a kissing of my Council ring. Monica took notes and I assured them all that I would mention it to the Council at some point. We called the brothers in last.

I went right into my business mode and told them that I was impressed. Their uncle and the King took an oath to vouch for them, so I was comfortable making them an offer. "You know who I am," I said. "I have some years to go before I will become a completely active member of the Body of the Council so at this moment I still have some options open to me. I aim to take advantage of this by building a staff of qualified and loyal individuals. You two are not, but you can be." I took a moment for my point to sink in. "Would you like me to continue?" They answered with, yes madam! "I am not proposing to veer the course of the world in a different direction. I am only replacing the empty spaces of the old guard with the new as they become available. To do this, I am considering the idea of collapsing part of the family lines into one. I know this will encounter a great resistance. The folding of the lines is not a new concept, but it is still a radical one. Just saying it aloud to myself invokes a psychological reaction. Now, unfortunately you two have only a small part of the Second Line and are therefore ineligible for ascension onto the floor. However, you can be part of the few trusted leaders that help run the European Military end of my personal staff." They looked at each other. "One day you may be Generals, but you will be called on to make mountains move long before that time." I paused again before standing up to allow them to kiss my ring.

I knew these guys walked into the room expecting something completely different. I also knew that those two young men knew more about the inner workings of the world than I ever wanted to. Their uncle had explained to them long ago what the Council was and how powerful it has been. But being outside of the Line (so to speak) they were content to watch from afar. I was offering a change of fate and that is why they accepted my offer. What I didn't say was like I did to the Society members, I would have to test their loyalty at some point.

Their adopted father on the other hand was of the Bourbon family and like his King, he could trace his line through the Capetian Dynasty and all the way back to Robert the Strong and his grandfather Robert of Hesbaye in 770 AD. He is directly related to Louis the XIV of France and Leopold I of Rome. All were descendants of Alexander and his Somatophylakes who were the original First and Second Lines. By his blood rights and his honor, he was granted membership. His sons were his proof and needed no test.

All and all, it was a real good outing. Now I had someone in my corner I could depend on. Duke Philip and his nephews were the first to be recruited onto my private Council staff. They would now be required to make their own connections and do their own recruiting. I didn't know them, but I did know that they would sell their souls for this opportunity, so I felt confident at the time. This action, as well as my other plans, could have been derailed by the Body of the Council but I hoped that Uncle Lloyd would back what should appear to look like a pure and honest effort to prepare for my next phase of ascension. To be on the safe side, I called Lloyd the next day.

He told me that King Juan Carlos had already spoken to him and convinced him that what I did was brilliant. The King told him that he had encouraged me to do it, but Lloyd said he knew that it was my idea. Lloyd also told me that he made the arrangements to have the Ball and was behind the suitors' attempts to woo me. He had hoped that I would become taken with someone and at least entertain the thought of marriage to a real man.

The Tripoli and Cairo visits would be on hold for now. Lloyd estimated that the areas would be unstable for many months to come. I was free to return to England or continue touring until he needed me, and for the first time in a long time I heard someone say something that I was not used to hearing. "You've done a good job so far." He went on to say, "If you were my daughter, I would feel very proud."

I was instantly overtaken by emotion. Tears rolled down my face and my nose began to run a little. I felt happy and sad at the same time. I didn't have the chance to bond with my father and when I did see him, I never got any compliments. Of all my childhood accomplishments, there was never a "good job" from him. He wasn't a bad man per se, just a poor father. But, there was more to it than that.

It was then that I fully accepted what had been obvious to everyone else. I was a girl. A walking, talking, breathing, real live, anatomically correct, girl. I had spent so much time studying, practicing and pretending to be a girl that I lost track of how it was affecting my mind. I had turned from acting the part, to being the part, and I don't remember when it happened. "You are my father," I answered him. "You have always been."

I hung up the phone and started crying. My ladies rushed into the room and wanted to know what Lloyd had said that upset me. When I told them that he said he was proud of me, they started crying too. I tried choking it back, but I couldn't fight it. I had truly crossed over to the other side. (What the fuck). I was dripping snot, rubbing my eyes, and the ladies were hugging, wiping my face, and babying me like something was wrong. It was just like before in that Georgia hospital only this time it was all real.

Now I had to re-revaluate what I was doing with my life. This took quite a while to do when I considered all the factors. There was nothing about me that was normal and there was nothing about me that was going to be normal. I guessed that at some point I could actually marry someone. After all, that is what my new father wanted for me. Acting in a submissive way was part of my initial cover. They were always the best qualities I had felt a woman had to offer. I took great pains to learn how to quietly sit and let another dominant person be in charge when I knew that I was the better and smarter leader. I let them lead because I looked like a kid that looked like a girl. It was part of my MO.

Sitting with my head down or standing with my mouth open and head to the side makes me look innocent and vulnerable. To some, that makes a girl seem even more attractive. It was a turn on for Miss Janet and it always drove Twister wild. I wouldn't respond to yelling but when they called I would bashfully come to them even if they were a little nasty. I mastered the sad, nervous, and crying looks too. The only thing I had not done as a girl was the one thing that my body was designed for: sex with a man. The very idea of it still made me feel sick.

In my old life, I never gave any of this much of a thought. I admit the fact that I was one of those 'hit it and quit it' kind of guys. The passion play meant only a waste of time to me, so the mental aspect was completely lost. Now I understand how important those things are to most women but at the time I gave no frills or thrills and I'm sorry about that. I was hard headed, and I didn't really care about how or what she felt. It took a crazy change like this to make me see the light. I have changed so much since my death and I'm not just talking about the outside. However, a big part of me will always be a guy.

I love the girl-on-girl action more than I thought possible, especially when I'm one of them. If you want me to, I will lick all the taste out of a pussy. I will kiss her, hold her, suck her nipples, and even let her pee on me if she wants. I can and will do whatever makes her happy, and knowing that, will make me feel happy too. I always loved having sex with a woman and my transformation has only made the feeling greater.

There was no doubt that I would greatly enjoy the feel of a dick sliding in and out of my vagina. As I said, it's in the design. I had been putting small things inside of me for more than two years and it was wonderful each and every time. But having a man insert himself into me still seemed way beyond being something I was not. And a blow-job was definitely out of the question.

I knew that sex would have to be a major part of a husband/ wife relationship. If I had a wife that looked like me, I'd be bending her over at the drop of a hat whether she was ready or not. It wouldn't matter what she said or did, that pussy was going to be fucked (a lot). And with that thought, I decided to ponder this dilemma at another time.

I'm Just on Vacation

I wanted to see my brother but before I arranged the flight my inner voice told me to call Sophie. She informed me that her brother (Pauly) was currently near Palermo working some deal for her father. She said that as a favor I should go visit him and that side of her family. I asked why.

She had wanted to go but her brother told her that she couldn't. When she mentioned to him that I was in nearby Spain, he offered the option to visit if I had the chance. Now since I had called and told her that I had some free time, Sophie pleaded with me to go and see what her brother was doing. She had a suspicion that he was sent to negotiate her marriage at her father's behest.

She warned me that this was an old-fashioned family he was seeing so I should be prepared to have an old-fashioned mind set. In other words, she was telling me that I couldn't take Twister the brawny butch, or my two tattooed Asian bodyguards. I had never been to Italy and it did sound very intriguing, but I had not been with Twister in a few days and the tension was starting to build.

We had a lot of offers to play a few gigs in Paris, Frankfurt, and Berlin before returning for a final run around London Town. Even Moscow wanted to be added to the list. It would be a great way to end the summer and the tour. Our agent needed a little time to make the arrangements, so we still had nearly a week to kill.

When I mentioned all of this to James he was excited. He said that I needed to have a heart-to-heart with Twister before I talked to the rest of the crew. I was to call him back afterward. I went to see her that night in town. I stayed at her hotel and she explained what James was talking about.

Twister was close to getting that deal she was working on. All the travel and interviews had hit a spot with the other producers in LA. The networks were on board for a spring debut. She had been sending recordings via the net and they loved the idea. All that was left was to discuss the product line and the legal red tape. She needed my permission to break her first contract as my bodyguard.

In the morning she officially left my employ, and my bed. I did still have a legal investment in Twister so when the lawyers were through I owned 20% of her show and the products, and Twister owned a 10% share. The other 70% was split between the networks and the other producers in LA. James flew out another great Sax player to take Twister's place but for Twister, there could be no replacement. For a time, I was really lonely and bummed out.

The new Sax man was an older guy that called himself Max Sax. Twister had a good and powerful sound but this 56 year old short black man wearing dark sunglasses, dark suit and a darker Fedora, was classy and smooth. While she brought raw strength, he gave a dynamic sense of style. He also came with a box of sound effects. Tito and the Sisters loved him and so did all his lady fans. The guy pulled women every time he played. He was laid back most of the time and seemed to have a funny joke for nearly every situation. But then there were times when he could get downright philosophical, especially when he had been smoking marijuana. He was the coolest guy I had ever met. He had other gifts about him that allowed him to sense and know things. I had the strangest feeling that if I got too close, he would find me out. So, I never bugged him about the grass.

James said that he was working on a deal that would have a big impact on our market. The producers of the LFL (Lingerie Football League) had approached him with an idea for a publicity stunt. They thought that if I were to date a girl from their stable of players, the controversy would enhance sales like crazy. He told them that I had a girl and they countered with a lot of money and a great triangle story. He knew I wouldn't go for it. James only mentioned it now because Twister was out of the picture.

At that moment the deal on the table looked like a ½ mil in weekend resorts, game tickets anywhere, and a bunch of small photo ops. I would get to choose the girl from all who would be interested in spending some time with me. He said that it would be something to do after the concert and football seasons. I told him that I might consider it after I looked at some snapshots and profiles. (What the hell, right).

Still, I hated losing Twister. I knew that she had her own agenda and that her dream did not include playing in a backup band. I had learned so much from her about being sexy and just being a girl, that her influence became a part of who I was. We knew that being together was a temporary arrangement. Like with Mariko, it was all part of a plan. The only difference was that I loved her. So, when we kissed and waved goodbye at the airport, she saw a smiling happy faced girl. As soon as that woman left my sight, I flew into the ladies' room and cried until a security guard came in to check on me. I knew that's what would happen and that was the reason why I insisted we go alone. (Sicily now seemed like a real good idea).

I would need an escort, so I asked Duke Philip which of his sons would be better for a quiet outing in the Italian countryside. He said, "Take them both." Upon their return, they would be reassigned and promoted to the next military rank. A week together would give me a chance to really get to know them and it would give the powers-that-be an opportunity to move their paperwork around.

Maximiano, Miguelangel, Annette, and I were met by Pauly and his cousin Clemente at Falcone-Borsellino Airport in Palermo. After the introductions, we were quickly whisked out of the city and into the nearby Sicilian countryside. This area was magnificent and so were the girls we saw along the way.

We travelled light and dressed like ordinary tourists. Annette and I packed simply with nice mid-length skirts and short pants. The guys went for the business casual look. All my gifts were sent to England. The rest of the stuff went ahead to the next hotel. We wanted to appear like everyone else.

The Montano families were tied into a lot of things but what they wanted was a better piece of the exported wine business. Enough money flowed in from Chicago, New York, and Detroit to buy their way in, but a marriage would sweeten the deal and make them all one big happy family. Sophie was right. She was getting married. The only questions were when and to whom.

This was the thing Sophie had been born for. It was the reason for the grooming and the private education. It was why she had to keep her virginity and her looks. Like me, there was a plan to use her as collateral for a big deal down the road. (Boy, did I peg her right).

The Montanos knew only that I was a respected friend of Pauly and his sister. They sensed that an American-raised girl like Sophie might have reservations about the arrangement, so they did their best to sell the idea to me so that I could in turn, sell it back to her. The way I saw it, the choice was hers. It didn't matter to me if she were married. She could still remain as my second in the Society or leave the organization and be "happy ever after" as a wife in a wealthy Italian family just as her mother had been. I called her that night and as I expected, Sophie was very displeased.

The reason she linked up with me at school in the first place was in itself a show of defiance. It was her first step against a pre-programmed future that had been set in motion years before she was born. She never told me that she knew this day would come, but secretly she dreaded it. So, when I first talked to her about being and doing something more with her life, she saw a way out from the same fate that consumed her mother. She was compelling me to help her find a solution. I knew that there were rules to this kind of thing. Two powerful families were involved in this matter and they would both be insulted. Not to mention the possibility of cancelling their business deals.

After speaking to her uncles, her brother, and a bunch of cousins, other than faking her death I couldn't see another way of getting her out of this that would keep all the players (to include myself) alive. That didn't mean I wasn't looking for an angle. Yes, I'm sure I could have waved my hands and made the whole thing change, but that would be a bad idea. The Council frowns on the open abuse of power. We were in the business for routing the course of the planet, not arranging marriages (unless that marriage mattered). However this worked out, my attachment to the Council could never be known. I was just a singer, a business woman, and a friend.

The Montano compound was the old and the new worlds mixed together. The place had gardens, horses, satellite dishes, iron gates, and armed guards. It was a beautiful spread, and everyone was dressed like they were heading to the office. We stayed with them for two days before I, and a delegation of family members, headed off to the Florio homes and winery.

I had to leave Annette and the brothers with the Montanos. These people are real funny about bringing outsiders into family business. If not for the fact that I was in business with Pauly and a "friend of the family", we would never have been allowed to enter the Montano compound. Maximiano and Miguelangel were introduced as my guards and Annette as my clerical assistant, so they were also part of Pauly's business partners and therefore under his protection. They would be entertained and watched.

Jasmine on the Green was more of a business before it became a home. This place was both. Not only was it a massive winery that employed a large staff of family members, it was also a fully functioning hotel with a restaurant, swimming pool, and wine tours. The rooms were big enough, but the furnishings were just enough to fit your basic needs. It seemed to fit in with the local customs. You did have your satellite TV, internet, and complimentary bicycles to ride around the place. This week I would be the only customer.

The Florio families have been producing the well-known Marsala wines for nearly 180 years, so from our first moments on the grounds we heard words like Inzolia, Grillo, and Catarratto. The property was vast, and the grapes were everywhere.

It was close to the sea and they could drive you to see some of the ancient Greek, Roman, and Medieval ruins at Mozia, Erice, and the Segesta and Seinunte temples. I would not have known that the

Salt Flats there were just as famous to them as the "Flats" in the US were to me. I even saw a castle. In fact, the families tried to keep me so busy that I found myself cut out of the marriage plans and discussions altogether. The families did whatever it took to keep me distracted and I had not yet seen this guy. On day two, I told Sophie what was going on and she insisted that she had to fly over that night. I needed to meet her at the airport in the morning. I was not able to make that appointment for a number of reasons.

Even though the Montanos were much more business oriented when it came to negotiation, I found the Florio clan were equals when it came to deception. I first noticed this when Pauly and I were separated as soon as we got out of the car. Everyone wanted to see and speak to the famous singer. From the oldest to the youngest, they all wanted to try out their English and get me to say things in Italian right away. They wanted to know about the music and the places I had been. How did I meet Sophie and Pauly and could I sing something? I took pictures with everyone and was forced to taste a whole lot of wine. It seemed that no matter what I did or said, it was worthy of applause. I was only left alone in my room. (These people were good).

When I was alone, I longed for Twister and found myself in desperate need of someone to touch and hold me. My little fingers were doing the walking, but they weren't getting the mileage I wanted or needed, for that matter. It was more like a tease. After that very first time with Miss Janet, I had become dependent on the mind-numbing release of endorphins that sexual activity produced. (Built-in side effect). I was in a bad state of chemical flux, otherwise known as Sexual Withdrawal. So, when the lovely and talented Delfina appeared on that second evening (cousin to someone's cousin), I fell blindly into her trap. As it turned out, she was the mother of all deceptions. (And oh, what a mother she was).

Being me, I was much more attracted to the Sicilian women than I was to the countryside, the grapes, or the men, and anyone could see that. I was turning my head from left to right and had been working on a stiff neck since the moment I got off the plane. Maybe it was partly the wine, but I was jonesing so hard for some good pity-sex that even I could smell my own juices cooking. How could I be expected to think straight under those conditions?

I'm sure my reputation as a batter for the other team had been discussed prior to my arrival. They could have easily gotten that information from my website. So, it made sense to have a bombshell like this one on standby just in case they needed to go into "psychological warfare mode". I guess they figured they would offer this girl in trade for my allegiance if it came to that. The truth of it was never revealed.

After my phone calls to Annette, LA, and Sophie, I relieved myself with a little light masturbation before returning downstairs and into the courtyard for some live music, singing, and dancing in Old Italian style. It was in my honor, so I was more than obligated to attend. I knew that I would have to drink some wine. Beer, brandy, whiskey, and even wine, all have the same effect on me. As long as it had alcohol, I would get drunk pretty easily. So, I had only planned to drink as little as they would let me get away with.

Some of the kids were swinging me in a dance that flung me around and around in a circle. At the end of the song I stopped to lean back against a post to steady myself and allow the warm breeze to blow through the thin dress and onto my damp skin. I had a buzz going from the two glasses I already had but one of the old women insisted I try a glass from her favorite batch. I had just taken a sip of the nectar when the goddess herself walked towards me from the other end of the gathering.

Like out of a dream, this majestic being chose to walk straight up to me and stop just in front of my face. I remember thinking "is this really happening?" and "that skimpy dress is either partially painted on her or it's a part of her skin." She had on no perfume but with the aid of the bonfire and the evening breeze her flesh smelled intoxicating. In other words, she was ripe. A shiver crawled up the length of my damp spine and I almost dropped the glass.

She was 22 years old and stacked about the same as I was except she was taller, bigger in the breasts, and had those wild exotic features that only a true Sicilian girl can have. (OK she was not like me). Her ebony hair fell halfway down her back and her dark eyes seemed to draw in more light than they would release. But it was hard to understand her words. Truthfully speaking, she murdered the hell out of the English language. Because I knew Spanish, I had some idea of what most people were saying. But with her, it kept sounding like "I know you want me." She would open her mouth and her lips would move to say "blab, blab, blab", but what I heard was, "I know you want me." She was right every time she spoke.

At first, she spoke in Italian but then changed to broken English after seeing the look on my face. She was saying something about playing a guessing game. The first thing I thought of was, "If it's in your language, I'm going to lose." Using body language and her very bad English, she instructed me to take another sip of wine then put two fingers into my mouth. When I did, she slowly took my hand, removed the wet fingers from my mouth and placed them into hers and licked them.

The first person I had sex with was Jan Parker and the very first time we did it I came in my pants before I could take them off. This time, it was worse. I felt a second, but colder shiver, run up my back, quickly followed by the release of a hot fluid trickling down from between my legs after filling my panties. I had no choice but to stand there with my fingers in her mouth and let it happen. The fact that someone who was so much more exotic then I, wanted me, blew my mind. In that first experience I was 14 and about to see my one dream fulfilled. This time, I was with a Goddess of Olympic lore and I was more than half drunk. (Whatever game she was talking about, she had obviously won it).

Normally, this would have been chalked up as the most embarrassing moment of my female life. I was off balance, nervous, and totally defenseless when I came on myself surrounded by a bunch of people I didn't even know. It's the kind of thing that happens in a young girl's bad dream. But at the time, I didn't care. I just let her pull my hand as she led my wet ass up to my room like Bela Lugosi did in so many Vampire films. If she wanted, I would have become her slave. Her game was now clear. Her intention, bold as it was, meant to cause a reaction in order to distract me and boy, did it work.

That night, I found her to be many of the things Twister was not. She was soft, gentle, and a real warm cuddly bear of a girl. Twister might grab me, strap-on and fuck me until I would either pass out from exhaustion or collapse in exaltation. In total contrast, Delfina made sweet and passionate love with me (not to me). We both shed tears and she led me right to "the place with no name". The girl would not stop touching me, and I loved that. She even held onto me when I came, and afterwards I fell soundly to sleep on her breast like a baby. When I woke, she easily convinced me to go to a nearby private beach. It was a spot owned by a friend where we could have some topless fun in the sun. "Just the two of us," (I'm pretty sure) she said. I was spellbound.

The sky was partly cloudy, but the water was very warm and relaxing. I stopped trying to understand her words and just focused on the way her sounds made me feel. It was not to be overshadowed by the way she gently kissed and the silky smoothness of her skin as we rolled around on the beach blanket. I was so taken away in the excitement of it all that I didn't notice the little boat on the water slowly growing larger. By the time I felt the cool shadows over me it was too late to put up a fight.

I felt something calling to me, but I was way too distracted to listen. By the time I turned my head to see what the shadow was, a man's big hand slapped a cloth over my face. It's almost impossible to take any action without first taking a breath and that's what I did. I heard the beginnings of a scream but within seconds, I was out.

I've used chloroform myself in the old days many times. The smell is unmistakable, but the use is strictly old school. Not to mention that the skin can be irritated or even burned if not neutralized or washed off. Nowadays it's more popular to inject a victim using a dart or a syringe with a number of easily obtainable drugs. A man that uses chloroform is a man that loves the challenge of getting in close. Although he may be a deadly and highly skilled hunter, he thrives on proving this skill to the hunted. In any case, I never saw it coming.

The first time I woke was on the boat. I was still mostly naked. Meaning, I was partly wrapped in that same beach blanket that we were lying on. There were four men on this fishing boat. They all looked to be local thugs. Two of them were near the back with Delfina, one was in the front, and one was bending over me. The boat was anchored, and the sun was going down. It seemed as though we were waiting for something or someone.

Instinctively, the first thing my brain did was to tell my body to continue with the last thing I was doing before I lost consciousness. Without thinking, I turned over and started swinging at the first person I saw. I don't know what the bending man's intentions were, but he changed his mind when I drove two fingers into his left socket and pulled out most of that eye. As soon as I turned my body, I saw that the man was vulnerable to that kind of attack. I already knew it would work and the action was completed in my mind before I even lifted my fingers. It was more of a reflex action than anything else.

The orb was soft, slippery, and still tethered by the cords leading into the brain, so it was easy for it to slip through my fingers and spring back to slap the side of his face. As the man jerked back his head, he screamed and made a few attempts to grab at the dangling eyeball that I had squished into a completely different shape. As he continued to move backwards, he stumbled and fell off the boat and into the water where he began to splash and scream wildly.

The other men were so startled and distracted by the commotion in the water that I was able to quickly move up to the single man at the front and kick him before he could defend himself. He too, went over the side and into the water. By this time the other two men were making themselves ready for action.

It was then that I realized what they had been doing. From the way Delfina's body was propped with her butt up in the air on the wooden board that formed one of the seats on the boat, she was being raped while she lay helplessly unconscious. The top of her chest and her knees were flat on the deck. Her face (also on the floor) was wet from the water that moved from side to side as the boat rocked. I knew she was alive because bubbles came from her nose and mouth when the water went past her.

By this time the men had pulled up their pants. One went for one of the oars and the other took out the bottle of chloroform from the cargo pocket in his pants. I dove off the side away from the two floundering men and started stroking. I couldn't see land or any other boats around, so I just headed north. I thought I was doing pretty well until I looked back to see the boat gaining on me. I tried swimming under the dark water, but every direction seemed to be against the current. Not to mention the fact that I was getting tired. Each time I surfaced for a breath, they would spot me and toss things in my direction.

There were three men in the boat now. The Cyclops was nowhere to be seen. They thought it was funny to try and hit me with bottles, buckets, dead fish, and other things that happened to be lying around in the boat. When something did hit me, the men would celebrate. It would hurt, and the pain would make me swim a little slower. It was all fun and games until a block of wood hit me in the forehead and almost knocked me out. I wasn't going anyplace but I refused to give up until a weighted net was tossed over me. It was only a matter of fishing me in after that. I nearly drowned in the process.

Once aboard again, one of the men hit me on the legs with the oar a couple of times before he was made to stop. A few fish hooks that were caught in the net were now stuck in me and needed to be cut and pulled out of my flesh before the net could be removed. When it was, I was too hurt and too tired to put up a fight. They were obviously instructed not to rape me because they didn't. Instead I was tied up and made to watch them continue to rape Delfina with a vengeance. They were violent and brutal. At one point she came to, only to be beaten into submission and raped some more. Each man took his turn and took a turn again.

They didn't rape her because they thought she was sexy and loved the touch of her smooth and silky skin. They didn't rape her because they thought it felt good or that it would be a fun or cool thing to do. They raped her because they were angry. Their anger was partly due to the loss of their friend and the fact that I had caused his death. But mostly, I think they were angry because of what they had become. These men were not born this way. They just wanted money. And the need for it consumed who they once were. Nothing in their world would hold a candle to this need, not even sex. Still, it was the reason why Delfina was made to suffer, and I was made to watch.

I couldn't help flashing back to 'Nam. Some of the things I saw and did were more horrible to remember than they were to witness. Much of it I was able to block out with the help of time and a big adjustment to being "back in the world" (as we used to say). Thinking of Vietnam as another planet made it easier to deal with the 24/7 bizarre way we had to live. When we returned to the US, we were forced to relearn how to survive in another new world that used to be our home. We locked the monsters and the memories in the deepest pit we could dig. We threw a truck load of dirt on it, followed by lots of concrete. The rest became a part of who I was (who we all were). We didn't have a choice. (Survive or die).

It was a small piece of the master plan to win the war. We were told that the enemy would comply through humiliation and fear.

They were only partly right. The first time I was ordered to torture villagers I felt bad about it. Later, it all began to make perfect sense. Seeing it this time from the female prospective made me hate the old part of myself just as much as I hated these men in the boat. When it comes to rape, both persons become damaged. That is why I understood them.

I must have thrown up about a half-gallon of water, lunch, and breakfast, while watching them abuse that girl. Even when I closed my eyes, I could still see what they were doing. The oar man shook me, so I could see them drop Delfina's limp body over the side. He said something about "an eye for an eye." I couldn't tell if she was alive or dead at the time. Like the trash that was thrown out earlier, she just went down. (A few hours before I was fantasizing about a double wedding). I remember suddenly feeling cold and I began to shiver like never before. My teeth chattered, and my bones began to ache.

When I woke again, I was strapped on a gurney in what appeared to be the kitchen of someone's house. I was covered with a sheet. The windows were blocked out and the room was very dark. I saw light filtering in from under a door to another room and I could hear a girl being whipped with some kind of a strap not far away. Her screams and the sound of the strap seemed to wrap around the bare walls and echo into other places below me. I admit I was worried.

I woke again startled by the sound of a slamming wooden hatchway being opened five feet above my head. I was in a room underneath the house now. Someone had dug a large space in the hard, rocky ground and turned it into a small stone dormitory of sorts, for the temporary storage of young females to be sold as slaves. I lay on a filthy blanket over the floor next to five other dirty girls of varying ages. All of us were tethered by an ankle harness and lock, to one of many steel posts that were staked into the ground and fortified by concrete. We were all dressed in a pajama outfit and a pair of flip flops. Each of the items was numbered and I was number 6.

One of the girls looked to be about 10 and another looked like she was around 25. They were healthy, exotic, and all appeared to be from someplace off the Mediterranean coast. As it turned out, all seven of us were snatched up by the same men. We had all been sold to the managers of this house, one at a time. One of the girls had been in this pit for 4 days with only water to drink. She was number 1.

Two windows (or viewing screens) were built into the high ceiling of the floor above and were the source of our only light. From overhead, our captors and buyers could look down on us from the comfort of a couch without having to deal with the smells of the dirty girls and the overflowing pots of shit and pee that were emptied only twice a day by whomever the master wished to punish.

Number 1 later explained in Spanish that emptying the pots had an up and down side to it. The up side was that you got to go outside for a few minutes to breathe the fresh air and see the sun. The down side was that spilling the pots meant being hit with a strap and having to clean up the mess.

The normal method for this was to pour all the smaller pots into one or two big pots that were in a basket that were lowered into the cellar along with the key to one girl's lock. The man above would hoist the pots up and set the basket near the hatchway for the chosen one to carry outside and dump into a pit about a quarter mile down the path. Armed with a leather belt, the master would open the door and walk behind her on the path. Back in the pit, she would pass out bottles of water and collect the empties to be placed back in the basket. Once this chore was completed, the girl would not need the key to lock herself back onto the chain. After that, the master would remove the wooden steps and secure the trapdoor.

The crashing I heard was girl number 7 returning from her detail. She passed out the plastic refilled bottles and waited until we were all finished before she collected them to pile into the basket. Only after the door slammed closed, were the others brave enough to speak. In three different languages they all asked her about the weather and if it was foggy or bright. The smallest (number 3) wondered if the plant with the yellow flower was still blooming. I had to sit up and think about what I was dealing with. The very idea that a plant was more of a priority than escape made me weak in the knees.

When questioned, none of the girls could remember how many masters they saw, what kinds of locks were on the doors, or even if a clock was on the wall someplace up top. I wanted to know where we were. How many people we were dealing with? If there were some items we could smuggle in and use to help in our escape? The girls were no help with any of this.

What they did know, was how hungry they were. That mixed with how much they missed their parents and this whole thing being their fault for being alone someplace they shouldn't have been, was all I heard. Not to mention, someone was always crying. That alone made me feel sick, but the overwhelming smell of the dirty pots and people, caused me to throw up twice before I forced myself to get used to it.

Not only was the thought of working as a team to get ourselves out and away a hard sell, getting them to help me get the tools I needed to do it was almost completely out the window. I realized very quickly that I had to do whatever I was going to do on my own. I also considered the possibility of at least one of them telling our captors what I was doing to try and gain some favor. I decided to just be quiet, heal myself, and keep my actions secret. For all I knew, one of them was a plant.

Believe it or not, number 3 (Nahid), the little girl from Tunis, Tunisia, was the only one I found to have any enthusiasm. She and her parents were visiting some family in the port town of Bizerte when she was taken out of the water and away from the beach in much the same way I was. She was playing with some other kids she met and strayed too far from her parents. She and another girl were snatched at the same time and they were both drugged with the chloroform. When she came to, she found herself in the dungeon shackled next to girls 1 and 2, but her playmate was no place to be seen.

The sun loved her and gave a bleached light brown color to her hair. It also gave her a glowing brown skinned complexion. Despite her crying, she was polite, friendly, and smiled when I spoke to her. It was easy to see that she would grow into a beauty one day and I was certain she was taken for just that reason. I knew that she would most likely die in a brothel either to drugs or disease, and the light she carried would be permanently removed from the face of the globe.

I was able to convince the girls that the best way to survive this ordeal was to sleep as much as possible. "If you can sleep, you won't be crying all the time," I told them. "Sleeping will conserve your strength and energy. You won't feel the pain in your stomach if you are asleep." And that's when it got a little quieter.

I asked Nahid to try and find a small thin piece of metal on her next trip up the stairs. A bobby pin or paper clip would do. She was told that if she couldn't get it without being seen that she should let me know where she saw one. I eventually got her to draw me a picture in the dirt of part of the house and the path she took to the dump. We only spoke when the others were sleeping and then only in whispers.

Of course, I dreamed of the Destroyer. It would have been an easy bet to make, and it almost would go without saying, except that this time I saw him three nights in a row. After most every violent waking episode I would usually follow it up with a terrifying dream. The other disturbing thing was that for the first time, the other girls got to live a small part of it with me.

In both lives I had always been a quiet sleeper but for some unknown reason I had now begun to talk and even yell during my "monster dreamtime". Apparently, I was the new "Harry Caray of Nightmares". I gave a play-by-play on how I coached the other me through her action. I was told that I said things like, "Go to the right! You have to run faster! That way is too hot. How can he get there so fast? Everything is on fucking fire!" It was quite terrifying for the girls who all thought I was pursued by a demon. Even the kidnappers were troubled to watch me through the glass ceiling.

The only thing I could think of that made any real difference between these dreams and the others was the fact that in this instance, I was still in the midst of great peril. (The shackles, the injury, and the hunger). Every other time I was forced into mental and physical trauma, I would wake in safe surroundings. This time, it was not the case. I yanked the shit out of the ankle chain each time, and that created a painful bruise. When my body healed the dreams stopped.

Over the course of the next days, little Nahid was not only able to map out the pathway, but she was able to count two of the men that were holding us and the one female that acted as the medic. This information matched the voices and the footsteps I was hearing over my head.

It took two more days before I was allowed to emerge from the dungeon. I had been hearing frequent yelling and a lot of heavy footfalls. We had still not been fed and girls 1 through 5 were growing weak. We weren't really abused per se, but we were a bunch of starved little hamsters lying in the dirt. I'm sure that they planned to feed and sell us soon but, in all honesty, I knew those kids wouldn't last another week that way. Something up top was wrong.

On this afternoon, I felt other footsteps. Nahid called them "new feet." She had learned to tell the difference, too. She also knew the difference between the steps of a person just walking around and the steps of a person that was getting ready to do something with us. For example, someone about to prepare the water bottles or open the hatch to empty the pots was an easy one to predict. But I knew who was about to look into the glass floor and so did Nahid. The others had no clue.

We were all called by our numbers but until now, they had never called for me. The basket was lowered and when I got the key I automatically went for the pots, but I was told to leave them alone and just come up. Once I did, I was ordered to wash my face in the sink. (No one had ever been asked to wash). I knew from the pipes that the trapdoor was in the kitchen. This was the same room I was in when I first awoke. My blanket was just underneath the sink and a little to the right.

The man in the kitchen looked like an old boxer. I was mistaken on how I had imagined him. For a man, he was short, but stocky, and had the scars and marks of many fights that must have dated back for 30 years or more. He was in his 50s and walked with a limp, but his upper body was solid. His voice was soft but firm. He briefed me in Italian that I should not speak unless I was asked a question and to keep my answers short. He also said that I should always keep my head lowered and my eyes to the ground. If I didn't do what I was told and when I was told to do it, he would beat me and rape my cold body when I was dead. After which he would chop me into small pieces, so I could be cooked and fed to the other girls in the hole.

I didn't know if he was serious or not about that last part, but I did know that none of us had eaten anything and all the girls were still alive. It was because of me that they were conserving energy and possibly staying healthier longer. We had all lost weight but after hearing this, I felt that I could shed a few more pounds before I was ready to eat a person. In any case, I was certain that this person would not be me. To tell the truth, I wasn't wholly convinced that we would be made to eat a human child. However, I did get the impression that this man would be willing to chop one into bite sized chunks (alive).

Up to this point, I had played the part of the frightened young tourist girl too far from home. I was meek, humble, and as innocent as I could appear. It seemed that no one knew who I really was, and I thought that it was a good idea to keep my identity concealed for a lot of reasons. This all started to change when I walked into the main room to meet what I thought was the buying agent.

Besides Mr New Feet, the nurse (who was about 30), and a younger man (in his 20s) also stood in this new room. The nurse looked to be going through withdrawals. She twitched and scratched at her skin as if she didn't want it on her body. The young guy looked too military to be anything else. As young as he was, he could not have had any rank or status. He was either a recent reject or he was still in someone's Army. Either way, the sneer on his face looked like bad news for someone.

An older man stood on top of the glass part of the floor in what could be described as a viewing room. End tables and chairs were placed in a way so you could sit and have a smoke or a drink while you watched the girls in the dirty hole. This man wore a suit jacket, slacks, and a white T-shirt (the old "Don Johnson Miami Vice" look). He held a camera in one hand and a cigarette in the other. He had the look of a Greek man in his 40s. I had been hearing a little Greek on my travels and his accent was a match. I also noticed what looked like some kind of police badge holder on his belt and the impression of a gun clipped to the belt near the middle of his back.

I guessed that he had finished his duty day and came out of his way to meet with his slaving partners. He was most likely the brains of this part of the operation. He was the middle man that made the deals. Having status and connections, he was obviously the leader and the others worked under him.

The boxer told me to tell the boss where I was from and what I was doing in Sicily. With head down, I used English words and said that my name was Stacy from America and I was visiting a school friend. I must have said, "I'm just on vacation" three times. The boxer smacked me in the back of my head so hard that it knocked two teardrops from my eyes and threw them two feet in front of my flip flops. I saw stars and would have hit the floor if the "GI Joe" guy would not have steadied my left arm and shoulder.

My strategy was to maintain ignorance mixed with a little defiance, so I turned to the boxer and said "Ouch!" He raised his hand to smack me again and I had already gone through four different scenarios that all ended with me putting two rounds in the chest of everyone in that room, but the "Great White Hope" was prevented from smacking me and so was my first opportunity to make a move.

"She is American, Boomer!" The Boss called out in good English. "It is in their nature to be difficult. The most you can hope for is her broken head or your broken hand and I want neither. The best medicine for the sting of the tongue is the prick of the needle." He moved his head closer when he bent down to get a better look at me and drive home his point. But like all cops will do, his stance guarded his weapon and I was still too far away to make a go for it.

I put my hands together as if to pray and dropped down to my knees. The move took me about a foot and a half closer to the Boss man. "Mister, I am sorry" I said. "I don't know what I did wrong, but I know that you are the Boss right now." I began the creep a little closer. "You're talking about drugging me, right? I don't need any drugs. I'll do whatever you say." I touched his shoe. "I had a summer job last year and that Boss wanted me to stay on because I was the one that did everything right. I had to go back to school, so I did. And this summer was my big chance to see Italy. I couldn't pass that up." I put my hands on his left leg and made every effort to look pathetic. "I'll be just the way you need me, Mister." I began to move up his leg. With tears in my eyes for effect, I looked up to see the barrel of his Sig Sauer an inch away from my forehead. The cigarette was now in his mouth.

I recognized it as the P226 Blackwater Tactical. This model was discontinued after the name Blackwater was no longer found to be cool. I'd never shot one, but I had seen a few guys tote these in Afghanistan and heard that it was a real nice gun. They were company men and considered the weapon to be a kind of symbol of pride. Today a gun like this would be put in a case and displayed only in certain company for the rights to brag and say that you had "been there and done that." The only reason why a COP would carry it on duty was so he could whip it out to empress the other officers and show how much of a badass he was and still is. A Blackwater in Greece would be rare on the best of days. The odds were that he had to kill to get it. When I saw it stretching ever backward, I froze and lost my second opportunity for a go at that gun.

The Boss said something to the effect of "get this filth off of me" and that's when GI Joe grabbed a hand full of my favorite hair and yanked me back and to my feet. He pulled me to the wall where I stood when I first came in the room. My scalp was still tender from that head smack I took. For that instant, I thought that I would have rather been shot. For the sake of remaining in character, I turned to Joe and mouthed "ouch" but this time without the sound.

The Boss thought that I was funny enough to be liked a little bit. He warned that this part of my personality would also disappear after I was introduced to the 'needle's embrace' "That reminds me," he interrupted himself. He holstered the weapon and pulled from his pocket what looked like a small plastic bag of white powder that he handed to the twitching nurse. She snatched the baggy out of his hand and quickly disappeared around a corner. "My medicine," she said.

As far as I could tell, the Boss took about 10 pictures of me clothed and unclothed. I was allowed to drag a comb across my head but I'm sure that I still looked like hell. I didn't argue or say a word about it. I just did what I was told. It seemed to be the best move given the situation and I wanted to avoid any more thoughts about pain, shooting, or drugs. I saw no other opportunity to reach for the gun, either. However, I was able to palm one of the plastic teeth that broke off the comb.

As I was being led back to the trapdoor, Boom Boom asked me about the three small marks on my arms. I tried lying and told him that it was something silly I did just because it was cool, but Boom didn't buy it. He had fought a man with similar markings once and lost (badly). "You are not the average of schoolgirl on holiday," he said. "I will be watching for you." I knew what he meant.

Upon my return, I found that Nahid had fallen sick. Later that same evening, we all got our first meal. It was pita bread and some kind of soup that had noodles and a little bit of beef. I had to instruct the others to eat slowly and chew everything down to mush before swallowing. I yelled at #1 for eating too much and Nahid had to be force-fed. I felt good that no one had to die before I could finally eat something.

It took me a while to get to sleep at first but once I did, I was out like a light. I remember thinking that Boom Boom's attention to detail now made him an even greater threat than that dirty, girl-shooting, drug pushing, Miami Vice want-to-be COP. The Army reject seemed to be full of hate. I knew from his actions earlier that he was just chomping at the bit to do some violence. The woman was a waste of what money was spent for her education. They all deserved to burn in hell, but Boomer had to be killed at the first opportunity. He would also be the hardest to fight.

When I woke, there were five new girls chained to the poles along with the rest of us. It wasn't easy to do, but I was able to force my eyes open to see what I was hearing. It had to be something in the soup. These girls were pure African and looked to be of the same tribe. I tried to speak to them but they all ignored me. It was as if the conversation they were having was much more important than what I wanted to say. I remember thinking that I had never seen a person this dark up close. When I woke again, my # 6 blanket and flip flops were gone.

Those African kids ripped us off while we were asleep. It's not like we were dead or anything. We were just drugged, and those girls knew it. I guessed that they wanted to show their unity and establish a dominance over the rest of us.

Normally in this kind of prison situation, you want to wait until one person establishes themselves as the clear leader and then beat the hell out of him. I couldn't wait that long. If I allowed this to continue, they would cut the rest of us out of any other food we got and most of the water.

All my girls were missing something but #1 was completely stripped. She was still out cold and lay on the floor wearing nothing but her chains. I waited until I knew no one was watching us from above before I did anything about it. I also wanted to judge the other's reactions.

When I stood up all the Africans turned to me. I focused my attention on the one closest and said, "Give me my stuff back" in English. I knew from the way they were talking that these girls wouldn't know my words. They were not travelled or educated. They were each attractive, but their hair was so matted that it gave the appearance of having never been combed. They all had bodies like swimmers and appeared to be just ignorant fishers or daughters of village fishermen. The sea and the water was their life, not any school. The thieves gave me a dirty glare before turning to each other and continuing their conversation. Not one of them looked to be over the age of 17.

I side kicked the closest girl on her back. It lifted her a few inches off her feet and she went flying forward. She fell into the middle of her sisters like a bowling ball into its pins. This time I played the fisherman as I reeled her in by her leg chain while the rest were still rolling about. I grabbed her leg and drug her skinny ass out of the reach of the others, so I could choke her out. It was easy. The kid had no idea what was going on until it was too late. The others watched as I let her limp body drop to the dirt.

If I were locked in a room with men or even boys, my crew would have joined in and started swinging. Instead, the other girls just sat on the ground and looked at me. I would have liked to have seen more support but what could I really expect from a bunch of hamsters. I quickly discovered that I went nowhere trying to push the "us against them" button.

I took the arm of the unconscious girl, hyperextended the elbow and threatened to break her if I didn't get my stuff. I only got a couple of mumbles from the African's side. None of it sounded like anything I wanted to hear so I stepped on her shoulder and pulled back. It snapped, and everybody squealed. The girl awoke and started screaming, too. What a racket it was!

I moved as far as I could to the huddled group and yanked at another one of the dark sisters. I punched two of them before the others would let her go. Again, I pulled her back into my area, placed my right arm against her throat, took my right fist with my left hand and started to squeeze in. Just before the girl went completely limp, the others started to toss all the clothing and blankets they had, to include the items they were wearing, in my direction. I was Queen again. Queen of the hole in the ground, I said to myself. I dropped the kid to the floor.

After that, my will was law in the Pit of Despair. To keep up my status, I made the two that I choked out, sit next to me and claimed them as my property. I called one Broken Wing and the other Sleepy Eyes, because that's what they looked like when they were lying on the floor. I gave # 1 her blanket, but that was it at first. I had my girls fold all the other items I had won and set them in a pile behind me.

It was obvious that none of the others were real leaders. One of the Africans would have risen to the challenge, but I had just taken that all away, so I was unopposed. Since the other so called "white girls" were inclined to sit and let me fight alone, they could now sit and let me lead them. I wondered if maybe some of them would be good followers.

I thought it odd that no one had come down to see about the commotion. No one came to the glass floors and no footsteps of any kind were heard around the house for many hours. There was no telling where they were or what they were doing, but we did hear a cell phone ringing for a long time. That day we went without water. With the addition of these new prisoners squatting over the pot and the rest of us having had full stomachs the night before, the receptacles soon became overfilled. I had a bad feeling, so I took this time to set a plan in motion and put the girls through some drills.

The first thing I did was to make it clear that I didn't want any noise over a whisper. That went double for crying. I was able to convey the fact that I was willing to loan some of the clothing and blankets I controlled for other items or deeds. I wanted a knife, small pieces of metal, or some good sharp rocks for starters. At the end of the day, everyone had something to wear except the two girls I owned. Their lives belonged to me. Keeping them naked reminded the others that I was not to be trifled with. It was a simple but effective way to keep them all in line.

I did use one of the pajama tops to put Broken Wing's arm in a sling. Then I put her to work crushing tiny pieces of concrete into dust. The others collected small stones and began to sharpen them. One of the new girls gave me a fishing hook. Through a kind of sign language, she told how she saw it fall from the ceiling. This was one of the hooks that was sticking out of my flesh when I first arrived. I straightened it and started working on my leg lock. I got two other girls free before the hook broke.

When the slavers returned it was nearly morning. From the conversation they had we learned that Joe and Boomer had a problem with the vehicle they were driving. They couldn't ask for assistance, so they had to walk back. To avoid detection, they were forced to move off the path and made their way through the rocky hillside. The men called the house all day and used up their allotment of phone credits, but the nurse was too doped up to even notice. It sounded like they slapped her around pretty good and hit her with the belt, but I don't think she was in any shape to even care.

The men wanted to wash themselves and rest but knew that they had better check on their below ground investment before they did. As they prepared to retrieve the pots and lower the water, I readied the troops.

I instructed them not to answer when we were called. There would be no gathering the pots or passing out the water this time. Joe flipped a light switch and for the first time I saw just how dank and miserable our pit really was. We pretended to be sick. While we lay on our blankets moaning and groaning, Joe called to Boomer before climbing down the ladder to investigate.

Before Joe could place his foot on the last step, I signaled the Africans to take him. Joe was turning in my direction when he was hit in the eyes with the dust. Now blinded, he couldn't see the four Africans and two of the other girls rush him with a blanket. They wrapped his arms and forced him to the ground where they began to pound the pointed stones into him just as we had rehearsed.

I was proud of my little warriors. Their movements were quick and relatively quiet for the most part. Joe was able to make some noise at first, but it was not enough to sound a real alarm (or so I thought). The girls checked his pockets and found the keys and I quickly made my way up the ladder.

As soon as my head broke the plane of the floor, I saw Boomer coming towards me from the hallway carrying his belt. I quickly launched myself out of the hole and away from the trapdoor before he could get to me. He closed the trapdoor with his foot and stood on top of it preventing any others who would have appeared. I would now need to get past him to leave the kitchen and he had just effectively cancelled any help I might have received from the people under the stairs. It was just he and I.

Behind me was a wall of empty shelves and cabinets. Just in front of me was a wooden kitchen table full of dirty pots, pans, and plates. It seemed that everything that should have been in the cabinets was on the table. In front of that mess was Boomer and the trapdoor of loud angry females. Beyond that was the door to the hallway that led into the living room and my freedom.

To get to me, he would have to move and negotiate this table somehow. But he would first have to bend down and lock Pandora's Box before taking his feet off the hatch. If not, one or more of the other screaming prisoners could get out. But Boomer was smarter than that.

I was quick, agile, and very pissed off, but I still had to get past that big man. He had seen the marks on my arms and knew that if he flinched for a second, I would be over the furniture and down the hall in a flash. He chose to wait. One of us would have to make that first move.

In my old life, I fought guys his size and bigger. Sometimes it was straight-up and hand to hand, but that was only if I ran out of bullets and was too close to avoid the confrontation altogether. Mostly, I used a scope or silence pistol but when I couldn't, stealth and a knife to the gullet or between the seams of his plated armor was my preferred method when silence was paramount. A professional uses what is proven to work the first time and every time. A good policeman can track these techniques to find a murderer. But a soldier might use the same skills to win a war. That other fancy stuff and dialog you see on TV is just for entertainment. In short, you use what works and you don't change unless you have to.

This situation was different in more ways than I could count. He was over twice my weight, size, and maybe four times my strength. There was no way I was going to get close enough to let him grab me. I remember thinking that I would do better throwing Kung Fu books at him then trying to fight him with it.

He told me that I had one chance to submit. If not, he planned to pull my arms and legs off my body and eat them raw while I watched. It sounds funny now but at the time those words were visually horrifying. Then something clicked. I couldn't believe I hadn't thought of it before.

Every new day living in my enhanced mind surprised me. I had never been as quick with my thoughts as I was at that moment in time. But even with the supercharged memory and the ability to think on multiple levels at once, I just can't seem to get the fact that I am a girl. (I had to just accept the fact that I was probably never going to believe it no matter how hard I tried) but I could remember to act like one when needed. I picked up one of the unwashed iron skillets that was lying on the old kitchen table and said, "Then I guess it's dinnertime mother fucker! Get it while it's hot!" And like so many other girls before me, I began to toss kitchenware at the man. (An occurrence of which I myself have been the recipient on more than one occasion).

Since the rebirth, I had set out to deeply study "the art of girlyness" and I had that shit down cold (that is, when I'm not fighting or training to fight). I'm great at kicking, punching, running, and fighting with anything I can hold in my hands, true, but other than that I was all that a girl should be. So, when it came to throwing things at a moving target I have to come out and admit that at that time I sucked. It is safe to say that half of most other girls could die of old age without ever playing a sport of any kind. Face it, how many chicks do you see tossing a wad of paper across the room into a trash can and yelling "Kobe!" But if you would set me in a room full of those lace-panties-wearing and pink-nail-polishing girls, even they would have to vote me the most girly of them all. And a unanimous decision is not too far out on the limb.

I tried to hit him, but I needed it to be more of a distraction than anything else. What I really wanted was to get on top of that table. First, to take away his height and momentum advantage and second, to get to a better weapon. I saw a knife, but I really wanted those two long wooden ladles. After I ran out of things to throw (which incidentally were the same things he dodged and blocked), I got to the long spoons. With them I would at last have something I could fight with and I could keep him and his belt at a distance.

Out of the many things I tossed his way, a few actually did strike him, so the man was bruised and more than just a little angry. Once I had the spoons I was so confident that I could damage and humiliate this man Jacky Chan style that I jumped off the table and onto the floor in front of him. But I was wrong. The man must have reached back to Thursday morning to long punch through the spoons and knock me into Saturday night. Both spoons were broken, and I went sliding across the floor.

As my head collided badly with the broom closet door, a wooden mop fell across my legs. My left arm was slightly numb, but I was able to grab the mop and crawl under the table while he was latching the cellar door. By the time he smashed the table into small sticks, my head was clear, and I had removed the mop from the handle to make it the Grandfather of all Weapons.

His belt was rendered useless and any other attempts to attack or defend were met with pain. He couldn't get close enough to hit me and he couldn't get far enough away to avoid being hit. I whittled him down little by little like a large oak tree. I beat his arms first before I worked on his legs. It wasn't a quick or an easy feat, but I had trained for nearly two years for this single moment. As strong as he was, he eventually fell to the ground like so many trees to a woodsman's axe.

At the end, he sat on the floor and begged me to put him out of his misery. He said something about him being dead inside for too many years. He had lost his family or the idea of keeping them together or something like that. It was mostly a mumbled mix of languages. He also told me that if I didn't kill him, he would eventually find me and kill me as a payment for forcing him to live. I was partly afraid that he would try to grab at me when I came behind him, so I moved as fast as I could and struck from the side.

I found no joy in jabbing the pointed end of the dull carving knife into his throat, but it had to be done. I quickly drove the blade into the right side so far that it pierced through the left from the inside. I removed it just as quickly. Blood shot out from both sides of his neck, his mouth, and his nose as if I had turned on a fountain. His death sounds were wrenching to hear and the sight horrible to see. He sprayed all over me and a good portion of the room before his heart had no more blood to pump. When it was finally over, I added to the mess by throwing up on the floor next to him.

The girls were screaming like crazy, but I knew that I had better find that nurse lady before I let them out. I shouldn't have had to, but I crept around the house until I found her in one of the two bedrooms. She was dead and covered in her own filth. From the looks of things, she had laid there all day. She was so high that she either couldn't or just refused to get up. Instead she enjoyed a full day of undisturbed bliss and didn't trouble herself with checking on us or going to the toilet. It's possible that she wouldn't have known that she even needed to. It was no wonder the men were so angry with her.

When the men returned and slapped her around it must have disrupted part of her buzz. That may have been the reason why she took this opportunity to shoot up again. (One last time). Her neck was sweaty, but it was the only semi-clean spot of flesh worth looking for. It was hot to the touch, but I found no pulse. In truth, you could have pronounced her dead the moment that cop gave her "the medicine".

For fear of throwing up again, I closed my eyes, held my breath, and felt my way back to the trap door. I noted that when I returned to the kitchen to let the girls out all their noise had stopped. After I unlatched the door I had to yell at them to get someone to come close enough to the hatch to be seen. I guess they freaked out when blood started to drip on them from the door and the ceiling above.

Once out, every last one of them took a look at me, Boomer, the blood, the puke, and screamed. That is until they too, threw up on the floor. There was no getting past the mess without going through it. Some of them tripped or slipped and fell in the mess and got themselves all bloody and pukey, too. We were all in a real foul state. I was forced to open my eyes to get around the other girls and there was no way I could continue to hold my breath. I left what remained in my guts on that floor.

As the sun came into view, we exhausted what was left of the water in the outdoor tank showering two and three at a time. There was no soap so the PJ's (those of us that were wearing them) still looked really bad. I would have had to break another arm to get someone to go back in the cellar to get the other things, so we took the dirty sheets from the other room and prepared to get out of that house.

After charging the nurse's cell phone, we discovered that it was almost completely out of credits. We had heard the men say that they were all out of minutes so any long distance calls were out. We attempted to call the emergency number and found that the thing was set up only to receive calls. I sent a text to Sophie that simply said, "Find me." I didn't dare to hope that it had gone through. It was disappointing, but I kept the phone just in case.

It was foggy but from on top of the roof it looked like miles of nothing but hills, rocks, and trees in all directions. We saw no power lines, antenna, or chimney tops, but I could smell the sea. A larger hill was to the east, but the only path went west. The hill might have given us a better vantage point and if I were alone I would have gone that way, but the path had to lead someplace. Just the thought of the phrase 'some place' means 'an area of people' and 'people' meant help. We each took a bottle of water and started following the path.

About a hundred yards later we found an intersection and a voice in my head said "north", so we took the northern path. I remember thinking that this was not the normal voice I was tuned to. The frequency and tone were off. The voice that I had always known for most of my life was discovered on the football field and worshiped on the battlefield. At one time I ignored the voice and it almost went away. Later when I realized how vital its insight had been to my success, it became more defined and recognizable. It was how I was able to tune the other voices out. In these last two years, it had changed from the strong whisper of a man to the strong whisper of a woman but the channel it came in on was always the same. But as I said, this voice was different. Still, why not take the path, I thought. I saw no reason not to.

The landscape looked like nothing I had ever seen. The ground in the area was mostly comprised of stone and sand. As we moved up this one lane path, it all turned into rock. The trees got smaller and the rocks got bigger. Most of the girls had nothing on their feet so the going was pretty slow.

We walked in a staggered column formation. If the phone rang, I would answer it. If a car came by, we would ask for help and get in it. If that help turned out to be another trap, or if we saw anyone that looked like another slaver, we would stone the vehicle and split-up. That was the plan.

In less than one hour, the water was gone and half of us were weak and tired. I had no idea how far we had to go, but I knew our situation would worsen in the dark, so I forced them to continue moving but at an even slower pace. Besides the rocks around us, all we had were two knives and what little we were wearing.

The Africans seemed unaffected by the rock, the fog, and the lack of water. They sipped a little at the water they had and gave the rest away without me ordering them to do so. They helped the others when they slipped and acted a lot less afraid. The tallest one even volunteered to carry Nahid. Their advantage was in the fact that they had not been locked up and starved like the rest of us. But they also knew a thing or two about how to throw a rock.

I had been having a hell of a time concentrating on what I was doing ever since I left the house. I was fighting what seemed like a noise between my ears. I guessed it was the results of that round #2 knock down at the hands of Boom Boom. I didn't want to let the others know but my head was killing me, and it felt a little worse with every few steps.

When I heard the gunshots behind us, the static in my head was so distracting that I had to convince myself that what

I thought I heard was real. We were on a hill, so I had the tribe move off the path and hide. From that vantage point we could see a good strong 60 yards into the fog in all directions.

I started to clear up a lot when I saw the smoking car speeding towards us from the direction of the gun play. That same voice that had spoken earlier came back. It was garbled but the woman speaking had a British accent. She told me that we had to distract the man in the car. He was going to see us anyway. She tried telling me that he had something, or he was going to kill more people. It was hard to understand but it sounded important. I knew that I had lives that depended on me, so I had to make a choice.

The troops and I were already set-up for a hasty ambush, but the driver was going way too fast. I decided that I would use myself as a distraction. Maybe seeing a woman in the road would slow him down a little. Maybe he'd be slow enough to get one or two stones onto the window before he went past and would crash. The British chick would do the rest. It was the best I could hope for.

I had about 20 seconds to spread out the girls on both sides and instruct them to aim for the front windshield before I ran down the path to wait at the end of our line.

Just behind us was a curve in the path that led the traveler between two small croppings of large stone slabs. Unless you really knew this road and your car, a driver would have to slow down a little or he could risk damaging his vehicle as the many paint rubbings and pieces of headlights on the ground near the stones attested to.

It was my thinking that a person in the road would make your average driver either slam on the brakes or hit the rocks in an effort to avoid hitting this person. Then again, normal people wouldn't be fleeing a gun battle in a smoking car driven on a planet made out of stone at 60mph up a winding foggy goat path. So, it was very likely that this driver would just run into me, especially if he recognized me from the hole in the ground. (It was a risk to be sure). Still, I stood at the ready, wearing my bloody PJ's, holding a rock in one hand and a table knife in the other.

When the car came close enough to have a clear view of the driver, we recognized each other right away. It was that Don Johnson want-a-be cop. He aimed right for me and I was forced to drop my rock and run up the side of the stone slab and spring off and over the car to avoid getting hit. I hurt my ankle on some loose rocks when I landed. I guessed that he didn't like me anymore.

The car slammed into the stone and rode across the slab sideways on the passenger side sparking as it travelled about 30 more feet before it was able to stop on its own. A trail of smoke and steam from the bullet riddled Mercedes had been following behind the car, but now that it was stopped, the vehicle and the entire area around it was completely engulfed inside of a mist. This, mixed with the ever-persistent fog, made the car and its driver disappear before my eyes.

I was surprised to see him back so soon. I could only figure that by now he had to have run my image through some kind of police recognition software and discovered who I was. I wouldn't know his plans, but it would be easy to assume that he called to his minions at the house about it. When he didn't get an answer, he would have had to come by to investigate the matter for himself. Over the hissing of the radiator, I heard the creaking of an opening door and sensed that this man at the very least had bad intentions on his mind.

At that time, I could only guess what happened to put bullet holes into that nice Mercedes. The only thing I knew for sure was that he had to get out of it if he wanted to get his hands on me. Since the car was at a 45 degree slant, he was either going to have to roll open the driver side window and crawl out onto the ground, or climb up to exit from the passenger side and slide or jump off. The fact that I heard a door creaking told me that the window option failed.

The man heard something to the north and started shooting in that direction. Every shot fired seemed like an explosion in the denseness of the smog. I knew if I didn't stop him, he would kill one of my girls. As the weapon fired, the muzzle flash made a silhouette of the top part of his body and for that moment, he could be seen. That was where I threw my rocks. (Or should I say that was what I was aiming for).

The others heard the crashing of glass and metal and started throwing their rocks too. The Africans started to make a noise that reminded me of the wild Indians in those old cowboy movies I saw on Saturday afternoons when I was a kid the first time. The other girls made noises too. Altogether it was a strange and eerie sound that surrounded us from seemingly all directions.

As the man emptied two magazines into the mist, I got the feeling that the ghosts of all the girls he had bought and sold into slavery that died along the way had somehow returned for their moment of revenge. The spirits of the nurse and all the other drug deaths were howling. The drowning victims were whispering, and the suicides were laughing out loud. Delfina would have been there, cheering us on in her broken English. It would have been enough to drive a sane man mad if it were not for a lucky shot hitting one of the girls and bringing him back to reality with her cry. The yelping stopped.

As the man noisily climbed down from the high side of the car, I was almost close enough to cut him and I would have done so, if he had not fired a round in my direction. I had used all my knowledge of silence and mental misdirection to close on him. But the closer I came, the stronger my scent must have been. It was either a design flaw or an intentional side effect that makes me heat up and sweat so much. I understand how I can lose a pound or three running or having good sex and I am used to the fact that I can soak my entire wardrobe just by having certain thoughts in my head. My natural odor is distinct but normally inoffensive, but under the above conditions, I will produce a scent. That is why I will travel fully stocked with gentle soaps and lotions that will allow me to wash several times a day without hurting my skin. But this week I was 'roughing it' as one might say. Add shit, puke and blood into the mix and I would have been easy to follow.

The quick and cold showers we all took were only enough to get rid of part of the surface dirt. Without soap to kill the bacteria from that pit and the other filth from our own bodies still stuck in our pores, none of us were the least bit fresh. Not to mention, that being tasked to stop a speeding car driven by a killer with only a rock and a dull knife, can lead to some extra perspiration on its own. So, the others stunk too. We were all a bunch of over ripened fruit tossed on top of rotting meat. He only needed to follow our lingering odor to find us. As he made his way straight for me, I was forced to back off and out of the ghostly cloud.

When I did carry a weapon, I kept three loaded magazines. Two were on the belt and one in the weapon itself. I was told that the Blackwater came with four 20 round mags in the case. That meant that this man could have left the house with a minimum of 80 rounds. If he used one clip in the gun battle, he could have jumped into the car and reloaded while driving. He had just quite generously expelled two whole clips shooting into the fog at us. He could have had more ammo and he could have had less. But the safe money was that he could still have another 20 shots left.

I saw a few of the girls when I emerged from the thickest part of the smog. They had stones in both hands and were creeping up to hurl them all at once. With one scream, the stones flew, shots were fired, and the yelping restarted.

When someone finally connected it inspired us to throw harder and faster. The kids were like pack animals. They would pick up a stone, toss it, and move to get another. The man inside the cloud had no way of knowing where the next stone would come from. It was a beautiful thing to see and be a part of. That was, until James Sonny Crockett stepped out of the mist to put two holes into the back of the girl we knew as #7.

Parts of her lungs, heart, and pieces of her ribcage blasted out and away from the front of her thin body. She was dead before she flopped silently to the ground in slow motion. Her body lay in a strange position and the stony slab beneath her could be seen through the middle of her back. For the second time everyone turned quiet as we watched in horror. Later, the fact that the body didn't bleed much at all would be a point of conversation.

The man exited the void holding the left side of his bleeding head with his left hand and waving the gun with his right. "I'm going to my boat," he said in English. "I quit for this day. Move away and the rest can live a long life."

"You killed another one!" yelled #1 in her Spanish. He returned her Spanish by saying that three of his people were dead and he just had to kill his business partners. In his score chart, we were ahead. All he wanted to do was get the bag out of the car and go.

The steam and the smoke were starting to taper off. We stood and watched as the man popped the trunk, moved something out of the way and retrieved a green back pack. As he strapped it over one shoulder I was compelled to speak.

"You're spoils of war," I said.

He paused before pointing the gun and his English directly at me for a second time and said, "I'm on vacation! I'm on vacation! I don't know how you did it YASMEEN, but you took from me the only person that I ever liked! I knew Boom Boom when he was fighting on the side of the road," he said. "I saved him. I was fast in the mind and he was fast with his hands. I was the cop and he was my enforcer. We made much money. People said that he hit like, how you say …DYNAMITE is your word! When he was badly hurt by a small Chinaman, his body healed enough but his head would not let him know it. We had lost all the money and started slaving girls to make up what we owed. Last year we were all paid off. This year was for us. We were going to retire!"

"He asked me to put him out of the misery he was in," I told him. "He hated himself! He said that he had been dead for longer than he could remember. You didn't save him, you just killed him slow. Same as you did the nurse, this young girl, and a hundred others! You killed children, parents, and families! You're not just a slaver, you're a disease!" (The words just came out).

He moved forward and put the gun to my forehead, just as he had done before and said, "It would give me such joy to end you like you did my friend, but I am letting you live. One, is because I now like your music and two is because of you I am a rich man." He then turned, put the weapon in his belt and started to walk away. "The next time I hear you sing I'll be thinking, maybe this song she sings of me."

The voice signal returned. This time it was clear, sharp, and way too loud. "Thank you for your help. We will be in firing range in 15 seconds. We can terminate the target, or we can track him and have him arrested later today. Please indicate your preference by way of body motion."

I told the other girls to get back and called out to the cop to stop walking. The girls stepped away, but the slave trader refused to comply. This would have been a perfect moment to say something really cool, like Arnold did with "I'll be back" or Jack did with "Here's Johnny", but for the life of me, I couldn't come up with a good phrase in the allotted time. What I did do, was step up onto a large rock, lift my right arm into the air, close my fist, and I gave him a 'thumbs down'.

As soon as I did, a lightning bolt seemed to strike him from straight overhead. Just as a demolished building can be made to implode in an instant, it looked like the top half of his body was violently and suddenly smashed into the bottom half. Or maybe like the invisible 'Hammer of Thor' crushed him before what was left burst into flames and dissolved before our eyes. It took less than five seconds for his entire body to completely burn the fuck up, bones and all. All that remained were ashes, small clumps of charred flesh, most of the backpack, the gun, and the smell. It was all kind of clean really.

Later this event would be described as 'Fifth Generation Warfare'. First, Second, Third, and Fourth Generation thinking are well known to most military strategists. Fifth Generation Warfare will be known as "the ability to eliminate your enemies without sending troops of any kind." There is little to no evidence of a conflict. Even a living witness will not have the ability to describe what happened. The target simply disappears.

It gave me the dry heaves something awful, but I was able to get Crocket's bag that turned out to be full of Euros. Sleepy Eyes, #7, and another of the African girls were dead. At least Nahid was alive. We hugged each other and thanked God for giving us the strength to survive not to mention that bolt of lightning we just saw. I was suddenly inspired with a great line. "Let that be a lesson to ya!" (Bugs Bunny).

The experience was exciting, amazing, and a little mind blowing. For me, the whole thing started with doing my friend a favor. It moved quickly from boredom to fantasy followed by kidnap, murder, and starvation. I worked on my acting skills, I proved myself as a fighter, I killed a man, and I saw others die before my eyes. In the end, I had lost over 10 pounds and was holding a big bag of money.

I had survived due to training I had in my former life linked with the new experiences of my present. I felt proud that I had taught ignorant young women (children) how to kill and praised them for doing it. I was sad that I lost three people in our fight from slavery and who knows what other horrors, but considered it acceptable given the circumstances, the alternatives, and the fact that all our enemies were not just defeated, but dead. The others would need years of therapy but there I was reminding myself to look sad in front of the other girls. Inside, I considered this a more then minor compliment to my leadership ability. It wasn't until later that I recognized this as the point I first started to turn slightly back into the old me.

During this experience I was in lots of danger, but I was never truly afraid. The one thing I had that gave me the advantage and my eventual victory was the fact they underestimated me at every turn just because I was a girl. I used the cute, innocent, and scared look to hide my intentions and that helped a lot. Still, no one had a clue of the plans and back-up plans that ran through my mind because they all thought I was just a stupid female.

When the chopper landed two hours later to take us off the Rodopos Peninsula to the Kratikos International Airport, I could have kissed both Maximiano and Miguelangel on the lips as the two stepped out of the door and onto the rocky ground. (I wasn't locked up that long). They were in uniform and wearing the rank of Major now.

I wanted to go to a private hospital in Alexandria for treatment and to relax before splitting up the girls, but I was denied. Duke Philip had arranged something in Athens. So, we left the Island of Crete and flew by private jet into Athens International and from there choppered again to a special facility. On the way, the brothers told me about the events from their perspective.

The brothers were first alerted that I was missing on day two. Sophia called Annette, then her brother, to get one of her cousins to collect her from the airport when I didn't show up on day one. The cousin took her to the Montano Estate where she met Maximiano and Miguelangel. Pauly found the Florio family less than forthcoming with the 411 on their relationship with Delfina, so he fell back to the estate where he and his uncles put a plan in motion.

Sophie only knew what little I had told her about my family and the powers they possessed. She had however spoken to Ian the day we took down the Goldstein's. The conversation confirmed what I had told her and a whole lot more. He called and told her not to resist when his people came to investigate later that same night. So, when the brothers called Duke Philip, she was calling Ian and the two parties contacted each other. The Society was asked to do nothing.

While the Montanos pooled their resources and began a ground and sea investigation, my newly acquired First Line staff volunteered to head the Global Satellite search, Task Force activation, and Extraction plan. Agents and pawns for bait were placed around the area and tracked.

On day three, the Montano's discovery of Delfina's partly fish eaten body led them to a group of slavers they knew were active around the area. The investigation slowed when no amount of torture or killings could get them closer to the small independent group.

On day four, the group got approval to ping the chip in my head. Two British submarines were diverted and put on patrol. One sonared and pinged its way across the entire Mediterranean. The other travelled from Sierra Leone to France. The entire cone of the footprint encompassed all of Europe, North Africa, and the Middle East. Eventually the footprint was expanded in all directions for nearly 3000 miles. It stretched from the southern shores of Lake Victoria in Tanzania to the center of the Gulf of Bothnia in the north. It vibrated the eastern shore of the Caspian Sea and searched west of the Azores Islands.

I was trapped underground in an area surrounded by solid stone mixed with iron and other elements. That tiny section of the world was part of the original crust of our planet. It lay under the water for millions of years before it was thrust up by newer layers long before man walked on this earth. The signal never made it to my chip.

After 10 days the only continuing effort was a low intensity ping relayed off every global carrier to surround the entire planet. A small family dispute between the Montanos and Florios resulted in three deaths, no marriage and a renegotiation of the first business deal.

On day 12, the ping was returned once from someplace in southern Europe. The brothers put drones in the air and tightened the signal but widened the bandwidth.

Early in the morning of the 13th day, it was reported that I was not only returning the signal from Crete, but I was moving at a slow pace. The spy techs determined that I had to be walking and therefore alive. The brothers readied their standby team in Rome. Separately they flew to Athens, linked up and deployed to Crete in two choppers.

It was assumed that I was receiving the signal when I turned north but due to the conditions I could not be pinpointed. The dead bodies in the house combined with the missing slaves meant that someone was being double crossed. It was one man against six and the winner headed north. The drones spotted the firefight from over 50 miles away even under the foggy weather and saw two heat sources in the vehicle. The man was still too far out of range to shoot. It was believed that a lost agent and valuable resource was in the area, but it was also a possibility that she could be in that car. In order to stop the fleeing man, he needed to be slowed down. But until I stood on that stone with a rock in my hand, nothing was really certain.

Of the weapon, all I can say is that the man was taken out by a smaller version of the Rail Gun deployed from an orbiting platform that was originally conceived in the time of President Reagan. When he talked about Star Wars, this was one of the things he meant (Fifth Generation). Repositioning the weapon brought it across the sky and into a lower orbit. It gave another meaning to the phrase "death from above". The papers would later say that it was a Weather Balloon.

The voice I heard was the voice of the grateful cousin I had met at the Davenport Manor. By standing on the rock, I was not only acknowledging who they thought I was, but I was letting her know that vocal signals could be received by the chip in my head. Her voice, although way too loud, was able to guide me to a place where the weapon could cover us better.

The missing agent was in the trunk of the car, but she had been shot by stray rounds from the gun battle at the house. Her job was simply to gather information, but she went above and beyond. Having twice escaped on her own, this was the third time she had allowed herself to be in the wrong place at the right time. She died before the trunk was opened. The girls and I considered her a nameless hero in the fight against human trafficking. The hidden notes in her socks were later used to track down the two previous slave rings and destroy them.

Flash Back Who's That

Seeing Doc Stacy again was a surprise, shock, and a nightmare at the same time. If I would have known she was waiting for me in Athens, I would have pushed harder with my request for Alexandria. Then again, there was probably no way to avoid her. She seemed pleased to see me and I was sure that she was asked to be my therapist because she was familiar with my case. Still, I had the worst uneasy feeling about her.

I wondered if she thought that I had something to do with the accident, incident, or whatever they were calling what happened at the Georgia sanatorium. It's still possible that someone found my set up before it could destroy all the records and body parts. Either way it went, I was the only one that tried to escape that day, so I had to at least be the prime suspect for sabotage. It was safe to assume that she received some heat when I injured myself trying to escape from the mall. I knew she would want to talk about that and more. There was no genuine reason she should have been smiling.

Last time she saw me as a retarded and shell-shocked little kid with no memory. I didn't have the sense to answer questions or know what I should be feeling then. This time she would see me as a semi-popular singer, business woman, a world traveler, killer, and possibly a spy. She would most definitely want to know all about that too. That's why I kept thinking that at some point I would wake up as the old me or worse. (A headless brain in a jar). I was compelled to execute another escape as soon as I smelled her scent.

All of the other would-be slaves were split up and put into nice two-person rooms. I wanted to keep Nahid close to me, but Stacy and the others did not agree, and I was alone in my own room. All of us were scrubbed from head hair to toenails and everyone but me was given shots. I had refused mine. I knew this would draw more attention, but I was as paranoid as I could be. I didn't know what these people were going to do with me. The staff persisted and so did I.

I demanded to see Annette, Sophie, and the brothers before I would take any medicine. I said they were my bodyguards and I needed them in the room. I knew that the brothers would have found some way to retrieve my phone and I wanted that, too.

What I didn't know was that the brothers were busy controlling the security on our floor, the roof, and in the parking lots. Annette, Sophie, Joy Bird Song, and Jacky O were being held in one of the lower levels of the building and were not allowed to see any of us. We were quarantined.

It was only after I hit one of the orderlies with a bedpan and pushed another into a glass cabinet that security responded. They called Miguelangel for guidance. He thought I was going nuts, but I ordered him to release my friends and escort Stacy and whomever did not normally work there, out of the building.

It was my first "Rich Bitch Power Flip" and it was a good one. It was a shock to everyone that knew me, and I guess I had come way outside of the bag to get what I wanted. In my mind I was convinced it was a trap. That woman wanted to get into my head one way or the other. When Doc Stacy said that it was a normal reaction and started quoting psycho mumbo jumbo, it took two men to hold me back from choking her. While they had me, a third one stuck a needle in and like the good book says, "The evening and the morning were the next day."

While I was out, I heard a voice hiding behind other voices. It was an impossible voice. Like a faceless memory it refused to come into view. It was a ghost of a voice that said, "What a mess," just like it had before.

I woke to Sophie's sad and beautiful face floating over me. If it wasn't for the restraints I would have tried to choke her, too. After struggling for a few seconds, I realized I wasn't going anywhere. Sophie refused to unshackle me until I first promised not to hit her and then sang "You've Got a Friend" written by Carole King. (Believe it or not).

It was a good choice. In spite of all my anger, she forced me to remember the birthday party I gave her earlier that year. I sang this song for her at a restaurant in Miami and she cried, I cried, and everybody else cried, too. I wasn't ready to acknowledge her apology, and this was another way of telling me that she was sorry for asking me to step in her family business. True, she should have just married the guy and saved a lot of lives, but I didn't have to go into all of that. We hugged, and I had to let it go. She gave me some nice flowers. (What could I do?).

Once I was dressed and supported by my people, I felt a lot better. The brothers kept Doc Stacy's people at bay while I visited, kissed, and hugged all my girls, goodbye. I instructed the men to personally supervise the girls' return to their homes when they were ready. I took the rest of my stuff and got on the first thing smoking to Lebanon.

Nabeelah had been trying to contact me for days. She had no idea that I was missing until I called her back and told her. She knew that I had stopped the extra shows I was doing and wanted my help with her niece again. She promised that I should prepare myself for something too outrageous to be explained over the phone. When pressed, she told me that the entity asked to see me. (My fans).

I waited until I got on the plane before I spoke to Lloyd. I knew he would be HOT and boy was I right. I countered with threatening to end my own life if any of those people touched me again. I told him that they represented the ending of all I knew and the beginning of all I had lost. He seemed to understand that point of view but kindly insisted that I would have to meet with another professional that would report to Doc Stacy. It was not an option. It was a necessary evil if I wanted to continue on with his plan.

I asked him to send me someone that both he and I could trust. I would meet them in Beirut, but I wanted a few days first to eat, sleep, and relax with my close friends. He agreed to give me four days and then put my brother on the phone.

The kid seemed awake but still distant in many ways. He said what you wanted him to say and did what you wanted him to do but that was it. I had to remind myself that he had always been like that. To me, I had the feeling that there was something about him that was missing. Sure, he was not yet three years old, but by that time I thought that I should be seeing some unique sign of a personality emerging. Then again, what did I know about kids? It was most likely a side effect from the process that saved his life. How could he and I ever be expected to classify as normal? Still, if you would have asked me at that time, he was the one that could have used the shrink and not me.

Sophie needed me to speak to the Society and Annette insisted that I had to talk to James. The ladies were happy and relieved to see my face and hear my voice on the internet. They all wanted to ask questions about the experience and offer their support. It was nice, and I appreciated it, but it was much more girl talk than I was in the mood for. I had to cut the whole thing short. On the other hand, I was relieved to speak to James. It took him only 10 seconds to sum up his joy in seeing me alive and moved quickly into business. (It was refreshing).

The band was in the studio and had already worked five tunes. Two of them had what he thought were good lyrics, but the others were not so good. He loved the music and wondered if I wanted to try my hand in writing at least part of a song before he farmed the job out. It was possible that he would give me all the writing credit if my words were good enough. As he uploaded the songs to my phone I didn't have the heart to tell him that I was thinking about quitting.

He also spoke more about that deal he was working with the LFL. He interviewed 15 girls from different teams around the US and one from Canada. I needed to check all the profiles, teleconference with whichever ones I liked, re-interview them and pick one. The season was about to start up again and the league wanted to capture as much media as they could. I looked at all the files.

I remembered Delfina. She may have tricked me into distraction, but her passion was real. I could have lived with her on that sandy beach for a hundred years. It would be nice to have a steady someone. Someone that wouldn't go away. What a thought. To the old me, that would have been the sappiest thought I had ever had in both my lives. Still, on this day it was the truth. I needed more than just sex. I wanted to belong to someone. I needed love. But until I found it, I'd take as much sex as I could get and just fantasize about the rest. Someone once said, "You can never gain without risking loss." (Unknown).

On the ground there was no shopping, checking in, showering, or even a change of clothes. Nabeelah had a car pick us up at the foot of the plane and drive us directly to a special site in the very ancient city of Jubayl, 25 miles north of Beirut. My hair still looked like a bird's nest but there was no time.

Gebal is one of the earliest names for this town that some believe it to be the oldest continuously inhabited city in the world. The Greeks called it Byblos and the Crusaders called it Gibelet. Jubayl is more of an Arabic name for this community that has supported life long before 7,000 BC.

Aleaha's aunt had turned in desperation to a secret society that specialized in hunting things that called themselves gods (or so she thought). This top-secret location was layered with security. In the end, only I was allowed to pass into unearthed chambers that were dedicated to gods before the time of gods as we know them. The three men guiding me through the underground temples were wearing red robes with gold trimmings. Before we entered, I had them assure me that they meant me no harm and that I would leave the same person as I was when I walked in. Due to the desperate nature of my recent events, they allowed me to take a knife. (I was in no mood to be nabbed again). They did warn that I might become more enlightened before the day had ended.

I counted 45 men who seemed to represent a wide span of nationalities. Glancing at the baffling array of equipment I saw along the way, I figured I passed the work station of every type of engineer there was. I saw computers attached to things that looked as if they came off the set of a science fiction movie. I also saw what looked like potions being made and walked past some giant gemstones and a few crystal balls.

My escorts explained that there are millions of entities that are known to us as godlike. "Some have always existed and always will," said the first man. "They are the greater gods. Others were born, reborn, created, or given this status by other gods. They are the medium level of godliness and they all have a purpose. Then there are other lesser gods. Some are ascended creatures and other beings that we ourselves created. Many of these creatures have turned against their creators. Their quest for a status that they cannot achieve has made them petty and cruel." He went on to say, "It is our belief in these lesser gods that gives them power over us. But human beings have recently earned the power to mentally evolve while most of the lesser of these entities still do not. This is not because they lack the ability. Their only failing is a lack of humility. Many gods of legend were vanquished because they underestimated their human foes. Their arrogance made them as vulnerable as any normal man. If you were born one thousand years ago, you would not know how to use a computer. If you became a god one thousand years ago, you would think it was too beneath you to even learn."

The second man began. "When the ancient people would outgrow one of these false gods and when I say 'false' I mean not worthy of worship, they would no longer need them anymore. A god of this kind that has no worshipers soon dissipates and the power that at one time was his alone bleeds away to be passed on to the general masses. Every new cognizant life in the effected realm now has a chance to learn part of this free-flowing ability and it is only in rare cases ever given to just a chosen few or one person. As mankind continued to grow, their need for the minor gods became less and less. Our order was formed long ago to see an end to all of the false or unneeded gods so that a more mentally aware form of life can take their place."

"In a sense that day is already a reality," the first man told me. "Consider a man having two conversations at one time. One conversation is with a person thousands of miles away, about a lost package that did not arrive for his brother's wedding. At the same time he is on the phone, his wife wants to discuss the reasons why they will be picking up his dry cleaning on the way to the airport. First of all," the man explained, "no one in the old times could multitask. Not all of the ancient gods could fly. Almost none could speak at great distances. If they didn't have wings, they were forced to send messages by others or use things they created or built just for that purpose. We surpassed their power with the invention of the telegraph and the airplane. Now, due to discoveries in science, medicine, and a better diet, we are starting to extend our lives. And we don't have to be magical or mythical to do it."

"You can't hope to extinguish the light of all the gods, so you can absorb the power of the universe, do you?" I asked the men.

"No," the third one replied. "The greater gods have control over the very forces that allow life to exist not only in this universe but in others as well. Our focus is on the ones bound to this planet for now. When the time comes to venture beyond this veil, we will be prepared. Besides, more souls are ascending every day and thanks to this effort, many of them are from our own world. Our best plan for success in that new form is not to be merely concerned with governing the affairs of mankind. It is in the learning, growing, and expanding of our mental potential that will make our godhood useful and everlasting. The next great frontier is not outer space, but inner space. That is how we will take to the stars and maybe someplace beyond even that."

They told me that they were at a critical point in expelling the entity called Euterpe from Aleaha's body. The spirit was cooperating nicely up until the point it asked to speak to me. These priests were in the business of expanding life, so they wanted to avoid killing the girl if given a choice to save her.

As we started to enter the chamber that had Aleaha strapped to a stone slab and covered only by what appeared to be an elaborately colored bed sheet, the first man said, "Sometimes these false gods try to avoid extinction by attaching themselves inside the bodies of living people. As a spirit, these things are elusive, but their life is short without a host. It could find safety sleeping among other resting souls and could hide virtually undetected for hundreds of years, but that's no fun. The point of being alive is to live. But when it binds itself to a human host like this one has, it's basically trapped itself until it's forced out or the host dies. We know of this one. It has been on our list for more than two thousand years and we are well prepared. It is very strong but the powers of other entities both new and old assist us in this sacred ritual. The self-destructive nature of this creature is too dangerous to be allowed to pass through these walls and therefore must be utterly destroyed. She is fighting but the appearance of you and your power will push things well into our favor. This child might yet live."

I touched my knife and asked, "You said that you would leave me be. Do you mean to take some kind of power you think I have and break your promise?"

"No," said number two. "You have two strong spirits, but they are from the same soul."

"You'll have to be more specific, gentlemen," I politely stated.

The men told me that I am the proud owner of an old spirit that is fighting to wake up and a young spirit that is fighting not to go to sleep. The one that is awake should have gone to sleep and the one that is asleep should not be waking. A third one is dead leaving only a weak trace of her spectrum. They surmised that the third somehow sacrificed itself to bring the others together (it was her choice). They were curious how both live spirits were able to exist in the wrong time. (As if unbound to or trapped outside of time). They had never seen a situation quite like this. It was argued that existing in all times at the same time would be the pentacle in our understanding of what the ultimate power could be. If I somehow found a way to understand how to use it, that would border on immortality. But, since none of the three lives that had shared this same bodily shell have the ability to share the life knowledge of things past or future, and the fact that I am affected by normal time makes me mortal, that theory was thrown out.

It didn't mean that Alexander could not awake at some point and live inside of Robert's mind as one single entity. I would know everything he knew, and he would know me and all the things I had done as Jasmine. I would see, know, and feel things as if I had lived in both times. What the men in red were really talking about was that waking Alexander might actually give me the power to travel back into time or be in another time of my choosing. I would bring the knowledge of today to the experience of yesterday and that would be god-like.

They openly debated the how and why, while I stood watching them. As did the monks in that California Temple, they expressed a great desire to study me further, but they too saw a greater destiny in letting me go. Besides, the impact I would make could likely help this society's plans in the long run. "That is if you survive the rebirth of the other", they said. (Something to look forward to). I wanted to ask them about the man in my dreams, but I was afraid that it might change the way they felt about me.

The third man reminded us that Euterpe was ready to leave and needed to speak to me now. It was something so important that she would hold Aleaha's life as a ransom to ensure I got her message. Nabeelah was told of the situation and insisted I be allowed to visit and that was the reason they allowed me to bring a knife.

Although connected to every manner of medical monitoring apparatus I could think of, Aleaha was not receiving any fluids or meds. This they said would force the body to shut down on its own. The spirit would be compelled to leave the body or risk dying with it. They tied a silver chain around my waist and pointed me ahead and into a tunnel of contraptions that surrounded the girl from every angle.

The event was being recorded and the area was surrounded by cameras and blasted with lights. Microphones were mounted and dangled from above and onlookers stood taking their notes. As I approached, the limp body seemed to lift gently off the slab and began to glow with an orange and silver tint.

The kid was sweating like crazy. The liquid filled the sheet and rolled off the stone slab to drip onto the floor. Even through the covering, I could see that her wrists and ankles were stretched wide and bound, causing her mid-section to bow upward. Aleaha would have raised to the roof if not for these restraints. She looked near the end of her tolerance and was too weak to even turn her head or open her eyes. But she could still whisper.

The sounds she made were more like hissing noises in two voices that came from one breath and one mouth. Aleaha and Euterpe both began to talk very slowly at the same time in different languages. One was in that same ancient tongue that I had heard in Dubai and the other was in the modern Levantine Arabic that is commonly spoken around the area she lived.

At the time, I couldn't really understand anything they were saying. The slow words seemed to connect to each other and the two soft voices led more to my distraction than an understanding. It was not until I was handed the written text that I was made aware of what the words really were.

The hissing was followed by faded mumbling until it too, tapered into silence. The body slowly and lifelessly dropped back to the slab and the glow terminated. I was reeled back and away as a steamy mist began to escape from the child's nose, ears, and open mouth.

The force of men, machine, sound, and light formed a visible electronic and ethereal screen of energy that encompassed the area of the slab as soon as I was jerked away. The essence was held and slowly depowered inside the shell before it was devoured by some of the red robed people before my eyes.

When it was all clear, ten of the twelve men that took what was left of Euterpe's essence, walked away. One came to me and the other went to Aleaha along with five medical staff members. The man that stood in front of me put the palm of his right hand on my forehead and said, "Receive your gift and your reward."

I cannot explain the warm energy that filled me from my head to my toes, but I knew it was something of the gods. I knew then that I would no longer have to guess or be confused about my music. From now on I would know. I now understood everything music related that had taken place. I also knew that I could never quit making music or performing. To even consider quitting was a stupid thought and now out of the question.

It seems that this was one of those rare times that a power would be given to a chosen few. "Music was never a gift to our world, it was won on the battlefield many thousands of years ago," explained guide number three. "The survivors are the ones we call the lesser gods. The ability to create art and music spilled out in all directions, but the power to make your creation live in the minds of all men is still very rare. Euterpe won that ability and kept most of that power to herself, but she specialized in music. The power to conjure a vision and convey it in a way that will compel or inspire the listener to perform a desired action or feeling, is as close to a supernatural ability as humans have come. It ranks very high in our mental evolution. The next logical step would be to heal the sick and raise the dead. Only a few humans have ever been able to connect to those abilities on their own and even they could never control it. The ability usually controlled them." He said that the popular tale of the Muses is not too far from the reality. "There are beings that do influence a few men from time to time to create great works. Often, these works inspire other men to do other works. But the Muse enjoy the Arts far too much to merely sit back and watch others create. Sometimes they want to be the creators. To do so, the Muse needs a human host. But this pure and complete form of the power is too much for our less evolved material form. As in the case of Aleaha, combining two life forces and this great ability in the same body, is more than any human can handle. It usually drives the host mad. This smaller portion of the gift you were just given is equal to the rare free flowing amount that attached itself to Michelangelo, Bach, Van Gogh, Wagner, Beethoven, Picasso and the others that we call Masters of the Arts. In the past it was common to wait two or more generations between one and another of these great improvisers to surface. Now more recently we are seeing the likes of DeMille, Presley, Warhol, Hendrix, Dylan, Spielberg, Petty, and Jackson impacting minds all at the same time. You and Aleaha have very expanded minds and should be able to control this power better than most others before you. It will be a burden and a responsibility but used wisely and carefully it will work to all of our advantage."

The man that gifted me spoke up. "We will now look for ten other enlightened minds and together you twelve will begin to change the sound this world makes. If more people had the ability to inspire, then our imagination would have no limitations and our ascension would be that much closer. This day brings us another step closer to immortality for the entire species of man."

On the way out, I met Aleaha's aunt, mother and father. I was able to tell them that I last saw her moving her head and breathing on her own. Nabeelah insisted on setting us up in the finest hotel, all expenses paid. I was given a written copy of the message from Euterpe and advised not to look too deeply into it for any real or hidden meanings. "It's likely that the entity was just biding for time," they said.

The Arabic version talked about imposters that would fool me into protecting an artificial man, made real. The other translated message warned of long lines of small numbers that have the sum of many minds hiding in a box of light and living in a crystal crown. Then there was something about the intended jar being too small to hold them.

Arabic is not blunt. It is a poetic language of many varieties. Most written communications are standardized but when spoken words are re-translated into a dialect, it is best to know what you are talking about and to whom you are talking, or the meaning could be completely lost. The dead tongue was much simpler, but it was clear that the speaker replaced words for things she didn't understand with the words she knew. I wasn't sure what she was telling me and neither did the members of the Order.

I gathered my small crew and went to the hotel where I quickly discovered that I could not sleep alone anymore. I could nap a little but to just let go and pass into deep REM sleep was out the window. The girls pitched in and took turns lying in the bed next to me. Neither Sophie, Annette, Jacky O, nor Joy Bird Song were lesbians, so all I ever got was the sleep. What I did get was the warm touch of a hand, leg, or a breast pressed nicely against my back to give me comfort. But if that chick moved to the other side of the bed or got up to go pee, I became wide awake. Even with their help, I was still restless. I was told that I may have said some things in my sleep that were not nice, but I don't remember doing it. (Nobody was crying in the mornings, so I guessed whatever it was, wasn't too bad).

The shrink showed up right at the five-day mark. His name was Gene Harlow (no relation). It took me about 15 minutes to give him that as his official nickname, "No Relation." Each time he would say his name, I would quickly throw-in the 'No Relation'. Everyone said they thought it was cool and funny, but I thought I was the only one that ever really got it.

His job was to ask questions, observe my behavior, and report all the findings to Doc Stacy. She would give him the follow-up questions and let him know what actions or tactics she wanted him to try.

He was a smart white guy from Boston, 6-3, with glasses, around 30-35 years old at about 190lbs. He was real fit for a Head Shrink. When he wasn't in my ass with probing questions, he was in the gym or at the pool. The other girls were all ape about him. They followed his every move as if his ass was made by Prada. In the end, he turned out to be a great gym coach. I think he and Annette got it on once.

In the four weeks I had with him (one was in Alexandra and two at Jasmine on the Green). We did not talk about the dream monster (Destroyer), the spirit giver (Euterpe), or my real feelings about my brother (Little Arthur). We didn't talk about the three separate personalities occupying the same body or if a soul could or even should live in two different times. We didn't talk about how proud I was to have only lost three children escaping when they all could have lived longer as slaves. He would have thought I was as crazy as that sounds.

I did talk to him about the mysterious voice I heard in the hospital and he wanted to hypnotize me. That voice and the words it said had been bugging me but not enough to allow my mind to be opened up for him and Doc Stacy to look inside. For all I knew, it's just what she and the others wanted. Besides, some of the old information I have locked in my head can still be used to topple some of the strongest governments. Add that with the new info and the fact that I am really not who I say I am, Doc Stacy would suspect that I was potentially the most dangerous being on the planet. I would have to be eliminated.

I admit that my biggest concern since my first days as a "military operator" was to have my mind down-loaded (or whatever) and the files sold off to the highest bidder. One way to do that was with hypnotism. Another way is to do whatever Doc Stacy's friends had done to me. The Old Code told me that if I couldn't avoid that kind of situation and was unable to escape from it, I had to find a way to take my own life.

Life since my rebirth has been so new and exciting. The prospective alone has been eye opening. I was rich, a performer, and soon to be a leader in the oldest secret organization there is. There was no telling what potential I could look forward to. If I could just keep a lid on my past, learn all I could in my new situation, and eliminate my enemies quietly, I would end up as that person that literally knows everything. That was always my true hidden fantasy and the main reason I had not revealed myself to anyone.

When I confessed my new fear of the dark and asked if that was a bad thing, he told me that I feel a need to have people around me not for attention, but for affection and protection. He thought my phobia for doctors and hospitals was understandable given my history. The man said that I was mostly just lonely and that I needed to start singing again and find a friend despite my fear of going outside in public again. We agreed.

By the time Gene left, I had gained 6lbs of muscle and felt good enough to try my new songs in public. Also, with Gene's help I had narrowed down the eager crop of LFL ladies to two. He told me to express my feelings, so I told the prospects that I wanted a real relationship with lots of sex and that "I want to be held all night when I sleep." Six girls said they could do that but after talking to them all, I was able to get it down to Betty, AKA Touchdown Betty, and Tammy, AKA Tammy the Sweet.

These girls were not star players and had no real stats to speak of. They were both pretty and their tight bodies looked good in oil and shoulder pads. In truth, they spent most of their time on the bench but took great pictures. Betty played for Las Vegas and knew a lot about martial arts, so we had something in common. Tammy, on the other hand, played for Chicago. She wore the number 34 and took Payton's handle so that got my attention too. I had to meet them both and that meant going to the US. It was also time to record again.

A hard sell, but Lloyd allowed me to take my little brother back to Los Angeles. I had to take Freda and another woman by the name of Ms Bonnet. Bonnet was a private tutor for the gifted and the special. She was a tall woman in her 40s that dressed and acted as if she lived 100 years ago. No matter how much we disagreed, I was under strict orders not to fire her.

I also had to bring a security man named Barton. Barton was a strictly business kind of guy. He was a "half cast" (British for half white and black) man in his 50s and I could tell that at one time he too, was a real operator. He was one of those guys that didn't exist. What he lacked in agility, he more than made up for in experience and firepower. He didn't speak much at all but was always in the right place at the right time. We had more in common than anyone else I knew, but that was something I could never say to him. I had no idea how a man like that could end up protecting a child. I could only think that he was hired to protect him against me if necessary. In any case I admired and respected the man, but I couldn't get over the idea that I might have seen him before.

And Those Hollywood Nights

The Factory was no place for a little kid to play in. I leased a Hollywood mansion in the Hills that came with a small day staff. It cost me $52,600 for each month but the quiet and the view of the city from the Santa Monica Mountains was just about worth it. I decided against the optional car and driver.

The Britten home near London was not what you would call a single-family unit. It was built for the entire Britten clan to come and go as they pleased. Jasmine on the Green was nice but it's not what pops in my head when you think the word, home. This seven bedroom, seven and a half bath, had everything I could ever want. I had seen bigger and nicer, but this had a pool, view, space, weather, style, and one thing more, it felt personal. It felt like I could live there. Each night I'd step out on the deck and hear that old Bob Seger song play in my head and think, "This is truly one of those Hollywood nights."

The place had enough space to put myself into the master bedroom, Little Arthur in a nice one, Annette had hers, Freda and Bonnet shared one, Barton was near Little Arthur, and I brought Jane and Gabriele over to enjoy the fun and share the sixth room. The seventh was for any visiting Society member that came by or if the others needed some privacy. Deak rode up on his bike and used it twice.

I used a den area for my personal security detail that consisted of four people with one of them on duty outside and inside at all times. Jacky O and Joy Bird Song were working on their comic book so the entire security force that was in town had a chance to work the house, grounds, and hangout at the pool off-duty.

James and Tito had tweaked together a sound and video version of our tour and wanted my opinion before pushing it out. I had some ideas, but the product was sound enough to let it go as it was. It never pays to over think these things. I decided to focus more on the new songs and took this time to craft an even better performance into this, the third recording. It all seemed so much better now. Almost as if the songs told me how to sing them. But that was only the smallest part of a universal spectrum of change.

Before, I was good because I had the advantage of a near perfect memory. I memorized my music like I memorized sexiness. I heard or saw the behavior I was asked to mimic, and I did. But I had to break it all down into tiny segments, choose the small parts I wanted in that segment, and build that action until I found one sequence or several I was happy with. Then I would memorize the complete action and add it to a list of many. I used the mirror, the camera, and my mentors to help me. I weaved it into something that looked original, but it was really just a mix of something different people had already done. In true definition, it was good, and I was good at it, but as I have been made to understand, it was not real art. Not in its truest form.

But after I received that special gift from Euterpe and the Order, things changed drastically. It's hard to describe but I could liken it to a piano. All the notes, the scales, the theory, and the rules about how to play it, are crucial if you want a good piece of music. And if I want to, I could hit the little button on the side and the thing would play all by itself. Is that art? No. The mechanics alone may sound good but that's not was art really is.

What is art in its truest definition? It is creation, innovation, experimentation, and improvisation. Once you're skilled enough, you can take all the rules you've learned and bend them into something else. And Jazz (as we know) is meant to be a little bit different every time anyway. That's what I did with those new songs and it worked. Or should I say, that's what the new songs did to me.

It made James cry. The man kept saying, "That's it! That's it!" I couldn't tell him what had happened that made the big difference, but he did ask me. He thought he was going crazy and brought his father all the way from the East Coast into the studio, so he could confirm what he was hearing. That man cried too.

I took Little Arthur to all of the cool places a kid would want to see, and I tried my best not to argue with Bonnet in front of him. By agreement, I had to also take Freda and Barton everyplace we went. I wanted to do something alone with him, so I insisted that every night I would read or tell him a story before he went to sleep. He seemed to like it quite a lot but if he had not fallen asleep before I was through, I might have to lie with him until he was out. After all he was the prince in the family, not I.

I got caught up on our Society business and contracts, worked out, visited everyone, and even made a surprise visit to the set of Twister's show. We filmed an impromptu interview, tried some of her "new same old food" recipes, discussed strength verses flexibility, and I sang a song with her band. It was a good show despite my shy act. But then again, I was with Twister.

James Town Productions was slowly making its way into the black. We were getting offers from a lot of overseas clients that liked the unique sound effects and video mix our studio provided. James was able to use this income to promote some of the newly signed acts, pay his staff, and cut his main investor a percentage of the remaining profit (meaning the Princesses).

Before the end of this month Mr Gaddafi had been overthrown and Bubba Smith had died. I, on the other hand, did two nights in Vegas and got into a big fight. Little Arthur was not allowed to go with me and it turned out to be a good thing in the long run. I was forced to read to him over the internet and at the time I felt that I was being cheated. (But that was before the fight).

James set me and the band up with a spot to do two one-night shows. We would do the new stuff and some of what he called "Deep Choice Classics" like Ella, Etta, Nina, and Sarah's greatest recordings. The numbers got flipped around and I know firsthand that these things will happen. I also know that business is business, so I could not blame James for what he did. Still, I hate surprises and this one turned into a little something more that got recorded on video.

Once I arrived in Vegas, I learned that the deal had changed. Instead of doing just one full show at 2200hrs on Friday and Saturday nights, I was going to do four songs at 1300hrs at one hotel, then the full show at 2200hrs in another spot, for both days. Although the early shows were just warmups, they turned out to be more than just four songs. Famous people came up on the platform that wanted to sing with me, or play for me, and I was not able to get out before 1600hrs both times. Sure, we took pictures, I got autographs and they treated me real nice. But that gave me only six hours to eat, nap, shower, and get my head and body pumped up before the big show later that same night. It was ass kicking and I know now why many artists take drugs. But that's not all that happened.

Just before I went on stage for the Friday night show, I was introduced to Sweet. James knew that in the past I had to have time to get psyched up to don the guise I portray on stage. But ever since my last Lebanon visit, I found that I would actually become the persona that is "Jasmine" and hold it for hours after the singing, recording, show, or interview was over. In a situation like this, when there was virtually no break, I found that I could be stuck in this mode for days. At the time, I could only assume that he had reason to break my rhythm by interrupting with a girly and a photographer. Again, I hate surprises.

I was standing in the dressing room working on a few of the speaking lines I was planning to use on stage. Part of my act is to set or reset the mood by talking to the audience in my shy and somewhat sad style. I was still in character from the early show and only needed to set my mind into the flow of the act. My dressers were fiddling around with my hair and gown while I spoke out loud to the imagined crowd before me. I had become used to this treatment and as they worked, the women fell into the background of my mind.

When I was mentally prepared, I headed backstage to feel the vibe before stepping out. I could hear Max bleeding in from the closed door and the man was turned all the way on. I wanted to get out of the room so that his sound could fill my soul, when I was stopped just outside the door.

I don't see a lot of James on the road, but he would come from time to time, so it was not a surprise to see him. Sometimes he would bring one or two people with him that he is trying to impress, so that's not a surprise either. When he does show, he likes to be in the background. He may speak to me and then again, he may not. A few of those times I didn't even know that he had come. But this time he came with a cameraman ready to get my surprised reaction to meeting "Tammy the Sweet".

She was a very tasty looking, 5'7", 135lbs, 34C, dark brown headed girl wearing a tight fitting black and yellow leather motorcycle outfit with the words "Tammy the Sweet" on the back. The suit had tassels on the legs and sleeves, and the jacket was zipped just enough to see down into those plump ripe melons that decorated her chest. And yes, they had an oily sheen. She had a picture of me in one hand and a striped helmet in the same colors, in the other.

"Jasmine," James started the introduction. "Tammy the Sweet is a big fan of yours. She rode all the way from Chi Town to meet you."

The camera flashed as she moved up to hug me and said, "If you sign my picture, I'll let you ride on the back of my bike." When she pressed herself against me I got a scent of how hot she was, wearing all that leather without the benefit of blasting wind to cool her down and dry her skin. The mix of perfume, sweat, olive oil, warm leather, and a little body musk told me that she really did just ride in from someplace. She felt real and smelled like she was on fire.

I had to hand it to her. Like me, she too was playing a part, but the girl swooped in and hugged me like she knew me from childhood. Like a real natural, she turned to the camera to get the shot and then turned back to me and did the most amazing thing. And that's when I understood why she was given her nickname.

It was her brown slanted eyes, the long black hair that couldn't stay out of her face, her puffy baby cheeks, her pearly white teeth, and the way those swollen dark red lips parted when she girlishly smiled. She wasn't called Sweet because she wore the 34. She was called Sweet on account of that heart melting smile. I think that number was given to her after she showed them her teeth. Her act was fake, but her face showed what was truly inside of her. Seeing it was like breathing in sunshine and it made me smile back. I sensed that she wanted to take me to "the place with no name" and I wanted to find out if she could. (I would have to wait and see).

I must have looked a little silly, being stunned and pleased at the same time. She saw that and returned the look with a giggle. The two of us shyly smiling at each other with grade school grins on our faces reminded me of what people say when they look at cute pictures of kids and dogs in the family album. "Oh, isn't that sweet." At that moment I felt like someone gave me a small gift. It was unexpected, and I would have to say that I was very surprised. And that's the way it looked in the newspaper the next day.

At the time I was unable to formulate a sentence. I later got word to her through James that I wanted her to meet me at 1100hrs for that ride she promised. I first had to do my act and that meant getting to the stage. As I walked around the corner I heard her say to James, "She is so incredible. Do you think she could even like a girl like me?" I was flattered that a girl so hot, so sweet, and oh so cool, could think that I was too classy for her. (The encounter almost threw me off).

The show went very well, and in the morning I went shopping so I could find something to wear on Sweet's bike. My hips didn't make it easy, but I was able to meet her at about 1130hrs. She had to bring me to the early show at 1230hrs, so we only had one hour to ride up the highway and back. It was a wild ride.

Few things are cooler than a pretty girl on her own Harley. (You can quote me on that). The Night Rod Special was black with yellow lines and stripes. This was a 2008 and had seen some road but it was still in real great shape (the girl was extra hot too). I could see that she put as much care in the bike as she did herself. As a cruiser, you wouldn't expect to see the speeds that you would on one of those Japanese crotch rockets. But a Power Cruiser like this may do around 135 mph. This one in particular had some nice after factory modifications. I gave my security detail a break and walked out to meet her alone.

She and I had both signed up for a publicity event, but I wanted more than that. Sure, I could have asked her to have sex with me and she might have just said yes. But I was lonely for something else. The thing I had with Twister was special, but it was done. Everyone I had met since was either too awed or too intimidated to get any genuine emotion out of them. I wanted to be with someone who would honestly enjoy being with me. I thought this girl was pretty cool and the bike and football thing seemed like the makings of another wild fantasy about to come true. I didn't want to scare her off too soon and since this was a take it or leave it deal, I had to make some kind of impression.

Sweet asked me if I had ever ridden on the back of a bike before and I answered, "Yes, but it was a long time ago." (At 19 how long could that have been). She had to think that I was lying. What I wanted was to make her feel that she was better at something then I was. I also wanted to feel her out and see what kind of person she really was. As it turned out, she had the same intent.

I asked her about the bike but pretended not to care when she started to talk about it. I was testing her by acting girly and she got a little offended but sucked it up. When I asked her to help me on, I knew that she wasn't happy. She only helped me because she was a nice person. But I could tell that she didn't want me on that thing. I could only imagine what she was thinking. Then it was her turn.

Through the headset, she talked to me. The first thing she said was that she had a test that she always performs to see if she can be friends with a person. She told me that she was going to go so fast that I was going to scream, shit, or both. I told her that unless I thought I was going to die, I was not going to scream, and that my outfit was too new, too expensive, and way too tight to shit in, so that wasn't going to happen either. She replied with, "Consider that as the test," and released the clutch.

For the sake of honesty, I have to mention that a motorcycle can sometimes come close to mimicking the same effect as those Davenport horses did to me. Each kind of bike gives a different feeling, but my preparations must always be the same. That's why I could do a free commercial for my favorite panty liners. As uncomfortable as they were, those things can hold a lot of fluid, especially when you stack them. But for long rides on a "real bike", nothing beats long leather pants and tall boots. (I can't go without a matching jacket). You're going to smell me when I take them off, but no one outside of the bedroom would ever know how much I enjoyed that ride. (Except of course the dry cleaners).

The newer style bikes are mostly electric and give a girl no more of a thrill then sitting on top of the washing machine. A bike built in the classic US style on the other hand, is best enjoyed from the bitch position. That way, I can just hold on and concentrate on my breathing. Now, with my arms wrapped around the person in front of me and all the wetness confined to the inside of my leathers, I don't worry about falling off or leaving a trail. Throw in a few bumps in the road and I can call it a night.

I wrapped my arms around her waist and thighs over her butt, closed my eyes and held on. I admit that women drivers have always made me nervous, but if I can jump out of a perfectly good airplane into the wide blue yonder, I can certainly ride on the back of a bike driven by a 22 year old, thrill seeking girl. I wasn't afraid, I was just trying to maintain control of myself. But she didn't have to know that. I think it worked because she gave me a real ride. I figured I'd just be quiet and wait until it was over, besides, holding her was fun.

She knew I wasn't looking at the road, so she talked me through everything she did. "I'm about to do some doughnuts." "Let me know before you get sick!" "Look at all the smoke and dust." "I like the way you stick to the seat girl!" "Did you see how big that dead dog was?" "This is a wonderful day to ride." "Do you think I can pass all these cars at once before that truck comes up?" "You're a good hugger. I like that." "I can tell you like doing these curves, don't you?" "Did you feel that? I just ran over that dead dog." "I can hear you breathing." She went on like that and had a good time with herself. I didn't say a word.

When we finally stopped, I felt like my feet were swimming inside my boots. She had me remove my helmet to check my color and see if I was OK. I asked her if I had passed her friend test and she apologized for trying to scare me. Some friends had told her that she was too boyish and crazy for me, so she thought I was not going to choose her.

I apologized too, and said that many of my friends have bikes, to include my adopted father. "I was riding on the back of his Ducati two days ago. I just wanted to make you feel good."

"Oh," She said. "I thought I was playing a joke on you, but you were playing a joke on me at the same time. Are we bad people?"

She hung out for the afternoon show and I took her back to the hotel later. We talked a lot about the lime light, sex, love, and the business of show. She had a unique way of looking at things that reminded me of T Dog. She stayed while I napped, and we rode together to the show later that night.

You ever meet that girl that was so cool, fun and great to be around? Not the one that has to steal the show and all the light away from everyone else. She is the one that creates the atmosphere that the show is built around. There are no dead moments with her. When the mood should be calm and quiet, she can do that too, but her gift is fun and laughter. In a sense, she is the show. Tie that with the smile and that girlish grin and you have Sweet.

In the profile that was sent to me, it said that Tammy the Sweet was part South African and part Brazilian. The truth was that her mother was of the mix of red and brown people that are Cherokee Indian, and her father was of the mix that is white Australian. She was conceived in Sidney but was born and raised on North Carolina Native American Indian land.

Her mother was a brilliant law student and the pride of the community. They sent her to Harvard and she excelled. Just before her graduation day she was picked up by a low-level diplomat that worked for the US Ambassador to Australia. While in Sidney, she very quickly became pregnant by another low-level aide to the Australian Prime Minister. When she was fired and sent back to the US alone, she had no place to go but back to Reservation Lands to have her baby.

The father never visited but sent money for about ten years. After that, he was never heard from. Sweet's mother said, "It's likely that he is now married to a White woman." The mother said she didn't hate the man but whenever Sweet's father was mentioned in any conversation she would call out the words "Old Pale Face!" The meaning is "people without color", or whites. But that is just part of it.

Ancient Indian folklore says that they were the first people of the earth. When the Whites arrived in the world, they refused to blend into the land like the natives did. Instead, they became a contrast to all of creation. These white men were experts in the art of destruction. Their skin reminded the natives of ghosts and the death that the Pale Faces brought, walked among the trees and destroyed everything in its path. The Pale Faced people were bypassed as much as possible until their greedy reach could no longer be avoided. But the Indians acted too late.

The native people, who believed that everything in the world was alive and that those lives deserved respect, could not have won against a people that were willing to kill in order to possess everything they could put a fence around. Those people arrived from another world with documents of ownership on lands that were gifted to God's own people. The very idea of ownership was as strange as the Pale Faced men themselves.

The Pale Face term was once used a lot in old movies about the Great Wild West. You don't hear those words much anymore, so for Native Americans, hearing them can be both an insult and a joke. It all depends on who's doing the talking.

May Starr named her daughter Rena but her tribal and home name was Ayita (meaning, "first to dance"). Rena's mother became a lawyer and the two of them fared better than most. But May's new resentment for white people and most of the men she met, was the reason she stayed in the Nation and why she never married. Her daughter became a soccer champion and played on a small professional women's team for two years. But like her mother, Rena needed more challenges than the Reservation and the area could provide. So, when Chicago called her, Sweet got on her bike and rode off into the sunset like so many Cowboy and Indian stories, comics and movies of those earlier times. Her mother did not object.

Touchdown Betty on the other hand, was a different animal altogether. She and a few friends from the Vegas team arrived backstage early that night and were taking pictures in their football uniforms and giving autographs before Sweet and I arrived.

Betty was a blonde, 5'11", 165lb, long legged, ex-basketball and tennis player that had a black belt in Shotokan karate. Her bio said that she was an expert with the Tonfa, the Nunchaku, and other exotic weapons. It also said that she was born in Houston, Texas, 25 years ago and that she joined the Vegas team right after she left the Lady Raiders hanging high and dry after an argument with the coach.

What she told me via email, was that she was cut from the team when she could not return for the second half of the season, after her father was badly injured in a farming accident. After he died, an LFL recruiter gave her a call. She said that she wanted to open her own Karate Studio and just needed to earn a little cash first.

Typically, my personal security will travel with me but since the whole 'napping incident, Nick Parker required that another security detail be on the ground at least two hours before I was. So, when new faces showed up without James to escort them, security limited their access. The five ladies had passes and were very pissed off that they were stuck in a back hallway. When they saw Sweet and I walk in together, the Vegas girls flipped out and had to be escorted out of the building. That was also caught on camera. The next day I had to meet with Tammy, Betty, James, and two LFL promoters, Leonard and Steven, in the lounge of another hotel at High Noon.

The promoters all loved the pictures and were eager to discuss the best way to spin the stories. What they didn't like was that it seemed like I had cut Vegas out of the action before the choosing game had officially started. They were calling a flag on the fact that Betty was not given a fair chance. So, for the rest of that day I had to be filmed hanging out with Betty.

I probably should not have even been in the meeting. But as part owner of the company and the main participant, I had an interest and I needed to agree to the deal. It's just that with my new-found passion I was now oozing out with each song. It was exhausting to say the least and I was in a daze the whole time. I only shook my head a few times then looked at the wall until I quietly fell asleep at the table. In no way was I in touring shape. So, for the rest of that day, all they got from me was Zzzzzs.

The next day I met Betty at the karate school where she attended and taught. I was unhappy with it from the moment I walked in. The standard of teaching, discipline, and the level of respect for the art were so low that I would have been surprised if anyone learned anything. The more I looked around, the worse I felt and that is why a challenge I made to the head instructor (that was not even there) quickly turned into a big fight.

The advance security and I arrived at the same time. I like getting to my appointments early if I can and I couldn't pass up a chance to maybe get in a workout with some new people before the camera and the show arrived. In this case it may have been a mistake.

I was asked to meet Touchdown Betty at the overpriced, watered down, candy ass studio at 1300hrs. I was going to be filmed watching her go through a few forms and a weapons demo. Later, we would do some light friendly sparring. It was supposed to be fun. But from the moment Katy Kick, Frazzle Dazzle and I walked in the door two hours early at 1100hrs, we had one problem after another that added up to a fair challenge that was not answered with honor. And that is why Katy and Frazzle beat down eleven people before the master of the school arrived.

Katy's real name is a bunch of Korean sounding noises that no one seemed to be able to say correctly. Her accent was so bad that it was actually worse than Iko's ever was and her education was poor. Most of the time, nobody knew what she was saying. She was fresh off the boat when our Safe House for runaway teens called us. The kid knew no English at the time.

When I say "fresh off the boat" I mean that she was a stowaway on a cargo ship. The small 17 year old girl and her 15 year old boyfriend nearly died of starvation before they were discovered by security. Once she was healthy enough, the San Francisco Juvenile Hall had plans to transfer her to the hands of the Korean government for deportation. She overpowered the guards during the handover and fled into the city. A week later she was with us. It had been six months and still no one could understand the words coming out of her mouth.

Even though her name and nationality are now changed (on paper), her past and the friend she once knew will never be spoken of. That is the way she wanted it. In return for saving her from her past and the authorities, she offered her continued service and her skills in the Taekwondo and Hapkido styles. She was also a demon with the baton, nunchaku and the rope. (Very gifted).

Frazzle Dazzle, AKA Niga-peno, was born and raised in the Philippine Islands to a Philippine mother and a Black American US Navy father. At 23, he was arguably the best stick fighter in the state of California. His past may not have been as colorful as Katy's, but he had more trophies and awards that I had seen in one place. He was one of our best trainers and did not believe in a single school or style but embraced the best of anything he could learn. We made him an offer the day he won the underground Kumite, held in Frisco.

Katy had an awful time with anger and it seemed that only Dazzle could keep her under control when she was upset. In Taekwondo she would have been rated as a 2nd degree and that alone made her a dangerous opponent but her fearless rage kept her away from competing in the ring. The two of them formed a kind of sign language and started a love relationship. As a security team they were only so-so. But as a fighting unit, they were something to behold. The voice told me to bring those two this day.

When Katy attempted to correct a student, she was challenged to perform the same maneuver by the class leader. After the class leader was corrected he became insulted and wanted to spar. Dazzle warned that it would be a bad idea and the man pushed him. I stood in a corner and watched as my two bodyguards beat down nearly everyone in the building like it was a Bruce Lee film. The head instructor, his girlfriend, and the promotion photographer walked in just as the last willing student fell to the mat.

The leader wanted to call the police, but I told him that the whole thing was a misunderstanding that turned into a matter of honor. I said that it was not the fault of the students that they have a poor Master and I challenged his School Master to honor the "Old Code" by shutting down his school or giving the people their money back. I told him that it was not in my authority as a

Shaolin Master to close a Shotokan school, but that he should do it out of honor and respect for the arts. I used the term "Mc Dojo", after the popular fast food chains that you can see on the corner of every main street in every town. They are known for looking and tasting good, but the menus are the same and none of the products are good for you.

He called the Master, who happened to be the owner of the school and told him what had happened. I'm not sure what the Master told his 3rd Dan Instructor, but it must have had the words "kick her ass" in part of that conversation 'cause that dude came to me swinging.

I waved my guards off and let the man attempt to impress me by breaking a table and a hand painted bamboo screen. I spent the next several minutes deflecting his forceful punches and kicks into the trophy displays and the walls. I took pleasure in embarrassing him further by calling out names of the moves I used to manipulate and redirect his every attack. I used the techniques called "Leading the Way" and "Mounting the Horse". Without landing a blow, I had him destroy the main hall before he got tired and stopped fighting altogether. He bowed to me and the fact that I was able to do this in a short skirt and heeled shoes. The other students who were cheering him on before, had now become silent.

The Master and Betty met at the door from different directions on the street. The 40 year old, white American, 6th Dan Black Belt was livid. He berated the instructors immediately upon entering the building. He kicked everyone out of the Dojo except for his two trainers, me, and my two guards. He said that he was an official board member of some Nevada Martial Arts Association that represented 12 styles, 19 schools, and that he was going to show me how things were done in his town.

He wanted proof that I ranked a Shaolin Master and I volunteered my forearms. After making a phone call, we waited for 30 minutes for his council members to arrive. They knew that they would have to come through a security check, so the three men were not alarmed when they were patted down and escorted into the building. Now we were eleven in the room. It was the six of us that were not thrown out, three new Masters, and two members of the outside security team.

The Masters introduced themselves and their credentials politely so that there would be no more misunderstandings. All three were in their 50s or older. One was Korean, one was Japanese, and the other was Chinese. They asked me who I was and from where did I hold the honor of Master. After I told them, we all sat on the floor as Frazzle and the school instructor explained to the visiting Masters, what had happened. Then I was asked to present my marks to be inspected by the Masters, and I complied.

After what was a heated but formal discussion, it was decided that Master John Larson and I would have a contest. If I lost I would pay for the damages, admit defeat, and not practice martial arts in any form in the state of Nevada for a period of five years. If Master John lost he would admit defeat, be banned from teaching for five years, and the association would offer 15 months free training to all John's students (past and present) under other Nevada Masters of their choosing. I wanted 24 months, but my mouth was going dry. We agreed and since it was John's house, he was given the choice of the form of combat. He of course chose weapons. We would fight in two days. The only real rule was that this was not a fight to the death, so that meant that the weapons would be blunt, and I was asked to cut my nails.

Like before, the entire event was recorded on film. The promoters were mixed but I was bound to the fight by honor and I was going to keep mine, win or lose. Betty wanted nothing more to do with me, so Tammy won the deal by default. It was for the best and turned out to be the third greatest thing since I was reborn. The second being that I discovered music and the first was the fact that I could breathe again.

I spent the night back at the house to be with my brother but returned the next day with him and a crew of 65 of our best people once I heard that the contest would be in an open auditorium. John's association would use this to promote some students and give out awards. There would be some demos and an 'All Styles' open competition. This was 'year book stuff'. Our spies expected to see over 120 association members and it was feared there might be some activity if John lost in the Grand Finale, so I came mentally and physically prepared.

James didn't want me hurt and showed his protest by not attending. Deak showed up with some friends. Twister brought her show and competed. All my FLC girls that were not on assignment came down on their bikes. My buddies from Camp Pendleton surprised me by entering in some matches. Word had gotten out over the internet and some of my fans and other entertainers came. All and all 484 people entered the doors of that building and I knew the names of 133 of them. 175 other people came just to support me. The association signed in 126 card holding members that day and some of them were Jazz fans. The LFL was represented and some of those fans came too. Flags and banners were posted everywhere. Tammy and Little Arthur were with me and I was sparking with electricity.

The contest was a lot less enjoyable than the fans were. At first there was tension in the crowd but after it was obvious that the association people were outnumbered in the hall and outmatched on the floor, the mood soon changed. There were friendly jeers from fans of a particular form or style but that made the vibe even more exciting. The competitions became lively, fun and the spectators were thrilled and really enjoyed the evening. In the end, just about everyone was pleased. That is to say, everyone except Master John Larson.

I was invincible. My newest gift transferred over to the martial arts abilities and I saw everything differently. No longer did I need to use the math of A action, plus B reaction, giving a C result. Now, I saw everything there was to see, heard everything there was to hear, and felt all there was to feel. Each vibration of any of the muscles on his body meant something to another muscle. I already knew everything about my training and what my body could do. All I had to do was take advantage of what I sensed from my multi-level thinking. He was an open book and I was born to rewrite his chapters.

When he chose the Tonfa to start, I picked the Three Section Staff knowing I was going to show off with it. Later he proved better with the Nunchaku, but he couldn't land a blow with that either. After dropping it, one of his students tossed him a Fiberglass Bow Staff. I knew it would take away my reach, so I back-stepped and motioned for my favorite Wooden Long Bow. (The Grandfather).

He was stronger than I was and could bring much more momentum in his strikes, so his plan was to overpower me with force. I took advantage of that force and turned it into a weakness the same way I bested his lead instructor by using finesse and deflection.

He was too strong for me, so I had to really hurt him and stop the fight before he could hit me. He showed courage by trying to do like the guy in that "Last Samurai" movie by getting up again and again. The old me would have broken his skull just to keep him from stabbing me in the back at a later date. But rules are rules and I had to act with some kind of decorum, so I waved his team over to take his bloody ass off my floor.

I bowed to the table of Judges, I bowed to the crowd, I bowed to my brother, and I bowed to Master John Larson and his trail of blood. The crowd was on their feet and I started jumping around and waving to people I knew like I was a little kid on a parade float. The panel repeated the same announcement about the terms of this unusual but honorable contest. When they pronounced me the winner the place went nuts and so did I and my team of helpers.

As we were celebrating, a man got on the microphone and started yelling in Japanese. When someone came to get the thing away from him, the yelling man kicked him into the crowd of fans. That was an attention getter and it nearly started a riot. People began to push each other back and forth. Another man grabbed a different mic and started to translate.

The angry Japanese guy was John's old Master years ago. He was against the public display and accused me of having an unfair advantage. He had found that even though I was young and a female, I was of a much higher rank than John. That being said, he felt strongly that the contest was invalid. He also said something about Karate always winning over Kung Fu in a fight that has no cheats. (Ooooh).

The Judges and most of the folks were not in total agreement with these statements. I was reminded again of my favorite movie and the quote, "Bust a deal and face the wheel." People started to yell and throw things at each other. This was what that man really wanted; to see this place explode in all directions. If things got out of control and people got hurt, it would have looked very bad for so many of us. I had to do something.

I whispered instructions to Battle Angel and sent her to the second microphone. She said, "Master Omoto, I understand the pain of a fallen student. Surely the Master cannot be blamed for someone who has lost his faith in the discipline of the Noble Arts. As we have seen, this one did not fully embrace the lessons that you hold in such high regard. You sir, are not to blame and are in no way obligated to fight to regain your honor. You are excused!" The auditorium went nuts. There was no way he would challenge an 18 year old girl to a full contact fight. He had to shut up and bow out, or so I thought. I was wrong of course.

Omoto was outraged and claimed that he was dishonored again. He demanded an apology or satisfaction through a sparring competition. I guess he figured that I would never get into the circle with a 9th Dan. He also made other attempts to shadow the name of Shaolin Kung Fu. The Judges and other Masters rushed to Omoto and small fights (mostly loud talking) began on the floor.

It was at that time that I walked to the middle of the floor stretched out my arms and became the White Crane. Omoto saw it as another taunt and hurried over to call my bluff. Did this go over well with my crew? Hell no! They wanted me to leave the building. Even the usually reserved Mr Barton yelled at me to get off the floor. Omoto was reputed to be one of the best fighters in the association and I was about to face him unarmed. My inner voice instructed me to remain and so I did.

Omoto came with a flurry of speedy punches and kicks, but I was able to avoid or deflect them all. I knew that one mistake on my part could cause me a broken arm, leg, or worse. For about two minutes, all I did was defend my body. I could read his movements, but the man was like lightning and unlike John, he was a true Master. He was 57 years old, in top shape, and very pissed off at this female.

He came at me in a straight forward fashion. His technique was clean, crisp, and regimented. His movements broke through the air with the sound of a cracking whip and were a blur to see. This was not a mere demonstration lesson for his students and fans, this was him avenging his school, his honor, and his favored student.

I on the other hand, moved in circles large and small. At one point, he made a small mistake and I was able to deflect and counter with a paralyzing strike to the nerve center on his right bicep. (Cobra shoots his venom). For a short time, this greatly reduced his strength and speed from that muscle group and he felt pain. It gave him something to think about and everything changed after that.

He changed from his straight line attack to a box defense. He attempted to bait me with his injured arm, so he could set me up for a spinning kick or a back fist. Instead, I made him the center of my circle and started to pick away at him piece by piece bruising other pressure points as they became available.

Once his extremities were less of a threat, his entire core was vulnerable to my attacks. I then began to tighten my circles and work on his vital areas causing stiffness and pain to the rest of his body. After that I was able to use the pretty strikes and breathtaking kicks that we all love to see at the movies.

Master Omoto acknowledged his defeat by bowing out. Knowing he could no longer compete, he prostrated himself face to the floor, knees down, and his forehead on the mat. The translated version of what he said was, "Please accept my humble apology." I graciously accepted by returning his bow from the standing position over him and felt as if I were on top of the world holding a flag.

I was so happy to have fought the greatest hand to hand nonlethal battle of skills that I had ever seen or heard about. It was near legendary. Not only did I win, but I won without suffering great injury to myself. If I would have had the energy to do so, I would have loved to do one of those 'football touchdown dances' when the building erupted all around me. In truth, I was so tired and so bruised on my arms and legs, that all I wanted to do was lie down in somebody's tub.

I had to get escorted out, but I posed for people and signed autographs on the way. Later there would be interviews, plaques, certificates, school patches, and a lot of invitations to teach my philosophy. I was even offered lots of money to have my name placed on door signs as an endorser of their school. But on that night, my new girlfriend and I got a deep massage and I sweated my pains away in the hotel sauna.

The next day we were back to the Hollywood Hills. Mr Barton asked to speak to me privately. He said it was very important and since he had never said more than three words to me in a row, I was quite interested. He wanted to go someplace private and refused to say another word about it until we walked into the Factory.

We took Sweet with us and it gave me a chance to show both of them around the place. Nick was teaching an advanced class of leaders and Barton acted as if someone had given him a treat. I showed them the range and they both wanted to fire some weapons. Sweet was having a blast and Barton was completely out of character. After a quick bite, I asked Barton if he planned to kill me. He assured me, "No", and we went alone to my office to talk about what was on his mind.

Once in the office we sat down, and I asked him to put his hands on the table. Then I warned him, "I know a man like you wouldn't take a job as a child minder unless it was a means to an end. So, if you are planning to do me harm, know that I don't feel like dying today and if I do fall, you could never leave this place alive."

In his London Cockney accent, he began with, "If we can agree that I could not have acquired this kind of job with this kind of clientele if I were thought to be insane, I will begin."

"Agreed," I answered.

He continued, "Then know that I speak the truth when I say that I have been looking for you and it has taken the whole of my life to finally reach that moment in time."

I didn't know what to think so I said, "Go on."

"I'm hoping that you can understand what I am about to say and if you do, you may be the person I think that you are."

"Mr Barton," I interrupted, "I would hate to grow old during this conversation."

"This is a critical matter Jasmine, and you'll just have to indulge me." I acknowledged, and he continued. "I've spent my life searching for an idea. A quest if you will, for something or someone to believe in. I've been given gifts and I have learned a lot of valuable skills. I have had the opportunity to use these skills in the service of many important clients. My reputation in this business alone is my CV. In these past 20 years, I've made a lot of money and I've seen and learned so many things, but in all my traveling and working, at no time did I find any one individual that was worth dedicating myself to. That is until now, if I may be so bold. I accompanied your father on many of his trips. I found him to be an honorable man. He was able to influence people without making them feel less than human. He had great potential, but he was only the man he was trained to be. He played his part with dignity and there is much to admire in that, but he was no leader. He lacked the will to think outside the box. You too have potential, but you are more than just your father's daughter and there is no box big enough to hold your deeds. I can't believe that I'm saying this to the same kid that had drool running down the side of her face just two years ago."

I thought the man was only trying to lower my guard but that last note rang a chord. "You knew me then Sir?"

"Oh, you were more of an empty shell than your brother is now," he said. "That's why you can't remember anything, not that it even mattered. Forgive me, but I don't know how you got through a day without drowning in your own saliva. It wasn't your fault, but you were a real mess! At least your little brother is dangerously close to knowing he's alive."

"A mess you say. I've heard you say this before, haven't I?" It was him. He was the mysterious voice that had been bugging me. It was his words that I could only now identify. "You were in Athens!"

"Yes. I was in LA too. Before that I was in Delaware. Before then, I was in Atlanta. Each time with orders from the Council to put you out of your unnatural misery and each time the orders were rescinded. Your awakening has caused a rift in the Council's Heart. They see you as an unplanned destiny forcing itself into being. Some see you as something of Alexander himself and it has them uneasy, as quiet as it's kept. You may be a sign that the great leader has returned to retake what is rightfully his. There is talk that his spirit is unhappy with what they have done and that he has come at their weakest hour in order to set things right. And there are others who say that he has sent a phantom to destroy their souls for the abomination they are about to commit. All of these scenarios can be viewed as both good and bad.

I myself see this as an opportunity to re-chart the course of this world and still fulfil your family's role as leaders. The options are vast, and it is for that reason that I was compelled to speak, but the choices will be yours. I can give you guidance and support in whatever you decide. The Council however, is another matter. You should be afraid."

"And why exactly is that Mr Barton? So far, the most threatening thing in recent memory has been this conversation." I was desperately trying to understand the whole purpose of this business lunch we were having but up to this point, he had yet to produce anything tangible to chew on. It was then that he told me the reason I had not been given any training on my true role was because I was already playing it. I was poised to be the next "Great Distraction", he told me.

A lot of people get famous and are popular, but he was talking about something more. There have been others who were used, employed or contracted if you will, to control the eyes and ears of a certain voting population, age group, race, or even a country, but only a small few were empowered to distract or keep the interest of the entire world. (These people agreed to a deal).

The way he explained it was if the world was focused on me, they wouldn't be as focused on other matters. The media is always desperate to promote the weird and outrageous. It wasn't always like that. Recently, a small but important government erupted in a revolution while one third of the United States was talking about how cute I was in the new motorcycle outfit I wore to a Chicago Bears football game, or the fact that I bought nine seats so my friends and I could promote our minibikes in the stands that day. Some smart person just happened to buy stock in that brand of bike just the day before and that same person negotiated a seven billion dollar relief deal that this small but important government could not possibly pay off. I could say who this individual was and who he was ultimately working for, but that would get some people killed. And that is the reason that most media networks didn't even cover the war that day. By the time the 'regular guy' heard about the conflict, it was old news and not worth reporting anymore.

To make this role exciting and believable, you need charisma and talent. It seemed I was a natural and required little real training in these areas. Lloyd had sold the idea so well that it got me into the Body of the Council. If and when the Council made some earth shattering move, I would also be put into action as a diversion from the raw truth as it unfolded. In the meantime, I would just be my unpredictable self. This is a position of great influence and power, but one envious enemy in the Counsel could have me replaced and in a matter of no time, I would be forgotten like so many other media grabbing superstars of the past.

The key to this role was to just be me. The problem with that was that I didn't really stand for anything moral. I showed great respect for music and martial arts but the lifestyle I led brought corruption on them as well. The old me, having a solid base in a different idea of decency, would have looked at the new me as foolish. He would have ignored my antics and chalked it up to "rebellious attention getting" but he would have been fooled just as much as all the rest. The new generations have no idea of what is right and wrong, they believe only what they see and hear. And the more they see it and hear it, the more they copy it. In a nutshell, my job was to "blur the lines" of conventional thinking and I was not the only one doing it.

Anyone over 30 can see that in the United States alone, the moral fabric and financial stability have been degrading for generations. You can thank popular music and movies for that. Education is not worth the outrageous cost and healthcare has made us all slaves to the medical machine. Not only can we not buy our own cure for our ailments, but we don't know how to make what we need ourselves.

Barton drove the thought home with, "The moments of life you are currently enjoying depend on how well you perform the part you are already playing. You have no choice in this area. Then again, you're one smart little cookie. What I am proposing is something much bigger than you have ever imagined. Still, I think you can take what your people have given you, to not only save the souls of you and your brother but the lives of millions, or even billions you could never know." He continued, "I want you to understand that the destiny some have planned for your brother clashes with what I am now proposing for you. Even if you cooperate with what the Council wills in every way, your famous unpredictable nature alone makes you the worst kind of threat to them. If you travel your own path, (our path), some will want to eliminate you if they cannot be convinced to come onboard, so either way you are in the same danger you have always been. It's my hope that you will entertain my suggestions but if not, I would still pledge to sacrifice my life to protect you and your mission. I'd die knowing it was for a worthy cause whatever that cause happened to be. The only question is, what path calls to you?"

There was a manufactured moment of silence. Barton leaned back in his chair and watched me think. I considered the fact that he could be telling the truth about most of what he was saying. Nothing he had said so far was not a thought that I had not entertained at some point. Still, he had a lot more he was dying to tell me, and he had purposely not made any key points. Just hearing more of these unverified claims about the Council would cause me to appear to have leaned one way or the other and like everything in life, there would be a cost. I felt I was now being made to choose between the red and the blue pills at the point of a gun. I also considered that maybe he was sent to test me, but by whom?

Mr Barton was a very clever man. He spoke like a devoted crusader, but he was forcing me to make jihad against someone. My next words would mean my demise or my destiny, and there was no telling which one was which. He wanted me to think that he was offering me a better way but what did he really want? The only information he had really told me was that I was a pawn in a game that surrounded my baby brother (I knew that). I could make the obvious choice and choose Arthur (Lloyd's plan) or make the bolder choice and choose myself (Barton's plan).

Barton was saying that I faced danger on either side (perhaps). I'm sure there were other factions with other ideas, but one group wanted Little Arthur to restart the family and another did not. There was no doubt that Lloyd allowed me to run loose to be a distraction to all the players while he readied himself.

Without asking any questions, I had no idea who would ally with me and what I could offer them to do so. There were so many things I didn't know, like who these other players were and how much power they had. But those were questions a politician or businessman might ask. Is that what this guy wanted me to say?

Another way of thinking could be, "What option would keep me alive long enough to gather the information I needed to make a better decision?" That would be the logical thinking of Robert Blake. Then again, I could just say, "What do you think I should do?" That could buy me some time, but did Mr Barton really want another follower or did he want someone that could lead?

I considered trying to have him killed and pretend we never had this strange conversation. If I succeeded, I could have made up a story about how he died saving my life or something. Little Arthur and I would be pulled back to London for safety and no one would be the wiser except of course the tester (if there even was one). I would still have to watch for my enemies and without Barton, I would not know how to start looking for them. How much more time if any, would I gain by his demise? Besides, the only people I could vaguely trust were the ones I had recruited. It might be better to stay away from London for as long as I could. My little voice whispered, "Alexander."

Again, it was time to pick one of the pills and gaze into the looking glass. The blue pill meant that I would learn and do nothing more than I was already doing. My destiny would still be in the Council's hands and I would go on living or die at their whim. The red pill meant that I would be faced with a challenge greater than I had ever faced before. My brother and I might still die, but it would have been my choice. In the end, it didn't matter if Barton was testing me with bullshit about "billions of lives" or just setting me up. A "battle of all ages" could determine the fate of many, beginning with my next words. If I were really bold, I would have asked him if he knew my real name, but that would have been too trusting. Instead I asked, "Who called in the kill orders, who rescinded them, why is my brother an empty shell, and what is this abomination you're talking about?"

THE END OF THE REBORN-RUDE AWAKENING

About the Author

KR. White is a former US Air Force member who acted as a Force Security Manager for most of his active duty. Until recently he worked as a Force Protection and Base Defense Operations Center Manager in the role of Battle Captain as a civilian contracted to the Department of Defense and stationed in the Green Zone of Baghdad, Iraq. As an Experienced Operator he studied Trends and Analysis (the art of gathering information from multiple sources and the planning of long term strategies). Many of his correspondences have been viewed in one form or another by the highest levels of military government. Trained in a variety of weapons, tactics, vehicles, fighting skills and surveillance systems, he is also a student, teacher, song writer, singer, poet, father, and a great saxophone player. He has worked and lived in Europe, Asia, the Middle East, and throughout the United States. Between contracts, KR lived in the Philippine islands, but currently resides in Atlanta, GA.

https://www.facebook.com/smoothoperationsarehere